# MERIDIAN

*Also available*

ARCLIGHT

# MERIDIAN

## JOSIN L. MCQUEIN

First published in the USA 2014 by Greenwillow Books,
a division of HarperCollins Publishers
First published in Great Britain 2014 by Electric Monkey,
an imprint of Egmont UK Limited, The Yellow Building,
1 Nicholas Road, London W11 4AN

Text copyright © 2014 Josin L. McQuein

The moral rights of the author have been asserted

ISBN 978 1 4052 6395 5

52459/1

Typeset by Avon DataSet Ltd, Bidford on Avon, Warwickshire
Printed and bound in Great Britain by the CPI Group

## EGMONT

Our story began over a century ago, when seventeen-year-old
Egmont Harald Petersen found a coin in the street. He was on
his way to buy a flyswatter, a small hand-operated printing
machine that he then set up in his tiny apartment.

The coin brought him such good luck that today Egmont has
offices in over 30 countries around the world. And that lucky
coin is still kept at the company's head offices in Denmark.

# CHAPTER ONE

## TOBIN

We're at Day 49 AF—days since the Arc fell.

Almost two months ago, a group of kids with rocks took down the security lights that had guarded this compound for generations, and the Fade walked through. No one died. No one was stolen away to the Dark. In fact, it was the opposite. They brought back the people we'd written off as lost.

Everything changed, but you'd never know it the way things have settled.

Walk the perimeter. See nothing. Report nothing.

Test the lights.

Walk the perimeter. See nothing. Report nothing.

Lock step and follow orders.

Training for a security position should involve more action, but that's all been past tense since the night my friends and I brought the Arc down.

"Twenty-seven?"

Mr. Pace's voice crackles through my radio, at the same exact second he calls every night.

"Present, Teacher," I say, using a voice I know he can't stand.

"That wasn't even funny the first time."

"Present, *Elias*?"

"Tobin . . ."

"Sorry."

"And I'm pretty sure I've warned you about lying to a superior, too."

"So write me up for apologizing. I dare you."

He's got no one to report me to. With our former leader, Honoria, hiding in the lower parts of the compound, he's as high up the chain of command as you can go.

"Keep it up, and I'll do you one better," he says sourly. "I'll tell your father."

Okay, that *would* be worse than the write-up.

Things have been weird with my dad since he came back from the Dark. I don't mean to avoid him, but the Fade are *in his eyes*, all silver and shiny—everyone sees it, and everyone whispers when they think he can't hear them. It's worse being in the same house and wondering if the hive sees what he sees. Thinking about it makes my skin crawl, and that reminds me of *them*, too.

We're supposedly in a state of neutrality with the shadow crawlers, but I can't shake the idea that *neutral* is a code word for something we haven't anticipated.

"You have to take this seriously," Mr. Pace says. "It's not a drill anymore."

"Assign me something more interesting than watching the sun set and I'll take it as seriously as you want."

"Interesting is overrated. And *stop* staring at the sun; you'll go blind."

"Would that get me another assignment?"

"The system's about to cycle." Mr. Pace sighs. "Keep your eyes on the perimeter and off the flaming ball of solar gas."

"Yes, sir."

I wish the cameras were online. I'd salute, just to piss him off.

The radio goes quiet, matching the rest of my assigned perimeter stretch, only quiet never makes it all the way to silence anymore. I can't say for sure that my hearing's sharper since *he* did his little magic trick and healed the gunshot wound that should have killed me, but I'm definitely more aware of my surroundings. I listen harder and look deeper. I never take for granted that what I see is all that's out there. And I never forget that the white nightmare drew blood long before Honoria did. If he hadn't recognized Marina when we went hand-to-hand outside my door, he wouldn't have stopped with slashing me across the shoulder. He probably would have taken my head off.

Marina never thinks of him as anything other than "Rue"— short for rueful—"*sorry*."

More like sorry-ass.

He's a walking pile of genetically altered apologies with a broken heart. She swears he never intended to hurt anyone that day he took on five of us, but it's not that simple. Thanks to the emergency share of his nanites, I know that the Fade don't hate *humans*, but I also know that there is *one* Fade who does hate

3

*me.* I know exactly how close he came to saying no when she begged him to save my life.

He still wouldn't have gotten what he wants. Me dead wouldn't make Marina more Fade or less human.

I stop at the center of my assigned route, something I've done often enough to leave footprints.

"Ready," I say into my radio, and start a mental countdown. The lights in my section go through a prearranged pattern of tests before blazing full bright. In my head, it's set to music. A billion notes blended into the current.

"How's it look?" Mr. Pace asks.

"Same as yesterday."

Things repeat so often around here, I'm surprised I haven't been hypnotized.

"Good, then the reroutes haven't done any new damage."

Most of the damage Annie and the others did to the lamps was superficial, only requiring new bulbs and covers, which would be perfect except that while it was happening, the techs panicked. They thought the problem was more complex than broken bulbs, and they tried to force more power into the lights, causing massive shorts in the system by routing too much voltage. Now all that damage has to be unraveled like a giant, layered knot.

"There's a pulse headed your way."

"I'll be here."

I step back from the perimeter, and wait for the heat.

A pulse is exactly what it sounds like. Mr. Pace takes each section of the boundary in turn and sends high power bursts through the lamps, so we can highlight any points weak enough to buckle. The bulbs come on so strong and hot that they cook the fog right out of the Grey for several feet around the Arc. There's something about the uncovered desolation that gives me chills, even though I'm sweating from the burn.

It's depressing. *Lonely.*

On the short side of the Grey, where Annie and I had crossed to go after Marina, the Dark's so close that you can see it, even through the fog. When the lights go bright on that side, the trees shudder from the shock, but here, there's nothing. The Dark sits below the horizon, dipping out of sight in the extreme distance. It's easy to pretend there's nothing out there beyond rocks and tree stumps and trash that's blown into the Grey as a reminder of the world before.

"What's the damage?" Mr. Pace asks.

"They're holding."

"Good. I'll give you a heads-up before the full-perimeter burn."

"I'll be here," I say again. The lamps cut off, leaving me with a predusk sky for light.

Time for target practice.

They don't give trainees guns, but I can improvise. I bend down for a couple of stones that are just big enough to fit my hand. There's a felled tree with its roots sticking up that I've been using the last few days. From my angle, the roots form an almost perfect circle.

The first rock hits the tip of a root about an inch from the center, sending a rain of dry dirt shaking off; the second clips one off the outside ridge. I reach for a third and pitch the rock high, but it must have been cracked. It splits into pieces that drop to the ground, except for one that bounces off something midair. Suspicion creeps up my neck, ticking the back of my ears.

*It hit a tiny root,* I tell myself. *Or a knot on the trunk that's just out of sight.*

I crouch for another stone, then fling it sideways, two feet off the ground. This one hits something, too, but not my stump. The rock bounces off something beside it. Something invisible.

"Bring up the lights," I whisper into my radio, standing slowly, my eyes skimming the Grey for any hint of shimmer that would tell me a Fade's using the fallen trees for cover.

"We're still checking other sectors, Tobin."

Anyone from Marina's hive can walk safely up to the boundary now. The curious ones come every night. So why would it hide?

"Is this a drill?" I ask

"These are the same tests we've run for the last week. I'm not sure—"

"Not the lights—out in the Grey," I say.

"Did you see something?"

"I *didn't* see anything—that's the problem."

6

*Maybe it's shy*, I think, *or scared*. It could be a kid, like Marina's little sister, but staying camouflaged is asking for trouble. It's not even full dark. Why would it be here so early?

What if it's more than one? We could be surrounded.

I'm going to kill Silver for skipping out on patrol and leaving me alone. Then I'll have my new invisible friend heal her, and I'll kill her all over again.

I take another shot at the stump, aiming for the opposite side—nothing but air, so I turn back to where I'd hit before. The rock goes sailing, but at the point I expect an impact, it changes direction. Something's batted it away.

A stick snaps in two, displacing the dust around it, though I can't see the foot that must have stepped there.

"If this is you getting back at me for joking around, tell me now," I say into the radio.

"I'm not doing anything," Mr. Pace says.

Maybe it's *him*, come to keep an eye on me.

"Hey!" I shout. I move forward but don't cross the Arc. Staying on my side of the line makes me feel better, lights or not. "I know you're there!"

I pick up another stone.

"We're the same height, Nanobot. The next one's coming straight at your head!"

The invisible something moves again, shuffling away so fast that it bumps my target, snapping several of the roots. This isn't Rueful. If he wanted to screw with my head, he'd have dropped the invisible act right beside me, just to prove he could get close enough to do it.

"Tobin!" Mr. Pace is shouting. I must have tuned him out.

"I'm here."

"I heard. Can you confirm it's Marina's buddy with you?"

The lights come up.

"It's not him, but there *is* something," I tell him.

"Sykes is headed your way. Scope it. Tell me what you see."

When Rueful came for Marina in the hospital, Mr. Pace was able to track him with the infrared from his rifle, so each trainee was assigned a light to use in situations like this. I forgot, the stupid thing's been hanging off my wrist the whole time.

I aim the beam at the stump.

"There's . . . *nothing*. There's nothing there."

I sweep the light side to side, up and down, but I never see more than the targeting dot against rocks and brush. Another dot appears next to mine, and I turn to find Lt. Sykes has joined me.

For a second I think he's on my side. He's got his rifle tucked in tight to his shoulder, with serious concentration on his face. He gives the Grey a much more thorough check than I do, turning the search into a grid and covering each section in a square pattern, but ultimately, Sykes drops the rifle to his side and picks up his radio.

"It's clear," he says. "If there was anything out there—"

"There was! I swear." I sound like a kid throwing a fit.

"It's gone now," Sykes says, staring at me, but he's not listening to me anymore. "No trace."

"The stump has plenty of traces," I say, pointing to it.

Sykes turns around and walks a few feet off, but my hearing's a lot better these days.

"He's exhausted, Elias," Sykes says. "The kid's got circles under his eyes dark enough to pass for Fade-marks, and his posture's shot. Anything he saw, *if* he saw anything, could have been in his head. I don't want him on the perimeter. Not like this."

"Agreed. Send him home."

When Sykes turns to deliver the message, I'm right behind him.

"You shouldn't eavesdrop, kid."

"You're not old enough to call me kid, and I'm not hallucinating!"

"No one said you are."

"That's *exactly* what you said!"

"I said you're exhausted, and that's the truth. You've been covering your duty and Silver's for days—we've noticed. It's burning you out."

"I can—"

"You can find your friend and tell her to pull her share of the weight, and then you can take a nap. But first show me which stump, so I can scrape for samples. Being exhausted doesn't make you wrong."

Maybe not, but the possibility of being right makes me never want to sleep again.

# CHAPTER TWO

## MARINA

*I chose to work in the Arbor*, I remind myself. *It makes me happy.*

But right now, it makes me annoyed. Someone took my stepladder—*again.* Every time I have to track it down, I end up off schedule, so I thought using an upturned bucket made sense. But it was stupid. Really, really stupid and wobbly.

I still have to stand on my toes and stretch to reach the branch I need to sample, but if I can tip myself just a little bit more, my shears should be long enough to—

"Ow!"

The bucket topples out from under me, and the falls sends the points of my shears into my hand. But I got my trimming. *Ha! Take that, ladder thief!*

I can't stop myself from checking the blood.

It's red. Nearly two months from my last breath off my old inhaler, I still bleed human red.

I hold my hand down, watching the drops run and collect on my finger, ready to drip onto the potting soil below. A million billion bits of genetic code that could tell me what the color

10

my eyes and hair would be had I been born human rather than turned into one.

Blood remembers everything. It could tell me the name of the father I still don't know, but it just hangs there, turning tacky in the Arbor's humid air.

*You should be more careful*, a snide inner voice taunts. *Humans are imprecise.*

Sometimes I wake up in the middle of the day while the rest of the Arclight's still sleeping. My dream-fogged brain tries to convince me that my skin's the color of ash and that what thrums in my veins is thick and black, teeming with the tiny machines that used to fill and form my cells.

On those early mornings, it all comes back. I smell flowers and know my little sister's close. The sting of pine needles tells me my mother's there. All the layers stemming from the Fade's connection to one another wrap me up in a whirlwind of comfort.

I remember my real name. I'm the warmth of a new day filtering past the Dark's canopy, and the promise of adventure on an errant wind. *Cherish*, and cherished. I belong.

Then the hive's voices dull, falling away until only Rue's remains.

*Never alone*, he said, but his final words to me were a promise he couldn't keep. I'll always be alone. No one else has ever been Fade, then human.

In the end the moment passes, and I've lost everything.

I *always* lose.

"Stop it," I say out loud, bracing myself against the workstation. The *s* comes out as a hard hiss. "Go away!"

I plunge my hands into a bucket of irrigation water, watching the blood sink to the bottom among the falling silt.

*You go* is the answer I get.

Weeks ago, when I was released from the hospital, I told Dr. Wolff and Tobin and everyone else that I had control of myself after the suppressant was out of my system. I didn't know it was a lie. My memories were trickling back, but they brought something else with them—*Cherish.*

I thought she was an echo. I'd say or do something routine but feel a twinge or hesitate because it didn't actually *seem* normal. Something as insignificant as sitting down with a tray at meals or opening my mouth to speak to Anne-Marie felt alien and uncomfortable.

*That's not how we eat,* I'd think. *That's not how we speak.*

As my memories returned, they were the memories of a Fade. I thought my brain was just having trouble filtering, but it escalated. I'd reach for a fork at my next meal, and my fingers wouldn't move. I could see the fork, and I'd want to pick it up, only something interrupted the brain signal required to do it.

*That's not how we eat,* my inner voice insisted, until I finally realized it wasn't a memory. Something inside me was trying to control my movements. Something that still thought of me as part of a hive—the voice never said *I,* it always said *we.*

The Fade are dual creatures. They can exist as an individual or as part of a hive mind, and the residue of the life I left in the Dark was still trying to make me act like a Fade. *Cherish* was trying to send me back to the shadows.

Things would be so much simpler if I could talk myself into taking the suppressant again. One puff off my old inhaler, and Cherish would drift back into stark-white nothing; I'd forget she ever existed. But if I let go of her, I lose my family and Rue.

I don't know what to do.

I can deal with Cherish for another day. Just one. Just today. If I keep telling myself that, I may string enough days together to last me the rest of my life.

I dry my hands, reaching for the bulky gloves I'm supposed to wear.

Cherish doesn't comment, but I know she hates them. Fade prefer to feel the soil, and it's usually easier to humor her, but today she's being difficult. She doesn't get her way.

"Good children of the Arclight don't search for ways around the rules," I tell her. "We do our jobs and move forward."

*We are not the Arclight's good child.*

"I will be," I say. I can't be a Fade, but I can be the best human girl I can be. I have human responsibilities to the Arbor; she won't distract me from them anymore.

*The creatures are here again*, she says smugly.

Sometimes Cherish is more sixth sense than annoyance. She notices things I don't, by virtue of the enhanced hearing I never lost. I'm busy snipping and cataloging leaf samples in jars, but she's hearing the swish of a cat's tail through air.

Something whisper-soft brushes against my legs, weaving around my ankles in a figure eight. I bend down to pet it.

"I wonder if those came from Mom's monsters."

A real voice startles me as Tobin's boots shuffle into sight on the other side of the work-station. Even if Cherish heard him come in, she wouldn't tell me. She doesn't like him.

"Hey," I say, as though it's not odd to see him down here.

"Hey."

He smiles, reaching out to stroke the cat's ruff. It springs free with a hiss at the first touch of his fingers, and he laughs.

"Definitely Mom's. They always hated me."

He told me a story once, about how the cats in the Arclight came from his mother's efforts to save a litter of abandoned kittens she'd found outside the boundary as a girl. He takes the Arbor cat's disdain as proof that his mother left a mark on this place beyond the research Honoria used for my so-called cure.

"Is the shift over already?" I ask. I could check my alarm band, but I've spent weeks breaking myself of the habit of answering to that stupid screen on my wrist. I'd rather get my information elsewhere. Somewhere not controlled by the people who nearly killed me.

"I've been sent in search of Silver. She didn't show up for rounds, so she's become their latest excuse to get me away from anything interesting or important."

"That bad?"

He shrugs.

"If you need someone skilled at watching lights flick on and off, I'm your guy."

I toss my cut branch into an envelope, stick a label on the front, and set it aside with my other samples. Someone else will come to test them again, but they'll do it after I'm gone. That way, they think I won't realize they're watching me.

"Have you seen her?" he asks.

"Silver doesn't come down here." Since hiding in the tunnels with Rue, she breaks into hives at even the mention of the Arclight-below. She claims she caught claustrophobia from Anne-Marie.

"Didn't think so." Tobin hops up onto the workstation

"Isn't sitting down the opposite of finding someone?"

"I asked Annie first, and now she's got me looking for Dante, too."

"Which means they're together," I say.

"And not wanting to be found, so I consider myself on break. I thought I'd see if you wanted to be on break, too."

Cherish suggests the Arclight's good children don't take breaks.

"You look terrible," I say, ignoring her.

He's shaking, scanning the room over and over. Something's rattled him—bad.

"What's wrong?"

"Nothing. Just insomnia." Tobin picks at the clods of dirt around him, crumbling them into powder. He shakes my collection jars. He never looks at me when he's lying. "I've slept about two hours in the last four days."

He grimaces, grinding at his eyes with his palms.

"Tobin! You didn't tell me it was that bad!" I sling my gloves off to take his hand and pull him to his feet. "I'm taking you to Doctor Wolff."

This is a switch; usually, he's the one threatening me with the hospital.

"I don't need a doctor," he insists.

"He'll give you something."

"Like he did you?"

"Low blow, Tobin." Dr. Wolff giving him a sedative is nothing compared to my being perma-drugged to kill my memories. But if Tobin's using that against me, this is serious. "It's Doctor Wolff or your father. Pick one."

"Marina, stop . . . please," he begs. He's got his feet planted, leaning back as hard as he can. If I were still Fade, I could move him, but plain old human Marina? Not a chance—and Cherish doesn't miss the opportunity to point that out.

"You're scaring me," I say, letting go. "What's so bad you'd rather dance around it than tell me?"

"I don't want to sleep."

The hairs on the back of my neck shoot up, tingling from an electric current straight off my nerves.

"You said the nightmares stopped," I say.

After Rue healed Tobin, and we were released from the hospital, Tobin started having dreams where he was consumed by the Dark, drowning under a wave of black water. He claimed it was post-traumatic stress, but their voices remained in his head for way too long.

"They did stop *for a while*," he says, mumbling the last part. "But they're back—sort of. They're different. It's weird."

*Weird* and *Fade* are two things that do not need to occupy the same space as nightmares. Bad things happen when they do.

"Sometimes I can't tell if I'm awake or asleep. I hear—"

"You hear the Fade?"

A long absent dread uncurls inside my throat, spiraling toward my stomach, where it turns cold and sharp. Only this time, I'm not scared for me. Tobin shouldn't be able to hear the hive.

"Not like that," he says quickly. "And not always. It just drifts in sometimes, like a nightmare. I just don't want to explain that to anyone else. You understand; they won't."

"You're sure?"

"Yeah. I haven't heard or seen your boyfriend since it happened."

Calling Rue my boyfriend is like using "it" to encompass everything that happened to us. Tobin's still dodging.

"They're just your average, creepy-feeling, shadow-filled, something-awful's-going-to-happen-if-I-fall-asleep nightmares," he says again, with a half-choked laugh. "Though if you want to double-check and ask your ex, I won't object."

"I can't hear Rue anymore," I say. He hasn't so much as come into view since the night we brought Tobin's father and the others back.

My mother was here once—close enough to touch—but she didn't bring my sister, and she was only interested in getting me to follow her into the Grey. I wanted to—I really did—but I was afraid of what would happen if I returned to the Dark. Cherish would have the advantage there. What if she's stronger than me?

*We are stronger than you*, she says, making me certain that I had made the right decision.

I can still see the mix of anger and sadness in my mother's expression, and taste the way the air turned, like it was suddenly infused with bitter lemon. Even now, the memory makes my eyes sting.

Tobin leans forward and grabs my hands as I do. "You're bleeding."

Once, those words were enough to make my heart falter, but now they're just a reminder that I pulled my gloves off fast enough to break open the cut from my clippers.

"I got careless taking samples," I say. "It's nothing."

"Nothing doesn't leave bloodstains." He wipes my palms with a towel dipped in irrigation water and then bends down to pick up the gloves I dropped. "Here," he says with a lopsided grin.

Usually, that's enough to foil my attempts to stay annoyed, but this time it's not his lips that have my attention, it's his eyes and the metallic, silver shine in them.

"Tobin?"

The effect lasts a blink and a skipped heartbeat, and then his eyes are back to brown, and I'm back to remembering how to breathe.

"What's wrong?" he asks.

"Did you really come here looking for Silver?" The question's a toss-away to help me collect my thoughts.

"Mostly, but Annie also wants me to remind you that you promised to help with her rotation. I think I was even threatened with food poisoning if you don't comply . . . No, wait. That wasn't a threat. That was Annie reminding me about dinner. She really does want your help, though."

"I guess I'd better get going, then."

"And I'll get back to not finding Silver or Dante," he says. "Why can't they just use her room? I know Dante's folks don't want him home much, but Silver can come and go. They'd be a lot easier to avoid if I knew where not to look."

I nod, washing my hands mechanically at the spout on the wall without sparing another look at Tobin's face. When I pass the incinerator meant for burning rotten plants and refuse, I throw in my gloves and the towel he touched.

*Just in case.*

# CHAPTER THREE

## MARINA

Events that change the world seem like they should come with a herald or harbinger, but that's not how it happens. The moments that mean the most happen in the pauses between breaths—easy to miss if no one knows they should be looking.

What did I miss with Tobin?

I should have noticed something before now. Tobin's eye shine is more than a whisper of warning. It's a plunge into an icy stream so cold, the surface grows solid over my head. It's the pull of water away from shore before the waves crash down to drown us all in his nightmare.

"Tell me this is you," I hiss to Cherish while in an empty hallway. Hardly anyone comes near the Arbor at this time of night, and I'm grateful for their avoidance. No one can see me talking to myself. "Tell me you're playing with my head, or thinking about Rue, and somehow that made Tobin look different to me."

But Cherish stays stubbornly silent.

If I call it stubbornness, then I can believe she's really the cause—not Tobin.

The halls of the Arclight-below pass in a blur; routine by now, so I don't think about where I'm going until I reach a door and need my wristband for access. Down here, you don't need permission just to enter; you need it to leave, too. Every time I have to wait for the red light to turn green and let me through, my breath hitches and I wonder if this will be the day they change their minds. The point they turn on me and lock me away again.

Those fears have grown weaker the last few weeks, but if Tobin's eyes are really silver . . .

The door snaps open, and I shoulder through as soon as I'm able, holding my breath when I pass the alcove that houses both Honoria's office and the White Room, where Cherish died and I was born. *This is nothing but a routine shift change,* I tell myself.

I pass the familiar scrawl of USAF that someone stenciled on the wall between embossed stars; streaks into a line at the corner of my eye. One of these days, I'll ask someone what it means. By the time I reach the final panel that allows me into the Arclight-above, I've denounced and defended Tobin a dozen times.

*I should tell Dr. Wolff,* insists the part of me indoctrinated by the Arclight's rules. Nightmares, plus voices, plus eye shine, equals Fade.

Rue swore to me that the Fade don't take unwilling hosts anymore. Tobin loathes the Fade; he's terrified of them. No way would he agree to let them stay inside him by choice.

Did Rue lie to me?

*Negative!* The suggestion makes Cherish angry. *Deceit is not a possibility.*

"Okay, maybe it was an accident or an oversight."

Nanites are tiny. Rue could have missed some when he took his back. Cherish has lasted this long, there's no reason Rue's contact with Tobin couldn't do the same.

*But where are the marks?* Tobin's skin is clean.

*Where's the sensitivity to light?* The arbor's full of sunlamps. Tobin works on the perimeter with the high beams every day— no Fade could stand that.

And his father would have noticed. Wouldn't he?

Turning Tobin in would bring suspicion to our whole class, and at least half the upper-years. Anne-Marie and her brother Trey, Silver and Dante—they all put themselves at risk. I can't tell them they might have been wrong. And I can't lose another life. The Arclight's all I have left.

If something happens to Tobin, it's my fault. *I* brought the Fade. *I* begged Rue to heal him.

"Were his eyes really shining?" I ask, but Cherish only answers with a reminder that Tobin left the Arclight for me. She nudges me to do the same for him. Rue's in the Dark, and he'll answer my questions.

She's baiting me, not helping. Her strength is in the Dark.

What I need is a cooperative Fade who's willing to come here. One who might understand what's going on, but who also knows why I can't mention it to anyone else.

I need Honoria's baby brother.

Schuyler Whit turned Fade in the first days, more than a century ago, and has lived as one ever since. I named him Bolt, for his appearance, with its sharp, slashing lines, and a presence that invokes the violent nature of a thunderstorm. I've watched people approach other Fade with curiosity when they venture out of the Grey toward the darkened sections of the Arc, but few bother with him. He looks menacing, but he isn't, and his connection to Honoria makes him taboo. It's a shame, considering he has a knack for defusing people's tempers.

My panicked heart begins to calm. Bolt comes at least three times a week. Once I make it through my promise to Anne-Marie, I'll find him at the Arc, and everything will be okay.

"Yay!" Anne-Marie cheers when I enter the midyear classroom she's been assigned for the night. "One of you showed up, at least."

It was no surprise when she declared her intention to follow a teacher's path the moment we were allowed to choose. Anne-Marie and her brother are a perfect split of their father's personality. Trey got Mr. Pace's desire for a security position, and she got the teaching bug.

"I don't suppose you've seen Dante?" she asks.

I'm still getting used to how different she looks with her hair cut so short that it barely rises above her scalp. It seems an odd choice of celebration, but she said the change was for her birthday.

I should figure out if I have one of those.

"Silver's gone missing, and you know if they're together—"

"No details in the kiddie classroom." She holds up a hand to cut me off. She'd probably cover her ears if her other hand wasn't balancing an oversize tub on her hip. "Actually, no details on those two, period. Neither of them understands the concept of oversharing. Or locks."

Poor Anne-Marie swears she didn't sleep for days after walking in on the two of them in a closet; something about Dante having a really big, really weird birthmark.

There's a bluish aura around her, glowing brighter and bolder with her increased agitation. It's the way Cherish sees people who have touched the Fade but who aren't part of the hive. I've seen Anne-Marie's since I got my memories back, but it's especially vibrant today.

"Besides," she says. "I doubt Silver's with him, unless he's finally convinced her to go out on the short side with him. Every day, he skips out on rotation early and makes himself go a little farther into the Grey. You'd think he was hunting for buried treasure out there."

That's a conversation I have no intention of continuing. One person having Dark dreams is enough; I don't want to think about it spreading. Thankfully, it's only a passing comment, and Anne-Marie moves on.

"Could you get the chairs out of the way while I set out the cups and stuff?" she asks. "That was Dante's job, but he's useless."

Easy enough, and if I'm both lucky and quick, I'll make it out of here in time to beat Bolt to the Arc, so there's no chance of missing him.

"Why are you setting out snacks like for a baby class?" I ask offhandedly, as I stack chairs against the wall.

"Mid-years get snacks." She stumbles but catches the cup she drops before it hits the floor.

"They do?"

The air between us hardens, developing the sharper edge of a knife drawn to keep me back. It's been a few days since I've experienced an emotion so strong I can taste it, and it takes a steadying breath to reacquaint myself with the phenomenon.

"Sure. On special occasions," she says.

"Today's special?"

Did I miss another holiday? There are so many days on the calendar, I can't keep them straight.

"Birthdays are special," she says stiffly.

Anne-Marie won't look at me. The scent of oranges, which usually hovers around her, turns as acidic as the toner used to strip down tables in the clean rooms of the Arclight-below. It burns my throat when I breathe.

*She's hiding something*, Cherish warns. *Danger. Flee.*

But I'm not the one who looks like she's about to dart out of here.

"Anne-Marie?"

"Do the last row, would you? I have to pick up the kids from orientation."

She swings the box off her hip, toward me, so I can either catch it or let it fall as she rushes for the exit.

"Anne-Marie!"

She stops, shoulders rising with a sigh, without turning.

"You have to face her sooner or later, and the longer it goes, the harder it will be," she says. "You're my friend, Marina. I hate what she did to you, but we need her. So long as she's avoiding you, she's no good to us. This place will fall apart."

"What are you—"

I don't have to finish the question, and Anne-Marie doesn't have to answer it. The room changes in a way she can't sense, with explosive rings spreading through the air from the door. Into the void behind them, steps a person who sets my every nerve alight with panic. Cherish becomes a wild animal running amok inside my skull.

Honoria hasn't made many appearances since she shot Tobin while trying to prove he was no longer human. She's avoided me altogether, which suits me fine, but to my continued annoyance, most everyone has fallen onto the same side of the argument as Anne-Marie. They think Honoria's countless years here are an asset—no matter the mistakes she's made or crimes committed. Even Tobin's father has tried to get me to talk to her.

They don't understand that when I look at Honoria, I lose myself.

To me, she's the woman who almost murdered Tobin for the sake of her misconceptions. She's the one who ordered me kidnapped and altered. She's the one who tried to exile Tobin's father and those who went with him into the Grey. She's the one who tortured Rue.

Honoria's a monster, and she's staring at me like I'm the one who doesn't belong in a room meant for human children.

I don't, and that's her fault, too.

"You can't leave me alone with her." I make a desperate grab for Anne-Marie's arm, and the box nearly topples to the floor when she steps out of reach.

"You don't have to forgive her; you don't have to like her, but you need to find a way to live with her so things can get back to normal."

Normal for the Arclight means sleeping all day and hiding under lamps at night, jumping at shadows that never meant us any harm. That's not normal, nor is it an existence I want to return to.

"I don't care if you have to draw a line down the middle of the building and pick sides, just do something. *Please try*," Anne-Marie says, rushing back to hug me for some, inexplicable reason. She lets go and turns very serious, scolding me with a pointed finger. "If either of you are dead when I get back, I'll be really irritated."

Then she walks out of the room, leaving me to face the one real enemy I have in the world.

# CHAPTER FOUR

## MARINA

Honoria's expression holds no emotion; there's no hint of the decades she's seen hidden in the colorless gray of her eyes. We don't need to paint lines to divvy up space; this classroom might as well have the White Room's safety pane running down its center. She stays on her side; I stay on mine.

"Do I need to tell you this wasn't my idea?" she asks. For once, I'm sure she's not lying. Her shock's palpable.

Tobin says Mr. Pace took away the silver pistol she always kept tucked in her waistband, but I'd feel better if I could see her back to know for sure.

"Door's open," I say. "Feel free to leave."

But no one's going anywhere.

I step sideways and set out a bowl of cookies from the tub Anne-Marie left, but I never take my eyes off her. Honoria slides into the room, just as guarded.

I place another bowl; she moves another step. Bowl, step, bowl, step, until we settle into predatory symmetry, like the films we've seen in science class of long-gone animals fighting over territory.

With my focus on Honoria, it's easy to forget the cushions on the floor that have replaced the chairs I moved. On my next step, I hit padded cotton rather than floor, and I drop the entire tub off my hip. Cookies go flying. Bottles of juice shatter, soaking into the napkins that land on top of them. And I blurt the first curse I've ever used in my life as I bend down to clean it up.

"Tobin's rubbing off on you," Honoria says, right beside me. Someone her size shouldn't be able to move that quietly. "I wonder if you've had the same effect on him."

"What's that supposed to mean?" I snap. Hopefully, the look on my face is closer to a glare than "you terrify me." How does Tobin flip the switch from fear to rage with barely a thought?

My hands are trembling now, so I cover by scrubbing at the spill. It's grape juice, the purple color close enough to red that I'm having flashbacks of trying to stop the blood from Tobin's chest.

"You realize those napkins are useless?" she asks rather than answer me. "You'll go through the stack and only push the mess around. There should be towels in the cabinet."

I crawl backward as she moves forward, furious that I let myself lose my footing with her, and end up sitting when I run into the cushions behind me.

"I don't need your help," I say.

All I need is to make sure that she never finds out what I saw in the arbor. I refuse to have Tobin's screams haunt me every time I close my eyes because she decides to turn him into an experiment.

For once, Cherish seems in total agreement, echoing my fears with *protect* and *conceal*. It's the way of the Fade—if you don't want it stolen, keep it hidden from human eyes.

*Conceal*, Cherish repeats, following the order with a burst of flaring light across a darkened sky. She's named Tobin after the star shower we shared the night I followed Rue into the Dark. She doesn't want me to go through the agony she felt when Honoria separated her from Rue; she'd have to feel it again. Honoria won't touch Tobin—not if we can help it.

Cherish names her "Destroyer," a raging flame that lays waste to the Dark and everything in it.

My attention drifts back to the lake of juice that looks more like blood the more it dries.

"Being stubborn only leads to a bigger mess," Honoria says, still tracking me.

"Speaking from experience, are you?" The napkins have turned to a ball of soggy glop in my hands. I stop trying to sop up the juice, and reach for the broken bottles to put them back in the tub. "I said I don't need your—Ahh!"

I pull my hand back with a hiss. A long shard of glass has imbedded itself into my hand, in nearly the same place I cut it earlier.

Honoria's on me in an instant, as though the smell of blood draws her close. She tows me up with a gloved hand around my wrist, bringing the wound close enough for inspection. I glance at the blood to prove to myself it's red, even as Cherish goes feral in my mind.

"Let go!" I order, bracing myself so Honoria no longer has control over where I stand or fall.

"Annie?" a voice calls from the hall. "Has Dante come back this way? Because I really can't find him."

*Tobin.*

A meteor shower goes off inside my head as Cherish calls his name over and over.

Translation: *He's not Rue, but he'll do.*

"Tobin!" I call when he reaches the door.

"Marina?"

He's stunned for a second, and I can only imagine how we look to him. Me bleeding. Honoria standing over me. Broken glass.

"What happened?" he asks, entering cautiously. "Where's Annie?"

"She left," I say.

"Marina's hurt," Honoria says at the same time. She jostles my hand to show off the glass. "And she's acting like a child."

"I broke a bottle," I argue. "That's hardly hurt."

Getting shot is hurt. Being burned by lights until the lines that used to run my arms and legs melt off—that's hurt. This is a scratch.

"Let her go."

"You're *both* acting like children," Honoria says, digging at the piece of glass. Either her gloves are too thick or my blood's too slippery because she can't get a decent grip on the shard without driving it deeper.

"Ow!" I do the only thing I can think of—kick her in the shin. Honoria glowers at me, but she lets go.

Two months ago, I wouldn't have challenged her outright. I didn't understand why I feared her until I saw the recordings of my torture in the White Room. I still feel that threat with her this close, but I'm stronger than I was then.

*We are stronger than you*, Cherish intones.

Honoria grabs one of the fingers on her glove with her teeth and tugs until it comes free, then holds her bare hand out to me. Her skin's nothing but crisscrossing lines of scar tissue from her fingernails up past her wrists, where they disappear beneath her sleeves.

She gives me an annoyed scowl and zero warning before yanking the glass out of my palm.

"Ow!"

"Keep pressure on it," she says, pressing another towel and Tobin's hand down over the free-flowing blood when she's done. "It shouldn't bleed long."

"Ow!" I'm too shocked to say more.

"And close your mouth, you look like a fish."

"You touched her—bare-handed," Tobin says.

Of all the people inside the Arclight, Honoria is least likely to break the rules of contact with someone Fade-touched, and she's always seen me as contaminated. What gives?

"I don't wear these to protect myself; I wear them to protect everyone else. With you, there's no need."

She fixes the glove back in place and drags a chair across the room to the front.

"Are those burns?" I ask.

"Collateral damage," she says in a weary voice. "I made a choice many, *many* years ago, and that was to not be like those who live outside this compound. I'm not like you. The suppressants help, but I can't be cured with a dart and an inhaler. If I want to stay free of the Fade, it costs me."

She can't honestly think going from Cherish to Marina cost me nothing.

"The nanites have never stopped replicating in my system; when they start to spike, I do the only thing that works: I cut myself, drawing them to the wound, and burn them out again."

"You *kill* them for trying to help you!"

"Help is a subjective concept."

The only things keeping me in my skin and in this room are Tobin and the sound of laughter and feet. Anne-Marie returns with a line of students who go silent when they see Honoria waiting at the front.

"Everyone, stand to the side and mind the glass," Honoria says. "Once it's clear, you can take a seat."

The children all file into a line against the wall, as though this were a Red-Wall drill. Anne-Marie joins me and Tobin as we lean against the teacher's desk at the back while Honoria quickly clears as much of the mess as she can.

"What happened?" Anne-Marie asks, looking at my hand

and at the towel wrapped into my fist.

"You abandoned her," Tobin says, but she doesn't take the bait.

"Marina?" she asks instead.

I can't really explain beyond saying, "It was an accident."

She scowls at me, as though dropping bottles of juice was a violation of her order not to try and kill Honoria.

"Uh-huh." She crosses her arms and sets her sights on the front of the room, where the children have started to chatter nervously in line.

"I thought she left," one boy whispers.

"She didn't leave, she went nuts," another beside him answers.

"Why's she here?" a girl asks nervously.

"No one's told you?" Honoria asks, silencing them. Her hearing's as keen as mine—she caught every whisper. "Usually, those with older siblings get clued in early."

She shoves the bottle bin under her chair and takes a seat. A reverent hush falls over the faces watching her with absolute attention.

"I'm here to tell you what lies beyond our borders, lurking out of the light."

She raises her head, looking me straight in the eye.

"Today, I tell you the truth about the Fade."

# CHAPTER FIVE

## TOBIN

Marina twitches, ready to jump up, but Annie's hand nails hers to the desk.

"This is how things work," Annie says.

"How they stay broken, you mean," Marina mutters, pulling her hand free to tuck it under her arm. Her other hand tightens its grip on the towel, but she doesn't argue.

She should—and a lot more.

Honoria's twisted truths nearly forced a war between us and the Fade—one we would have lost.

"This is her first chance to make it right," Annie says. "I want to know if she takes it."

"You think she will?" Marina's hoping for a yes, I can tell, but she should know better.

"This is how we find out." Annie shrugs. She pushes off the desk to replace the shattered juice bottles with new ones from the room's snack dispenser.

"You don't have to stay," I tell Marina.

"I want to," she says. "If Honoria's going to lie, let her do it to my face."

It wouldn't be the first time.

I take a seat beside her on the desk, too tired to stand without moving. Every time my eyes relax, they conjure up shapes and shadows in the corners. I shake my head and focus on the front of the room, where the lights are brightest.

The scene's surreal. Aside from Annie and the juice stains, it looks exactly like it did the day Honoria gave our class this speech—right down to the cookies and the cushions on the floor. The patches on the kids' sleeves are the ones we wore. Honoria's holding the same book she read to us. We could be watching a recording of that day, her voice is so similar.

"Sky's gotten worse since he saw Dad beyond the safety fires. He wanders a lot, talking to himself. He doesn't eat and doesn't sleep. I catch him staring out the windows into the darkness, and I know we're going to lose him, and soon."

"Are you awake?" Marina asks, and I realize I'm drifting.

I was out of it just enough that the sequence Honoria read played out in my head, as though it was happening in real time.

I blink, and Marina's hair turns to tarlike sludge dripping down her face. There's an ocean of it all around, so deep that only the kids' heads are above it. It's over my ankles.

I wrench backward to pull my legs free, but they're clean and dry, and the room is normal again. No one noticed a thing—except Marina.

"Tobin?"

"Sorry," I say, lowering my feet off the desk. "Dozed off."

She looks at me weird, but only for a moment before turning back to Honoria. I look for something sharp to hold in my palm. If I can squeeze it, the pain will keep me awake.

I don't remember Honoria tearing up when she read this to us, but she is now. The light pinging off her eyes turns them shiny. It's an illusion, but it makes me shiver.

She does the same and has to take a drink of water before she can read more.

"It's how Tracey acted before she changed," she says, monotone now. "And how Major Gardener used to stare before he went after his wife. Sky's not listening to real people anymore. All he hears is Jimmy, and Jimmy's been gone a week."

Marina's enthralled. This all new for her, and she's probably hoping Honoria will share something worth her attention, but she won't. Honoria won't even admit what she is—not here.

Her eyes don't glow like a Fade's, but she's not completely human. She's a freak of nature. Frozen, like the memory of the people in that book. Too many of our elders use that as an excuse for pity.

*Her snapping was understandable,* they'd say. *It's remarkable she fared so well for so long.*

What a load of crap.

They're lazy.

They're so used to her doing the hard things and making the difficult decisions for them, they've put her on a no-fault system. *Whatever she did, she had a good reason.*

They've forgotten how to think for themselves.

Even Dad, with his: *She was a kid, too, Tobin. She made mistakes. You don't know what it took for her to become the woman she is.*

Like he knows.

How can he buy into it, knowing she was going to let him rot outside the Arc? She hasn't done a thing to keep people off his back when she's the one person around here who could.

So his eyes turned silver—So what? Why can they accept her and not him? She's had Fade in her blood a lot longer than he has.

*Her eyes are silver now. Lines spiral out across her face to match the ones creeping down the walls.*

I have to shake myself awake again.

Honoria's rules won't last. Not once our group ages up enough to have a real say in things. We brought down the Arc; we can bring her down, too.

These kids are already questioning her.

"But we know the Fade aren't dangerous anymore," a boy near the front says. No one in my year would have had the nerve when we were his age.

Honoria's attention goes straight to him, as though he's spoken some blasphemy. She turns her book in her hands, so that bits of gold and silver catch the room's overhead lights where metallic lines are embedded in the shape of a bird and a bell. The gilded pages glint along the edge.

"Is this normal?" Marina asks.

"No."

Usually, Honoria doesn't stop talking long enough for anyone to pick out the holes in her story. And in a normal year she doesn't lose their attention, but as Annie paces the room, doling out refills, the whispers start again.

One kid says her older brother is taking her out to the Arc, maybe even across it—*Does anyone want to come?* Another says he went far enough into the Grey that he couldn't see the compound. Each claim gets bigger, counting numbers of steps as proof of bravery until the contest is settled by a boy in the back.

"I touched one," he says. "I went right up to him and shook his hand."

"Where?"

"When?"

"Which one?"

"A week ago," the boy says. "And you know—*him*. The weird one."

"They're *all* weird."

Marina cringes and says something under her breath I can't hear. She's locking down.

"They don't mean you," I tell her, squeezing her fingers so I don't press her hand by mistake and make it bleed again. "You're human now."

"I know," she says, but I think she means something else. She's watching the boy at the back, like everyone else, including

Honoria. The kid doesn't even realize he's the center of attention.

"The one with the slashes on his face and arms," he says.

*Schuyler.*

Marina calls him Bolt, but his *real* name is Schuyler. He told me. I've never told anyone that I heard him speak because he didn't say it out loud; it was a one-time thing. It's not worth spooking anyone. I know, and that's more than enough.

Honoria's hands tighten on her book. She clears her throat, and the whispers stop. The kids all look ashamed, caught in the middle of breaking a rule.

"The Fade are being hospitable at the moment; that doesn't make them less dangerous," she says. "Appearances of safety often mask unknown dangers."

She glances at Marina, and Marina's still grumbling. If Honoria doesn't stop baiting her, she's going to regret it. Anyone who can find the guts to hold a burning knife to my skin and save my life can find a way to do worse and save her own.

"You know what—forget this." Honoria pitches the book onto the floor beside her. "I don't need my journal to tell you what happened."

Her journal? That's a new one.

When Honoria gave us this speech, she told us it had been found in a scrap heap and that we should be grateful there was an account of what had happened. This group gets one less lie.

Annie rejoins us in the back, but she sits cross-legged on the floor, like she's one of the kids hearing this for the first time. She holds a bowl of cookies on her head so I can take some.

*My hands are corpse white, smudged with charcoal lines. Annie's hair sprouts long tendrils that wrap around her neck— choking her.*

"Toby?" she asks.

*How can she talk when she's being strangled?*

"Toby! I said, are you done?"

I shake myself again, and my hands are still in their gloves and still in the bowl. Annie's looking up at me from the floor, like nothing's wrong, because it isn't—not for her, anyway. Sykes was right. I'm losing my mind.

Annie puts her bowl in her lap.

"What's going on?" Marina asks, nibbling on a cookie.

"Two hours of sleep in four days," I remind her.

"Then go home."

"Not a chance." I jam three cookies into my mouth. Maybe the sugar will keep me awake.

"I didn't live here when I was your age," Honoria says. "This was the military base where my father worked. He made wondrous things; good things. In the beginning the Fade were a tool meant to help people."

"He made the Fade?" a girl asks.

"He created machines called nanites that were so small, they could fit inside a cell and unravel disease. Sounds like a good idea, right?"

They all nod.

41

But they can't see what I see. Their shadows are pacing the wall, moving without them.

"I thought so, too," Honoria says. She keeps swallowing, pausing for half beats in the wrong places. "But someone made a mistake, and they malfunctioned. My father tried to fix them, but the machines moved faster than he could. It wasn't long before they covered everything."

I remember us being the ones uncomfortable when I was listening to this as a kid, but now she's the one who's jumpy.

"No one called them the Fade, then; that came later. We called them the Darkness. The Shroud."

The whole story comes out a halt, a skip, and a falter at a time. I wonder if she's ever told it all before. How she was at school when the alarms went off and everyone thought it was drill, until the trucks rolled by and they knew it wasn't. Her dad came home shaken but telling her everything was fine—then he disappeared.

My head droops toward my chest, and my cookies fall from my hand to the desktop. I know I'm falling asleep, but it's getting harder to fight.

"Hey!" Marina punches my arm.

"Thanks," I say. The sting stops the crawling tingles I feel every time my eyes close. Honoria's still droning in the background.

"Men from the base came to our school. They pulled me and my brother aside to ask us questions. The kind they'd only ask if something had gone so wrong, they couldn't make it right again."

"She should have told us this," Annie says. "It's better than the book."

Maybe it is. I don't know. Everything's spinning.

"After that, my friends changed and disappeared. It spread. The world fell into a panic, all because my father thought the Fade were harmless. *They're not.* This base thought it was secure. *Nothing is.*"

"So we should still be afraid of them?" No idea which kid said that. They're all a blob of uniform blue with too many heads smashed together, bobbing in black water.

"Go home," Marina says to me. "You're about to drop."

*She looks like a Fade. But if she's a Fade, she'll go back to the Dark.*

"Tell Rueful it won't work."

"What?" she asks.

"Nothing."

She's human again. White-blonde hair. Blue eyes. Marina, not Cherish.

"Nothing to worry about," I say.

*Is Honoria still talking?*

"Vigilance isn't fear. Keep your eyes open and be familiar enough with your surroundings to recognize changes if they come. Never forget that it was a single mistake that put us all over the edge. Now get out of here and go home. No classes tonight."

The kids stand. Some are happy they can skip out on class, but the rest—the majority—aren't smiling.

"Do you still want to go out?" asks the boy who had met Schuyler.

"No," the girl beside him shakes her head.

"How about you?" he asks another kid. "I bet he's there."

This one says no, too. He shrinks from the braver one. The one he'll never forget has touched a Fade.

"Tobin!" Marina shouts in my ear. Annie swats my leg.

"Huh? D'you say something?"

"Snap out of it, Toby," Annie says.

"Can't." I shake my head, but I've already lost the battle. Sleep's going to win this round.

"Can you make it home?" Marina asks.

"I'll be fine once I'm moving. Shouldn't have sat down."

"You look like trash," Annie says.

*Yeah, well, you look like one of them. Spun black crystals for hair, glowing eyes, and lines dripping off into the rising dark.*

"I'm fine," I say again, then ask Marina: "Are you okay?"

"I don't know what I am."

Her mouth doesn't match the words, but it sounds like her talking.

"Home," she orders, followed by Annie's "Now!"

Lights flash in my eyes, and suddenly, I'm down the hall, standing at the mouth of the domicile wing. *The lights are out.* Then I'm at my door, *and there's something crawling on the wall above it.* Now falling onto the couch—*I hear them click-clacking all around.*

Everything's heavy and slow. I'm alone in the Dark.

*And then they come.*

I hate this part.

# CHAPTER SIX

## MARINA

"Do you think he made it?"

Tobin left the room at a half-drunk lurch, his final words to me and Anne-Marie slurred into gibberish. I think he said something about Rue.

"If he goes facedown between here and his apartment, someone will roll him the rest of the way," Anne-Marie says.

I hope that's humor.

She starts grabbing cushions off the floor. Honoria's picking up discarded bowls, stacking them to put in the wash. I reach for the nearest chair on the wall, ostensibly to put it back in its proper position in the room, but I really just want something physical between us.

As usual, Honoria's the one to break the silence.

"I was surprised you never came downstairs to find me," she says. "You've seemed *confrontational* since you came into your . . . shall we call it an inheritance?"

"Might as well. It's what I got after you killed me." I slam down the chair and drag a desk over to go with it.

Anne-Marie glances at us, but it's more warning to behave

than concern or curiosity.

"Pouting and angry gestures," Honoria says. "How very *teenage human* of you."

"That *was* the general idea, wasn't it? Take a Fade and make it human?"

Anne-Marie drops a bottle into the collection bin hard enough to rattle it, but she doesn't have to worry. Once I'm done, I'm out of here.

I take more chairs and return them to the room's center.

"Believe it or not, I understand," I tell Honoria. She looks at me like she's never seen me before, a silent nudge to prove I could possibly see things the way she does. "The Fade flipped your life upside down, and you want to reset the balance." I get that better than anyone, I imagine. "But the world's changed. People are supposed to change with it."

"You think it's that easy?"

*We adapt easily*, Cherish says.

"I think it's *possible*," I say.

"You have no idea what you're talking about."

Yes, I do. When Rue and the others crossed the Arc, the human world flipped again. Everything they thought they knew about the Fade, and the dangers they posed, changed in an instant.

"I know you're the last constant this place has," I say. "The Arclight needs that. They need to see you adapt, so they can, too."

I want to say more, but an alarm goes off on Anne-Marie's

47

wrist, and despite myself, I flinch, though we've had fewer drills lately.

"It's my mom," she says. "She wants me home."

The alert sounds again, and I realize the ping is nothing like a Red-Wall signal.

"Leave the rest." Anne-Marie glances warily between me and Honoria. "I'll make Dante finish it when he decides to show up."

"Dante was supposed to be here?" Honoria asks, suspicion in her voice. She presses a button on her wristband. "Blaylock, Dante: locate signal. If he's in the compound, I can—"

"He is," Anne-Marie says.

"He snuck off with Silver again," I add before Honoria can head into full-blown paranoia and send a security team to investigate a midnight hookup. "No big deal."

Her bracelet beeps and she frowns.

"Auxiliary storage unit nine," she says.

"Told you so."

"Happens all the time," Anne-Marie says. "He really will make it up—he always does, so you don't have to stay," she adds, to me.

The alert pings again. Her mother's not exactly patient.

"Last one," I promise. "Go on."

She runs out as I push a desk into position with its chair and then start for the door.

"You were wrong, you know," Honoria says.

I pause, knowing that's what she wants, but don't face her.

"You said I wasn't human enough to regret what I'd done—you were wrong."

It takes me a moment to realize she's talking about our confrontation in the White Room two months ago. Tobin and I had found files documenting the torture I went through to transition from Cherish to Marina. It was raw footage of me burning alive under the heat lamps while Honoria watched, dispassionate and unconcerned. She thought there was no cost too high to achieve what she wanted, and for that, I accused her of being the soulless monster she believed the Fade to be.

She acts like that moment just occurred rather than being in the past.

Does she feel time differently because she's been around so long?

For her, maybe the rise of the Fade wasn't an eternity ago. It was yesterday and still fresh in her mind.

"I regretted every step I took down the path that led to you," she says. "You were a last resort. And I am *not* the only constant this place has. I'm not the only one who remembers the world before. I'm simply the last to give up hope of reclaiming it."

I turn toward her.

Other people here who were alive in the first days? There can't be.

"There are others like you?"

"Five, counting myself, who live here now and lived here then."

"Who?"

"If they wanted you to know, they would have told you." A small mocking smile creeps into the corners of her mouth. She tosses me something and then walks out of the room.

I catch what she throws without thinking. It's solid and square, with smooth lines etched into it.

Honoria's given me her book.

What most people call "my quarters" is the single bedroom I was assigned. My walls are pink now, instead of white, matched to the flower bush my sister's named for. I put one in my corner so I can see it when I miss her. It's strange to feel homesick for a place I can't actually live in.

Anne-Marie used me once as an excuse for an art project when she ran out of ideas, so my bed's covered with the most tragically jumbled quiltish thing ever made. I like the lack of symmetry and the way one part drags lower than the others, like it's melting toward the floor.

Tobin's favorite snow globe sits on my side table. His mother had dozens of them, and this one, a desert beneath a night of falling stars, is the one he re-created for me in the Well. It was a magical idea—a place so full of light and heat that humans would be free of the Fade. Giving it to me couldn't have been easy.

My secret is that Rue hangs on my wall. No one knows he's what the cut-out image of the bird I tacked there means. The page came from Tobin's paper stash—something called a word-of-the-day calendar—and apparently, June seventeenth was a day for ornithology. My space wouldn't be complete without Rue.

This room is tiny, to hold so much.

It's where I met myself for the first time, standing as I am now, in front of the mirror. My skin's still pale, but no longer ashen, now that the Fade no longer block the melanin. Dr. Wolff says my hair is likely to darken, along with my eyes, but I think I may be stuck with white blonde and ice blue. I'll never know what I should really look like.

Honoria's book burns against my back, where I stashed it in my waistband.

I sit cross-legged on the floor, in an empty corner where the bed will hide me from view if anyone comes in unannounced, and open the book. This paper is heavier from what filled Tobin's magazines. It turns slowly, dragging across the facing page. Someone's sewn a pocket to the inside of the front cover and then stuffed it with folded scraps and pictures. I'm not sure I should risk touching those. The pocket's aged and is as brittle as the satin covering the book. It might give way.

A card fastened to the first page reads:

*Our Wedding*
*~ Rashid & Trinity ~*
*May 15th*

I turn the page and hit an unexpected obstacle. The words aren't typed like what we read for class. They're handwritten in blue ink, so the letters loop and swirl into lines I can barely make out. Everything's thin and tilted.

Someone—Honoria, I suppose—marked through the word *Guest* at the top of the page and replaced it with a date.

> May 19
> Dear Rashid and Trinity, whoever you are.
>     I'm sorry I took your guestbook, but it was the closest thing I could find to a journal in the salvage pile. We're past the 15th, anyway, so I guess you didn't need it. Nothing spoils a wedding like the apocalypse, eh?
>     Sorry, that was mean.
>     Wherever you are, I hope you're together, and still human, and that you found a way to get married, even without the pretty white satin. I'll take care of it, I promise. And if you somehow end up here, or I end up where you are, I'll give it back.
>     Sincerely,
>     Honoria Jean Whit

I've never paid much attention to how something sounds in my head while I read, but it's Honoria's voice I hear. She's younger, unsure of herself, and quick to apologize. I wonder if any of that has survived.

The next entry is on the same page as the first.

*Also May 19*

*Dear Rashid and Trinity,*

*Sorry to keep bringing you into this, but it's easier if I can pretend this is one long letter. If I'm writing to people who might still exist, then there's hope the world's still working.*

*I am such a head case.*

*I'm holed up in the corner, bunched up in a sleeping bag, and writing letters to strangers with their feather wedding pen. This is stupid.*

The entry stops there. There are a couple of drawings in the margins of a woman in a long dress and a man in a suit, but no more words for several days.

Loose pages are stuck between the bound ones, where she scribbled things down and pressed them in. These are sheets of lined paper with holes in them, not guestbook pages.

The entire chronicle of how mankind fell to the Fade is here. She filled in the gaps by memory, adding details of the run from her house to the Arclight and how they almost didn't make it.

She focuses on her family—especially her little brother. He was sure the army would fix things, and then they could go home.

*We burned our house today*—begins one page dated before Honoria started writing in her book. It's sandwiched into a stack containing details of her father's disappearance and worry over a friend whose dog had wandered to Honoria's house half starved and filthy.

> One of my teachers is here, isn't that
> weird? I don't think school exists
> anymore, but I can only think of him
> that way.

There's an entire list of entries like that—short sentences about people she noticed at random. They're scribbled on squares of colored paper and glued into the book.

> • The kids are getting quieter at night.
> They've figured out crying doesn't fix
> things. It doesn't bring back parents or
> stop friends from leaving.
> • One of the base officers is kind of
> cute. He's nice, too. He gave me an extra
> apple at dinner because he thinks I'm
> getting too skinny.

This one's stuck to a whole page with *Kevin* written in different ways.

> • *The colonel's watching us. He thinks*
> *we're dangerous because of Dad, but*
> *he's the greater threat. I saw him burn*
> *his hands. He'd only do that if one of*
> *them touched him. It won't do me any*
> *good to tell, no one listens to me. I'm*
> *just a kid.*

The colonel.

*The* colonel. It's not a name; it's a title. Col. Lutrell's name is James. Lt. Sykes's first initial is *K*, according to his name bar. For *Kevin*, maybe?

Colonel and lieutenant are designations from the world before the Fade, so why do both have them when no one else does?

Could Tobin's father be as old as Honoria? Older?

Tobin's good luck charm is that photo from the world before. A boy on a beach who became his father's namesake, but what if it's a picture of the colonel himself. Did he lie to his own son?

That would mean Honoria *didn't* lie to me.

Now it's more than curiosity; I *need* to read on.

The entries become sporadic, jumping dates.

July 6

This morning I realized the 4th had passed with no fireworks. A couple of hours later, it sunk in why—there's no country anymore.

No one's celebrating anything after the rain last night, anyway. It cost us the bonfires. We hadn't had darkness in weeks, besides that black shroud that's swallowed everything we left behind.

People were screaming and crying, scrambling to find candles and flashlights. They tried to get all the doors and windows shut, but there was so much howling and scratching and noise ...

There was Spacey Tracey, sitting by the exit, in the dark. She laid her hand against the door, and said, " I know, I will" to nobody. Mom says she's talking to her family, that she can't deal with what's happened to them, but Mom's wrong. If Tracey was talking to her family, she'd use their names. She doesn't.

And her eyes were not that blue

*last week. They're nearly silver. No one
notices things like that, but they should.
I saw Dad's eyes. I remember them.*

*That nuthatch is going to break and
run one of these nights, and I wish ...
I wish they'd get rid of her. There—I
said it. I know it's horrible, and I know
it makes me a bad person, but I don't
care. I don't want her around.*

*I heard the adults talking. These old
ventilation pipes catch everything and
broadcast it like stereo. They don't know
what to do, and that scares them.*

*No ... I think what really scares
them is that they do know, and no one
wants to do it. Not to pretty Tracey,
who used to be so sweet and so smart,
but they don't get it. Tracey's gone.*

*I hate this place.
I want to go home.*

Things change after Tracey. People Honoria mentions on one page are lost within the next three. She kept a list, tracking who left on what day, through several sheets held together with metal clips. I bet she didn't miss a single name.

Pages and pages are doodles of trees without leaves. Their

branches are spindly and gruesome—*ominous*. The first few are practice for one that takes up an entire page of meticulous detail. I start to trace the outline with my finger, but draw back at the feel of the paper along the lines. They're rigid and sharp, as though she was caught up in a frenzy while making them. Discolored patches on the page look like dried blood that's deteriorated over time.

Here, in the middle of the book, are the sections Honoria's marked to be read in class.

She's scribbled over her original entries, rewording them. She's marked things out and replaced them, adding notes on yellow squares. She's highlighted and underlined obsessively. Her changes support the assumptions she's made over the last decades when the original text may not have.

I don't know why she kept the original words. Why not rip the pages out and replace them altogether?

The last entry about Tracey mentions how the girl stole a box of pens and used them to draw lines all over her skin. I check the list and find that Tracey Malone walked into the night a few hours later. Honoria was very matter-of-fact about it—in the rewrite. She'd struck through the response she had in the moment so fiercely that it cut the page, and she replaced it with a clinical observation that Tracey's fate was inevitable.

She's tried to change the past, and in a way, I guess that's what she hoped she could accomplish with me. If her attempt to uninclude someone from the Fade's hive had worked, then it might have been possible to reclaim the world for humans and undo the damage of the last several decades. Too bad it's harder to mark through time than ink.

The thought causes a chill I can't shake. It gets into my blood and down to my bones. The only time I've felt anything close to this was when I stepped into the Dark as Marina for the first time and believed I'd walked into my own execution.

"Cherish?" I ask out loud; my voice is a victory. I was afraid *she* was the chill. That she'd figured out how to take me over. "Cherish?" I call again, but still there's no answer.

Shadows grow from the ceiling, gathering like cobwebs in the corners and trailing toward the floor. I reach for my lamp, to raise the shade and make the room brighter, but the bulb shatters in its socket.

The shadows turn to vines, slithering over everything. They reach my beloved sister-bush. I lunge forward to save it, but my feet are ankle deep in sludge so thick, it holds me fast, forcing me to watch as the bush is ripped to shreds. The vines strip the leaves and choke the bush, filling the room with the scent of ruined roses, and then it's gone. Nothing but leaves drifting down with the sound of my sister's broken laughter in the background.

My pink walls scorch black. The paint blisters up and boils away. When the shadows reach the cut-out bird, it comes squawking to life and flapping for all it's worth, but there's nowhere for it to go beyond its page. The shadows flow over it like poured tar, leaving it struggling beneath the weight until it goes still.

And the sludge around my feet grows deeper, up to my knees.

Half the room has crumbled to nothing. The shadows become snatching fingers, ripping and tearing by the handful. Anne-Marie's quilt goes next, soaking up the darkness to become a sodden abyss. I try to save Tobin's snow globe, but my arms are tethered, pulled flush to the wall. Darkness descends upon the globe like settling smoke. It passes through the glass to mingle with the water, churning and spinning until it goes so fast, the glass bursts, leaving the stars to ooze over the sides and into the sludge where they sink out of sight.

The darkness is to my waist now.

Something drips onto my head, and in the mirror across my room, I watch it slide through my hair, staining it black.

There's a flash of movement. I turn my head to check the last standing corner of my room; empty, but when I focus on it in the mirror, what I had taken for my shadow separates itself from the wall. Just a shimmer at first, slowly defining itself as the edges become clear and take on a human shape.

*No—Fade-shape.* It's a Fade coming into view, clinging to my wall, but still only in my mirror. Pale skin appears against the black background. Feathered wisps on her cheeks and short stripes wrapping toward her mouth. My eyes, only shining silver instead of flat blue.

*Cherish.*

"Help," I try to say, but cords of shadow wrap around my mouth.

This can't happen—Rue promised. The hive only accepts the willing.

I glance to the corner where Cherish should be, but she's not there. In my mirror she crawls down the wall, reaches out with clawed hands and breaks the vines around my mouth. She holds her finger to her lips, warning me not to make a sound, and then tears at the restraints around my arms, dropping into the sludge beside me.

She's fighting for me. She wouldn't fight the hive.

Once my hands are free, she dives for my feet, still unnoticed by the shadows as they destroy everything else, but they're closing in on my mirror.

What is this?

My hive celebrates someone coming home. It doesn't drown them. Where are the voices? Where's the harmony? Where're the warmth and welcome?

This isn't right. This isn't my Fade.

The sludge is up to my chest.

Do Fade need to come up for air? Cherish is still below the surface, picking at the bindings around my feet to free me. I can't do anything but stand helpless. I scream as sludge pours in from all sides, quickly rising to my neck and chin and higher.

Cherish reappears. For a second, I'm staring at myself. And I'm absolutely terrified.

My own reflection appears in Cherish's eyes, our expressions identical. As the sludge comes up, covering my mouth so that I have to struggle to keep my nose above the tide, she wraps her arms around my neck and literally goes to pieces. Her entire body becomes a shield made of nanites, trying to cocoon me away from danger, and so save herself, too.

But it's not enough. She shatters, and we're both washed away.

That's when I wake screaming into the light of my bedside lamp, still clutching Honoria's book where I fell asleep reading it, but it wasn't Honoria's dream I had—it was Tobin's nightmare.

Humans don't share dreams.

*We share*, Cherish says.

"No, *we* don't!"

Tobin is *not* a Fade. I'm no longer in the hive. I can't share what others see and hear. It was just a nightmare. *A run-of-the-mill creepy nightmare that leaves me with the feeling that something terrible is coming.*

I lay the book aside and head for my sink to splash water on my face, careful not to look up, in case the dream's still there in my mirror.

I reach for a towel, but while drying my hands, I realize something's missing—the sting. Between the cut from the arbor and the broken bottle, my hands should be burning. I glance down and find them impossibly perfect. The skin's healed over, without so much as a scratch.

Humans don't share dreams, and they don't heal in the course of a catnap.

"Cherish?" I ask, turning my attention to my reflection. "Did you—"

My voice chokes off, startled silent by the sight of myself in the glass. I'm still human, with blue eyes and white-blonde hair, but I'd swear—just for a second—my shadow moves without me.

"Cherish?" I call again, turning to check the empty room behind me. When I face the mirror again, all is as it should be, only now I can't lose the feeling of being watched.

# CHAPTER SEVEN

## MARINA

It's impossible to tell time in a dream. I've been out so long, I nearly missed Anne-Marie's birthday dinner.

Unlike the hinged door Tobin's dad installed at their apartment, Anne-Marie's is a standard sliding panel. I knock, and her smiling face appears as it moves into its pocket, leaving a clear path inside.

"She's here," she yells over her shoulder, and I'm yanked inside.

I was expecting something like Tobin's house, but this one's mostly metal and ceramic—inorganic materials considered safe from the Fade. There aren't any rugs, and the lights are stark white. Pictures of Anne-Marie and her brother cover the walls, and while I see a few of their mother, there aren't any of Mr. Pace.

"Mom!" Anne-Marie's still shouting, even though her mother's in sight. "Marina's here."

"Hi, Marina," her mother says.

"Hello, Ms. Johnston."

"None of that, now. My name's Dominique. You two go sit

down. We'll eat in a few minutes." Anne-Marie's mother smiles at me before turning her head away with a scowl. "Trey! I want you out of that room in five minutes!"

She swirls past us with bowls in each hand, only stopping long enough to deposit them on a clear glass table.

"She's, er . . . different."

"She's got help in the kitchen," Anne-Marie says, tugging me over for a look.

Mr. Pace is here, but I'm not sure I'd call what he's doing "help." He's picking at the food from a large bowl on the counter. When Anne-Marie's mother warns him off, he flicks part of what he's eating at her. She stomps across the room to take the bowl, but he hides it behind his back until she makes a grab for it, and then he pins her into a hug that quickly turns into a kiss.

Dante and Silver are bad enough, but parents? *Ew.*

"He's over a lot more since the lights went down. Mom's been floating."

Arc Fall seems an odd reason to visit family, but what do I know?

"Trey, five minutes! I'm serious!" Anne-Marie's mother pokes her head out the door of the kitchen, not smiling for the moment it takes to yell her son's name down the hall.

"That's his fourth five-minute call," Anne-Marie says, rolling her eyes.

"Is he in trouble?"

"Nah. Just Trey back to his normal, antisocial self. The

record's six days, but he was sneaking out during the day to snag food, so it doesn't really count."

It seems like siblings should be alike, but Anne-Marie and her brother don't even look all that similar. They're both tall, and both dark, but while Trey turns more into a Mr. Pace clone by the day, Anne-Marie looks like her mom.

Connections are so confusing.

*Not at home*, Cherish offers. I have to bite down on the response I want to give.

Thankfully, a knock on the door interrupts her at the same time loud laughter comes from the kitchen.

"Get that, will you?" Anne-Marie asks. "If I don't set the table, those two will forget we need plates. Honestly, you'd think *they* were the teenagers."

She heads for the kitchen with a hand over her eyes, declaring, "I'm coming in! Act parental!" while I go back to the door. So this is what it's like to have a home that people want to visit.

*We can return to home*, Cherish says. *Remaining is selfish. Stupid. Inferior.*

She doesn't usually go for insults.

"Hey," Tobin says when I open the door. His eyes are brown—I check. Col. Lutrell's are still silver.

"Hey."

I want to say more, but I can't decide what should come next. Maybe it's Cherish sabotaging things from the inside, but every time I see Tobin now, it's like a wall goes up between us. I swear

66

sometimes he actually looks blurry, and when I try to talk to him, like I did in the Well, I can barely string a sentence together. I want to hold his hand, but mine won't move.

He doesn't move, either, so maybe he doesn't want me to.

"Are we late?" Col. Lutrell asks.

"Not really. Anne-Marie's mother's sort of caught up in something."

There's another snort of laughter from the kitchen, followed by Anne-Marie's frustrated groan.

"Daughter still in the room!" she shouts.

"I can imagine." Col. Lutrell grins, winking at us as he excuses himself to go back her up. I wonder if he can tell something might be wrong with Tobin. Could he have seen Tobin's eyes? Can sense my suspicions the way I sense emotion? I know his hearing's sharp, but I don't know what other Fade traits remain with those exposed yet not included in the hive.

Maybe that's why he led the not-rescue mission when I was taken. If he's the colonel from Honoria's book, it would have been safer for him to risk the Fade. He'd already lived through contact.

"I thought I'd slept through dinner," Tobin says, but he doesn't look like he got much rest. "Dad said I was screaming so loud, he thought I was in pain."

"Nightmares?" I ask.

He nods, face paler than I've ever seen.

"What'd you tell him?"

"That I dreamed I got caught on the Arc when it was turned on, so I was burning up. I don't know if he believed it or not."

I wish I could get him to say more without telling him I had a nightmare myself. Maybe mine wasn't an exact copy.

"Trey, get your butt out of that room and into this chair *now*!"

Anne-Marie's mother sweeps back into the room with another set of steaming bowls.

Cherish leaks through, assigning Ms. Johnston a Fade-name that encompasses steam for her temper, mixed with something diamond hard and bright.

"Trouble?" Tobin asks, to shift the conversation off dreams.

"Anne-Marie claims it's normal, but it started with a countdown and progressed to an ultimatum, so I'm not sure I believe her."

"No, that's pretty much normal," he says. Everyone's moving toward the table, so we join them.

Anne-Marie's mother and Mr. Pace—*her father*—tote the last of the food out with Col. Lutrell bringing a large tray to set in the center.

This doesn't smell like dinner in the Common Hall. It's not wilted or reeking of vitamin supplements, and the plates aren't flat squares broken into sections. They're round and made of glass with blue flowers at the edges to match the blue glasses beside them. The plates sit on plastic mats with the silverware set out on each side instead of rolled into a napkin that smells like bleach.

"Nique's stuff is great," Tobin says when he realizes I'm staring at the food.

He's said before that if it wasn't for Anne-Marie and her mother, he'd have starved the first few days after his dad went missing. They even tried to make him move in with them, but he wouldn't leave his apartment, or the Well it conceals. It seems a silly secret now that the stars are there for everyone to see, but neither we nor Tobin's father have shared the knowledge of the door in their closet that leads to the Arclight's tunnel system.

Another shiver goes down my arms, acknowledging another clue. If the colonel's been here since before, it would explain why his room has access to the tunnels that others never knew about.

"Why isn't Jove here?" I ask Anne-Marie. "I thought you invited him."

"*Un*invited," she snarls. "I only eat with people I like."

*Oops* . . . I missed another fight.

"And I *don't* like people who tell me I look like a dandelion stalk with the fluff blown off now that I've cut my hair." She stabs her table mat with her fork.

I would have thought getting his jaw broken for running his mouth once would have made Jove more careful.

"Trey!" Anne-Marie's mother leans back in her chair to shout down the hall. This time, the scowl doesn't ease when she turns her attention to the rest of us. "I don't know what I'm going to do with him. Do you know he wanted me to invite the Fade who healed him to dinner? I mean I'm grateful for what it did for him, but dinner? Do they even eat?"

I cringe at the *it* and find myself mumbling an answer to her question, though I wish I'd remained silent. Cherish is fuming.

"They're vegetarians," I say. At least the ones who began as humans; it's a little more complicated for the ones who are born Fade. Either way, their bodies need fuel.

"Oh . . . Marina, honey. I'm sorry. I don't mean it like that. Trey's just been so odd since, well, you know."

"I know." I nod.

"It's driving me crazy—and it's only getting worse," she says. "Maybe I *should* invite that Fade over and see if it knows what's going on in his head—*Trey!* That's it."

"Uh-oh," Anne-Marie says as her mother runs out of patience. The countdowns are done.

Mr. Pace leans over and whispers something, but it doesn't help.

"No, what I'm going to do is drag him out of that room and down the hall by his collar. I've warned that child. . . ."

She throws her napkin onto her empty plate, storming off down the hall, still demanding her son come out. The shouts stop, replaced by a beep loud enough that we can hear it at the table. Tobin glances down, embarrassed, and the two men snicker.

"Parental override," Anne-Marie says. "Trey's too old, but his door hasn't been rewired, yet. She can still open it."

Just as I'm debating whether or not to crane my neck and see if Anne-Marie's mother makes good on her threat to haul

Trey to dinner despite her diminutive size, a shriek from the hall stops the laughter around the table. It's the same sound Anne-Marie's mother made the night she thought the Fade had taken her children.

"Stay—" Mr. Pace starts.

"Here," adds Tobin's father.

They're on their feet and running in nearly perfect sync, the way the Fade do, and I'm the only one who notices. None of us obey. We rise as though we all have the same disobedient thought at once and race after them, in time to catch the last of what Anne-Marie's mother tells them.

"His eyes . . . his face . . ."

She's got her back to the wall, outside Trey's room, and then slides down so her weight's on the balls of her feet. Her hands are to her mouth, holding in another scream. She doesn't move until we try to pass her. One of her hands shoots out to grab Anne-Marie's.

"Don't, baby. Don't go inside."

Anne-Marie's the picture of silent terror, probably as sure as I am that her brother's dead. Dead eyes and a corpse's face, what else would make her mother act this way? She gives me a panicked look that's very clear: find out what's going on.

*Listen*, Cherish says suddenly. *Hear.*

But what good is it to listen if no one's speaking?

*They are speaking*, she says. *You haven't heard. He hears.*

I enter Trey's room slowly. Mr. Pace, Col. Lutrell, and Tobin stand on the other side of the threshold, with a wide gap between them and Trey's bed. He looks fine.

Trey's sitting cross-legged on his bed with a pad of paper in his lap. His room's full of discarded pages—on the walls and floor, haphazard piles of them on the desk and chair.

*He drew home,* Cherish says. *He sees home. Sick.*

She doesn't mean homesick. Trey's pictures are all sickened versions of the Dark, even though he's never seen it. The buildings are strange and unfamiliar, the animals menacing. Fade I don't recognize with distorted bodies, and horror-stricken people I don't know. Trey's still drawing in a frenzy when his mother finally collects herself enough to come inside, holding Anne-Marie behind her.

"Trey, honey, can you look at me?" she asks. "It—it's dinnertime. Please stop."

"Almost done, Mom, I swear." He sounds normal enough. It's like he doesn't know he has an audience, and he didn't hear her scream.

"Trey, are you okay?" Anne-Marie asks.

I've crept closer to Tobin, leaning my cheek against his arm; his fingers twine between mine as the air compresses from the weight of worry flowing off so many people. I could choke from the stench of it.

"And . . . *done!*"

Trey's answer is the final flourish of whatever he's working on. He turns to face us, beaming and displaying the image of a ferocious tusked pig surrounded by ominous shadows.

"Any idea what this is?" he asks. "Wait, what are you all doing in here?"

No one answers. No one even breathes.

Trey's face is swirled with Fade-marks, and his eyes are gleaming metallic gold.

# CHAPTER EIGHT

## TOBIN

"Get out of here," Dad orders me.

"What's wrong?" Trey asks. No one's told him how he looks.

This pretty much blows Rueful's "only willing hosts" line to bits. Trey has no idea what's happening to him. How can that be willing?

So much for neutrality.

Mr. Pace starts stacking Trey's drawings into a pile, as though that's the problem.

"Am I in trouble?" Trey tries asking Annie.

"Move!" Annie's mom pushes her to her room and uses her override to lock the door.

"Let me out!" Annie screams from the other side. She's beating on the door, but she won't even make a dent. "Mom, please! Let me out! Mom!"

Nique won't do it. She'd rather have Annie locked in and scared than free to roam and turning Fade like her brother.

"What are you doing?" Trey asks. "What's wrong with Annie?"

"Nothing," Mr. Pace says. He grabs Trey's wrist when Trey tries to leave his room. "You stay here."

"But what'd I do?"

"Go." Dad shuffles me and Marina out the door when we don't leave on our own. "Marina, you're welcome to stay with Tobin, but I want you both out of here. And I'm checking the entry alert, Tobin. You have two minutes to get to the apartment and ping me, or I'm coming to find you."

Marina doesn't say a word, but I know what she's thinking, and none of it's good. When we get to my place, she keeps going. I'm not stupid—she'll go to *him* to sort this out.

I go inside and then stop the door so it can't close all the way. Once I've tripped the entry sensor, so Dad will get the ping to tell him I'm home, I head back out, allowing the door to close behind me. Hopefully, he's too busy to notice my tracker heading toward the Arc.

If Trey turns, I'm next.

No, Annie's next. She was exposed first.

What am I thinking? *Everyone* is next.

"How did you beat me out here?" Marina catches sight of me halfway across the quad and crosses the rest at a jog. "How'd you even know I'd be here?"

"Closest crossing point. I took a different route."

She stops beside me, at the edge of the Arc. The lamps are conserving power right now. They give just enough light so people can see where they're going and find their way back. No one's panicking yet, but they will. Then the lights will go completely hot.

"Were you put back on duty because of Trey?" Marina asks. "Are they tightening security already?"

"They wouldn't start with me, and they wouldn't put me here." Sykes would be patrolling the short side. Trainees get dumped in low-priority sections. "The lights would be brighter."

We'll be at Red-Wall as soon as our elders declare Trey a security breach.

"How long have we got?"

"As long as Dad and Trey's parents can buy us." So, not long.

It'll only take minutes to get Trey to the hospital, so long as he doesn't flip out and fight them. Mr. Pace and Nique can stall Dr. Wolff for an hour or two before he either alerts Honoria out of habit or she hears about Trey herself. If they're lucky, no one will see Trey en route and they'll be able to lock down the hospital without details circulating.

*Crap.* I'm starting to sound like Honoria. Worse, I'm starting to understand her.

The only choices are to hide what's happened or to start a riot with full disclosure. They've got to get Trey contained.

And then they'll come for us.

Marina knows that, too. It's why she's here.

"You're going out there, aren't you?" I ask.

"Like you're not here for the same reason."

I'm here because I don't believe in coincidence. Trey's bait. The shadow-hugger probably planned this. He left Marina a trail of Fade-crusted bread crumbs, and she's going to follow it until she loses her way home.

"It's too dangerous," I say.

"If Rue or one of the others knows something, then—"

"Then *what*?" I snap, harsher than I mean to. Louder, too.

She flinches back, and I tell myself to get a grip before I scare her and she goes looking for *him* to protect her from me. I'm too jumpy. The nightmares were bad enough, but seeing them on paper, like Trey pulled them out of my head, was too much.

Touching those things changes people, no matter what they say.

"What if they expected this to happen, Marina? What if Trey's just the first?"

"I don't believe that."

Of course she doesn't. All she can see is the tragic hero who risked his life to save his lost love. Rueful's a fairy tale. How do I compete with that?

"We should wait and see what Doctor Wolff says," I suggest.

"I don't trust Doctor Wolff."

Right.

"Then we wait here. Honoria's brother might show. We can—"

"Take a look, Tobin. What do you see?" she says.

I turn back to the Grey, but there's nothing there.

Nothing. No one, and no Fade. There hasn't been a night without at least a handful of them hovering in the Grey until sunrise drives them back. Tonight, there's only the fog, coming too close and making my skin crawl. I can almost hear the click-clack of tiny feet marching up my arm.

I reach down for a rock and throw it, but it drops out of the air on its own without hitting anything.

"Bolt's not coming," she says. "No one is."

Our night started with an invisible Fade on the front line. Now they're at full retreat, and Trey's jacked into my nightmares. What's next?

"I can stop you from going," I tell Marina.

"You're not going to hit me."

"No, but I can hit my wristband and send us straight to Red-Wall." She might hate me now, but she'll thank me later. "For all we know, Trey had a bad reaction, like an allergy. If it was serious—"

"Your eyes were silver."

Her answer's ice water to my face, knocking the air out of me.

She's lying. She has to be. Marina picked a sore spot because she knew it would get a reaction.

"You don't have to make up—"

"Your eyes were silver in the Arbor, when you saw the blood on my hand. Look at my hands."

She removes her gloves and holds her hands out, palms up. She turns them over to let me see both sides, and the perfect, unscarred skin that's replaced the cut I cleaned and the one from the broken bottle.

"What happened?"

"I fell asleep after Honoria's presentation, and had a nightmare—*your* nightmare. The cuts were gone when I woke up. Your eyes were silver, and I'm healing like someone's reknitting my skin from the inside out. We shared a dream, Tobin. Whatever's happening to Trey, he's not the only one. I'm not waiting. I'm *going* to find Rue. I'm not giving him a choice but to help—the end."

"Wait." I grab her by the shoulder as she steps forward. "What if it's not a dream? What if it's a premonition?" My voice sounds strange.

"It's not."

"What if the Fade are spreading again and we caused it by bringing down the Arc and letting them in?"

*Never forget,* Honoria's voice drones in the back of my mind. *It was a single mistake that put us over the edge.*

"Tobin, listen to me. Rue will fix this."

Sure he will. The mighty Fade Charming can fix anything.

I pull my gloves off my shaking hands, searching them for lines on my palms and knuckles. I check between my fingers in case they're hiding, but it's just skin. A fading tan from wearing the gloves so long, and fingernails that are clean, except for the one I tore trying to bite off a hangnail.

"You don't have lines," she says. "Neither do I. The silver was only a flash, but it was there."

"Maybe it was trick of the light."

"That's what I thought. I thought it was Cherish, and her mind games, but now—"

"You said you couldn't hear them anymore." I take a step back. I want to throw up, but my stomach's got a giant knot in it that hits my throat every time I try.

"Not *them*," she says. "*Her*. She messes with my head sometimes."

"But she's you, isn't she?" And since when is there a distinction? The shadow crawlers are an all-for-one deal. If you hear one, you hear the rest.

"I thought so, too, but I'm not sure about anything tonight," she says. "Something must have gone wrong when Bolt and Rue healed you and Trey."

I'm more concerned with the idea that something went right, and this is stage two. She might be convinced that the Fade mean no harm, but their definition of help isn't the same as ours— that's why they've stuck with Dad. We don't always speak the same language. This could be their idea of "better."

"You should have told me," I say.

"I just did."

Marina stands on the Arc with her foot hovering above the ground, but she can't manage to take the first step.

"What if she's stronger than me?" she says, but more to herself than me. She flinches, slapping at her ears. Did one of *them* say something back?

"If you're crossing, I'm going with you, and it has to be now. Leaving after the Arc goes hot will set off an alarm."

"This is a bad idea," she says. "But I don't have a better one."

She takes a breath, closes her eyes, and steps over the boundary into the Grey.

The short side used to be most dangerous place I knew; it's where we were most vulnerable. Anytime the Fade tried to break in, they did it here, because it's the only place you can cross and get back in a few hours. Now it's simply the most convenient. A couple of other people are already out here, barely within sight of the Arclight, but none of them are the kids from Honoria's speech.

"Tell me your dream again," Marina says after we're past them.

"I'm standing on the Arc, when it comes on and fries me where I stand."

"Now tell me the real one."

I don't want to. If I recount it, then I have to think about it, and if I'm thinking about it, then I might as well be living it.

"Why?" I ask.

"Because maybe I'm wrong," she says. "Maybe mine wasn't the same and I only convinced myself it was."

"That's probably it. I doubt your brain is as twisted as mine."

"I saw the Dark, Tobin," she says. "But it wasn't the place we went before, with the houses and families. It was like Trey's drawings. The whole thing was one writhing monster, ready to devour the world."

"I call that variation two," I say. Number one is worse.

We've reached the point where the terrain begins to change. Murky water appears in puddles and then turns the ground to mush that sucks against the bottoms of my boots. That's the only sound here beyond the wind and the occasional movement of the water.

This is part of the dream, too.

A creature I first mistake for a log makes a whipping motion with its long snout and tail before sliding into the water with barely a ripple. Its eyes shine red beneath the surface, where it lurks, watching.

"So, once we're in . . . *there* . . . how do we find the nanobot?" I ask. "Do we call its—"

"His!" Marina snaps.

"Fine. Do we call *his* name or try to find our way back to the settlement on our own?"

"I think Cherish can call him, but I'm not sure I want—"

"Stop."

I throw my arm up so she can't walk any farther. Finding the Fade won't be a problem; they're here. She should have heard them before me.

The terrain shimmers and then splits, forming two solid bodies with ash-pale skin marked with nanites. They head straight for us.

One's female, bigger than Marina, but not by much. She has a broad nose and wide eyes framed by spirals. The male's a head taller than me, but it's his hands that stand out. Most of these things come pretty evenly marked, unless they're hurt and the nanites go to the wound, but this guy's got nano-doodles all over his hands. He's scarred, too. A jagged ridge cuts through his scalp, leaving him with a bald spot.

I don't know about the female, but he was definitely human before he was Fade. They're both dressed in fatigues similar to the ones our security personnel are assigned.

"What do they want?" I ask Marina as they fall into step on either side of us.

"They didn't say," Marina says, cocking her head like she's listening to something. "I think they're escorting us in."

"What's with the silent treatment?" Maybe the ones born out here have trouble with words, but someone who started off human should be able to speak. Honoria's brother can.

"They didn't say that, either."

They urge us onward and set the pace. If I fall off cadence, one pushes me so I'll keep up.

Once we're at the Dark, they show us where to enter through the trees and vines, cringing away from a burst of light that ignites the sky behind us.

The Arc's back on full power, burning across the short side. A moment later, there's a siren wailing in the distance, calling everyone to safety while the alarm on my wrist and Marina's flash red.

She looks at me, and I nod.

*Honoria knows.*

# CHAPTER NINE

## MARINA

We've moved fully into the Dark, walking shoulder to shoulder with the unnamed Fade on either side.

*Are they a good thing or a bad thing?* I ask Cherish.

*Guard,* she says, but is that a warning, or does she mean they're a guard detail?

*Why would we need guards?* I ask, but she doesn't have an answer for that.

Instead she says, *Home.*

That's all she cares about—getting home.

She *wants* to be here. She *wants* to stay.

The moment I pressed my toes into the Arc, Cherish was pushing me to leave so hard, I could feel hands at my back. Other hands were reaching out for me the way they do in my dreams of belonging, promising to pull me home.

*Home,* Cherish says again.

*Not for me,* I say back.

It's chilly here. The Dark's always cool because of the shade, but this is more. Tobin's hand is a block of ice inside mine. The heat flows off my body, siphoned away so I'm left shivering.

The leaves and branches rattle, but there's no wind. They're shivering, too.

The Dark's afraid.

"They're scared," I whisper back to Tobin, casting a wary glance at the male Fade beside him. Even if they don't want to answer us, they can still understand us.

"Because the lights came on?"

"I don't think so." The Arc has kept the Fade away for decades. Crossing it is painful for them, if not outright lethal, but the lights don't reach this deep.

*What's wrong?* I ask Cherish.

I expect her to answer the way Rue would, by allowing me to touch the hive's mind, so I brace for the flood of noise and emotions that comes with it, but it never happens. She might as well have plugged her ears.

"She's locked me out," I say.

Cherish is doing this on purpose. She's hiding something.

"You try," I suggest.

"Try what?" Tobin asks.

"To talk to them. Try to hear."

If Tobin is turning, he'll be able to.

"I don't know—I mean, how?" Tobin asks uncertainly, but he never suggests that he might not be able to hear them. Our shared nightmares, and Trey's drawings, are coming from somewhere, and the hive is the only source out here.

"Act like you're trying to get someone's attention in a crowd.

Pick someone you know and then shout."

Tobin stops, bringing us all to a clumsy halt as he closes his eyes.

"I feel like an idiot," he says. His face draws up more like someone in pain than attempting communication.

"You *look* like an idiot," I say, and he scowls. "Did you hear anything?"

"Does my spiking blood pressure count?"

Sigh. I'll take that as a no.

"It was worth a shot," I say.

And, if nothing else, there's a renewed sense of peace to Tobin's demeanor. The hive didn't answer him. They don't answer humans.

Maybe that's why they aren't answering me. I chose a human existence; this is the cost.

*Continue.*

As if to prove me wrong, the male Fade speaks.

I'm not an outcast, I'm a misbehaving child, only allowed to speak when spoken to. One being told to stay out of the important conversations.

*Motion*, says the female. *Forward*.

"We should go," I tell Tobin, and we head deeper into the Dark, hand in hand.

The Dark's always moving. Nanites swirl across their hosts' skin, displaying emotions better than any expression. Lines of black crisscross the ground and snake up trees, altering their appearance in a neverending crawl. If they stop the cycle, the ones on top creating the canopy will die from too much sun exposure. They mourn every voice lost and try to preserve as many as possible. Here, the greater good is distilled for the good of one.

Haunting reminders of the world before the Fade appear without warning. Some are subtle, like the painted lines on the ground that peek through gaps of rolling Fade, only to be covered again a second later. Others, like buildings that stand in various stages of decay, are harsher.

Eyes watch us. Ghostly faces appear and disappear at random; shimmers follow us from high up on the trees. Here and there, fully formed Fade approach from the remnants of houses, and I can't help but wonder if they're the ones who were human in the beginning. Were these their homes?

"You think they'd at least tell us their names," Tobin says after a while. "They have names, right?"

I hear a growl, so close it makes me jump, but Tobin doesn't move until I do, so the sound has to be for my ears only.

"What now?" he asks, tightening his grip on my hand. His eyes and ears don't adjust as fast as mine. Here, *I'm* the one protecting *him*.

"I think he heard you," I say. "He growled."

*Negative*, says the male Fade, followed by the same fearsome sound.

He lifts the sleeve of his jacket to bare his arm and then points to a shape drawn with colored lines. They're static, and not crisp, until a rush of nanites darkens them, highlighting the image of a vicious animal lunging off his bicep, mouth open in a snarl.

"Is that your name?" I ask.

He growls again, replacing the sleeve over other pictures, including the obscure outline of a woman's body on his inner forearm. The Fade have tried to mimic the ink he had tattooed on before they came.

"They call him Dog," I say.

"Does that make her Cat?" Tobin snorts.

*Shh.* The impression of a sharp hiss of air comes from the female. *Speak softly.*

"Speak—Oh! Your name's Whisper."

The female gives me a sharp nod, the only truly human gesture I've seen from either of them.

"We're Marina and Tobin," I say.

Invisible water washes over my legs, just as it did when Rue tried to make me understand that Marina was the place where he lost Cherish. Honoria made it my name, and now Whisper and Dog have, too.

After the water comes the streak of light Cherish attached to Tobin, but it's only Whisper repeating his name. No one could have told her that name but Cherish.

Somehow Cherish can talk to them without me hearing it. I can't shake the feeling that my Fade-self is lurking in the secret parts of my memory, using my own brain to plot against me. If I can't hear her, I can't anticipate what she's planning. I can't protect myself.

This is my body; I should have the advantage, not her.

"This looks familiar," Tobin says of the deeper parts of the Dark. The relief's so thick in his voice, I could pluck it from the air like fruit from the Arbor. "Either it's all running together, or I recognize this place."

He's right. The monotony has broken, giving way to familiar trees with distinct roots and knots that mark the gates of the human-neighborhood-turned-Fade-settlement. The first houses are visible as swaths of white and blue, where metal siding has resisted both Fade and time. Birds a light on the eaves, trilling out a sound that can't really be called a song, but it's comforting. They sound like Rue's real name. Flowers and ornate fungi spring up out of the ground as we pass, creating a path to lead us the final steps.

The color's a spontaneous display of relief. Tension settles out of the air now that we've reached the place the Fade consider safe. They were worried we might not make it.

What could scare a Fade in the Dark?

"I know I was preoccupied the last time we were here, but this is . . . *not like it used to be,*" Tobin says.

More guards like Whisper and Dog mill the fringes in pairs. *Security patrols.* The loose nanites, which usually hang from the trees as moss, now form a fence, joining the trees together. The leaves rustle overhead, and Tobin points up. More regimented Fade are folded into the branches, clinging to the trunks with the claws that only appear on their hands when they need to climb. They're all on alert.

We gain followers, so that by the time we reach the middle of the neighborhood, and the crowd waiting for us there, another has us penned in from behind.

"Bolt!" I cry, recognizing him in the group. I wave him over, but he turns and disappears. "Wait! Come back!"

"I really hope I was wrong about this being a setup," Tobin says as one of the few Fade we know on sight deserts us.

"Me, too."

Otherwise, I don't think we're going anywhere.

Maybe ever.

# CHAPTER TEN

## MARINA

*Pine needles.*

Evergreen.

"Mom!"

The ashen blur of faces parts to allow my mother to the front, and the scent of pine fills the air, calming as a tranquilizer on my nerves.

"Why didn't you come back?" I ask. "I kept looking for you at the Arc."

*Searched*, is her answer, but she didn't have to look for me. I'm not the one who left.

She stretches out her hand, grasping mine. I'm pale compared to most of the people in the Arclight, but there's a difference in human pale and Fade-white. Her skin's warmer than mine, her pulse a mix of blood and nanites flowing through her veins.

I'm no longer the same species as my mother.

The lines uncoil from her arms, rushing toward her hands and mine in greeting. Tobin grabs her wrist.

"Don't," he orders.

"She's my mother, Tobin. She won't hurt me."

"No, she's a *Fade's* mother. You're some human girl she met once."

"Let her go," I say bitterly, but I'm not sure he's wrong. Evergreen braved the Arclight to retrieve her stolen daughter, not knowing I was going to stay Marina and leave her alone.

Her face stays passive, but the lines on her skin flatten out into wide blotches, giving her the appearance of deep bruises.

"He's not threatening you, Mom. Things have been pretty rough tonight, and—"

*Outsider.*

She places a hand over my mouth, cutting me off and glaring at Tobin.

*Speak*, she says.

"You know him," I say, muffled.

*Speak.*

My mother doesn't like my voice. She wants me to talk like a Fade.

She holds out her hands again, this time waiting for me to take them, and I do.

"I'll be okay," I tell Tobin over her head.

The marks on my mother's hands slip on to mine, bridging the gap between human and Fade. It's still not the full connection, where the hive chatters away with a million voices all saying shades of the same thing, but the sense of belonging is there. Expressions of worry and relief tumble from Evergreen's side of the link, followed by warnings for carefulness without context.

She sifts through my thoughts, pleased to see the Arbor. It seems I've always liked plants. There's a warm glow for the scenes with Anne-Marie, at least until she reaches the horror of being abandoned in a room with Honoria Whit.

Thoughts of Honoria bring my mother's attention to my hand, bubbling with excitement when she finds it healed. She seeks out every reference to Cherish I've locked away, dredging them out as if to say *look here* or *be this.* But I let go, stepping away with my hands behind my back before Cherish can reconnect with our mother.

Evergreen stares at me with glistening eyes and a sense of hurt so real that I may as well have slapped her.

"Why are you crying?" Tobin asks.

I didn't know I was.

*Separated,* Evergreen charges at the sound of his voice. *Disconnected.*

"It's not his fault," I insist.

*Why do you not speak?* she asks. *Listen.*

"Fear," I say.

*Which fear?*

How am I supposed to put that into words?

I show her a piece of my nightmare in hope that she'll understand that it feels like the shadows are choking me.

*I'll drown,* I say. *The Dark will bury me.*

*Negative.*

*Affirmed,* I argue. *I've seen it.*

I show her the tidal wave.

"I don't want to be washed away," I tell her.

*Seen where?*

The question is more forceful than the others. Desperate.

Fade drop from their perches, creating new rings around us, so escape moves further out of reach. Dog and Whisper inch closer.

"What's happening?" Tobin asks. "What did she do?"

"It's not her. It's me." I've triggered something, causing the whole hive to thrum with tense hostility.

We're surrounded.

*Show them*, my mother says. *Where was the Darkness seen?*

*See*, the others echo, hissing like a tangle of snakes. *See, see, see.*

The Fade surge, shrinking the space Tobin and I have left. There's no grass anymore, no colorful foliage. Everything's gone black.

"What do they want?" Tobin asks.

"Our nightmare."

"I'd say they've got the basic idea."

The nanites cling to his clothes and mine where our trouser legs brush against them. He shakes his foot, stepping high, but they hold fast. Hands and fingers grab at my arms and face, each covered in nanites seeking a connection.

"Back up," I say. "Back off."

My mother shifts her grip on my hands. There's nothing

welcoming or warm about the gesture, and she won't let go. She's holding me still.

*See. Show.*

"It's a dream!" I shout. *Not real. False.*

The concept of dreaming doesn't translate. They crowd closer, leaving no space between them. I can't see anything but Fade with angry, churning lines of nanites. They grab at me, trying to make contact, but there are too many.

"Let me breathe!"

But they don't. Nanites rush my skin from every direction, pouring in like a flood. They burrow in to find the dream and go zipping through, viewing it from different angles as it speeds up and slows down, so they can focus on the details they want.

"Stop!" I shove out with the hand my mother isn't holding. "Stop!"

*Cease!* Cherish says with me.

And, finally, they listen. The result is instantaneous as the command ripples through. The Fade go still, but they don't move even an inch. Tobin and I are back-to-back, a breath from the closest faces.

"Nice trick," he says. "Now get them to back up."

*Remove*, Cherish says.

They seem to ignore her at first, but only because there are so many. It takes time for space to open and allow them to comply.

The crowd dissipates, returning to doorways and broken windows. Scrambling up trees and into the brush. Some disappear but remain as shimmering lines nearby. They give us our space, but none stop watching.

"Why did you do that?" I demand of my mother. She finally releases me. "We came here for help. Why did you attack us?"

*Negative. I do not attack mine. Endanger mine.*

"Well, I *feel* endangered."

"So do I," Tobin says. She scowls at him again—one of the few emotions I've ever seen on a Fade face.

"If this is your idea of help, we're leaving." Coming here was a mistake. "Tell Rue it would have been nice to see him, but I guess he couldn't be bothered."

So much for "never alone."

I refuse to look to either side as I head for the archway we passed through on our way in. I don't doubt the others are moving with us.

"Are we really leaving?" Tobin asks quietly.

"Unless they—"

A wall of four Fade appear in our path, bodies forming one nanite-infused cell at a time. Behind them, the archway closes off, sealed from top to bottom with a flowing blockade of nanites.

"Stop us," I finish.

"Move," I say. I even try Cherish's version: *Remove.*

*Wait*, they say.

"There has to be another way out of here," Tobin says nervously.

"They'd beat us there and seal it. They say to wait, but I don't—"

"M'winna!"

*Blanca?*

A wave of unabashed excitement rolls over me, accompanied by the scent of flowers. My baby sister may be small, but she makes up for it in personality.

"M'winna!"

She squeals, throwing her arm around my leg and hugging tight. She's wearing the same dress as the last time I saw her. It dulls from blue and red to grow into a duplicate of my uniform. I'd wondered how the Fade's clothes managed not to rot like the buildings did and why the Fade left the Arclight's refugees to wear dirty and bloodstained things when their own clothes always look clean and new.

"Finally, a friendly face," Tobin says, reaching down to tug on one of Blanca's heavy curls.

"Tibby!" Blanca throws her other arm around Tobin's knee, holding us together.

"I think that's probably supposed to be Toby," I say, snickering at his annoyed face. "She learned most of her words from Anne-Marie."

I lift Blanca away from Tobin, and she squints, sending a flood of flowerlike shapes and scents directly into my mind.

"I remember," I assure her. "I won't forget you again."

She squeals again, nearly choking me.

"M'winna hears!"

"Sometimes."

"Love you."

Her voice is shaky, and she looks up with those huge, questioning eyes to see if the words are right. I hug her tighter, kissing her on top of the head.

"Love you, too, flower girl."

Pine needles, sharp and biting, imprint over the petals, and an irritated Evergreen appears at my side. Her arms are out, demanding possession of her younger child, but Blanca doesn't want to let go.

"M'winna me!" she cries.

"I think you'd better listen to Mom."

A sullen and dimmed Blanca allows herself to be shifted to our mother's side. I want to promise I'll say good bye before we leave, but the way Evergreen's holding her angled away, I'm not sure I'll be able to keep it. My mother's treating me like poison.

Does she think that by staying too close, Blanca will be contaminated and go silent, like me? If I infect Blanca with my humanity, she won't have any children left.

"So is Rueful actually not here?" Tobin asks. Normally, I'd call him out for mocking the name I gave Rue when we first met, but I've heard him say worse.

"I don't know. I thought there'd be—"

*Something.* Suddenly there's definitely something.

It starts like breaking dawn, spilling sunlight into the darkness. Tobin's oblivious, but inside my mind or my heart, maybe some shadowed recess Cherish has carved out for herself,

I feel the change and turn toward it like an early morning bloom seeking the sun.

Bolt went to get Rue, and now they've returned, walking side by side toward us.

Tobin speaks, but his voice is dull static, making no impact beneath the flood of sound from the hive. They're speaking now, in a frenzy, but not to me. Cherish gains the upper hand and charges toward Rue on my feet, nearly tackling him to the ground.

I can't stop her.

# CHAPTER ELEVEN

## MARINA

"Marina!"

It takes Tobin shouting that twice before I remember he's here. Twice more, and I remember it's my name.

The connection between Rue and Cherish is open. He's trying to foster the link, as someone would blow across struggling embers to rekindle a dead fire, but he's too late. The spark's gone.

"Put me down, Rue," I say.

Heat infuses my cheeks, turning them at least pink. Fade don't blush. Their faces are always pale, no matter what they feel, but the human me can show embarrassment just fine. I don't even want to think about how stupid I look.

My voice is stronger, and despite Cherish's attempts to anchor herself, I shove her back until she's caged again.

I'm still in control.

Rue's not letting go, though. I've unwound my legs, but he's still holding me up, letting my legs dangle until Tobin clears his throat.

"You are not staying to home." Rue loosens his arms and lets me drop. I'd say he's scowling, but he always looks like that.

My stomach clenches. He thought Cherish had come back to him.

"Home is safer," Rue says. "You have seen the Darkness. You should stay to home."

"This *isn't* her home." Tobin goes zero to fury in four words.

"I can handle this, Tobin. We didn't come here for a fight."

"We didn't come here to move in, either," he says. "That goes for *both* of you. I can't drag half of you back across the Grey, and I'm not leaving any of you behind."

He starts pacing the settlement's central area.

I sense movement behind me and glance back to find my mother stalking off with Blanca in her arms, but that's a pain for another day.

"I can't stay, Rue," I say. "We're here because we need your help."

"You are unhurt."

I'm grateful he's speaking out loud so there's no need to translate.

"I'm fine, but someone else might not be."

He glares at Tobin, assuming he's the only reason I'd be here and not staying. I guess the concept of a visit isn't familiar to him.

"It's not him. Well, not *just* him. Please, Rue, what difference does it make who needs help?"

"I've helped already. We have helped."

His speech is stilted by agitation but more natural than I

remember, as though he's been practicing.

"I know. You healed Tobin for me. You brought his father back, but—"

"We're still helping."

Rue's physical tics are very particular. The way he tilts his head, cutting his eyes up—he's searching for the right word, not arguing.

"Helping how?" I ask.

"Holding back."

"Try sentences longer than two words," Tobin grumbles.

"I need more, Rue," I say. "What are you holding back? Say it any way you have to, just help me understand."

His answer is a rush of overwhelming Darkness. Thick and clinging, with a dragging weight that attaches to my arms and legs, crushing the air from my lungs. Clouds and tides, of choking black smoke. They surround the Arclight, breaking over the top to wash away everything inside. It's all gone. There's nothing left.

My nightmare, and Tobin's.

"You're holding back the Dark?"

"We prevent the Dark," he corrects.

"That doesn't make any sense. You live in the Dark. It's all around us. What—"

"He's stalling to keep you here," Tobin cuts in. "Ask him what they did to Trey, so we can go home already. I *want* to go home."

*While we still can.* I finish in my head.

"What is Trey?" Rue asks.

"The boy Bolt . . .er . . . *he* healed." I nod Bolt's direction, unsure if Rue knows the names I use for other Fade. "Something's wrong with him."

"He had marks," Tobin says. "Like yours. His eyes were shining."

The general wariness that's been present since we entered the settlement ratchets up to something more tense.

"Could you have missed some of the nanites when you took them back?" I turn to Bolt.

"All of mine are present."

"You saw the lights come on tonight, right?" Tobin shoulders past me, so he's facing Rue and Bolt.

"Yes," Bolt says.

"That's your sister. She's got some serious paranoia issues."

Everyone wanted things back to how they were before. Somehow I doubt they'll enjoy getting their wish.

"And because of that, the dividing line's back up." He turns to Rue. "Tell us how to fix this, or the lights stay on and you're stuck your side. Without Marina. You won't be able to come back."

Rue's marks draw tighter as he struggles to keep his own temper in check.

"I told you he hasn't been back," I say.

"He hasn't been *seen*," Tobin corrects. "But he's been back. And he's sent others—haven't you, Nanobot? I caught your invisible buddy beyond the lights."

"I sent no one," Rue says.

I back away, intent on not becoming the catalyst for a fight, only to be caught off guard and off balance when Blanca bursts straight out of the ground and back into view.

"M'winna me!" she cries, distraught, lunging for my leg. The impact's slight, but it's enough to take me down and bring her with me.

"Blanca?"

"M'winna me!" she bawls into my chest, curling closer. She buries her face in my hair, whining "Mim" and reeking of singed pine.

"Is she hurt?" Tobin asks.

"I think she's mad at our mother," I say, struggling to my feet while balancing Blanca. "She'll be okay."

"How about you?" Tobin asks, picking at my sleeve. The tumble's pushed it up, and I skinned my arm on the gravel. I hardly even feel it.

"Heal?" Rue offers.

"It's nothing," I assure him. Blanca's already winding down to sniffles; I'm not about to set her down over a few scratches. "I get worse than this in the rec room during class."

"Nothing doesn't leave bloodstains," Rue says, startling me so bad that flames ignite behind my ears.

"What did you say?" I ask.

"Nothing doesn't leave bloodstains," he repeats, precisely in the same tone and cadence as he'd said it before, only neither of them are his. The rhythm's wrong.

"It was you!"

I always thought the idea of a person snarling was fanciful language meant for stories, but it is, indeed, possible. Blanca wriggles out of my arms. Bolt, who is nearby, tries to calm me down, like he's done before with others, but he backs off when I glare at him. Cherish must have a nasty temper.

"You're the reason his eyes turned silver," I rage at Rue.

"What?" Tobin asks.

"Those were the exact words you said to me when your eyes flashed. He was listening to us."

That's why Cherish wanted to protect Tobin from Honoria! He's her connection to Rue.

"What did you do?" I demand.

Rue stays silent, both in speech and thought. He doesn't deny anything.

"Are some of those . . . those . . . *things* still inside me?" Tobin asks, shaking. He's about a half-breath from coming unglued.

"Rue! Answer him!"

"Cherish did not return to home. Home remained to Cherish."

"You left them behind? To what—spy on me? To make sure Tobin keeps his distance?"

No wonder Tobin has been awkward around me; there's been an invisible Rue wall between us.

"Get them out!" Tobin loses it. He's slapping his hands against his arms and sides, scrubbing at his face and clawing through his hair. Bolt steps up and puts a hand on his shoulder, but Tobin is beyond calming. "Get them out of me!"

"They are not harmful," Rue says.

"That's not the point! You can't garrison someone's body without asking. This is exactly the kind of thing Honoria expects you to do, Rue. Get them out of him—NOW!"

"Now, for M'winna!" Blanca adds with a stamp of her little foot. She hooks Tobin's leg again. "Now, for Tibby!"

Reluctantly, Rue walks over to Tobin. A flare of panic crosses Tobin's face as Rue reaches for him. Tobin cringes back, fists up. It's a reflex. He's too unsteady to really defend himself.

"Don't look at him, look at me," I say, taking his hand. "Rue has to touch you, but you don't have to watch."

Tobin swallows so hard it looks like the spit sticks in his throat; his breathing's erratic, but he nods.

Of all the things Rue could have done . . .

Exposure to the Fade cost Tobin his mother and almost lost him his father. There's no nightmare greater for him than losing himself the same way.

Tobin's fingers tighten on mine until I want to scream, but you can't scream and gasp at the same time. Swirls of Fade-lines bleed into his skin, dancing across his face and neck. The black crystal nanites ooze from his pores, flowing to Rue's hands, and with one final flash of silver in his eyes, they're finished.

"Are you okay?" I ask.

"No." Tobin walks away, still trembling, still swallowing, and trying not to hyperventilate. I let him go.

"Are they really gone this time?" I ask Rue.

"Returned." He nods.

"All of them?"

Cherish lets out a mourning wail inside my head. I'll take that as a yes.

"Good. Now go get the ones you left in Trey," I tell Bolt.

"I left nothing behind but my other," he says.

"Then what's wrong with him?"

Silence.

My question is answered by absolutely nothing, followed by the sequential slamming of doors as the hive tightens its hold on their secrets.

"Tell me!"

They refuse.

Evergreen returns, accompanied by a male. His eyes are round saucers, like Blanca's, but the rest is me. My pointed chin. My nose. He's my father, I'm sure of it. I try to get a fix on him, but like with the others, everything's gone. He's blank.

"How did things get *weirder* around here?" Tobin asks, taking my hand again.

"Something's got them spooked, but they don't want us to know what it is."

The crowd's gone completely still. They're a living photograph, frozen in place. Bolt and Rue look like marble statues. Fade-lines drop from their bodies and onto the ground, mingling and then shooting back up on their bodies.

*Communication.*

Either that's Cherish or a memory. I'm not sure which, but this is some Fade version of a town-hall meeting.

Blanca flees across the open square and leaps into our father's arms, suddenly terrified.

When the pulsing exchange of symbionts between the Fade stops, Rue makes a gesture that causes the rest of them to scatter. Only Rue and Bolt remain with our guards from before.

"Remain or return," Rue says.

*Choose.*

He emphasizes the word with a finality I don't like.

"Are you asking if we want to stay here?"

"Marina, we can't. If they've initiated the SOS protocols . . ."

Then the clock's ticking. If Col. Lutrell checks his alarm and finds Tobin missing, or if they do a head count and we're not there . . . We can't miss the window for reentry. We'll be assumed unsafe and shot on sight.

"Remain or return," Rue repeats. "Home is safer."

"We have to go back, but Trey needs—"

"Then we will return you. You will show me your Trey, and we will prevent the Darkness."

Rue and Bolt take up positions in front of us. Dog and Whisper file in behind us. We needed two guards to get in and four to get out. This is not comforting.

"Rue, what aren't you telling us?" I ask.

"Mouth closed politely," he says, heading for the short side's exit and the lights waiting on the other side.

# CHAPTER TWELVE

## TOBIN

Schuyler detours at the edge of the Dark, returning with a dingy bundle that holds the robes the Fade wear to get close to the Arc. They reek, rotten as decomp, but Marina acts like she doesn't notice.

The lamps are still burning across the Grey like midday sun.

"How long can they keep that up?" Marina asks, shielding her eyes.

"All night," I tell her. "But they'll fry the circuits." The system isn't ready for this kind of stress.

"Approach this direction." Rueful veers into a diagonal, away from the brightest lights.

I knew he was lying about watching the Arc.

"We're moving toward a dimmer section," I say.

"So?" Marina asks. "You know they can't cross on the ultra-brights."

"The only way Nanobot would know where the dim lights are is if he's been there to see it."

"You saw, I saw," Rueful says, and suddenly I can't breathe. How much did those robo-bugs tell him about me?

He must keep talking because Marina's face is getting more and more sour.

"That's not funny," she tells him. "You had no right."

We walk a few steps, and then: "I sound angry because I *am.*"

More steps, and: "That's not an apology, no matter how high you make your voice go at the end."

I don't think she knows how weird it looks when she speaks to him like that. Just like I doubt she notices that she's stepping in his footprints. I glance back, and Dog and Whisper are doing the same thing. Only mine are out of step.

"Were you serious about there being a cloaked Fade at the boundary tonight?" Marina asks. It takes a minute to realize that one's aimed at me.

"Who's asking? You or the ink blot?"

"Tobin . . ."

"At least I insult *him* to his face," I say.

"It's a figure of speech, Rue," she says, annoyed. "He knows that's the back of your head."

A pause, and then: "Because that's what a figure of speech is. You say one thing, and mean another."

Another pause, and she's rubbing the back of her neck and grumbling.

"No, it's not the same as lying."

"You should answer her question," Schuyler says to me, to end their argument. "Without speaking in figures."

The first half sounds almost entirely human, but the end doesn't.

"Was something observed on your perimeter tonight?" he asks.

"If there's something dangerous lurking between here and the Arclight, I'd rather know," Marina says.

I hadn't considered that it could be something other than one of Rueful's hive-mates, but when she says it like that, and with the Fade acting the way they are-

"It stayed hidden," I say. "But it kicked up dirt when it moved, and it was smart enough to get out of range when I chucked a rock at it. By the time I thought to use my scope for a better look, it had gone."

"Change course," Rueful says, shifting us another few degrees to the side.

"Why are we taking the long way?" I ask.

We're close enough to the short side that we don't have to deal with the wind spouts that blow through the wider regions. Here, there are rocks and trees to break them, but Rueful's directional shifts keep slowing us down. The Fade keep stopping, reacting to things beyond my senses.

"Rue says there's danger," Marina says.

"Can you hear anything?" I ask her.

"No," she says, mumbling. Then, "That's what scares me."

Her senses are nearly as sharp as theirs. What's stealthy enough to evade that?

I stop walking and try scanning the area with the light hanging off my wrist, but it's clear.

"Continue, or return to home," Rueful prompts.

"You're going to stretch this out so long, the sun will rise before you have time to get back," I tell him

"This way is unobstructed," he says, nodding the direction he wants us to go. He starts walking again. The other three do the same, in perfect sync, herding me and Marina along with them.

"What's *obstructing* the other way?" I ask.

"Nothing," he says.

"Then why—"

"He doesn't mean there's nothing there." Marina's face pinches as she deciphers whatever hacked-up hash of an explanation he's given her. "It's nothingness. A void."

"This is the Grey," I say, sweeping my arms around. "It's *all* a void."

"Not like this," she says, and shivers. "It's there; it's dangerous, but you can't see it. It's watching us."

We stop talking, or at least I do, and if *they* still are, it's not out loud. Rueful slows to a halt once we're a few hundred meters from the Arc. There are trash piles and mounds of dry brush waiting to be used for bonfire fuel, but other than these, all that separates us from a straight shot back into the Arclight is fog.

Dog breaks right, and Whisper left, patrolling the Grey. Schuyler sticks with us.

"They observe the Dark," Rueful says before anyone can ask.

"Tell them to make a diversion while they're at it," I say. "We could use one." A glance at my wristband says we're still at Red-Wall.

Getting help to Trey isn't going to be as simple as visiting the hospital. This is security containment, and I really hope they haven't finished repairing the White Room. If they have, that's where he'll be. We won't be able to talk our way inside like the night Rueful was taken there.

"Tobin." Marina taps my elbow. "We have a problem. Look—embers."

She points to bits of burning grass floating through the air, too light to land before they're snuffed out.

"Watch fires," she says, grabbing Rueful's hand. He draws back.

"They're using them to fill the gaps where the Arc's dimmer," I explain. "That means heavy patrols—two watch the boundary, another two tend the fire. We can't go that way."

"Between is not safe," Rueful says. "Choose a home—yours or ours."

"We already chose. Follow me." I head back for the brighter part of the Arc and then tuck myself behind one of the felled trees, where I've got a clear view.

"They can't cross here," Marina says.

"If security's pumping this much power into the lamps, then they're going to have skips."

"What's a skip?"

"Watch," I say, waiting for the signs of an oncoming power cut. An embedded lamp flickers, sputters, then dies, leaving a narrow access point. "The connections are weak. I've counted that pattern out for four nights straight. It always cuts a ground light."

"I guess you really are the guy to call if I want someone skilled at watching lights flick on and off."

The light hums loudly, fizzling as the current floods through it again, and a column of bright white threads into the rest of the barrier.

"How often does that happen?"

"Every time they push the power. The blackout's random, but you'll see the top lamps flicker. The light below them goes dark."

"Will we have enough time to make it across before the lights come on again?"

"We should," I say, turning to Rue and Schuyler. "But we still have to watch for patrols."

To prove the point, Mindy Olivet tromps by with her partner.

They stop near our glitch-point, scanning the area, and I stop breathing. Marina shrinks away from the guards' shadows, but our stump's not much cover. The lights have thinned the fog. Mindy will see us for sure.

Rueful grabs Marina, cupping his hand over her mouth.

"What are you —*mmph*."

A hand clamps my mouth, too.

"Mmph!" I try to pry Schuyler's hand off, but it's stronger than cement.

The haphazard lattice of lines and dots from his hand passes to mine and morphs to mimic the mist, matching my skin to his and burying us both beneath a layer of artificial color. My face tingles with sleeping nerves as those *things* try to talk to me.

I'm Fading—like one of *them*.

*Get off! Get off me!*

I fight his grip, but he won't let go, and the guards can't see us.

*Calm. No danger. Concealment*, he insists.

Mindy hears something, and she shines a light our way, but it's only the flashlight, not the infrared.

"Nineteen clear," she says into her radio. "Proceeding to twenty."

She and her partner move on. My skin reappears as Schuyler collects his nanites and lets me go. I shove him as far as I can.

"*Never* do that again. I don't want those things anywhere near me!"

I'm shaking and can't stop. The last human he touched was Trey, and now Trey's eyes are shining. I don't want eyes like that. I can't live with people looking at me like they do my dad.

"It's okay," Marina says, reaching for my arm, but I jerk away.

I don't want to be touched by anyone right now, not even her. She had nanites on her, too, and they could still be there, ready to jump.

"They were helping," she says.

"I don't want their help." I gulp air, trying not to hyperventilate. The creeping chill of fading still sticks to me like cold slime. "I don't want them here. I don't want anything from them at all."

*Anything else.* I already owe Rueful for saving my life.

"Blinking," Schuyler says, getting our attention.

The lamps are dimming. When they settle, the one in the center goes out, leaving a gap.

Rueful darts forward, taking point. Marina goes next, and I follow her as the heat from the rest of the bulbs burns through my clothes. If it's this intense for a human, I can't image how it feels to a Fade, but Schuyler comes through behind me.

Making it through is a hollow victory. Even with my knowledge of the Arc, getting in was too easy. How do I know we're the only ones who've made it across the line? The shadow crawlers are smart.

"Maybe you two should be less visible," Marina tells them.

As much as I hate the idea of these two skulking around unseen, we're already tempting fate and Dad's temper—not to mention Honoria's. The last thing we need is to get caught breaking protocol on a high alert.

The Fade's features blend away, leaving us momentarily with a pair of robes, and I shiver again, scrubbing my arms, in case I missed something. Then the expanding nanite webs overtake the robes, too.

"If our luck holds, Dad won't have checked his parental

trace, but we still can't go through the main doors. They'll be locked down."

"Then how do we get inside?" Marina asks.

"Trust me." I can't believe I'm about to show this to a pair of Fade. "This way."

I head for the side of the building nearest the outside garden and enter the equipment shed.

"Dad showed me this once I chose the security team as my focus," I say, feeling my way along the back wall.

My shadow casts long on the side in the light from the Arc, where it shines through the windows. I put my hand to a shelf bolted to the wall.

"Get on the other side and push on my count," I say. Marina leans against the far side of the shelf.

Dad's going to kill me for this.

"One, two, three—go."

We push together, shoving the shelf into what should be a solid wall. The back of the shed gives way, rolling into the main building, and exposing another entrance to the tunnel system below.

"Careful," I warn, stepping inside. "There're stairs, but they're steep. If you don't look for them, you'll go straight down. Don't ask me how I know that."

Marina trips over a ground-level track every time we use the hidden door in my apartment; unlit stairs could kill her.

"You two still there?" I ask in the direction I think the Fade are standing. "I'll have to take the lead for a while."

Marina snorts out loud, then coughs out: "Sorry. Rue says lead the way."

Sure he did. Not killing that guy on sight should seriously count as payback for my life debt.

# CHAPTER THIRTEEN

## MARINA

Tobin's tunnel leads us under the Arclight, into the maze of concrete walls and pipes that served as emergency entrances and exits in the first days. This looks like the path to the Well.

We don't have enough light to give me much of an idea what's ahead; just the glow from our alarms and a pale track of rope lights set into the ceiling. I hope we don't run into another patrol down here. With the Arclight at Red-Wall, and Trey possibly turning Fade, we do not want to get caught sneaking Rue and Bolt in through a secret tunnel.

"Where does this go?" I ask.

"Same as the one in my apartment. This tunnel's on the opposite side of the compound, but the design's the same. Once we hit the junction, we can get to the hospital."

We reach the junction as he mentions it, but the directions are reversed on this side. When he turns toward the hospital, it feels like we're moving backward.

"What the—"

Tobin stops suddenly; I stumble into his back. Rue or Bolt, whoever's directly behind me, can't stop quick enough to prevent a pileup. Tobin reaches out to poke the empty air, as though he's hit something solid.

"Is something in here with us?" I ask.

"Your boyfriend doesn't follow directions well." Tobin seizes a handful of air, yanking it toward us.

Rue pulls out of his grasp. Fully visible, not at all where he's supposed to be, Rue.

"I told you to stay back," Tobin says. "I'm not running through these tunnels looking for you when you get lost."

Rue turns to me, catching my eye. Like the first time I questioned his ability to navigate the Arclight-below, a schematic of the tunnels appears in my mind, with one, distinct path illuminated by a bright pink line.

"He says he knows the way," I tell Tobin.

"No, he didn't. He didn't *say* anything." He bounces forward, sparring for a fight.

"I know the way, *Tibby*." Rue turns the nickname into a challenge, meeting Tobin toe-to-toe.

Tobin draws back, ready to unload the full force of the night's rage on Rue's jaw, but I intercept his hand.

"Don't."

I have seriously got to stop putting myself between people's faces and Tobin's fist. I don't even know *how* I got between them in time to catch his hand, but mine's stinging.

"You should have let me hit him," Tobin says, pulling free.

"Just get us to the hospital," I say. "Trey is more important than a fight over line leader! Rue, stay with Bolt."

*Negative.*

"Not asking. I'd rather have you watching my back, okay?"

"Not okay, but yes."

"Close enough."

"Good, now *follow* me," Tobin says. "We're almost there."

This tunnel isn't a complete a copy of the other one. There's no stagnant steam here and no smell of mold. Thin gas and water pipes still run the length of the ceiling, but without the red wheels that control the flow. While Tobin has markers to use, I don't. To me, it's all a loop of endless sameness, and it's a relief when he finally stops.

At least until we hit a wall instead of a door.

"This shouldn't be located here," Rue says, stepping forward. "It doesn't belong."

"It's a security panel. Someone's sealed the exit," Tobin says, running his hands over a metal plate. "This wasn't here before."

We're stuck. The door's locked, and going back means we sit and wait for security to find us because there's no other way in.

*Suffocation.* Cherish's voice surfaces, dredging up her greatest fears. *Crushing. Choking.*

She goes berserk, throwing one horrible memory of being confined at me after another.

I brace my hand against the wall, fighting the lightheadedness from the imagined lack of oxygen, and try to even my breathing. I end up gasping instead.

"Are you all right?" Tobin asks.

"Panic attack. Cherish doesn't do well with enclosed spaces."

"Right," he says, facing the seal, like it's a riddle he needs to solve. "So, what do we do?"

"Find a way to open it." I'd shout it if I had the air. I'd also call him a few things I'd have to apologize for later.

I feel a hand against my back—Rue, reaching out to Cherish. *Calm,* he tells her. *Still.*

I don't move. If Tobin sees Rue with his hands on me, it'll lead to another fight.

*No danger is present,* Rue says.

The familiar sensation of cool water hits my arms and legs.

I didn't realize until now, but it's part of my name. He's calling Cherish by her real Fade name.

Rue's presence soothes her, and in return, I get peace.

"Any ideas?" Tobin asks, glancing back at me. He has no clue what's just happened.

"It doesn't look new," I say. It's not shiny like clean metal, and there's no evidence of installation. "Maybe it's been here the whole time."

"If it's a pocket panel, Dad may have had it open when he showed me how to get here. I can't tell."

"Can you unlock it?"

Tobin raises his wrist, lining it up with the scanner on the wall. His security trainee status should open most anything, but the scanner doesn't beep or blink.

"Nothing," he says. "Either it's dead, or this is a high-security seal."

Rue and Bolt jostle past me in a space so tight, only one can pass at a time. Bolt, being taller, grips the sliding panel near the top of the seam where it meets the wall; Rue crouches down, doing the same at the bottom. Their hands sprout claws, and together they heave.

Those claws can tear through concrete and steel girders; they can crack reinforced glass that a bullet can't shatter, but here, the door stands solid and unmoving. Bolt lays his palm flat against it until the slashes from his arm transfer to the door. They run the edge, draining through the seam.

"What are they doing?" Tobin asks as Rue sits back on his haunches, waiting.

Tobin can't hear the tiny breaks and chips between the wall and door, like I can.

"Picking the lock," I say.

It doesn't take them long to finish. The nanites trickle back through the seam to return to Bolt's skin. He and Rue resume their previous stance, and this time the door yields an inch.

"Help," he says, facing Tobin. "Add your hands."

Tobin takes the middle position on the door, wriggling his fingers into the notch created as it moves. All three of them strain, pulling until their bodies shake, and then suddenly, the panel slides away, leaving only the same sort of door that caps off every tunnel I've seen in the Arclight-below.

I tell myself that it's mostly the Fade's doing. Rue's symbionts aren't inside Tobin anymore, and he and Bolt had only needed a little extra help to break through, but that panel flew open. None of them were caught in the momentum. Most people would have fallen, or at least faltered when it released, but Tobin didn't even wobble. How can he be that strong?

Tobin faces the newly exposed door and tries the switch again, but the automatic slide doesn't work. He presses it into the wall by hand, opening it barely a crack, so we can see into the hospital without exposing our presence. The malfunction's an accidental blessing.

The hospital's full, and no one looks happy.

# CHAPTER FOURTEEN

## MARINA

Honoria, Dr. Wolff, and Lt. Sykes stand huddled up with Mr. Pace and Col. Lutrell; no one's smiling.

If I'm right about Lt. Sykes and the colonel, then the others could round out Honoria's five. They all hold positions of authority here, and she *did* mention a teacher in her book. But what would that make Trey and Anne-Marie?

Parents pass things to their kids all the time. Maybe Bolt isn't responsible for triggering what happened to—

Oh God . . . Tobin.

If Mr. Pace passed the Fade to his kids, did Col. Lutrell do the same to Tobin? Is that why his mother was working so hard to find a cure?

*Where is your Trey?* Rue asks.

"Behind that drawn curtain, I'd guess, but we can't go out there until they cool off." I crouch down so there's room for the others to peek out the opening, too.

"Agreed," Tobin says, whispering.

*Disagreed,* says Rue. "We help. We leave."

He steps forward, folding his hand around the edge of the

panel to open it all the way. I can't reach his arm, so I grab his ankle.

"Run into that room, and there's no telling what they'll do."

*Stalling*, he says.

*Strategizing*, I correct. "You can't even go out there invisible. They'll see the panel open if you push it that wide. Wait for some of them to leave."

Preferably Honoria.

A door opens in the hospital, stopping our argument.

"Go home, Nique," Mr. Pace says. "Keep an eye on Annie."

"It's Anne-Marie's mother," I say, knowing Rue and Bolt won't recognize her name. I try and repeat the one Cherish gave her.

"Annie should be in the safe room with the others," Honoria says. "And you shouldn't be here."

All my hopes of getting through this unnoticed vanish. Of course Red-Wall means everyone's in the bunkers. They'll all be wondering what the danger is, now that they believe the Fade aren't a threat. And they'll notice we aren't with them.

"Unless you want every child in this building to know what's happened tonight, the last place you want my daughter is locked in a room for hours. Now tell me what's going on with my son." Ms. Johnston moves into my line of sight, but Honoria doesn't relent.

"Go home. Make sure Annie's where she's supposed to be—*this time.*"

"Don't you dare. She went into the Dark to save her brother

and her friends. You're not going to vilify her for it. *You* started this. You and your lies."

Normally, Anne-Marie's mother would lash out with more than words, but too much has piled up on her too fast. She grinds the heels of her hands into her eyes, pushing back the tears.

"What's important is making sure Annie stays safe." Lt. Sykes becomes an unexpected voice of reason in the room. Ms. Johnston startles like she'd forgotten he was there. "If she's by herself, she's more likely to do something reckless. I'll have someone watch your door. You can stay here."

She's always nervous around him, but it's more than the silent way he moves or the way he seems to watch everyone and everything—she knows.

Every adult must know about all five of the originals, but Lt. Sykes is the first one they grow older than. As a child, Ms. Johnston would have seen him as an elder, but now she looks like she could be his superior or teacher. Her own son is his age.

"I'll send someone to your place. They won't even go inside—I promise." Lt. Sykes squeezes her arm; she doesn't quite manage to stifle the flinch.

"Thank you," she says. I honestly hope he can't smell the ashy unease from her.

"Get a head count on the kids," Honoria says. "If anyone other than Annie is missing, I want their names, and I want them found."

"Channel two on the radio," Lt. Sykes tells her. "Ten minutes." He hurries out the door.

"That's not a lot of time," Tobin says, giving me a hand up.

"I know."

Bolt moves for the first time since we opened the panel. He takes my place, staring into the hospital.

"If you can tell us anything about your sister that might help, now would be the time," I say. She's still our greatest point of opposition, and her presence here says she still holds sway with the others.

"Waste of time," Tobin says. "I've known her my whole life. Dad and Mr. Pace are our best shot."

"She helped," Bolt says.

"Yeah, and I've seen what happens when she tries to help. So have you." Tobin rubs the spot near his heart where Honoria's bullet left him scarred.

"She helped ours."

"She *shot* you. How's that helpful?" I say.

"She helped ours to see."

He faces me, locking eyes, and suddenly, I'm in his head. He and Cherish shared the same hive mind; his memories are a part of her, if she wants them to be.

I hear Honoria's name, spoken by a human voice and translated into the raging burn the Fade associate with her. My mind's on fire—no, my head. My head's on fire, my skin's melting, about to burst into flame. I smell my own flesh singeing as the voices of the Fade scream in confusion as to why I'm hurting myself. They plead for me to stop.

"It's not me," I say.

It's not me, it's—

"You felt Honoria burn herself out of the hive?" I ask. "Is that why her name means fire to you?"

"She helped us see," Bolt says, and turns back to the panel's opening. "We will help her see."

Honoria's still shouting.

"This was *always* a possibility—you *both* knew that." She gives Mr. Pace a sour look.

"You can scold me later, Honoria. Right now, we need to focus on helping my son."

"There *is* no help," Honoria says, her voice softening in a way that shocks me. "Have you honestly forgotten that? It's past contact—they're in his organs. Likely, his brain. We can't burn them out; at this point, even the serum would be risky. If we kill them, there're enough that the dead will poison him as they decompose."

Anne-Marie's mother chokes down a sob, turning her face into Mr. Pace's shoulder.

"We had some early success with dialysis," Col. Lutrell suggests. "Filter his blood as they die, so they don't have a chance to reach lethal toxicity."

"That's never worked long term."

"We have to do *something*," Mr. Pace says.

"I'm not gloating, Elias," Honoria says. "But you knew the risk and you still took it."

"The only risks I took were for my family," Mr. Pace argues.

"Your family's dead. You should have left it that way."

Anne-Marie's mother lunges toward Honoria; Mr. Pace grabs Nique up off the floor so she can't reach.

"Sometimes I think your body's the only thing about you that aged, Honoria Jean," he says. "Inside, you're still the bitter little military brat who used to cheat on her exams."

If he *was* her teacher, then how did she end up in command?

"That's enough—all of you!" Dr. Wolff steps into the middle of them, waving a folder. "The bickering is getting us nowhere. I've checked and double-checked Mr. Johnston, and the nanites are *not* spreading. This isn't an exposure issue."

"You mean he's not turning into one of them?" Anne-Marie's mother asks.

Hope calms her down like a shot of tranquilizer; enough so that Mr. Pace decides it's safe to set her back down.

"The markings on his face have dissolved; they never appeared elsewhere. He's calm, and was even presedation. There aren't any spikes on the monitors. I believe what you witnessed was a result of dormant symbionts in your son's body reacting to live ones when he was healed."

"But it's been almost two months," Col. Lurell protests.

There were so many drawings in Trey's room that he could have used them for wallpaper and rugs. That could have easily taken two months, but how did he not show signs?

*Uninjured*, Rue supplies. Dr. Wolff seems to agree.

"They've had no wounds to treat, so no reason to replicate for healing. They've likely been building steadily in his system since contact with the live specimen."

"You said dormant," Trey's mother says. "He's had them all this time?"

"It's possible that he's had them from the point of conception. I wouldn't doubt that Annie and Tobin have small numbers of them as well."

"What's he mean?" Tobin asks me. I shrug. He doesn't need to hear from me that his father could have passed the Fade to him like an errant gene.

Or a disease.

"We know the Fade can procreate," Dr. Wolff says. "The only difference is, in this case, one parent is fully human, and the one exposed has kept his nanite load suppressed. The children were born with no indicators."

"So Annie, too?" Mr. Pace asks.

"I can test her, but the nanites she came into contact with were never active in her bloodstream. However, the same isn't true for—"

"Tobin," Col. Lutrell finishes for him.

I glance back at Tobin; he's looking at his fingers, shivering.

"They're gone," I whisper to him.

"I know." He nods, but he still wipes his hands on his pants.

Back in the hospital, Honoria snatches the radio off her belt.

"Sykes," she hisses. "Collect James's son and bring him back here once you're done at the safe rooms."

"Problem?" Sykes buzzes back.

"The way this night is going? Almost definitely." She clicks the radio off, hooking it back on her belt.

"This is *not* a disaster," Dr. Wolff says. "The sample I took from Trey is inert, and I'd rather not spark a panic by implying there's a risk of an outbreak."

"Then why were his eyes shining?" Honoria asks.

"It's part of the reaction, but considering the appearance of Marina's eyes, and those of our people who were treated long term, it won't be back. The shift to light blue is likely a side effect of the nanites' melanin-blocking properties."

"Trey's eyes turned blue?" Anne-Marie's mother asks.

"Once the suppressant was in his system, just like with Marina. But unlike her, the concentration of nanites wasn't high enough to affect Trey's skin or hair. He's showing no lingering signs of contact. You're all worried over nothing."

"*This* is not nothing," Honoria insists. She snatches up a pile of Trey's drawings. "He was connected to them, and if he still is—"

"It was just an accident," Tobin blurts, rushing into the main room and exposing us all.

I don't think he could take hearing any more symptoms or guesses. He wanted them to stop talking so he didn't have to think about all the things that could have happened to him if Rue hadn't taken his nanites back. But Tobin can't smell the shock for his sudden appearance, and he doesn't know there's an explosion building to critical mass inside Honoria that's worse than anything I've ever registered from her.

"They've come to fix it."

"Tobin?" Col. Lutrell says. "What—"

"We went to get help."

"Help?" Mr. Pace asks, squinting toward the tunnel entrance where the Fade and I are still mostly hidden by the sliding panel. I step into the open, reaching back to bring Rue and Bolt with me.

"He's the one who healed Trey before," Anne-Marie's mother says. She starts toward Bolt, but Mr. Pace holds her back.

"Don't," he warns.

"But if he can help—"

"Give it a minute, Nique."

It's not Bolt who Mr. Pace is wary of. Shadows are banking up around Honoria like clouds on the verge of a gale. He doesn't want Anne-Marie's mother crossing in front of her.

"*You* brought them here?" Honoria goes perfectly still.

"To help Trey," I say, risking another few paces into the room and hoping Honoria's grip on her sanity holds out, but she's cracking. I can see it.

"We're at high alert," she says. "And you brought them *here*."

"The alert hadn't sounded when we left," Tobin said.

"Honoria, I—"

"Stop!"

She cuts me off in every sense of the word—voice, thought, and motion, and suddenly, the silver pistol that nearly killed Tobin is back in her hand.

# CHAPTER FIFTEEN

## MARINA

Everything from the most chaotic night of my life floods back.

All of us packed into this room. No patience to spare. And Honoria with a gun pointed straight at my chest.

"You gave her the gun back." I state the obvious because it's so ridiculous that it has to be another nightmare.

The uneasy tilt of déjà vu throws everything into a spin. The walls close in from both sides. No, not walls—Tobin's back, and Rue's. They've stepped in front of me, leaving a narrow gap between them. It's wide enough for a bullet to pass through, and Honoria's a crack shot.

"Explain yourselves," Honoria demands. Her aura crackles with fury, but outwardly, she maintains her steady calm with only a tremor in her voice.

"Stand down." Col. Lutrell approaches her cautiously. "You heard Tobin. They're here to help."

"If they help much more, we all might as well move into the Dark."

"You gave her the gun back." It's either repetition or screaming bloody murder, and I've had enough of blood and murder.

"Seal the ward," Honoria says.

"Wait," Mr. Pace joins Tobin's father.

"The situation—"

"Is Trey, and he's contained. Hear them out before someone says or does something that can't be taken back."

"You gave her the gun back! Do you honestly not know she'll shoot Anne-Marie or Trey the same as she did Tobin? Because she can pull that trigger a lot faster than you can stop her."

"We needed the extra hand," Mr. Pace says.

The hospital seems infinitely smaller. There's not enough room to move or air to breathe. Honoria's attention is honed in on me, between Rue and Tobin, as though getting rid of me will negate all her mistakes, but she has to know how reckless this is. Can't she taste anxiety's crush or smell the burnt fuse atmosphere that's so much like the bite of cordite after gunfire?

"Everyone take a step back." Col. Lutrell puts himself beside Honoria. Mr. Pace closes in on her other side. "Give me the gun, Honoria Jean, or pass it to Elias."

I can see the argument forming in her mind as though letters are flashing in her irises, but there's something about the way they use her name: Honoria Jean. It's what she answered to as a girl, when she wasn't in authority. It has a definite effect.

I focus tight on her hands, picking up every aspect of them in razor-sharp detail, from the way her fingers tighten on the gun's grip, to each individual wrinkle of her gloves where they bend at the joints. But this time *she's* the outlier, and she knows it. Honoria makes the only choice open to her, which is to surrender the gun—though she pointedly hands it off to Dr. Wolff rather than Mr. Pace or Tobin's father.

"Now, everyone sit," Mr. Pace says, pointing to the empty hospital beds on either wall.

Tobin pulls me with him toward the bed nearest his father. We sit on the edge, stiff and still. Neither Rue nor Bolt move. Bolt hasn't even left the threshold of the tunnel.

*Rue,* says Cherish, using my name for him for the first time. *Rue . . . imploring. Please.*

My leg begins to throb again, over my scar.

She's begging me to call him over, so she'll feel safer, and I have to agree. We're all better off with Rue close.

I reach out to him, silently so Tobin can't hear, pushing the urgency in Cherish's voice at him. He keeps his eyes on Honoria, but comes our way, and sits in the chair beside the bed. Cherish's voice dulls to a hum, matched to the pulse of his aura. No matter the choices I've made, or the distance I've put between myself and her, the connection between Rue and Cherish hasn't died.

Bolt leaves his hiding place and takes a chair, too, leaving the middle of the room empty, until Dr. Wolff steps in to address us.

"Given the circumstances, perhaps it would be best to make sure everyone's who and what they claim to be. Then we can move on to things not requiring threats of violence."

He thinks we're like Trey. Delayed-reaction Fade-bombs, waiting to go off.

"I'm Tobin, she's Marina. The end," Tobin says bitterly.

"Not the time." Col. Lutrell gives him the warning look Anne-Marie's mother uses when she's upset. "What do you need, Doc?"

"A pinprick of blood on a slide should be sufficient. Even in the early stages of exposure and replication, the nanites will show under magnification."

"Give him your hand."

If humans could growl, Tobin would be.

"You can check mine," I say, offering my hand.

"Thank you," Col. Lutrell says quietly. "Nique, a little help?"

Anne-Marie's mother nods, relieved to have something to do. She follows Dr. Wolff to the cabinet, waiting for instructions.

Honoria paces, as she always does when she's nervous or losing control of herself. I can imagine her wandering the halls below at odd hours, stricken with insomnia and walking through her boots, constantly fidgeting with things, trying to keep an eye on everything at once, but I doubt she's ever realized why she does it. Nanites never stop moving. They're still influencing her.

"Hold still, okay?" Anne-Marie's mother says to me. She has a lancet in one hand and a box of glass plates in the other. "I'm shaking bad enough for the both of us."

I barely feel the needle. I pick a slide with a yellow sticker on the end and touch my finger to it. Rue bristles at the sight of my blood seeping red, but he stays quiet.

I hold my breath, half expecting the tiny wound on my finger to heal over, but it keeps trickling.

"Pinch it off," Tobin says. "It'll stop faster."

He holds his sleeve cuff against his own finger once he's pricked it, so I do the same, strangely relieved by the sting.

"Well?" Honoria asks. She's already made up her mind; she's just waiting for those little slips of glass to agree with her.

"Patience," Dr. Wolff says.

The room dims, allowing a projector to shine on the wall.

Dr. Wolff adjusts the scope, sliding Tobin's plate into place over the light, and the wall turns red. But this is nothing like a security alert. It's not vibrant or blaring. The darkest red forms dots that float around, bumping off one another. Between them are specks of black dust.

Nanites.

*Fade.*

"He's infected," Honoria charges.

Tobin becomes the center of attention. He eyes the nearest curtain, as though debating whether or not he should pull it shut around us.

Is this why he protected me? Or why Anne-Marie risked talking to me that first day in the Common Hall? Were they only responding to the familiarity of the hive—not me at all?

"I'm not infected," he insists.

Rue agrees, telling me that Tobin definitely cannot hear the others.

"I'm seeing evidence to the contrary," Honoria says, staring at the wall.

"Actually, you're not," Dr. Wolff says. "If this was a contact situation, the machines would be active and inside the cells, not floating in plasma."

Tobin moves, trancelike, from the bed to the wall, putting his hand into the projection to try and wipe the dark patches out of his blood, but they're not dirt or scratches on the lens. They stay put.

"Is he safe?" Col. Lutrell asks.

Dr. Wolff doesn't get to answer.

"How can I have Fade in my blood?" Tobin asks. "Nanobot took them back—I saw it."

"The nanites you're seeing here are inert," Dr. Wolff says. "They're as benign as the day you were born."

I see the exact moment he knows he's said too much. He meant that last bit to be reassuring, but Tobin heard something else.

"We're born with those things? Like one of them?"

He glances back at Rue, horrified.

"Not everyone," Dr. Wolff says, like that makes it better. He starts to explain, but cuts himself off and pats Tobin on the shoulder instead.

"Dad?" Tobin asks, but Col. Lutrell won't look at him. I don't think he wants Tobin to see his eyes right now.

It's not fair.

Until now, Tobin's faith in his father was unwavering, even when he found Col. Lutrell among the Fade and even with silver eyes. Watching that die as the colonel's secrets emerge breaks my heart. I know how it feels to realize everyone in the room knows more about me than I do, and know they're keeping the secrets I've been killing myself to try and uncover.

At least I knew parts of my past were missing; Tobin's been blindsided.

I stand to bring Tobin back to our seat as Dr. Wolff removes the slide with his blood from under the microscope. Tobin startles from the change.

"How is this possible?" he asks me.

Another slide—*my blood*—replaces his in the projection circle.

"When this is over, talk to your dad," I tell him, staring at the blood cells on the wall. My sample looks almost identical to Tobin's, though there are more nanites present, and they're ringed neatly around my cells. None are moving.

What if this happened another way and they'd tested us before we went into the Dark? Would Rue's nanites have shown up active on the screen?

He could have ruined everything.

*Remorse,* Rue says. *Apology. My intent did not equal the result.*

*Then what did you intend?*

*To hear Cherish.*

*But you can still hear her,* I say.

*Because you are near. Once I return to home, there will be silence.*

142

The familiar heartbeat sound dies to nothing.

I don't feel so good. His regrets infect Cherish, and she passes them to me, filling my insides with the fear of separation.

I thought breaking away from the hive would allow Rue to move on, but he's no better off than when Cherish was first taken. What have I done?

"It appears that both of our boundary-challenged young people are human," Dr. Wolff says.

I used to think that was what I wanted.

Dr. Wolff turns off the projector, bringing up the room lights as Honoria huffs into a chair.

"Does that mean you'll let Bolt help Trey?" I ask.

"Perhaps I can undo what was done by others," Bolt offers, but Honoria's already shaking her head. His voice makes her cringe. "No."

"Why?" I ask. "What could he possibly do to make things any worse? You already think Trey's a lost cause. What are you afraid of? That they'll fix this, and then you'll have to acknowledge they aren't monsters?"

The others look at her expectantly, but she refuses to answer. Bolt goes to Anne-Marie's mother.

"May I see your Trey?"

She's torn, her face a mirror of Anne-Marie, with her lip pulled into her teeth. She knows Bolt's helped Trey before, and she knows that he's never been aggressive, but he's still the "it" she wouldn't invite to dinner.

Her regrets smell of burnt fuses. Shame is worse—curdled milk and vinegar.

"I . . . I don't know. Elias? What should we do?"

"Can you really heal him?" Mr. Pace asks.

"I promise the attempt, not the success."

"Then do what you can."

Honoria's foot starts tapping on the tile. Dr. Wolff points down the row of beds.

"Don't be alarmed that he won't wake up," he says. "It's best if he sleeps through this."

"Best," Bolt agrees. "We are the same."

"They put people to sleep to heal them," I explain, knowing Dr. Wolff won't find a healing stupor to have much in common with chemical sedation.

Bolt disappears behind the curtain, which no one moves to pull aside. They don't want to see what's happening, and they certainly don't want to see failure, if that's what's coming.

"I still have a question." Honoria's out of her seat, pacing again, flicking her radio's power switch on and off. I check the counter to make sure her gun's still where Dr. Wolff left it. "I'm willing to believe that *these* two Fade have no particular ill intent. And I'm willing to extend that belief to the idea that *you* brought them solely to benefit Trey, but that neither explains nor excuses your presence in a sealed access point. How'd you get through the perimeter?"

"We got lucky," Tobin says.

"I doubt that," she says.

"There's a short in the lights," I blurt. Tobin glares at me. I don't trust her any more than he does, but something out there is scaring the Fade. We need all the holes in our security net plugged tight. "Anyone can run through."

"You knew about this?"

"Not until tonight." For me it's not a lie. "When we saw the fires, it was either take a run at the lights or go the long way around to the old tunnels under the Grey. They flickered, and we took the chance. We got lucky."

I see her weighing my words for a hint that they mean more than their face definition.

"There's something out there, Honoria. You need to close the skips before it finds its way inside."

"Did you see something?"

"No, but *they* did." I look at Rue, who mimics Tobin's scowl to the finest crease on his face. Exposing human secrets doesn't bother him, but Fade concerns are another matter.

"The Fade are guarding their territory from something. They're guarding *us*, too."

"Guarding?" Anne-Marie's mother asks.

"We have our patrols; they've got theirs," Tobin says.

"And theirs are backing ours up," I add. "Curiosity didn't bring them into the Grey. They've been standing watch over us—every night. Something changed when our lights went down. They're terrified."

Rue stays silent. To deny it would mean a lie, and he won't do that.

Dr. Wolff, Mr. Pace, and Col. Lutrell all exchange looks with Honoria—nearly identical to the ones the Fade wore when they were talking to one another. But this time, there's nothing being said. They don't *know* what to say.

"Ask Sykes," Tobin says unexpectedly. "He tested the samples he took, didn't he, Mr. Pace?"

"Elias?" Honoria asks.

"He took them, but we got a bit sidetracked." He glances at Trey's curtain.

"Has the hive told you anything?" Col. Lutrell asks me.

"They're hiding, almost like radio silence. I think they—"

Honoria's walkie cuts me off, crackling into a transmission so garbled that nothing coherent comes through.

"Sykes?" she barks, shushing us with a wave of her hand.

"We've got a situation," Lt. Sykes says.

"It's handled. Tobin and the girl are here."

"No. Tess Blaylock's boy—"

A horrible sound overruns his voice, made worse by the static. It sounds like a wild animal howling in pain.

Then dozens of voices scream.

"Stop him! Bar the door!" Lt. Sykes shouts.

The shouts give way to gunfire and then more screams.

"Blaylock?" I whisper to Tobin. "Isn't that—"

"Dante."

Somehow, we're back on our feet. Everyone's moved closer to Honoria, watching her radio like it's a vid-screen.

"Get them out of here!" Lt. Sykes orders. "Everyone stay clear—Silver, don't. Don't touch him, sweetheart. Please don't touch him."

"What's happening?" Anne-Marie's mother asks.

Honoria's paralyzed, unable to answer. Mr. Pace takes over on the radio.

"Tell me this is not what it sounds like, Kevin."

"Get down here now—Silver, don't! Get her away from him. Hold her on the other side of the room."

Silver doesn't go quietly. The sound of her struggle comes through loud and clear.

"I need a containment team," Lt. Sykes says, breathing heavy. "He's turning, Elias. The boy's gone Fade."

# CHAPTER SIXTEEN

## TOBIN

They should have cleared the bunker and locked Dante in it. He's raving, fighting Dad and Sykes with all he's got. Trey didn't do anything like this.

I wonder if I will.

"Dante, stop!" Silver shouts over him. "They're trying to help you!"

He's been shot. There's blood on his leg, but none running. His body's healing faster than Marina's.

*The boy's gone Fade.*

He still looks human.

I had micro-bits of the shadow crawler in my veins and never changed, either. This could be me.

What if Dr. Wolff's wrong and the ones in my blood aren't dead but asleep? What if they're getting ready to wake up?

"It's not the same," Marina says out of nowhere. "Dante's not like you and Trey."

Sometimes I swear she's reading my mind. The only question is whether or not she's doing it on purpose.

Mr. Pace moves to help while Dr. Wolff attempts to find an

opening wide enough to fit a tranq so he can sedate Dante. Nique hauls Silver away from the scuffle.

"Should we help?" Marina asks.

I should. I'm security, but my feet won't move. Our elders put Dante on the floor, facedown.

"How can this happen?" Marina asks.

"Ask the nightmares," I tell her.

"His are not ours," Rueful says, and she can't back him up fast enough.

"They didn't do this," she swears.

How can she be that naive? "He doesn't have a cold, Marina. There aren't a lot of options for carriers!"

Am I a carrier? Is that what nanites in my blood mean? I can poison others but stay safe myself?

Honoria's pressing Dante's shoulders down with her knee, trying to hold him still, but every time Dr. Wolff gets close enough to tranq him, Dante bucks up off the floor and the doc loses his shot. A wild swing sends Sykes flying.

"Maybe he asked to change," Marina suggests. "He could have been willing."

"Does this *look* like something he'd ask for to you?" I say.

Dante's been watching the Dark almost since the Arc fell, but no one would want this.

"Cherish says Dante touched the Darkness," Marina whispers to me. "He can hear but has no voice."

"And what does that mean in human?"

"I don't know."

Schuyler comes out from behind the curtain, either on some cue from Rueful or drawn by the commotion. He and the ink blot cross the room, in step.

Schuyler grabs Dante under his arms, brushing Mr. Pace off, while Rueful takes his legs from Dad. Honoria's the only one who refuses to let go until the three of them have put Dante in a bed.

"Best to sleep," Bolt says, leaning his weight against Dante's chest.

"Agreed," Dr. Wolff says.

They tie Dante down with restraints, but he breaks one of the wrist ties clean off the wall before the meds kick in. Even asleep, with a breathing mask full of anti-Fade smoke over his nose, he never stops moving. His skin's a kaleidoscope of shifting and swirling marks that never disappear long enough for Dante to look like himself. His eyes twitch while tremors shake his hands and feet. The muscles in his neck constrict.

"They've hit his nervous system," Honoria says to no one.

"You have to help him," Silver croaks. "You're supposed to protect the good people, and you shot him!" She punches Lt. Sykes in the side, screaming hysterically until Nique folds her into another hug. "He wasn't going to hurt anyone. Dante wouldn't do that!"

"Shh. It's okay, honey," Nique says. "He'll be okay."

"No. He won't," Honoria says.

"You could at least pretend to show some compassion," Nique spits. "We don't know anything yet."

"I *do*, and so do they." She points to Dad and the others. "We know *exactly* what this is because we've seen it—too many times and over too many years to remember all the faces. We've lived it, and *I* tried to warn you. You wouldn't listen, so try looking."

Honoria reaches for the edge of Dante's shirt, where it's come loose from the back of his pants, and yanks it up, lifting his body on the side where he broke the restraint. There's a black smudge focused at his spine and branching out along his nerves to his whole body.

"He didn't have that before," Silver insists.

"We called it the Death Tree when I was your age. Why don't you ask them why?" Honoria says.

"Dad?" I ask.

"Go on, James. Try telling him this truth and see if it lightens your spirits."

"We called it the Death Tree because once it took root, the only options were death or Fading."

We? He's talking like he was around when Honoria was a kid. I've never heard anyone mention Death Trees before.

"Never think I don't know," Honoria growls, dropping Dante's shirt.

Silver screams again, stamping her feet as she clings tighter to Nique. I reach for my back, sliding my hand under my shirt to feel the skin below it.

"There's nothing there, Tobin," Marina whispers, pulling my hand down.

"There has to be something we can do," Nique says.

"Containment," Honoria says grimly. "Dante's the only one symptomatic—*so far*. Hopefully, we can stop it before it spreads to anyone else."

"Spreads?" Silver sniffles, suddenly more alert. "Spreads how?"

"Contact with a carrier," Dr. Wolff says. "I'll reinstate mandatory blood screenings, starting with Dante's peers and their families. It'll take days to get through everyone, but if anyone else has been exposed, we'll know by then, anyway."

"What kind of contact?" Silver asks, quieter, and still. No one's been closer to Dante than she has. "Like *contact* contact?"

Nique curses into the top of her head. Honoria and Sykes go ice white.

Dr. Wolff heads for the cabinets where he keeps his syringes, preparing another one. Dad slams the heels of his hands into his temples. He used to do the same thing when Mom had a seizure he couldn't stop and he thought it would be the one that killed her.

"It's happening again," Mr. Pace mumbles.

Only Sykes remains as he was, waiting for orders.

"I'm not like him—I promise."

Silver tries to wriggle loose, but Nique holds her tight. "Let us see your back, baby."

Slowly, she raises the back of Silver's uniform; it only takes a couple of inches to see the streaks down her spine. Honoria kicks a wastebasket to the other side of the room, drowning whatever she says in the clang.

"She's branching," Sykes says.

Dante's over the line, and Silver's approaching it, but Marina's Fade stay ominously and suspiciously mute.

"This isn't what happened to me, or Trey," I prompt them. "What's happening to her?"

"Darkness," Rueful says. He glances at Marina.

"It's a tide," she says for him. "Dante and Silver are being washed away. Dragged out to sea."

"They are too many," Rueful says.

"They are aware." Schuyler.

"They are searching." Rueful.

"They are here." Schuyler.

They answer together, almost like they aren't the ones talking; it's just coming out of their mouths.

"Who's here?" Honoria asks.

"They have no name."

"They are no one. They are Dark."

That cleared things right up . . .

"Somebody please tell me what's happening," Silver's still crying.

Dr. Wolff comes closer, needle in hand, and Silver goes wild trying to get away from him. The more she thrashes in Nique's arms, the faster the black lines creep down her spine, sprouting feelers onto smaller nerves.

"Make it stop," Silver begs.

"The faster your pulse, the faster they spread," Dr. Wolff says. "You have to control yourself."

He gives her the shot.

"But I don't want to be one of them. I didn't even go out there—Dante kept asking me, but I stayed inside. I was good." She breaks and runs for the Fade, kneeling down to grasp their hands, begging. "I was good. Why did you do this to me?"

"These aren't ours," Rue says. "They won't listen."

"Dante and Silver are kids," Nique says. "Like you—you're kids, aren't you? Young? Marina, help me, here. I don't know how to say it so he'll understand."

Schuyler's younger than Honoria, but that's not saying much.

"Silver doesn't want this," Marina says. "It was a mistake, Rue. Can't you fix it? For me?"

They're the magic words. *For me* got Rueful to save my life when he wanted me dead. Surely, he'll help a girl who knocked out the lights for him.

"Take them back," Silver begs. "I won't even be mad, I promise. I just want to stay me." She even manages a smile.

Rueful stands and reaches down to draw her up, but Schuyler holds him back.

"They are not ours," he insists.

His voice sets Honoria off.

"Get a suppressant in her system," she orders Dr. Wolff. "We can beat the first replication spike; there may not be enough in her to be toxic yet."

Silver whimpers. She's shutting down.

Honoria softens her tone. "It won't feel very good, but if we can get ahead of them—"

"It made me human," Marina says over her. "That's all you need to know, isn't it?"

Silver nods. Honoria actually mouths, "Thank you."

"I'll get the meds." Dr. Wolff heads for his mixing room.

"I want this ward sealed, inside and out," Honoria says, making for the exit. "Sykes, get on that door. I'm rerouting power to the alarms in the subterranean areas since our current measures are obviously ineffective. We'll need new fires on the perimeter to make up for the dimmer lights, and, Dominque, be careful of her tears."

She and Sykes leave the rest of us. The main door snaps shut, hissing as the quarantine seal sets.

"I'm sorry," Silver says. She's blubbering, but she's calmer. The shot must have worked. "I didn't know . . . neither did he . . . He couldn't have."

Nique lets her cry, completely disregarding Honoria's warning. Rueful approaches them cautiously.

"Do you hear?" he asks.

"Of course. You're talking to me." Silver cringes back.

"He means the hive," Marina explains. "Can you hear voices? Sometimes it sounds like static."

"I don't hear anything. Is that good?"

"May I speak?" Rueful asks.

Silver looks to Marina for translation.

"He wants to know if he can touch you. Maybe he can help."

Silver holds a shaking hand out, whimpering when Rueful takes it.

"This isn't going to work, is it?" I ask, leaning close to Marina's ear.

She shrugs.

Rueful and Silver go still, both with their eyes closed. Mr. Pace draws Nique back, though she's reluctant to let Silver go. It could easily be Annie standing there with Fade trickling down her spine and rewiring her nervous system.

We're all just staring. It feels like nothing's happening, and then Marina smiles.

"They're synchronizing—we all are. All the beats are—No!"

Rueful flinches, like a muscle spasm that leaves him swaying. Whatever was working just stopped.

"Oh no," Marina whispers. "No!"

Rueful crashes down to one knee, and Marina runs to him. She touches his arm but pulls back.

"He's freezing."

His hands nearly burned my skin in the Dark. Cold can't be good.

"It's siphoning his body heat."

"What is?" Dad asks.

"Darkness," she says, touching Rueful with a finger before

pulling that back, too. She shakes her hand. "It hurts. Help him!" She looks at Schuyler. "He can't get free."

Rueful isn't holding on to Silver anymore; she has him and won't let go.

She progresses from tremors to full-body convulsions. Black marks explode onto her face and hands, stretching beyond her body in grotesque protrusions aimed at Rueful like spikes. His marks retreat, leaving his hand the color of blanched bone inside hers.

Marina reaches for Rueful at the same time Nique lunges for Silver, but neither makes contact. Mr. Pace and Schuyler intercept them both before I can move.

"Get them apart!" Marina shouts, kicking in Schuyler's arms.

My mind floods with an endless sea of white. Nothing but light in all directions.

*Light . . .*

It worked when Rueful was in the White Room.

I run for the switch plate near the door and then spin the dial to high power. Sunlamps ignite over each bed before the emergency blinders put us all into a white out.

Human and Fade scream through my hands covering my ears. I'm screaming myself.

"Turn them off," Marina shrieks. "You'll kill them!"

But I hold the dial a few more seconds before turning them down.

Silver's motionless on the floor, her face marked by receding patches of black that blur to gray. Rueful's marks return to normal, everywhere except his hand, which stays white. He's sluggish and uncoordinated. Schuyler crouches hidden inside a veil of nanites.

"Get him out of here," Marina begs.

The keypad on the door's already beeping with the sound of someone entering the code, which means Sykes, or worse, and neither he nor Honoria will wait for an explanation about what happened. They'll only see Silver corpselike on the floor and Dante with his screaming silent mouth.

"Get out of here. Your sister will kill you both," I tell Schuyler

Marina nudges her shoulder under Rueful and starts to lift him, but his muscles aren't working right; they drag, and his nerves are jumping under his skin. There's no way she can manage on her own.

I take his weight on the other side.

"Thank you," she says softly.

I can regret saving the ink blot later. For now, it made her happy.

Mr. Pace uses his wristband to override whatever Honoria's done to the security panel we used to get to the hospital, and it slides open.

Dad whispers something to Schuyler, who nods and takes Rueful from us at the entrance. Mr. Pace seals them in as the outer doors open.

# CHAPTER SEVENTEEN

## MARINA

I expect Honoria to charge after Rue and Bolt before they can escape, but she looks defeated. She sees Silver with Anne-Marie's mother hovering around her and raises her eyes to the ceiling, shaking her head.

I don't know what that means, but hopefully the pause is enough for Bolt to get Rue somewhere safe. He isn't in much of a condition to run, and with dawn fast approaching, and the ominous whiteness of the hand that touched Silver, Rue's ability to guard himself against sunlight is slim.

"What happened?" Dr. Wolff asks, emerging from his back room. He nearly drops the inhaler he's just mixed in his haste to get to Silver.

"Rue tried to heal her," I say. "It didn't work."

Fear returns to the room, whirling in like the dervishes that wind through the Grey at its wider points.

"We can't leave her on the floor," Anne-Marie's mother says, but she doesn't volunteer to pick her up.

Even Dr. Wolff, kneeling beside her, doesn't let his hands get too close. He holds them above Silver's skin, as though they're some kind of scanning machine that can read her vitals from a distance.

"Is she alive?" Honoria asks.

"She's breathing," Dr. Wolff says. "I hate to risk dislodging any of these growths without knowing their precise configuration, but I won't know her full condition until I can run tests."

And still no one tries to pick her up.

"Keep away," Tobin says when I kneel on Silver's other side. "You saw what those things did."

"She's terrified," I say, pulling loose. "Everyone standing around and staring at her won't make her any better. Until someone figures out how to move her, I'm going to make sure she knows she's not alone."

If she's turning Fade, loneliness is an added terror she doesn't need. There's enough of Cherish left to talk to Rue; maybe she can reach Silver, too.

"At least put these on over yours." Tobin tugs his gloves off and passes them to me.

I slip them over the ones I'm already wearing. My hands feel restricted but also safer.

"Silver? Can you hear me?" I ask.

She gurgles in return. The protrusions that broke her skin punched through so viciously, they've ripped it open, leaving blood to seep around the edges; one cluster sits directly over her throat. Tears stream down her cheeks, soaking into her hair on either side of her neck.

*Caution,* Cherish warns. *Your intent is flawed.*

She knows the checklist I'm making in my head, starting with clearing as much of the muck off Silver's skin as possible.

*Then watch my back.*

*Negative. Your hands require observation.*

"Give me a towel," I say. Anne-Marie's mother puts one in my outstretched hand. "Silver, it's Marina. I'm sorry if this hurts, but I want to clean these so Doctor Wolff can fix them, okay?"

Another gurgle. I hope it means "yes," rather than "That hurts so bad, I want to die."

*Going silent would be better,* Cherish says, but I can't accept that. Death should never be the best-case scenario.

I slide my hand into Silver's, happy to feel the pressure as her fingers close on mine.

"She's conscious," I tell the others. "She's trying to squeeze my hand."

"That's good, right?" Tobin asks. "If she knows it's Marina, that has to mean Silver's still in there, doesn't it?"

"Whether she can say it or not, she'll always be in there," Honoria says gravely. "That's what makes it so terrible."

I tune her out, refusing to let her negativity get to me, and focus only on my friend on the floor.

Whenever Silver was exposed, it must have been far after Dante. Her blood still runs easily, and her skin isn't sealing itself as I wipe it. I finish one side of her face and start on her collarbone when a hand clamps my shoulder and yanks me backward.

"Move away," Honoria says.

"I'm almost done," I tell her.

"Marina, let go," Tobin says.

*Observe your hand*, Cherish says.

I raise my hand, to reassure everyone that both pairs of gloves are still in place and that Silver's blood is still red, but Cherish speaks again: *Observe your hand.*

I look at the other one. Miniature versions of the nanite growths covering Silver's body have crossed from her hand to mine; they're consuming Tobin's glove.

I leap to my feet, slinging the glove to get the nanites off; they land on her chest.

It doesn't occur to me to remove the glove itself until Tobin cuts through the wrist strap with his field knife. I drop what's left beside Silver on the floor.

"Did they hit your skin?" Tobin asks.

*No damage*, Cherish offers. *I do not hear them.*

"I think I'm okay," I say. My hand looks clear.

"No one else touches her," Honoria barks. "Get her isolated, and scorch these floors!"

"Elias, take Dominique in the back and give her some scrubs," Dr. Wolff says. "We'd best burn what she's wearing."

This time, Anne-Marie's mother doesn't argue. She leaves with Mr. Pace, disappearing into the room where Dr. Wolff makes his medications and hides the incinerator.

"Marina, you, too," Col. Lutrell says. "You can get a new

uniform later. Get changed, and then I want you kids out of here."

I nod, still numb from the shock of what's happening, and start for the backroom.

"Just a minute." Honoria seizes my hand for another inspection, and it's only now I realize how lucky I am that this isn't the one I sliced with the broken bottle. A few missing scratches she'd overlook, but not a wound as deep as that piece of glass went.

She turns my hand in every angle before cutting her eyes back up to my face and staring, as though she's searching for something hidden there. I stop breathing, unsure what clue she's looking for and afraid that if I do the wrong thing, she'll think she's found it.

"Is she all right?" Col. Lutrell asks.

*Please*, I beg, willing her to hear me like Cherish or Rue would. *Please don't do this to me again.*

I don't want to go back in a box.

*Neither do I*, says Cherish.

"She's clear."

Honoria shoves my hand away. All I can think about is Rue with his bone-white hand, Dante with the Death Tree down his spine, and how I've come way too close to finding out how exposure to these new Fade would affect me.

"This way." Tobin takes hold of my fingers.

We go through the door, and I stop to close it behind us, then lean against it for a minute to catch my breath and my thoughts.

"You're okay," Tobin says, still holding my hand. He looks blurry. "That's the one thing I trust that woman not to lie about, anymore. If you were in danger, she would have kept you with Silver and Dante."

I throw my arms around his neck and hang on tight. He hugs me back.

"Hey." He pushes me off to look at my face because I won't let go on my own. "You *are* okay, aren't you?"

"Thanks to you," I tell him. "They could have gotten me. I'd be like Silver."

"You don't know that."

He squeezes my fingers, and that's when I really start to worry. The hand he held was the one those things tried to swarm. Those were his gloves I lost. Now we're both unprotected.

The blurriness gets worse.

What if some of the nanites got through? What if one or two of them made their way into my glove and then into my skin? They're microscopic; no one would know until they took over. They could have jumped from me to him because I was dumb enough to want someone to hold my hand.

*They do not speak*, Cherish insists.

Tobin's talking, too, but I can't understand him. Spots of light and dark blink in and out over his face, set to the beat of my heart against my temples. Is this what a panic attack feels like?

"Marina!" he says, stern and loud, and the film over my mind breaks. "I said, you believe me, don't you?"

"Those things hurt Rue. What do you think they would have done to me?"

"I think there's no point in making guesses about things we'll never know the answer to."

And I think that's empty hope. We're on the verge of more questions. The only way to deal with them is seeking out answers we might not want to hear.

Dr. Wolff's mixing room is belowground; I should have thought of that.

Tobin takes us down a set of stairs to an area full of boxes and shelves. "Scrubs" turn out to be the boxy monochrome sets of clothes patients wear in the hospital. I was in there so often when I first came to the Arclight that I thought I'd seen every color, but this is the first time someone's given me maroon.

I leave the changing area to rejoin the others, but Tobin's gone.

"His dad needed a word with him," Mr. Pace says as he throws my uniform into the incinerator. Blanca's flower's still in the pocket.

"Are they words about how he knows what a Death Tree is because he was around when you called it that?" I ask.

"How—"

"Colonel and Lieutenant," I say, rather than confessing I've read Honoria's book. "They're the only people here who have titles. After I figured that out, I starting paying attention. I haven't figured out why your eyes are still brown. Contacts?"

"They never changed; the contact was too slight, and I burned myself too fast. James's were green, until they healed him. Most people don't pay attention."

"I sure didn't," Anne-Marie's mother says. Her scrubs are purple. "By the time I realized they weren't aging, it was time for them to tell us the truth. That was an interesting day."

"It always is," he says. "You never know how people will react."

"Does Anne-Marie know?"

"Not yet," her mother says.

I guess this is another of those graduation surprises we have to look forward to, like finding out we're not actually on the verge of starvation and discovering that the woman supposedly protecting us from the Fade is riddled with nanites.

"Do I have to stay in the hospital?" I ask, picking at my scrubs.

"No. The clothes are a precaution."

That's a relief. I hate the hospital, especially when Honoria's in it.

I start for the door.

"Where are you going?" Anne-Marie's mother asks. "Your room or James's apartment?"

"My room."

"Not alone, you're not," Mr. Pace says. "They cleared the bunkers after Dante, but the living areas are on lockdown. You can't go up without an escort. In fact, I don't think you should be alone in your room, either."

"I'm used to it." And I want the chance to sort a few things out with no one but Cherish around.

"Not tonight—today, actually. It's nearly dawn." Ms. Johnston checks her wristband. "Today, you keep Annie company so I don't have to worry about either one of you being by yourself."

She hugs me again. It's her go-to answer for everything.

"Nothing's going to happen to you under my roof," she says as she steers me from the supply room.

She must have forgotten that all of our roofs are under Honoria's, and plenty can happen in her house.

# CHAPTER EIGHTEEN

## MARINA

Sykes kept his promise. A woman I don't know stands at attention outside Anne-Marie's apartment. She picks up her radio as we approach and presses the transmit button: "They're here."

She nods and tells us, "You can go in."

"It's my home," Ms. Johnston says. "I don't need permission." She unlocks the door with her wristband.

"Marina!" Anne-Marie pounces as soon as her door's open. "Are you okay? What happened? Are you hurt? Why are you wearing hospital clothes? Are you sick? Is it worse? Where's Trey?"

She must have spent the last few hours coming up with questions.

"I was going crazy in here," she says. Her eyes are red and puffy, with sticky patches on her cheeks. I bet she misses when her curls were long enough to fall forward when she tipped her head. They made it easier to hide when she was crying. "I keep hearing doors slam, but the alarms are still red, and no one came here, so I don't know—"

"Sit." Her mother points at the nearest chair, then pinches her fingers together. "And zip it."

Anne-Marie plops down, mouth snapped shut.

Is that all it takes?

Her mother gives her the short version of what's happened tonight, leaving out the darker details. Silver's ordeal gets sanitized into: "Dante passed it along." Anne-Marie gasps, anyway.

"But they fixed it, right?" she says. "Your Fade friends came and put her back the way she's supposed to be?"

"Not exactly," I say.

"Silver can't be a Fade, Marina. She can't survive outdoors. She can't survive without a hairbrush. Tell them—"

"They tried," I say. "It didn't work."

Ms. Johnston stands to leave and opens the door.

"I'm going back to the hospital, and you two are staying here," she says, pausing at the sight of the guard outside. "Do not leave this apartment for anything short of life or death. Elias set that lock, and there's no one out there who can break it. Understood?"

She looks at me, not Anne-Marie. The apartment's Honoria-proof. Got it.

I nod, and she leaves me alone with Anne-Marie and Anne-Marie's nervous chatter.

"Was it awful?" she asks seriously.

"Awful, bad, chaotic—just keep going down the alphabet."

"Did Trey—"

"He's still asleep, and he's not like them," I tell her.

Now she's hugging me, too, soaking my shoulder with tears the way Silver did her mother.

"Sorry," Anne-Marie says, straightening up. "Worry makes me weird."

"I know the feeling," I say. "Is there a bathroom I can use? I haven't had the chance tonight."

"Down the hall," she says. "If I'd seen someone turn Fade, I would have peed my pants."

I don't really need the toilet as much as I need isolation. That way, both of me can speak freely. I go inside and lock the door behind me. How can one night have been this long?

Silver was begging to not become the thing I was born. How do you forget something like that?

*Negative,* Cherish says, pushing me the image of Dante's marked back. *We were not this.*

Now, I see Silver on the floor with all those spikes coming out of her.

*We do not silence.*

Now, Rue's white hand.

*Her plea was to not go dark. To keep her voice. Included, she would keep her voice, and gain ours.*

*You make it sound like there's more than one kind of Fade out there,* I say.

She goes quiet.

*Cherish?*

Nothing.

"Talk to me!" I brace my hands against the sink's edge, staring myself in the eye. This is the only way I've ever truly seen Cherish, and this is a conversation that needs to be face-to-face. "Tell me what's going on."

What little pigment exists in my complexion drains. My hair goes the other way, charring soot black and taking on the crystalline sheen worn by the Fade. Thin, feathered wisps appear on my face, first at the chin and cheeks, but soon the patterns sketch themselves everywhere my skin's not covered.

I'm Marina; my reflection is Cherish. I have no idea which one of us is scowling.

"Tell me," I say, swallowing my nerves before she can realize she intimidates me. "Stop keeping secrets. Stop holding back. Tell me everything."

Her answer comes as a taunting echo—*Careful what you wish for.* She lifts the veil between us and lets "everything" come roaring through.

It's the full knowledge of the Fade. Through the hive, they disperse their knowledge through an infinite number of voices and thoughts and memories. It's too much for one human mind to hold; you can't pour the infinite into a finite container.

*Stop!* I scream to her. *Cease. Please!*

Cherish hasn't been selfishly hoarding knowledge that belongs to me. She's been functioning like a valve, allowing only as much information into my mind as it can process. She cuts back the flow, and I'm left with the static of a tuning radio.

I catch my breath, before trying again. "Show me what I need to know. What can I tell Honoria that will help them? There has to be something."

*Affirmed*, she says. *Forbidden. Guarded. Secret.*

"Tell me, anyway."

Everything nonessential drifts into to the background while Cherish arranges the imperative sequences in ultrafine detail.

My nightmares—what I *thought* were nightmares—aren't dreams at all. They're a peek through the cracks into the Fade's greatest secret.

*The Darkness.*

The answer.

"Thank you," I say.

Now I owe her. That's the excuse I give myself to reach out for Rue and see if he'll respond.

*Rue?* I call. *Can you hear me? Are you still here?*

*Affirmed. Present.*

His response is hazy, a conversation heard through too many doors, but he answers. Cherish thrills with the joy of hearing his voice and frets over his condition, turning my body flame hot from hair to toenails.

*Injured?* I ask. He feels so weak.

My hand goes numb—the same hand that stayed white on him after he was separated from Silver.

I flex my fingers as Rue tries to convey what's happening to him. Black lines stretch toward the back of my hand, but they hit

172

some sort of barrier at my wrist. They shrivel up and disappear. Each nanite that tries to heal him falls silent. Something's attacking him.

Someone bangs on the bathroom door, startling me.

"Marina?" Anne-Marie calls through the door. "Are you okay? You've been in there a long time."

She didn't hear me, did she? I don't think I was speaking out loud.

"I'm fine," I answer, shaking my still-numb hand. "I just . . . um . . . just give me a minute, okay?"

"You sound weird."

"Because I don't usually talk to people while I'm in the bathroom. I'm fine, I swear."

*Rue,* I call again, once Anne-Marie's stopped. *Can't Bolt heal you?*

*Negative!* he shouts with such force that I nearly stagger back. *Darkness. Infects.*

*He refuses assistance for fear of spreading the Darkness.* Bolt's stronger voice takes over.

*Are you safe?* I ask.

Through his eyes, I see them moving through the tunnels, but it's a temporary solution.

*We must return to home,* Bolt says. *I am insufficient. He needs home. My other must understand this.*

Rue's won't make it across the wider points, not with all the dangers of the Grey that lurk there. At nightfall Bolt will have a chance to get safely home via the short side, but only if Honoria doesn't tighten security to the point that they can't leave.

"I'll try," I assure him.

*Success is required. An attempt without success will bring silence.*

He doesn't say anything else.

"Can we do this?" I ask Cherish, looking directly into the mirror.

"Marina?" Anne-Marie knocks again.

"I'm coming!"

*Success,* Cherish says, and leaves the mirror, so my reflection is all that's left.

I can do this.

*We* can do this.

Together, Cherish and I outnumber Honoria. We have the advantage.


"What were you doing in there? I thought you had to pee," Anne-Marie says when I come flying out of the bathroom so fast, I nearly fall over my own feet. She looks past me through the door.

"I need Trey's sketches," I tell her.

"Wait a minute."

"I know how to help them—Rue, Trey, everyone," I tell her. "She told me how, but I need proof. It's in the drawings."

"She who? Who were you talking to in my bathroom?" Anne-

Marie shuffles after me, down the hall to Trey's room. The door's still unlocked, but the mess is gone. Someone's packed all of Trey's things into crates, stacked neatly on his desk and bed.

"What happened in here?" I ask.

"Honoria sent someone to search Trey's stuff. Mom threw them out before they could finish. Now who was in my bathroom, and what's in the sketches?"

"Me, and something he saw."

I tear the lids off one box after another, but only find clothes and mementos.

"You're not making any sense."

"I know." I reach for another box, but Anne-Marie takes it away.

"You want the sealed ones," she says. "What did he see?"

"Something big, if I'm right." I rip the tape off of a secure box on Trey's bed. As promised, it's nothing but stacks of paper filled with dark figures and shadow creatures.

*Pay dirt.*

"Do you see it?" I can feel the smile spreading across my face.

These images are exactly what Cherish showed me; I should have seen it myself. Anne-Marie snatches one out of my hand.

"I don't see the big deal. It's just a shadow monster."

"And Rue isn't one. If the Fade look like Rue and my sister, then what's this thing?"

The world's about to tilt again. I grab a handful of pictures off the top, then run for the front door.

"Marina!" Anne-Marie runs after me. "You can't just rifle through my brother's stuff and run out of here talking like a crazy person! Mom said not to leave."

But I have to. I need reinforcements.

# CHAPTER NINETEEN

## TOBIN

"Dad!" I call into the apartment.

Our lights are dimmed below half power, but turning the dial doesn't make them brighter. I was only below with Marina for a few minutes when he radioed Mr. Pace to send me home. I figured it was important since he left before I got back, but where is he?

"Dad?"

No lights. No Dad. No way am I staying here like this. One more try, and I'm gone. I'll wait in Annie's apartment; he can come looking for me, if he needs me so bad.

"Dad!"

"In here," he answers from the hall.

"Were you in the tunnels?"

"I had to check a few things."

"A few, or two?"

As in the two creepers currently hiding out from the sun in our walls.

"They helped us, Tobin," he says. "We can do the same."

I flop into a chair and toss my jacket and boots.

"What's with the lights?" I ask, ending the discussion of Rueful. "Did we blow a fuse, or did Honoria's reroute dip into the building's power?"

"Neither," he says. I hear a sound behind him, and I'm back on my feet. "I was making the apartment more hospitable for our guests."

"Guests?" That sound was the sliding panel to the tunnels in our linen closet. Surely, he didn't—

He moves out of the way, to allow Schuyler to pass. Rueful's leaned over his shoulder, barely able to walk; he can't even raise his head.

"I'm out of here."

"Tobin, wait," Dad calls.

"Not as long as they're here." Schuyler doesn't bother me, but the ink blot's got to go. I will not sit here with him in the room. "I'll wait with Marina."

"Dominique took Marina home with her, and we're locked down. No nonessential personnel's allowed out unescorted."

"Security, remember?" I ask, tugging on my trainee shirt.

"Consider your status temporarily revoked."

I reach the door, but it won't open. He's set the parental lock.

"You can't do this." The door should swing out into the hall, but it won't budge, even when I smash my shoulder against it.

"Stop before you hurt yourself," Dad says. "I've already got one injured boy to deal with; I don't need two."

"He's not a boy!" I snap, turning on him. Last night was

too long, and I'm too tired to do anything more than shout. Schuyler's made it to the table and put Rueful in a chair. "I can't believe you let him into our home. *My* home! You know what he did to me—you saw it. He put that junk in my blood; I don't know if I'll ever get it out."

*Negative*, Schuyler says.

"Positive!" I counter, spinning around to answer him to his face.

"Tobin?"

Dad's staring at me with the same blank horror he had on his face the day Mom died.

"What?" I ask.

"Why did you say that?"

"Because *he* keeps saying this isn't their fault, and it's a lie!" I keep trying to lower my voice, but it still gets louder.

*He removed what was his. Yours remains*, Schuyler argues.

"None of them are 'mine!' Humans *don't* come with nanites preinstalled!"

I try the door again; it's still locked.

"He didn't say anything, son. Neither of them did," Dad says.

"He did. I heard him. He said—"

*Negative.*

My hands start shaking, still holding the doorknob.

"Dad?" What's happening to me? I look normal—how can I hear them? "What did you do to me?" I demand of Rueful.

"It wasn't them," Dad says, taking a seat. His shoulders slouch and his head droops. He folds his hands into a fist, with his arms rested on his knees. I'm five years old, and he's about to tell me Mom's dead. "The nanites came from me."

Involuntarily, my attention goes to his silver eyes.

"Good guess, but no." He laughs. The nervous kind, used to buy time and calm down. "Tobin, how old am I?"

"I don't know. I mean, I guess . . ."

I *should* know how old my own father is, but I don't. We celebrate his birthday every year, but only with a single candle on his cake.

"Forty?"

"I was thirty-eight when I got these." He holds up his hands to show me his scars. "Elias was forty-three. Doc was seventy-one. Sykes was two days past nineteen and begged me to burn his neck because he couldn't reach. Honoria was younger than you."

"But Honoria burned herself in the first days, to keep the Fade from . . ."

*We called them Death Trees.* We.

"You were there?"

"He silenced his voice," Schuyler says, bringing me back to the kitchen. Rueful's slouched over the table where I eat my dinner, his head on his arm, breathing heavy and fast.

"You're human," I argue to my dad.

"And it's a constant fight to stay that way. The five of us burned the Fade out at initial contact, and we spent every day since making sure they can't replicate out of control."

"Why are you saying that? *You're human.* Is it them? Are they making you say it?"

"I know it's a shock, and this definitely isn't how I wanted to tell you, but—"

"No. You and Mom were human. You had a human kid."

"Tobin!" Dad grabs my shoulders and shakes me.

I need to hit something, like a wall or a door. Something hard enough to pulverize the Fade in my blood. I want to punch a piece of clanging metal so the sound will vibrate them to nothing. I wish the walking Rorshach would raise his head; I'd be happy to put my fist through that.

"What am I?" I ask.

"Same as you've always been."

"Trey's not."

"That won't happen. You're—"

"Don't lie to me! Am I going to turn?"

"I don't know, Tobin. None of us had kids before you, Annie, and Trey came along. Honoria was the only one who came close, and her nanites rejected the embryo."

"Did Mom know?"

"Everyone does, eventually. Honoria's gone further than any of us, trying to purge the Fade completely from her body, and it shows, but the rest of us don't age, Tobin."

At the moment I want to explode, an intense calm overtakes me, forcing my temper to simmer. I've felt it before, when Schuyler's stepped in to tamp down my anger. I should have known the first time he did that—Fade can't connect to unincluded humans.

"Say something," Dad says.

Instead, I walk past him to the hall. The tunnels are tempting, but I won't run away. I stand in front of the collage of photographs pinned to the wall. They're mostly me, with a few of my parents here and there. A very few are even older.

Dad's followed me. I can feel him behind me.

"You said you were named for your fifth-greats grandfather," I say, staring at the picture of a little boy at the beach, burying someone in the sand.

"I was."

"Is this him?" He never said it was, but I always assumed. The photo was taken before the Fade, so who else could it have been?

"My mom took this," Dad says. He reaches over my shoulder and takes the photo. "The boy's me. Your grandfather's the one under the pile. That's your grandmother's handwriting on the back."

*James making a sand daddy. The Cove '23*

I know the inscription by heart.

"I need to leave," I say.

My father's as old as Honoria—older.

My heart starts to race. Something taps on my head like it's trying to chip through my skull and burrow in. I'm freezing, and then I'm falling toward the floor, no longer able to stand.

"I can't be here."

Shadows appear on the walls, but there's nobody standing in front of them. They move toward the ceiling and grow long toward the door.

"Tobin, calm down." Dad's kneeling beside me.

"Get me out of here, Dad. I need to be somewhere else."

A clanging sound bangs inside the linen closet where something's trying to open the door. Something's in the tunnels, and it wants into my house.

"Tobin . . ."

"I need . . . I need . . . I need."

*My hands.* My hands are bare because the Fade ate my gloves the way they tried to eat Silver. Spiky growths sprout over my fingers and wrists, wrapping tighter and tighter until my hands are bound together. Sludge pours down the walls to soak the floor and furniture. All our photos shrivel up and dissolve.

I lose my mother. Her smiling face crumbles in front of me.

"I can't . . ."

"Tobin!"

Dad's shaking me again, but this isn't like waking from a dream. It feels real.

*Tibby!*

The name works my nerves like it has every time Rueful's used it, and flaring anger burns out everything else. I hear *Tibby* over the rush of waves and the tinkling feet of a billion tiny mechanical bugs. The tide recedes, draining through the corners, and it almost takes me with it. My arms buckle where

I've propped myself up on my hands, and I crash.

"What was that?" Dad asks. He puts a hand to my back, but he doesn't try and lift me up.

"Me, drowning in the Dark," I say, half into the floor. "It used to only happen when I was asleep, but . . ."

"You see the same things Trey did?" He checks my pulse and my forehead.

I nod, pushing myself up, and Dad leads me to the table to sit with Schuyler and Rueful.

"That was a bad one," I say.

*They are all bad ones,* Rueful offers.

"Could you not do the telepathy thing?" I ask.

"We fear the Darkness, too," he says out loud. *They have no voices.*

I glare at him for the silent add-on, but I think it was actually his idea of a joke. He's needling me. The idiot actually smirks before he winces in pain again.

If this ends up making me tolerate him, I'll chew every nanite out of my veins with my teeth.

"We need to talk about this, Son," Dad says. He pulls out the chair across from Schuyler.

"Later?" I say. "I think he needs you more than I do right now."

Rueful's head falls to the table. The crystals that stand in for hair cover most of his face. The hand that's gone white hangs limp past the chair.

"Fine," Dad says. "But I'm not letting this go."

He turns his full attention to the Fade.

"May I see?" he asks.

Rueful shakes with the effort to raise his arm, but it won't bend at the elbow. Schuyler reaches for Rueful's robe and pulls it over his head to show Dad how far the damage has spread. The unlined patch has moved from his hand, up his arm, and across his shoulder.

When we left the Dark, he'd been wearing the same shirt he created for himself the first time I saw the Fade settlement, but whatever took his marks has dissolved the nanites that created his sleeve. His arm's bare; the shirt doesn't reappear until it's nearly halfway across his chest. I can't see his back to know if there's a tree down his spine.

*Negative*, he says.

I must have wondered too loud. I will *never* get used to this.

"Can you change the configuration of your marks?" Dad asks.

"No."

"Can you dissipate the limb? Maybe it would separate the toxin out."

"No."

Rueful tips his good hand toward the table; his fingers turn to grains of black salt in a short heap. He raises his hand, and they sprinkle up into the shape of fingers again. The other hand shakes, but looks otherwise dead.

Dad places two fingers against his wrist.

"There's a pulse, so there's still blood flow. Do you have physical control of the hand at all?"

Rueful concentrates, succeeding only in bending his thumb, but it's more muscle cramp than movement.

"The lack of lines makes me wonder if the blood is filtering red. I wish I could do some actual tests."

No one has to say *negative* to that. Taking Rueful back to the hospital's a bad idea.

"Can we call Doctor Wolff here?" I ask. He treated me on this table when Marina burned the Fade out of me. Surely, he can take blood or tissue samples.

"His risk, his choice," Dad says, nodding to Rueful.

But Rueful doesn't answer right away. He and Schuyler go into that weird Fade-trance where they're talking to each other, but no one else is invited to the conversation. Out of curiosity, I strain to hear either of their voices as they speak, but I can't hear anything except someone knocking on our door.

"Move," Dad says urgently.

Whoever's outside doesn't let themselves in, but that doesn't mean they can't.

"If that's Honoria or Sykes—" I start.

"Get him out of sight," Dad says.

Schuyler and I lift Rueful by the arms and usher him down the hall into my room.

It's a lot brighter than in the main room. The lamp's hardwired to stay on, so I grab yesterday's shirt off a chair, and throw it over the top. Rueful relaxes as we let him down on the bed.

*Thanks,* he says. *Gratitude. Unexpected gratitude.*

"I know the feeling."

The lights in the main apartment brighten, shining under the door so no one will see anything amiss if they come inside. I crack the door just enough to hear what's going on.

"She made me."

*Annie's voice.*

"Hall access is restricted. How'd you make it here without getting stopped?"

*Dad.*

"We have an escort."

*Marina.*

Rueful tries to stand when he hears her, but Schuyler holds him down. He doesn't put up much of a fight.

"You should have stayed at Dominique's," Dad says. I don't know who their escort is, but they're going to be in trouble.

The outer door closes. I slip out of my room, careful of the lights, to find out what they're doing here.

Marina's shaking sheets of paper in her hand.

"You see it, don't you?" Marina asks Dad. "You see the difference?"

"I see something," he says. "Are you sure these are what you think they are?"

"Absolutely, but Honoria won't listen to me. I need your help."

# CHAPTER TWENTY

## MARINA

Rue's in Tobin's room. I can barely see him down the hall through the open door, but he's there and he's alive.

In *Tobin's* room.

It's shocking enough to see him inside the apartment at all, but Tobin actually gave Rue his bed.

"Is he—"

I start for Tobin's door, but the colonel won't let me pass.

"He's fine. He just needs rest."

He needs more than that; he needs the Dark. Cherish sobs in my head at the sight of so much of his skin missing its marks. Rue's taken off his robe, and from what I can tell, he's lost nanites in half his upper body, at least. The lines are lighter on one side of his face, too; his hair's turning white and losing its crystal coating.

Rue struggles to sit up, but he's not strong enough to stay that way.

*Can you hear me?* I ask him.

*Affirmed.*

He stops moving so much.

*Does it hurt?*

*It quiets. Silences.*

Worse than pain, for a Fade.

*I'll get you out of here,* I promise.

When I turn away from the door, Tobin's watching me.

"Thank you," I tell him. "For helping Rue."

"Sure" is all he says, but I can tell there's more he wants to say. The look on his face is muddled, part anger and part fear, mixed with a lot of regret. He's probably wishing he'd shut the door behind him when he came out of his room, then I wouldn't have seen Rue at all.

Anne-Marie's staring over Col. Lutrell's shoulder as he examines the sketches.

"There was nothing like this out there when we went into the Dark," she says. "They were all pasty, doodle people."

I wonder if her mother's sit-and-zip-it trick works for anyone else.

"You were out there for a lot longer than we were," Tobin says. "Did you ever see anything like that creature?"

"No," his father says. "No, I didn't."

"That's because this creature didn't come from the other side of the Grey where the settlement is," I say. "It came from somewhere farther off."

The colonel gathers up the rest of the pages I brought and heads for the door.

"Doc needs to see this," he says. "Marina, you're coming with me."

The hospital's quiet, except for the sound of the machines and Dr. Wolff making notes on Trey's sketches, comparing them to pictures and X-rays. This would not have been my choice for places to wait, but Col. Lutrell insisted. He left Tobin and Anne-Marie at the apartment to babysit Rue and told our hall escort to keep me here until he returned.

Her name's Snott.

Technically, it's S. Nott, according to her name bar, but she refuses to talk to me or tell me what the S stands for, so she stays "Snott" to me.

Tobin would find that funny.

Anne-Marie's mother gives me a stern look for disobeying her order to stay put, but she won't do more than glare.

All that's left to do is watch the clock and hope the colonel can convince Honoria to listen.

I hear them arguing before they reach the door.

"I don't see why you couldn't simply have brought them downstairs, if you want me to take a look. Why come all the way up here?"

"Because Doc's using them, and your office makes Marina nervous."

Honoria's head goes up on my name. She sees me sitting here and starts to leave before she's all the way inside. Her mood hasn't improved since Silver's attack, and the fact that no one has slept yet isn't helping.

"Hear her out," Col. Lutrell says, pulling her inside.

"Fine. Talk."

"It's a different hive," I blurt, but that is *not* what I planned to say. "That's what had Rue and the others on alert—look."

I shake a drawing at her. I didn't plan on doing that, either. I'm blowing this.

Honoria sighs, but she leans closer for a quick skim.

"Pictures of Fade. Like the dozen I've already seen." She reaches back toward the cabinet and picks up a folder filled with more sketches.

"These Fade aren't like the ones who've come into the Grey. Stand Rue next to a human boy, and aside from his marks, you won't be able to tell which one is the Fade. Your brother's even more human-looking than Rue. *I* looked mostly human as a Fade. *These* don't."

I shake the page again.

Trey's sketches are spiked shadows with teeth. They're all running, crouched at odd angles, suggesting their bones are no longer shaped the way they used to be.

I cross the room and yank the curtain away from Dante's bed.

"Look at what they're doing to Dante—don't you see the difference?"

Dante's rigid, despite the drugs keeping him sedated. His skin's being slowly enveloped by a layer of onyx seeping from his pores.

She slides the curtain back into place.

"The Fade who were here earlier have been inside the hive for years; of course they look different from someone being newly overtaken," Honoria says.

"Have you ever seen one Fade attack another?" I ask.

I don't have to pull Silver's curtain open. Dr. Wolff's already done it so he can check her vitals and reload the inhaler canister on her mask. The protrusions have gone, leaving her skin torn and ragged, but she has no markings. The only lines are in her hair, where the nanites have fled the poison.

"Of course not." Honoria isn't scowling at me anymore, but flipping back and forth between the pages, studying them, running her hands over the surface so they come away with pencil smudges. "The hive's a singular organism."

"The nanites on Silver attacked Rue. When we pulled them apart, his hand didn't heal. It turned bone white."

Honoria's face pinches; she looks to Col. Lutrell for confirmation.

"The boy was too weak to stand on his own, and he had his arm cradled to his chest like it was broken. He was in shock."

"They're *not* the same," I say again. "Rue's Fade retain their humanity, in part; whatever's taken Dante and Silver doesn't. They're not healing Dante; they're supplanting him."

These Fade are like the ones from my nightmares; they destroy everything they touch.

"It's a different hive. And now that the lights are down, Rue's Fade aren't the only ones coming in for a closer look."

Honoria and Col. Lutrell gather around Trey's drawings, joined by Dr. Wolff now that he's done with Silver's vitals. One by one, they consider the pages and then Dante. The pages and then Trey. The pages and then me.

"When Rue tried to communicate with the nanites in Silver, they defended their territory. They didn't recognize him as part of their hive. *This* is what Rue and his Fade call Darkness, and it terrifies them."

I slap the drawing in Honoria's hand.

"None of my father's notes mentioned anything like this," she whispers to herself.

"With the time that's passed, and given the independent evolution we've already seen," Dr. Wolff says, "it's conceivable that a new strain may have emerged. Hives in nature are known to split if they become too large for one central unit to control."

"Rue's Fade separated from the main hive to preserve what they could of their hosts. They've tried to put things back the way they were."

"Even if what you say is true," Dr. Wolff says, "how would Trey have seen them? It can't have been physical contact."

"You said the dormant nanites Trey was born with reacted those Bolt used to heal him. Nanites are machines; Trey's got turned on."

"He touched the other hive," Col. Lutrell says.

"And accidentally told them the Arclight still exists."

Honoria's defenses slam back into place so fast and hard,

I can almost hear the whoosh of air as the doors come down inside her.

"All nice in theory, but there's no way to prove it."

"Actually," Dr. Wolff says, "I think there might be."


"You're sure you can tell the difference between the nanites in Dante and what's inside Bolt or Rue?" I ask Dr. Wolff.

"If the variation is wide enough."

We stand beside the panel in the hospital, waiting for Bolt to answer my call. Honoria's promised that if his blood doesn't match the samples taken from Dante and Silver, she'll let him and Rue leave.

*Present*, Bolt says from inside the tunnel entrance.

"He's here," I say.

Honoria releases the lock and backs away, startling at the sight of a sedate Bolt waiting on the other side of the panel.

His marks are gone.

"It's spread?" I ask, panicked.

Cherish screams, calling out for Rue. Bolt was fine when we left him. If he's lost his marks this fast, then what's happened to Rue?

*My voice remains*, Rue says but weakly. Cherish calms to a tremor at the base of my skull.

"This way is easier for my other," Bolt says. "My sister." He pushes his sleeves up to show the concentration of Fade-marks below them. "I appear silent, because it is easier for my sister." He steps out of the tunnel, hands shoved into his pockets.

When Fade move, there's a fluidity to their steps. They're a little too fast and a little too smooth, but this—this is a human teenager. Bolt's copied Tobin's easy slouch perfectly. He walks straight toward Honoria and stops. The last time he did this, she shot him.

"Hello, Honoria," he says, voice heavy with the unfamiliar cadence of the words. "Or is it better to say 'Hey, sis'? I have missed your voice. May we speak?"

Honoria flinches back, wary of the hands she can't see.

"Human speak," he amends.

"Where's the other one?" she asks, eyeing the open panel. "The troublemaker."

"Fatigued," Bolt says. "Help me return him to home."

"We'll see."

"May I see your hand, young man?" Dr. Wolff approaches Bolt with the lancet in hands layered with gloves. He's shaking hard enough to rattle the slides in the box.

"Do you want me to do it?" I ask. It's not like I can re-expose myself.

"I always knew you had a knack for this sort of thing." He passes me the supplies, but he's wasting his breath. I can't stand the idea of spending my life in a hospital.

"We need to see your blood," I tell Bolt. "It doesn't really hurt."

*Affirmative,* Bolt answers. He cuts open his hand with his

own fingernail, giving no indication of pain at all, and holds it over the slide.

Rather than spreading out over the glass, his blood forms a neat black sphere in the center.

"*Very* human," Honoria deadpans.

"Not human, but not dangerous," I counter, handing Dr. Wolff the sample. "You'll see."

"Borrow, not keep," Bolt warns him.

Dr. Wolff dims the lights so we can see the projection on the wall.

I'm surprised. Magnified, and with the lights dimmed, Bolt's blood is human red, filled with tightly packed nanites. The blood cells are arranged in orderly lines, as opposed to the random, bouncing free-for-all of human blood.

"Borrow, not keep," Bolt repeats, holding his hand out, which puzzles Dr. Wolff.

"He wants them back before the lights fry them," I explain.

"Oh . . . right. Of course." Dr. Wolff fumbles with the slide. "My apologies. I wasn't considering the effect of the lamp on the sample."

"Mistakes are acceptable," Bolt says.

With the top plate removed, his blood reforms the sphere it had first been and then flows into his pinkie, leaving behind a red stain.

"Well?" Honoria prompts.

"His sample is in keeping with previous blood tests," Dr.

Wolff says. "And it's not at all similar to what's going on inside our own young people."

"He's been a Fade for decades; they haven't," Honoria says. "Are you sure the difference isn't due to initial infestation?"

"This is an image of the sample I took from Mr. Blaylock earlier." Dr. Wolff focuses another image on the wall. "I think it's clear that the two are unrelated."

The blood cells on the wall are damaged and bent out of shape, ripped open by a more vicious version of the nanites in Bolt's blood. Dante's aren't smooth. They're spiked, plugged in between the red blood cells like gears, forcing them to align as violently as possible.

Honoria eases toward the wall in a daze. Her back turns mottled red where it interrupts the projection. She raises her hand to trace it.

"He was exposed to a throwback singularity among the hive," Dr. Wolff continues. "Or what passed to him is not the same Fade that resides in this young man here."

"It is not us," Bolt says.

"They're trying to reshape him from the inside out," I say. "The others correct damage; they don't cause it."

"This is what we burned out of ourselves?" Col. Lutrell asks, advancing from the cabinets at back of the room to stand beside Honoria, turning red along with her. "It looks like a virus."

"They share physical attributes with the more basic viral agents I've seen." Dr. Wolff's voice gets softer, turning into a string of spoken thoughts. "I'd have to do some checking, but the possibilities . . . If the early samples were exposed by mistake. Perhaps an ill technician or research assistant. It could explain the Fade's change in behavior. If their earliest exposure was to a virus, then they could have taken on viral properties—"

"Absorb and assimilate." Col. Lutrell nods along. "The one who found Dante was a scout looking for any aberration, which is us."

"It came looking for what they saw through Trey," I say. "Rue's people have been trying to guard us, but something slipped through."

*Apologies*, Bolt says. *Remorse.*

"They evaded us," he adds out loud.

"Pull the samples Sykes brought in from Tobin's patrol," Honoria says. "Test them and see if they match. Find out if there's one of these throwbacks loose on our border." Then, with a curious softness that comes near hope as she goes back to Trey's pictures. "Colonel, tell me what you see."

She's never called him that before.

Col. Lutrell picks up the drawing.

"Look at the reflections," she says.

"Reflections?" I move to his shoulder for a look myself.

"My God," he says. "Those are faces. *Human* faces. Their hair. Their eyes."

They're hard to make out due to lack of detail and smudging, but if you hold the paper at arm's length, they get clearer. He's right . . . *people*. Their eyes aren't shining, or even pale. They're dark and wide and terrified, as though death walked in front of them and someone saved the image. Some have long hair, some have short. Some have curls, but not like Blanca's, where the crystals of her hair twist into spirals against her shoulders. There are no crystals here. The hair comes in waves that blow in the wind.

"They're human," I say.

"They're *strangers*." Honoria amends the words to something with more weight.

"There's another enclave?" Dr. Wolff nearly drops his microscope.

"What do you know about this?" Honoria demands of Bolt directly. "Are these accurate? Are there people out there who aren't part of you?"

"Others resist the Darkness," Bolt says.

*Affirmed.*

"You mean they're fighting the Fade?" Col. Lutrell asks. "Er . . . the Wild Fade?"

"Yes."

"If they're holding off active attacks, maybe they can help," I say. "Something's given them an edge if they've survived this long. What if they've found something like what you gave me, something that could save Dante and Silver?"

"I'm surprised you'd suggest such a thing," Honoria says.

"Dante and Silver weren't Fade-children taken from their

families. It's different." I watch the projection dim to nothing when the lamp's turned off. That monstrosity has nothing to do with me or those I came from.

"We may return to home?" Bolt asks his sister. "Promise?"

I know the value of Honoria's promises and how fast they expire, but this time we've got backup.

"By all means, stop breathing my air," she says. Surprisingly, she's not arguing against their release. "You can go at twilight, before the Arc ignites."

"Is it enough?" I ask Bolt.

"It's all you get." Honoria pauses long enough to glance up, then goes right back to shuffling pictures. "There's containment gear in storage. They can use that."

"It's reflective head-to-toe," Col. Lutrell explains. "Completely fireproof, and UV protective. He'll make it home."

Col. Lutrell, I trust.

He leads Bolt back to the wall panel. As Bolt relaxes, the marks return to his face.

"Go back to your friend and wait," Col. Lutrell says, never mentioning his apartment by name.

"We will wait," Bolt says, turning to his sister. "Thank you, Honoria."

She shoos him off with her hand.

"Love you, honeybee."

Her head shoots up as he disappears.

Whatever ghost from their shared past Bolt raises with that

name, it passes quickly. All that matters now is what Trey saw through the eyes of the wild hive.

"It's massive," I tell her. "Our Fade are drops of water in their ocean, but they came in on foot and got here fast, if they're why Dante's been going into the Grey as long as he has. If they're close, then so are the people they know. Maybe Trey could try to link up with them again and find out where they are, or—"

"Not necessary," Honoria says. She straightens the stack of drawings, preparing to take them with her.

"But—" The look on her face stops me cold. "You know where they are, don't you?"

# CHAPTER TWENTY-ONE

## TOBIN

Dad radioed around noon. "I'm on my way home. We're having company, so clean up your room."

Basic translation: I'm not free to talk. Move the Fade.

Annie and I wrangled Rueful into the tunnels. Technically, she wrangled him down the hall and refused to go past the door of the closet, but we got there as Schuyler returned.

"He can stretch out in the junction," I said. Schuyler nodded

I grabbed a pillow and blanket from the linen closet and threw them in after, just in case Fade use them. The panel slid shut, and by the time Dad got home, we were Fade free . . . unless the nanites in his eyes count. Or the ones I was apparently born with.

Now it's hours later, according my wristband, and for some reason, I've woken up on the floor of my room. I don't remember falling out of bed.

I reach up to poke around. Someone grumbles; a hand falls over the side and slaps me in the face. Oh yeah—Annie claimed the bed. Just my luck. I get a girl to stay over in my room, and it's not Marina.

Dad should have brought her home with him, not let her be sent off alone where there's no emergency tunnel access for help or escape. I need to see if she's okay.

I crawl away, not standing until I'm closer to the door.

"Dad?" I call in the hall. I thought he might be sleeping, but the commotion from the living room says he's still got company.

Sykes is with him, Mr. Pace, and Honoria, sorting boxes of paper on the center table.

"Here's another one," Sykes says. "Different angle."

Honoria takes a page from him and scans it.

"Definitely the same building," she says. "This statue sits out front. See the broken tusk? I helped break it."

She flips the page around. It's the picture Trey was working on during Annie's birthday dinner, the one with the pig.

"I never took you for a vandal," Mr. Pace says. "I don't know if I should be impressed or horrified."

"It was their own fault—they cheated us out of the title that year," she says with a smile that makes her look almost like a teenager. "This is Ridgeline South, complete with survivors. I'd bet my life on it."

"You are," Sykes says sourly.

"What's Ridgeline South?" I ask.

They all freeze, like a bunch of lower years caught misbehaving. Sykes tosses the nearest pages into an open box.

"I was there when they found Trey," I say. "His pictures aren't a secret."

Sykes puts the lid on, anyway.

"I thought you were asleep," Dad says.

"I was, but it's after six." They all check their wristbands. "What's Ridgeline South?"

"It used to be a school."

"And there are people—human people—in it?"

"Not likely," Sykes scoffs. "There can't be survivors within a hundred miles of here and us not know it."

"You never saw the place," Honoria says. "It's a geometric nightmare made of steel and glass. Everyone called it the Ice Cube."

Honoria taps the picture she held up. What I mistook for slashes of pencil meant to fill the background aren't random. They form a grid of windows and doors that reflect dozens of blurred faces. The pig's broken tusk juts into the image at the bottom corner.

Mr. Pace nods his head. "No grass, no trees, nothing to interest nanites. Just a massive block of ugly surrounded by a cement parking lot and outbuildings for a half-mile square. It could be defensible."

"If anyone's still there," Honoria says. "They're close enough that we have a shot at making contact."

"For real?" The words stick in my throat.

I don't even care that they're ignoring me. Our world just got bigger. All those pictures in my mother's books, and the cities in her snow globes, aren't fairy tales anymore. If this school exists, then why can't they? Someone could have saved them, too. They might lead to another point, and another, and another.

We're not alone.

"Close enough in which direction?" Sykes asks. "I don't know any that wouldn't mean a run through the Dark."

"James keeps telling us his friends in the woods mean no harm. This is their chance to prove it."

"We'll need transport," Dad says. "Can the equipment take that kind of a trip?"

"We've got no better time to find out," Honoria says.

"You *really* think this is worth trying for, Jeannie?" Sykes leans in closer to Honoria, his voice harsh, turning the conversation into a personal argument between the two of them.

"If not this, then what?" she asks.

"Can you take another disappointment?"

"No, but I can definitely handle a success."

"Then I guess I'd better go check the oil." He stands to leave, slamming boxes into a stack to carry out. She takes the rest. Dad motions me toward the door; I run to hold it open for them.

"Our goal is two days," she says, before leaving. "James, I believe you have some stowaways to escort off the grounds. See if you can't make them amenable to a path through their territory while you're at it."

Slamming the door behind them is a complete accident for the most part. That's my favorite thing about a swinging door. Sliding panels just click.

"He used to be such a good kid," Dad grumbles. He and Mr. Pace pick up the plates and glasses from off the table to take them to the kitchen.

"All I did was slam a door."

"Not you—Sykes. He had a very promising start to his career, then—"

"Then you had to burn him?" I ask.

"Yeah."

"You told him." Mr. Pace stumbles with the glass in his hand.

"No choice. He's seeing things, too," Dad says.

I wish he wouldn't say it like that. Sounds like I'm crazy.

"Due to contact, or are they all hitting some natural threshold?" Mr. Pace throws a long look down the hall, toward my room.

"If Annie's having nightmares, she doesn't show it," I tell him. "I think she's okay."

Besides, if it's based on age . . . She's two months older than me.

I start rinsing off dishes, mainly so I don't have to look at either of them.

"I don't know where to start with Trey," Mr. Pace says. "How do I tell my own son I did this to him?"

"Try not doing it while a pair of Fade are sitting in your kitchen. Definite improvement over Dad's method," I say.

Dad throws a dish towel at my head.

"You tell him the same way you do anyone else," he tells Mr. Pace.

"Do people freak out when they find out the truth?" I've known Dad forever, but there are still times that the change in his eyes makes him seem like a stranger. I've wanted to rip my own skin off to see what's below it since I saw my blood projected on that wall.

Great. That image will probably find a way to work itself into my nightmares now.

"There've been some hard years," he says. "A few of the early fights were so big, they nearly destroyed the whole place. There were more like us right after the takeover, but when the others realized . . ." He trails off.

"It got bad?"

"It became a witch hunt," Mr. Pace says. "Most of us didn't survive."

"But you heal so fast—"

"Witch hunts end in fire, Tobin; so did this."

It's impossible, but the knife-shaped scar on my back burns. I roll my shoulder and can smell the charred skin. I see the flames that destroyed our old carpet, and I imagine it all spreading.

Is that what Dante and Silver have to look forward to if Dr. Wolff can't fix them? Once people figure out what's happened, will they go after Trey because his eyes are blue now? Or will they turn on Marina again?

I have to get out of here.

# CHAPTER TWENTY-TWO

## MARINA

*Open the door. Open the door. Open the door.*

"Shut up!" I scream at Cherish's voice. She didn't respond when I only said it in my head. Saying it out loud doesn't do any better.

After Honoria kicked me out of the conversation and the hospital, I was dumped back into my room and told to wait. I burned a few hours sleeping, but now I'm awake, and my door won't open, and now I know why Anne-Marie goes berserk in tight spaces. Cherish is doing the same thing, and I'm coming out of my skin.

*Open the door. Open the door. Open the door.*

"It's a security measure," I've tried to explain. "We aren't prisoners."

*Open the door.*

I stood in the corner where Blanca's bush lives and breathed in the smell. Surely, our sister would—

*Open the door.*

I took her to Rue's picture and imagined the sound of the bird as it flies.

"Try thinking about—"

*Open the door.*

I picked up Tobin's snow globe from the table and shook it hard to scatter my frustrations with the stars inside.

*Open the door.*

Cherish hasn't deviated from that single thought in twenty minutes, other than adding the sound of a rattling door to the mix. We're still stuck.

"Stop it!" I command. "Driving me insane won't get us out of here. No one's allowed out. The doors are all—"

*Click.*

The doors *were* all locked, but mine's opening, and the person outside it is not a welcome sight. Honoria's never been to my room before.

"Who were you talking to?" she asks.

"Myself. The door was locked. I couldn't get out."

"Oh." Her face falls. "Claustrophobia's usually only a concern with Annie. I didn't think."

Was that an apology?

*Run. Hide. Conceal. Flee.*

Cherish's chant changes.

I seriously wish I could slap her.

"Is the lockdown over?" I ask, peeking into the hall, but it's empty.

"No. Come with me." It's not a request.

We start to leave, but I dash back into my room and grab

Honoria's book from under my pillow. She doesn't take it when I hold it out; she doesn't even acknowledge it, so I tuck it back into my waistband and follow her into the hall so that my hands are free.

"Your Fade got out, in case you were wondering," Honoria says.

*If you hadn't been so loud, we would have known that*, I tell Cherish.

I'd hoped to get the chance to see them off.

"According to James, they were well into the Grey before the lights came up."

That's an uncharacteristically kind detail to add. *What's happened to her since last night?*

The guidelines on the floor transition from the green that marks my home hall, past the main areas, where several other colors branch off to other sections. We're into red and gold, the colors used for high security areas.

"Are we going downstairs?" I ask, slowing my pace so a gap forms between us. If she thinks I'm walking blind into the section where the White Room is, she's crazy.

*Run*, Cherish says. *Flee.*

"We're going to the motor pool," she says.

The words mean nothing to me. Machines can have motors, but pools usually involve water. The two don't mix well unless it's a boat, and I don't think we have any boats here.

"Keep up." We pass the secure entrance to the Arclight-below;

she opens a different door, instead. I've never been this deep into the aboveground security sector.

"My legs are shorter than yours. If you want me to keep up, then slow down," I say. "And give me some details while you're at it."

"You wanted to know what I saw in that picture."

"And that's in a motor pool?"

"No, but the way to get to it is. We're preparing to leave."

"As in, into the Dark?" I ask. A human can't outrun a single Fade in open territory, much less a group of them on the hunt. "How are you going to outrun the Fade for miles?"

"We won't be running on foot."

Honoria opens the last door on the hall, revealing a room five times the size of the Common Hall.

*Dead*, says Cherish of the air. *Stale.*

It's dusty and full of old boxes. Tarps cover piles of things with no discernible shape. Scattered throughout are vehicles similar to those abandoned along the ruined roads of the Dark, only these aren't rusty. Someone's kept them clean. People in security uniforms mill about, uncovering equipment and moving it away from the wall.

I touch the vehicle Honoria stops at, running my hands over the smooth metal sides. It isn't warm, like I expect. I press a button, and a door swings open with a high-pitched creak that makes Cherish yelp.

"It's a truck," Honoria says.

Cherish supplies impressions, drawn from various Fade who remember their human lives: Trucks are smelly and loud, with the rumble of a storm.

"Can this really outrun a Fade?" I ask.

"This old girl got me here. She won't let us down."

"Us?"

"However you get your information, you're the closest thing to an asset we have. Once this vehicle is road ready, we'll need all the assets we can carry."

Something pops at the front of the truck where Col. Lutrell's propped a metal panel up on a long pole, exposing the parts inside. He pulls out different metal wicks, testing the levels of fluid on them, while Mr. Pace checks the tension on belts and wires. I hope they know what they're doing.

"How long?" Honoria calls up front.

"Considering the closest thing you've got to a mechanic is a high school teacher and a guy whose wife was the technologically inclined one?" Mr. Pace asks.

"Stow it," Col. Lutrell says. "We've got the battery charged, but she hasn't made a distance run in a long time. Three of these hoses need to go, and I'd feel a lot better if we replaced the fan belt. Coolant's going to be an issue, not to mention cold starting the engine. It could—"

"Get it done," she snaps back.

"Don't vehicles need some kind of fuel?" I ask.

"We've protected a small amount for our generators, so we

can keep the emergency lights burning and to use for fire fuel if we need a blaze quickly. Most of our salvage has evaporated over the years, but we've got enough to keep a truck going a few miles and back."

I hoist myself into the seat. The smell's unfamiliar, and it crinkles under my weight. The whole thing seems sort of boxy rather than maneuverable.

"Someone will take you to get your gear soon," she says. "Stay here. I want you in sight until we leave."

All my attempts to reach Rue fail, but I keep trying. Bolt doesn't answer, either. I get desperate enough to try for my sister and mother, but there's not so much as a whiff of flowers or pine. Just air that's thick with the smell of rubber and engine fluids.

I'm left to wander the room, peeking into boxes that have been sealed for years while the team trying to move them give me nasty looks. I wish I knew what this stuff was, but I've never even seen most of it in pictures.

I try sleeping in the truck's backseat, but there's too much noise, so I turn to the only thing I have left. I haven't looked at Honoria's book since my nightmare. Was that really only a day ago?

I open the cover and flip through to the end, skimming lines here and there.

K. Sykes is, indeed, "Kevin." He's also the officer Honoria found cute. There are several entries about him, all addressed to the Trinity from the book but not Rashid; they're too embarrassing to share with a guy. I'm not sure I'll ever be able to look Sykes in the eye again.

Honoria describes so much loss the first few years, I'm surprised anyone survived. And then behind the last page, folded up tight, I find one, final letter.

Dear Rashid and Trinity,
    You're dead.
    Not news to you, but it was a shock to me. Even if you survived the Fade, time's caught up with you. I guess that means you won't come looking for your book. You'll never know how sorry that makes me.
    Your friend,
    Honoria Jean Whit
PS Rest in peace, for those of us who can't.

The page is warped in spots. *Tears.*

She mourned them. They were more than a couple she never met. They were her imaginary friends after she lost the real ones.

Maybe she was mourning herself.

I put away the book, pull my jacket over my head, and cry myself to sleep.

Eventually, I'm woken up and dragged to a storage area. The clothes here are similar to our daily uniforms, but rather than the tiered monochrome of yearly designation, or the khaki Mr. Pace and the adults favor, they're shades of gray camouflage, but it's nowhere near as effective as the Fade's.

"I don't know how much good they'll do, but hopefully they're an advantage," Mr. Pace tells me as he hands me a folded stack.

The jacket's too bulky and the pants are too long. I can actually fit Honoria's book in a deep pocket. They're obviously not meant for a teenage girl, but I do my best to resize them with tucking and belts, and I finish just in time to see Trey ushered in by Lt. Sykes and Dr. Wolff.

Seeing his eyes the same color as mine against his dark skin is strange. They're so small a thing, but the change is huge.

"What are you doing here?" I ask.

"I hoped you knew the answer to that one," Trey says. "Doctor Wolff released me. I thought I was going home, but they brought me here. No one would say why in front of Mom."

"We're going outside."

"They're putting us out?"

"I will never let that happen—to either of you." We turn as Mr. Pace joins us, holding another stack of clothes out to Trey. "Didn't they tell you anything?"

"Sykes said something about my drawings, but I don't remember most of them."

Did they even bother to tell him his eyes are blue? If not, he's got another shock coming.

"Marina, can you find your way back?" Mr. Pace asks me. "Trey and I need to talk."

No, I don't know my way back to the motor pool, but I tell him the exact opposite and hope I stumble through the right doors.

Cherish chooses to be helpful. She doesn't know the twists and turns the way Rue does, and she can't draw me a map, but between us, it only takes me twice as long to get back to the motor pool as it did to reach the storage center from it.

I walk straight into an argument between Col. Lutrell and Tobin.

When did he get here?

"You're not going," Col. Lutrell says. "End of discussion."

"But, Dad—"

"Forget it. Absolutely not."

"But Marina—"

"Is possibly immune—you're not. And if Trey's anything to go by, you may be more susceptible than most. We're not giving them another contact point—especially my son."

Tobin stiffens, steeling himself for a fight, but his father knows him.

"Let it go, Tobin. I make a lot of allowances for a lot of things, but not this. I cannot make the choice between my son and what's best for everyone else. If you stay here I can do my job and not be a bigger failure as a father than I already am."

"You're not—"

They look my way, so I pretend I'm stuffing more of this awful uniform into my belt rather than eavesdropping. But staring at the pattern on my clothes makes me imagine Fade-lines and protrusions on my skin—a final warning from Cherish to scare me off going, I think. I shake my head, and the image is gone.

"Tell her good-bye, son," Col. Lutrell tells Tobin.

If there was a little more time, we could slip off to the Well, but as it is, Tobin and I take refuge in a tarp-covered truck that's missing its wheels. His father leaves us alone with our illusion of privacy.

"Whose jacket is that?" Tobin asks, helping me straighten it. The shoulders still droop where they're too broad.

"I don't know, but I think you could fit in here with me." I flap my arms to show off how ridiculously long the sleeves are.

"Careful. I might try."

"I'm not sorry your dad said no, Tobin."

Quite the opposite. I wish I had my father here to tell me this was too dangerous and that he'll handle things for me, but mine's in the Dark protecting his Fade-daughter. Tobin doesn't know how lucky he is.

He catches my eye for second, gets an idea that I practically see flash there, and looks away, suddenly interested in a shallow tray of junk attached to the console in front of us.

"Hold this." He picks up a paper clip, then fishes a rubber band out of the mess.

"What are you doing, trying to tie us together?"

"I'm being useful."

He ties the band to the paper clip and slips it over my wrist, sliding the clip through the jacket's buttonhole. The rubber band shrinks down, holding the cuff snug to my wrist.

"Now they won't drag," he says, grinning.

"Thanks, but I still agree with your dad."

The grin's gone. He changes the subject, snapping the back of his hand with a rubber band as he talks.

"It's getting tense up top. No one knows what's happened to Dante and Silver, but they know it's bad enough to close the hospital. Half of them think you and Trey are dead. Annie's a wreck; Doctor Wolff had to sedate her when she found out Trey was leaving."

"Your dad says Doctor Wolff's staying here."

"So's Sykes," Tobin says. "Just in case someone else . . . you know."

"How's Silver?"

I don't want to ask about Dante. I can't handle bad news right now.

"Puking her guts out. She keeps sweating out into the sheets, and every time she does, they branch black and have to be burned. They shaved her hair off to get the ones hiding there."

"Maybe one of Rue's people could try again now that there are fewer in her system."

"I don't really want to think about him right now."

He takes both of my hands so we're turned completely toward each other; leans his forehead against mine, so he's all I can see, and I'm the same for him.

"It's been weird since"—he rolls his shoulder—"but I didn't know how weird until your boyfriend took back his nanites. And then I had to help hide him, and—"

"Why do you do that?" I ask, dropping his hands.

"What?"

"Make digs at me, use Rue for a weapon. You do it every time you're upset, like it's my fault I was born a Fade or my fault I was with him before I even knew you." There's a panel of knobs and buttons in front of us. I twirl them to have something to do with my hands besides hold his. "Rue belonged to Cherish; I chose you. Actually, I chose *me* and got you in the bargain. Stop making me wonder if I made a mistake."

*Rue chose you,* Cherish says. *He waits for you to choose me.*

"I'm sorry. I just hate this. I know he's out there, and we both know he's going to be with you the whole way."

"He won't—"

"Don't tell me he won't." Tobin fixes the paper clip where it's come loose from the buttonhole. "If he's anything short of dead, he's not letting you cross the Dark without him, and I'm glad. I know how hard he'll fight for you, but I should be there if—"

"So what if Rue's out there? I *want* you here, so you'll be here when I get back."

I kiss him, quick, before I can change my mind or he can pull away. This time, there's no awkward moment; the wall created by Rue's interference is gone. But Tobin's still downcast.

"I usually get more than a frown for one of those," I say.

"Sorry, but I can't shake the feeling it's a kiss good-bye."

"I said I'm coming back. Mopey Tobin is making me want to smack him, and I'd rather not leave here angry with you."

"If it'll make you stay, I'll make you mad," he says. The offer's genuine.

"Tobin . . ."

"He thought you were coming back, too, okay?"

He spins the knob nearest his hand until it won't turn anymore, then makes it go the other way.

"Nanobot *never* stopped believing he'd find you. He did everything he could to bring you home, and you never made it. Things happen, Marina. You changed. I don't want you to change again."

A shrill whistle calls our attention, and I poke my head out of the truck. Mr. Pace and Col. Lutrell are loading large canisters into the vehicle we're supposed to take into the Dark.

"Let's move," Honoria calls, sweeping her hand toward it. Trey climbs inside, so terrified that he's stopped blinking.

This is it.

"Make them give you a second warning," he says. "It's not like they'll leave without you."

"Honoria already hates me."

"Then blame me."

"I can't stay, but I maybe I can give you something else to think about." I reach for the book in my pocket and hold it out. It's too bulky to carry, anyway. "Read this. It might give you the answers your dad won't. By the time you're done, we could be back." I kiss him again—on the cheek this time. It's not as disappointing when a kiss on the cheek is nothing special.

I lay the book on the truck's seat, before letting myself out of our bubble and back into reality. The cement floor's nowhere near as cold as I feel on the inside, and the sound of boots against it isn't nearly as hollow.

"Marina, wait!" Tobin calls after me, running to close the few feet I've put between us. He's pulling something over his head that I can't see until he slips it over mine. "Now you have to come home so you can give them back."

"Your mom's dog tags?"

He matches the kiss I gave him and stands there as I walk away.

*I'm coming back*, I tell myself.

There's an odd kind of relief when Cherish echoes with: *Yes, we are.*

"Let's go!" Honoria shouts, climbing into the back of the truck behind Mr. Pace.

I open the door on the other side, behind Col. Lutrell, and pull myself up onto the seat next to Trey.

"Hang on, kids," Mr. Pace says. "This could get rough."

The wall we're facing splits open. Col. Lutrell turns a small metal key, and the truck becomes nothing but vibration and sound before we lurch forward with a rumble.

# CHAPTER TWENTY-THREE

I refuse to believe people traveled like this in the time before the Fade. Normal trucks could not have been this loud or this full of fumes, and they couldn't have run with the people inside bump, bump, bumping along so violently that I have to hold my lunch in my stomach while holding the rest of my body in my seat.

The way Trey keeps swallowing and digging his fingers deeper into the back of the front seat tells me I'm not alone in my discomfort. He shifts, gripping the edge of our shared bench seat and leaning back on the headrest, eyes closed, like he's in pain.

Honoria's oblivious, swaying along with every bounce and rumble while hanging on to a ceiling-mounted handle above the door.

We run over something large enough to tilt the truck up on one side, and the momentum throws me to the floor, half leaning on Trey.

"Sorry," I mumble.

"If we'd gone up another inch, I'd have been down there with you," he whispers as I retake my seat. "At least we didn't go the other way."

He twitches his head toward Honoria to say he'd rather not have her land in his lap.

Trey's as easy to talk to as Anne-Marie. He's calmer, and he doesn't speak nearly as fast as his sister, but they have the same presence, and they sound strangely alike.

"I hate trucks," I say when we hit another bump that bounces me high enough to hit my head on the ceiling.

"Agreed."

There's no handle over the window on my side, only a space where one broke off a long time ago. I find a cold, metal buckle set into the cushions, but the button on it doesn't seem to do anything. I was hoping it would get longer so I could tie myself in.

"That's the release for the belt buckle." Honoria's watching me again. This time she's amused. "It won't work without the other piece, but you don't want to use it."

I completely disagree and start digging for the rest.

"If we have to bail out of here, you don't want to be tied down."

I find the strap but have to admit she's right. I don't want anything slowing me down if we have to run. I make do with hanging on to the pieces to stabilize myself.

"Is that the lake?" Trey asks, kind enough not to call it the marina. He rises up in his seat for a better view. "Annie never said it looked so depressing."

"That's where we started the fire that burned the Grey," Honoria says, unprompted. She angles toward the window, fingers against the glass. "When we got here, someone had broken the boats."

Her voice turns distant, and somehow heavier.

"As the sun sank, people started crying, screaming out because we didn't know how far we had left to go. Without light, we were as good as dead."

I bet she's never shared this with the mid-year classes. It's in her book, though, told in five pages of detail, back and front.

"There were these iridescent patches of oil and gasoline dancing across the water. I thought they were beautiful, but no one else noticed. They were all looking behind us at everything we'd lost."

She blinks up, toward the ceiling, wiping her face with her gloved hand.

"One of the soldiers called for a flare. It caught the fuel trail and spread so far, I couldn't see the end of it. People cheered, but that was the moment I knew the rules had changed too much. This was a world where water burned."

How long has she rehearsed that story, wanting to tell it? The words are too perfect to be new.

The marina passes out of sight behind us, and I watch it go. That water changed Honoria's life as a teenager; it did it again when Col. Lutrell and the others pulled me from it and brought me to the Arclight. The night she went out looking for her brother, she only went this far, according to her book. We're officially beyond the boundaries she's set for herself.

The view outside my window's a blur of gray monotony, broken only by stripped trees at uneven intervals. It transitions into the line of demarcation between the human world and that of the Fade.

"Is that it?" Trey asks, leaning forward again.

It's the sort of thing a person asks even though they know the answer. The unbroken shadow and gloom growing ahead of us can only be one thing. Col. Lutrell's already slowed down in the marshes that have developed where the marina's shallows touch the earth.

*Stop,* Rue intones as we near the edge of the Dark, and Cherish thrills at the sound of his voice.

*He's here,* she cheers. *He's not silent. I hear his voice!*

*So do I,* I answer back. Her enthusiasm's infectious.

I send him the impression of a wave, which he returns. I can't stop the smile appearing on my face.

*Tell them to cease the machine,* Rue says.

"Stop," I call out. "Stop the truck!"

We skid to a halt, tossing dirt up with the wheels. Everyone looks at me expectantly.

"What's wrong?" Col. Lutrell asks.

None of them truly expects things to go right.

Ahead, pale bodies shimmer into view, standing shoulder-to-shoulder in a mimic of the Arclight's boundary. Rue's in the middle, directly in front of us.

"James—" Mr. Pace says, tapping Col. Lutrell on the arm, but the colonel already sees them.

"They're everywhere," Trey says, sinking back in his seat.

"They were waiting for us," Mr. Pace charges. "They've blocked us in,"

"Drive through them," Honoria says.

"Rue says we need to stop." And since he knows this terrain better than any of us, listening to him is probably a good idea. "He wouldn't hold us back for no reason."

"I never said he had no reason."

There's no reaching Honoria once she's set her mind to something, so I don't bother. I open my door, grateful she warned me about making a quick and unrestrained exit. If she wants to go so badly, they can drive over me, too.

"Marina!"

Trey makes a grab for my arm, but it's either for show or Dr. Wolff's long-term sedatives aren't completely out of his system yet. I drop to the ground.

The other doors slam behind me, followed by boots running to catch up.

*Faster,* Cherish urges. *Go faster. We are faster.*

I choose to believe that the burst of speed pushing me toward the Dark is real. This is like the sudden healing of my hand, a latent Fade-trait I've somehow maintained, like my eyesight and hearing, to use when I really need it.

Rue breaks the line to meet me, scowling at Honoria and the others, now right behind me.

"You're okay," I say.

The marks are still paler across his palm, and nearly absent at his fingers, but they're there. He's no longer shaking.

Cherish begs me to allow her touch him, or him us. Why not? What could a hug hurt?

"I was so worried about you," I tell him.

*Home heals*, he says. *Home is safer.*

Then out loud: "You should not venture into Darkness unaccompanied."

"Running off seems to be a recurring issue," Honoria says.

She reaches out to drag me back, but Rue's recovered more than his marks. He moves faster than I can track, switching our positions so that I'm nearest the Dark and he's nearest Honoria. She curls her fingers into a fist before they can brush his skin, dropping her hand back to her side.

"Get back in the truck," she orders me. "And you," she snarls at Rue. "Get those things out of our way."

"You do not hear, and your voice is silenced," Rue says. "I will go with, not away from."

"You want to come with us?" I ask.

"Truck's full," Honoria says.

"They know the terrain, and they know the opposition. How is this a bad thing?" Mr. Pace asks.

"You want us to approach potential *human* allies in hostile territory, dragging a line of Fade behind us, and you don't see how that could backfire?"

"I go with mine. *They* go with mine. The others remain."

Four Fade, including Dog, separate themselves from the group. But where's Bolt? He's not here. Neither is my family.

"We are assets, not burdens. I go with mine or you go nowhere."

The perimeter of bodies seals itself into a solid barrier. I can still pick out individual faces, but in the gaps between each one, the Dark knits tighter. Even the trees cling to one another to bar our passage.

The Dark surrounds us; we're inside their cage.

"There's no going around," Col. Lutrell says.

"He can see and hear things we can't. Things *I* can't," I tell her. "Give him a chance."

Honoria locks her jaw, making her face more severe. She's not in control out here.

"Truck's full," she repeats, trying to salvage her pride. "If you come, you walk. Keeping up is your problem."

"I require a moment," Rue says.

"You get one minute."

There's no such thing as a battle too small to fight. Honoria gives Rue her back and returns to the truck. It's a show of will for someone who has never trusted the Fade enough to make herself vulnerable to them.

Rue approaches the wall of the Dark, disappearing inside. Whisper and Dog, who stand on either side of his entry point, kneel down and surrender their marks to the whole as the rest of the Fade take on that unnatural stillness. They stay that way until we're all back in the truck.

"What are they doing?" Trey asks.

Honoria's watching them, too, but with less interest than suspicion.

"Communicating," I say. "Probably telling the others we're here. They won't like the truck."

There are pools of nanites within the Dark, for whom the sound of a spoken voice is too much to bear. They don't bother with bodies or maintaining the illusion of human life. They spend their time enjoying the quiet so long as they can ensure the Dark stays in order. The truck's engine, and the vibrations it causes, would throw them into a frenzy.

"Forty seconds," Honoria says, checking the alarm on her wrist.

"You really think they want to help us?" Trey asks.

"I *know* they do."

Our Fade blame themselves for the end of the human world; they aren't looking for ways to betray what's left of it.

"Looks like the conversation's over," Mr. Pace says.

Something's happening at the door to the Dark. Dog and Whisper stand, their marks back where they belong.

*Go now,* Rue's voice drifts in.

"You can start the engine," I say.

The veil of black crumbles, a waterfall of jet sand, sifting into nothing. What's left behind is brown and green. Tree trunks and leaves that have been encased in nanites for years stand bare to the light of our lamps.

"They've cleared the road," Col. Lutrell says. He shifts gears, bringing the engine's idle hum back to a roar, and we're off, spearing through the open space that used to be the Dark.

# CHAPTER TWENTY-FOUR

## MARINA

"Marina?" Trey asks. "Am I hallucinating or is he actually *walking*?"

"I'm trying not to think about it," I say, like it's not a shock to see Rue keeping a steady pace beside my door. I wouldn't exactly call it walking, though. He looks like he's sliding along the nanite trails on the ground.

Dog's doing the same on the other side. I assume the other three are behind us, though the truck's now traveling much faster than it had when we were crossing the Grey.

"This is unreal," Trey says.

"Unfortunately not." Honoria doesn't find the situation as fascinating as I do.

Obsidian walls reach above our head on either side, where the Fade have pulled themselves safely away from the truck's lights, but the walls aren't static. Lines flow from top to bottom in their unending cycle to ensure that none stay in the light long enough to be damaged. Others are chaotic, spreading out to fill any gaps they encounter, so the whole thing writhes and pulses like a beating heart. Some of the Fade stand on our side of the barrier, watching us pass, but my parents aren't among them.

I close my eyes, straining for the familiar markers that represent my mother and sister, but all I get is the image of a rock in water.

*Home*, Cherish says wistfully. It tugs, along with the desire to reach out for the voices I know are waiting just behind the nanite veil. The veil's so close in places, I could open a window and skim it with my fingers. But if I do, the Dark might hang on and never let me go. Or worse, I think, I might grab the first hand that reaches for me and hold on tight, just to hear my sister laugh again.

I want that connection, but it terrifies me. I don't want to end up Cherish's prisoner in this body. They'll all speak to *her* and listen to *her* and maybe even love *her*, but I'll be lost and alone.

Cherish claims that things aren't complicated in the Dark, but she's wrong. Nothing's simple here, at all.

"Is this the right way?" Honoria says.

"Like they pulled the route straight off a map."

They did, just not one made of paper. They've used their bank of common knowledge, re-creating the route from those who traveled this road in the days before. Those bright yellow lines I'd glimpsed beneath the constant roll of Fade are clean now. They mark our path, stretching out for miles.

"We'll be there in a matter of hours," the colonel says.

"That long?"

"I don't want to push the engine until I have to."

Behind us, the corridor collapses, falling in on itself and making retreat impossible. Honoria stays rigid in her seat, eyes fixed on the back of Mr. Pace's head, refusing to watch the Dark pass by.

The road's smoother now that we're past the ragged bumps in the Grey. There are no gashes in this stretch, like elsewhere in the Dark. Without the jars and jolts, and the sound of air against the sides, and wheels against the road become hypnotic. Trey's head drops to his chest with the crash that comes after an adrenaline rush. Everything falls into a rhythm I can't help but set my breathing to. More than once I feel myself nodding off.

Sleep comes as bursts of light and dark. I blink awake, then drift again. There are violent collisions of fire, and sparks where the flares touch the shadows. I stand in the midst of it all, on a line between creation and devastation, sure that I'll be seen if I move.

A million fingers pull and pinch, testing my endurance, but I persevere. The lights fall back until all I can see is a darkness so deep, it makes me wonder if I've gone blind. The darkness rises up, drawing together into the monstrous form of a great beast whose skin is nothing but agitated grains of black.

The beast growls, but I stand still.

It roars, nearly blasting me off my feet with the force, but I don't fall. The hands and fingers that prodded me before, now keep me upright, pushing against my back so I can't sag.

The beast rears up, towering tall on its hind legs before

slamming down as a wave. I hold my breath as I reach out for something to hang on to beneath the deluge, and I'm surprised to feel another hand in mine. It's bone white, with wisps of smoke churning under the skin, and as my eyes travel up its arm to its face, I realize I'm staring at myself.

*Cherish.*

The dark water begins to spin, whirling with a maelstrom's fury until I'm certain we'll be washed away, but Cherish is beside me. Hand in hand, together we do not drown.

The storm ceases and the dark mass shrinks, condensing to no taller than me or myself. It grows arms and legs and forms a face, with a mouth and eyes that stare, but it's not human. Its hair is spikes, like the ones that grew from Silver's skin; more erupt from its hands and feet.

"Who are you?" I ask

"What do you want?" adds Cherish; the first time I've heard her speak out loud.

The creature steps forward, extending a clawed hand. I look to Cherish, but her face is Fade-blank, and with her outside my head, I can't hear her speak to me. The creature takes my hand.

My fingers freeze inside its claw, a sensation that travels up my arm and across my shoulder. My spine's speared by an icicle. The cold branches out along my nerves; once I'm frozen through and through, it turns to pain. Blinding and so cold, it burns.

Beside me, Cherish freezes, too. Frost grows on our hands where they're joined, and she screams, but there's no sound. The cold rips her marks from her, one microscopic cell at a time.

Our feet are stuck fast, tied to the earth. They become chains, so heavy I can't move, and when I open my own mouth to call for help, a flood of black sand washes down my throat.

I stare into the creature's eyes. Deep within the recess there's movement. A face begins to form there, morphing through features: Dante and Silver, then Tobin and Anne-Marie. Rue. My mother. Blanca. Every face is placidly blank.

But in their eyes there are screams.

I'm being pulled apart, drawn into the creature to be absorbed as the wild-Fade have taken so many others.

I scream once more, and then I'm gone.

I jerk awake, throat shredded from echoing Cherish's shriek. Trey's making the same sound, in nearly the same pitch, right beside me. The sensation of breaking apart and being devoured stops.

We're still in the truck's backseat, only now we're standing still. Honoria's shaking Trey so hard that I can feel it. My left hand's got a white-knuckled grip on the door handle, prepared to bail out and run, while my right's clenched inside Trey's, lying on the seat between us. My glove's come untucked from my jacket sleeve, leaving a gap where I can see my skin. For a moment I think I see lines swirl on my wrist, but it's only in my head. I snap myself with Tobin's rubber band to make sure I'm awake.

Trey looks blank. Eyes wide and unfocused, so the icy color is even starker. His chest heaves, like he has to remind himself to breathe in after each exhale. My breathing matches his; my pulse and the pounding in my head mirror the thump of the vein in his neck.

And Cherish is still screaming.

"What happened?" Honoria demands. She's yet to let go of Trey's arm, but she's stopped shaking him.

Neither of us answer. My mind's fried. I can't remember how to put words in order.

"You were both asleep," she prompts. "Then you started screaming."

"Both?" I test the word twice in my head.

"At the same time," Col. Lutrell says.

He and Mr. Pace are watching us, the question on their faces identical to the one Honoria asked

"One of you say something." The concern in Honoria's voice surprises me.

"Sludge monster ripping you apart one atom a time?" Trey asks, voice too light for what he's saying.

"While devouring everyone and everything," I add.

*Everything* is the important part. The wild hive won't stop until the entire world's been consumed and brought into their strict order.

"I thought it was a nightmare."

"It was," Trey says.

He opens his fingers, slowly, releasing my hand and then lays his head against the back of his seat, closing his eyes to force his breathing into a regular pattern. The jumping pulse in his neck calms. If he were his sister, we'd still be covering our ears to block the hysterics.

Cherish is close enough. I can still feel her shaking, though my hands are steady. That heartbeat sound that Rue uses so often is racing.

"You both saw the same thing?" Mr. Pace asks.

"I think so. Marina wasn't there where I could see her or anything, but that was definitely more than a dream."

"It was *them*," I say. "The wild-Fade are searching for us."

Taunting for sport is more like it, but the others don't need to hear that.

"How's that possible?" Mr. Pace is unnerved. He thought he was enough to keep his son safe, but now he must be wishing he left Trey behind with Tobin and Anne-Marie. "Trey's communicated with them, but they shouldn't even know you."

"I don't know."

It's a lie, and I know now why Rue's willing to help us cut through the Dark. Part of it's his love for Cherish, but only part.

*The enemy of my enemy is my friend.*

The wild-Fade don't just want the Arclight or humans; they want it all.

Rue's people were hit first and lost many voices to the darkness. A lament hangs heavy among the trees, mourning them, but still the wild ones press forward, chipping their way deeper, coming closer to the Arclight and the Fade settlement inside the Dark.

The entire world will succumb; there won't be any hope left.

They have to have a weakness. *That's* what I focus on. Cherish's hive—*my hive*—broke free of them before; she should be able to find out how.

We can stop this.

The others startle when the door shakes from outside. Honoria's hand goes straight for her gun.

"It's only Rue," I say quickly, grateful he's shown enough restraint not to rip the door off its frame, though that's likely plan B.

*Rue, stop! I'm okay. Cherish is fine.*

*The door has malfunctioned.*

He shakes it again.

I unlock the door, and it flies open.

Rue leans in from the step rail, his concern spoken only to me.

*Injured?* He reaches out.

*Words only,* I warn, pulling my hand away. *No nanites. You'll set off every human in this truck, and I don't want to get shot again.*

Honoria still has her hand on the gun's grip. Mr. Pace's rifle is back in his lap.

*Assessing,* Rue says. *Concerned. Worried.*

He replays the frantic heartbeat.

"Mine screamed," he says.

"It was a nightmare. I fell asleep—well, we did." I point to Trey.

It's easier if I just show him, so I send him the memory of the beast.

*Your sight was untrue.* He chases images of the beast devouring Blanca and my mother with a burst of flowers and pine.

*Their voices remain,* he says.

*Thank you.*

I'd feel better if there was a way for him to check on Tobin and Anne-Marie, too, but I'll take what I can get.

# CHAPTER TWENTY-FIVE

## TOBIN

I wasn't going to read the book. I threw it on the table in my apartment and tried to forget it, but I kept finding excuses to walk through the room, and it kept being in plain sight.

The front pocket's jammed full of paper and cards, a ribbon with a faded #1 on it. There are two pictures. The first, a photo of a boy in a blue cap, smiling with a metal bat to his shoulder. On the back: *Schuyler Whit* and the stamped image of a stitched ball. The other picture's black-and-white medical film. It says *Whit-Sykes, Week 20, girl*, with scratched-through names like Amelia and Josephine below it. That's it.

I skim the parts about Honoria coming to the Arclight, searching for references to "the colonel" and marking them with stuff from the pocket so I can read them all at once. I thought I'd be excited to find out more of Dad's past, but all I feel is nervous. It's a relief when someone knocks.

"Annie?"

She blows past me into the apartment.

"Want to come in?" I ask the empty doorway.

By the time I turn around, she's down the hall, with my

linen closet open, throwing towels onto the floor.

"Annie!"

"Where is it?" she demands. "Where's the handle?"

I catch the next stack of towels before she can send them flying, and she turns on me, trying to push me away from the closet.

"Where is it, Toby?" She's practically screaming. "I saw you open it from here."

She's been crying again.

I let go of the towels, so they fall into the pile with the rest. Annie turns for another bunch.

"Stop it!" I grab those, too.

She glares and kicks me.

"I don't want to stop!" she screeches. "I want the door open." She's too upset; she must have started this fit somewhere else.

"You don't have to tear the place apart," I tell her. "The switch plate's not even covered."

I flatten her hand against it, so the door panel slides into its pocket.

"Where's the light?" she asks, not giving me time to find out why a full-tilt claustrophobic is so desperate to find the entrance to the tunnel she refused to enter when we were carrying Rueful.

"There isn't one," I say.

"No lights?"

Finally, she pauses.

"I'll tell you where the flashlight is, if—"

"Kitchen cabinet, behind the cleaning solution." Annie ducks under my arm, and she's gone again, banging around under the sink. I limp into the room after her.

"It's not there," I say.

"Fine. I'll take the one in your bedroom."

"Annie—"

"I know this place as well as my own, Tobin. You don't have any secrets."

"Aside from the passage in my closet, you mean?"

She makes a face and then heads for the bathroom, likely to look for the emergency beacon in the cabinet.

I block her halfway across the living room.

"Question one: Where's your brain gone? Question two: Why are you acting like I won't help you with . . . whatever this is?"

"I need to get outside without being seen and without tripping any alarms," she says.

I knew she'd snap someday. As soon as it hit her that the Arclight is nothing but a cage on a bigger scale, her panic reflex must have kicked in.

Annie glances at the linen closet; I know what she's thinking. She's faster on open ground, but maybe not in here.

"It's an emergency exit to the Common Hall and the hospital," I tell her. "You can't get outside from here." Even the Well's enclosed.

"You sneak out of here all the time. That's the only door without a censor on it."

"No, it's not."

Annie handles the tunnel system better than I expect. She won't set foot downstairs, but she makes it from my apartment to the Common Hall, and then from the Common Hall to the shed.

"This is how you and Marina sneaked the Fade in?" she asks, breathing through her nose; she held her breath as much as she could while we were underground. "And where Rue hid everyone the night we took down the Arc?"

"There are passages crisscrossing all over. More than half are sealed; I doubt Dad's shown them all to me."

"How do we get past the lights?" she asks.

"You want to keep going?"

I thought she'd breathe open air for a while, and relax, knowing she can get out anytime she feels closed in, but she's moving away from the buildings, toward the boundary line and the Grey.

"Annie, wait!"

"I'm going crazy thinking of Trey out there. I have to go."

Crap. This isn't claustrophobia. I pull her back by the arm.

"You don't know what's out there," I say.

"Yes, I do—my brother, and *his eyes turned blue*. They had him, Toby, and he didn't know it. The bad ones could still have him, and he may not know it. I saw what they did to Silver and

Dante. I saw . . . I saw . . . I won't let that happen to Trey. I won't."

"What about your mom?" I ask.

"I left a note."

Annie takes a long look at the boundary, as though she's psyching herself up for a running start and a jump across. Even if I drag her back inside, she knows how to get around security now, and I can't change that without having someone lock the tunnels.

I'm an idiot.

We go out at almost exactly the same point Marina did. It's scary easy. As soon as the patrols start to switch out, we make a run between the fires. No wonder Honoria thinks we're always on the verge of a crisis.

"You didn't have to come with me," Annie says. "I could have made it on my own.

"I know."

But after seeing Dante and Silver, and hearing Dad talk about the people who survived the first days, no one should cross the Grey alone. If worse comes to worse, she might need someone to burn her like Dad did for Sykes when he couldn't reach his wound, or Marina did for-

*Marina burned me like Dad burned Sykes.*

Am I like them now? Will I be stumbling over explanations to my son in a century or trying to make him understand why I don't age?

"What's wrong?" Annie asks.

"I don't like it out here," I say instead of the truth.

How long will someone like me or her live? Or Marina?

Am I even human?

I don't understand any of this. I need my dad.

"Watch for shimmers," I tell Annie. "Nanobot and the others acted like they could hear something when we crossed before."

A stick breaks several yards off, and we both snap toward the sound.

"Something like that?" she asks, bringing up her flashlight.

There's nothing there, but another stick breaks. Leaves and dirt disperse as something walks through them. I raise my infrared and catch the outline of a leg.

"Should we be running?" Annie asks.

"Great idea—outrun a Fade at night."

A shimmer-line appears as it comes closer. It's tall and thin, with the outline of a hooded cowl; it's wearing a robe to protect itself from the Arc.

"Toby, behind you."

I turn around to find another shimmer approaching. The Fade raises its hand, but only to move the hood enough so that I can see her face.

"Whisper?" I ask.

"You know her?"

I nod.

"It's okay," I say. "She's one of the guards who patrols the Grey."

I turn back to the other Fade, much less nervous with

Whisper's silent approval of his presence, but it's not Dog. He's the wrong size and shape.

The second Fade reaches for his hood and pushes it back. "Hello, Schuyler."

# CHAPTER TWENTY-SIX

## MARINA

Two hours pass, almost three. The truck keeps a steady pace, but we'll have to move faster eventually. The cleared area is narrow, and only open for the time we occupy it, but I can tell things are different here. These buildings were framed with metal, and made of concrete instead of wooden beams, so more of them survived. They stand close together on both sides of a road clogged with abandoned vehicles that move out of our way before we reach them as loose nanites lift them up and shuffle them through the veil.

This was a city, where people lived and worked stacked on top of one another. I watch it disappear as nanites fill in the space behind us. On the other side the buildings grow smaller again, spaced farther apart.

Rue's hive is enormous, and they're barely a blink compared to the rest of the Fade out there. How are we going to do this?

"Not long now," Col. Lutrell says, automatically turning to read a green sign that's still on its post. "That was the only real city left between us and the capitol. The rest is rural."

Maybe that meant something in the days before, but not

anymore. There's only our territory and theirs.

The truck pops with an ill-timed recoil that turns our smooth ride into a stuttering crawl before we roll to a stop. Both men in the front seat say "Uh-oh," under their breath.

"What's wrong?" Honoria asks.

"Something gave," Col. Lutrell says. He turns off the truck, even though the engine's already quiet. "This thing's an antique. The stress was bound to show at some point."

Couldn't it have picked a point closer to the Arclight?

He and Mr. Pace climb out. Rue knocks on my window.

*Return to home?* he asks.

*I don't think we're going anywhere,* I tell him. *Something broke.*

A clang comes from the back as Mr. Pace digs through containers for the tool kit. Our view in front's been blocked by the truck's raised hood.

"Can you tell what's wrong?" Honoria asks, still in her seat.

"It's running hot," Mr. Pace says. He waves his hand in front of his face to clear the air.

"We might pull the last fifteen or twenty miles out of it," Col. Lutrell says, "but if you want to get home, it's going to take some tinkering."

"Tinker when we get there," she says. "I'd rather stay a moving target."

"Our space is the safer stop," Rue says.

"We're on the edge of Rue's territory," I say, interpreting his meaning. It registers as a bubble, bowing out from the relatively safe part of the Dark behind us but pressing against the unknown ahead. We've stretched it to its limit. "The wild ones are wary of approaching Rue's hive in noticeable numbers, but the closer we get to the edge, the bolder the wild-Fade become. Rue's people can't keep the road clear without endangering themselves, and we won't have another chance to stop before we reach our destination."

"*If* we make it," Trey grumbles.

I ignore him and keep talking. "If we stop here, they can still buy us time."

"We will observe the boundary line," Rue offers.

"Worry about your lines," Honoria says. "We've got lamps to draw ours. Work as fast as you can," she says to Col. Lutrell and Mr. Pace. "I'll start us a campfire."

She's out the door.

"You two stay put until we're sure it's safe," Mr. Pace tells me and Trey.

They drop the tailgate, grabbing equipment they need, and then they're gone.

"I'll scoot over if you want to get in," I say to Rue. Cherish and I both long for him to say yes, but he's already hopping off the step rail.

"I must see beyond," he says, leaving Trey puzzled.

"He's going to check in with the others before the lights come on," I explain.

As he leaves, Rue adds his opinion of the truck and its noise and smell, finding both so distasteful, he doesn't want to be anywhere near them.

"You hear more than the ones we can see, don't you?" Trey asks. He stares at his reflection in the rearview mirror, so only his eyes fill the glass.

"How—"

"You mumble when you answer, sometimes."

"Cherish—that's the human version of what they call me— she's still in my head. I don't know how."

"Perfect. I have seizures that make me draw things I've never seen, and you've got a dead Fade-girl taking up space in your head. I wonder what Annie will get—random dance numbers?"

"She'd probably like that."

We both laugh, but neither of us would find it funny if it actually happens.

"Please don't tell anyone about Cherish."

"I'm beginning to think secrets are the best road to survival," he says. "If you or your brain-buddy were dangerous, I think we'd know by now."

Through the window, I see the colonel approaching. Rue comes back into view, having finished his survey of "beyond," and falls into step with him, stopping when they reach the door. The other Fade, including Dog, have disappeared.

"Can we get out now?" I ask.

"Once the lamps are hot."

"The rest of mine have been warned. I remain," Rue says.

"I thought you'd say that." Col. Lutrell makes a circle in the air with his finger, and the lights flare in a ring around us. He slaps the side of the truck twice. "You guys can haul out."

My legs have recorded every bump and twist we hit on the way through the Dark, and as I stand, they play them all back at once.

"Whoa . . . ," Trey says, climbing out behind me. "Are you seeing this?"

He stops in a crouch, too stunned to stand up straight.

With the Fade pulled away, and the ever-present black shroud of nanites removed from the area, what's left of the world is illuminated by spears of light. It's no longer the narrow chute we drove through. Rue hovers near the edge, his muscles tensed from the sudden intrusion of light, but he's determined to bear it.

Mr. Pace and Col. Lutrell stare. Honoria stops fidgeting with the fire she's built. For me and Trey, the scene is new and fascinating, but for them, it's a ghost dragged screaming into view.

Side roads end abruptly where they've been torn or damaged. They lead nowhere, starting at buildings full of nothing. More vehicles sit in clumps, where they died as people tried to flee. Now they're scattered mementoes of the lost. Boxy bags spill clothes that must not have been organic. The devastation's endless.

This is a wasteland.

For years, Honoria and the others fought for the idea that they could return things to the way they were before the Fade, but there's no way to repair this; we can only start over.

"I think I'm going to go and see if they need another set of hands up front," Trey says. "I can't use the wrenches, but I can hand them out."

"Hey," I say to Rue, once we're alone.

I don't expect an answer. Hellos are a human ritual the Fade don't need.

"Are you okay? Inside the lights and all?"

"I can tolerate," he answers, after searching my vocabulary for the word. I feel like giving him a sentence as an example— *I cannot tolerate your barging into my mind*—but it would be futile.

"It's shaded in the truck, if you'd rather sit there."

"I do not like the truck."

He says *the truck* as one word.

"Are the others okay?" I try.

"They are uncomfortable, but close. They will be closer if needed, but then they will be more uncomfortable."

He's standing sentry, scanning the open areas and listening for anything that shouldn't be there—which would be anything at all.

Nervousness makes me twitchy. I find myself picking at the dog tags Tobin gave me and popping the rubber band against my wrist. If he was here, he'd be on guard, too, but not the same way. Tobin stands solidly on his feet, daring anyone to try and move him. Rue's agility incarnate, balanced on his toes and ready to run toward danger.

Thinking of Tobin sets Cherish off. She tries to nudge me closer to Rue.

*Don't be so pushy*, I say silently.

She answers back with a "push" so hard, it knocks me forward. Rue throws his hand out to steady me on my feet.

"Cherish is stubborn," he says. "She hears, but she doesn't listen."

"You really can hear her, can't you?"

"Marina often drowns Cherish out. She's stubborn, too."

"How do you hear her from inside my head?"

"She would not fit inside your head."

He begins to pace the perimeter, either for a better look or to cope with the heat generated by the back of the light stands. This is his way of saying our conversation about Cherish is over, but I still follow. Out here, I understand why silence means death to the hive. This is the held breath when walking over a fresh grave. Without nanites poured out over everything, there's no way to ignore the emptiness.

We walk side-by-side for a while, every step reminding me how awkward I feel. I don't like it. Rue's never made me feel awkward before. Even when I thought he was my enemy, there was something about him that made me think he was worth listening to, but now he talks *at* me instead of *to* me.

Our lights have trapped a squat, one-story building within the ring. It's got giant front windows and the spindly wires of an awning frame that's lost its cover. Both windows are broken, but one still has most of its glass. Large red letters read open 24/7, while smaller ones tell me that the Lucky Eight jackpot is up to two-hundred and seventy million dollars. Apparently, I could buy a ticket here, if I wanted to play.

It's tempting to dash inside for a look.

"Do you think it's safe?" I ask Rue, peeking through the empty pane of what was once a glass door.

"Shadows." He blocks my entrance with his body. Inside the building, shelves and big glass cases block the lights from reaching the farthest areas. "Cherish didn't listen. Marina should learn from her error."

He means the night he lost Cherish to the Arclight, when she went exploring alone and was imprisoned in the light.

It's the light Rue usually mistrusts, not the Dark. If he has reason to doubt the shadows, I shouldn't be so keen to see them closer. Despite the rising temperature from the fire and the burning ring of our lamps, I shiver, mesmerized by the layers of Darkness that deepen away from the door. My mind plays tricks, telling me these shadows are moving and transforming into the devourer from my nightmare.

"The voices here are different," Rue says. "We should move elsewhere."

He turns from the building.

"But what about our voices? Is it okay to talk?"

He holds his hand out, no real expression on his face to betray if he thinks I'll take it—or if he actually wants me to. Cherish wants to, and my hand lifts toward his. It has to be Cherish. I can't possibly be considering it on my own.

"Out loud, Rue." I snap myself, then tuck my hands into my crossed arms. "I want to ask you something."

"Ask what?" He drops his hand.

"You know my family, right? My mom and Blanca?"

Calming pine wafts in on a breeze that fills my lungs but doesn't lift my hair.

"I know them. They know me. We know you."

"What about my dad, my father, my . . . Do you know what that word means?"

He shuffles through my thoughts, bringing faces to my attention, then discarding them until he settles on Tobin and Col. Lutrell. Tobin's face dissolves, leaving only his father's behind. He repeats the process with Anne-Marie and Mr. Pace.

I'll take that as a yes.

"Evergreen is what I call my mother, because of the pine," I say. "Who's my father? I don't know his name."

Rue shows me the image of that rock set into the current.

If water is part of my name, then putting a rock in front of it clearly means "blocked." What's the big secret?

"Why doesn't anyone want me to know?" I cry. How can someone I don't even remember hurt me this much?

*Negative*, Cherish says.

Rue adds: *Inquiry.*

"Every time I ask about him, there's a rock in my way."

He laughs at me, and I don't find it funny at all.

"What?" I ask, angry.

"Your name is from his name."

*Water.*

Rue calls me by my Fade name and then shows the rock again. That's my father's name. He's a stone set so deep that a river bends around him. *Unyielding.* Stubborn.

"Then he was there when we passed through?" I ask. "He was answering me?"

*Affirmed.*

He came.

One of those reaching hands in the veil was my father's. I feel like crying again, but not from sadness.

*Pain?* Rue asks, confused by the reaction.

"Not anymore."

# CHAPTER TWENTY-SEVEN

## MARINA

Honoria stands alone in the middle of our camp, tending the fire she's built.

"You still move like one of them," she says without looking up.

"Do you want some help?" I ask. "I don't really have anything to do."

"Only if you can fix an engine as quickly as your guard dog can heal himself."

She leaves the fire to unpack a canvas bag full of wrapped packages that turn out to be food. Dried out and lumpy, but food, in theory. I should really stop complaining about Common Hall lunches.

She plops one of the bundles into a pan sitting on the fire.

"I'm not a Fade anymore, and they're not mechanics."

"Then we're even, because I am definitely *not* a cook." Another of the packages hits the pan.

That sounded disturbingly close to being a joke, and that's more jarring than Honoria with a gun.

"Tell your friend there's enough if he's hungry."

"Rue doesn't eat that way."

Born Fade *can* eat, and will on occasion, if they're curious about the taste or texture of something, but it's only the ones with hosts who have to ingest food.

"Then *you* can come back in half an hour, and he's free to keep pacing," she says.

Rather than take Honoria's words for the dismissal she intends, I find a rocky patch and sit down next to the food bundles. I pick one up and peel the wrapper off before holding it out to her—whether she wants it or not.

"Is this what it was like? In the first days, before there was a real perimeter line at the Arc?"

That question gets me a heavy sigh as Honoria accepts that she's lost the battle to make me leave. She throws a third packet into the pan.

"Actually, no. The first *days* were a lot calmer than this. It's similar to the first nights, though. Only we had more people and less food to go around."

She stabs at the stuff in the pan so hard that half a piece bounces out to fall in the dirt.

"It's not my fault," I say.

"I didn't say it was."

"It's what you think."

I hate Honoria's laugh. It's never a happy sound. "You are *nowhere* on the list of people responsible for this, Marina. What you are is a reminder of the mistakes I've made, and that makes for unpleasant company. Mistakes only end in tragedy."

"You really think that, don't you? You honestly don't know what you did to them."

She throws her fork down, leaving the food to sizzle while she faces me, arms crossed and glaring down. She's as unpleasant as I've ever seen her, but that only means she's out of options. Intimidation is her last resort.

"Believe it or not, I never did anything to them—or you—out of malice."

"Neither did they," I tell her, "but that's not what I'm talking about."

She looks puzzled.

"For someone who hears so well, you're a lousy listener. Have you ever heard what the Fade call you?"

"I can imagine."

"They call you Fire," I tell her. "I thought it was a warning or an insult the first time I heard it, but it's not. It's a reminder of the moment your voice went silent among them. They remember the girl who made a choice to disconnect and who showed them that their way of life was hurting someone else's. It took them a while to understand, but eventually, they got it. They stopped taking hosts. You *changed* them."

"Quiet," she snaps.

"Don't dodge this, Honoria. You can—"

"Be quiet!"

I know that look. This is the dangerous Honoria. The one

with her senses on high alert, gazing past me into the distance, head to one side as if to listen to something no one else can hear. She doesn't even uncross her arms.

"Something's moving out there," she says.

"Maybe it's the wind. It could be the wind, right?"

She steps away from the fire, reaching back to grasp the handle of her pistol.

"Wind doesn't walk."

I strain to pick up anything past the crackle of the fire and popping food, and I catch the sound of crunching leaves and breaking twigs as something moves toward us. *Fast.*

"Did you—" Honoria starts.

"I heard it. Someone's headed this way."

"Some*thing*," she corrects. "Stay behind me."

She's using the gun that nearly killed Tobin to protect me.

"Hold up my walkie."

I unhook the radio on Honoria's belt and hold it high enough so that she can speak while I press the button.

"We've got movement in the trees," she says. "Beyond the perimeter and gaining speed."

When she's done, I'm not sure what to do with the radio, so I keep holding it until the others trickle in. It doesn't take long; we haven't got a lot of space here, and it won't take many Fade to surround us.

Without any sort of real cue or prompt, Trey and I are pushed together toward the center of a tightening circle formed by Honoria, Mr. Pace, and Col. Lutrell. Rue keeps to the edge. The sounds from the trees grow louder as who- or whatever's approaching gets closer; they're headed straight for us.

*No danger*, Cherish insists. *Wait.*

Rue takes her side.

"No need to run," he says. "They irritate, but mean no harm."

"Who?" Honoria asks.

The bushes are moving now, being pushed aside as whoever's on the other side forces their way through at a suddenly slower pace, and with one last, loud crunch, the next sound we hear is a human voice cursing.

"It can't be . . . ," Col. Lutrell says.

But it is, and I've never been so happy to hear such awful things in my life.

"Tobin!"

# CHAPTER TWENTY-EIGHT

## MARINA

I run toward Tobin's voice

"Marina, wait!"

Trey catches my jacket, but it's so big, it's easy to shuck.

"It's him. Trust me," I say.

If this were a deception, Rue'd warn me. Instead, his marks tighten down, pencil thin, nearly writing out *hate* across his skin. There's only one person who can get that reaction out of him.

Tobin and I collide along the perimeter.

"Who's there?" he demands. He stumbles back, pulling us to the ground and into the outer glare; it's like the White Room from this side.

"It's me," I say.

"Marina? I can't see." He sounds like he's gulping air rather than inhaling it.

"Get inside the circle. It's not as bright." I wish I had my Red-Wall shades. The lights have left my eyes full of spots.

I crawl back the way I came, careful of the lamps. On the other side, I'm grabbed up and pulled away, but I can't tell by who.

"Hey!"

"Marina?" Tobin calls, worry in his voice. "What—Let go! Let go of me!"

His voice moves in the opposite direction from the one I'm being taken.

"Sit!" Honoria orders and then drops me.

*Should have remained with Rue*, Cherish tells me, smug.

Tobin's still fighting. I can hear him from here.

"Calm down," his father says. Col. Lutrell comes more in focus as my eyes adjust.

"Dad?"

Tobin turns and hugs him, like he's surprised to see us alive. "I'm never doing that again. I didn't think we'd make it."

*Tibby's scared*, Rue says, but I got that part already.

"Did something happen at home?" Col. Lutrell asks.

If what took Dante and Silver spread . . . Maybe there is no home.

"Why did you leave?"

"Where are Sykes and Doctor Wolff?" Mr. Pace asks as another voice bursts through the silence.

"Toby?" Anne-Marie crosses the lamps with her arms over her face. She's breathing hard, with so many leaves stuck to her that she looks like she's wearing a bush for a shirt.

"Annie?" Mr. Pace asks. "What are you doing here? Are you hurt?"

"I don't think so." She checks her arms to make sure. Her

aura's blue and bright; it barely wanes at all when she sees Honoria with her gun. "Are you going to shoot us? Because that would make this whole trip a colossal waste of time."

She's giddy.

Honoria puts her gun down and picks up her radio from where I dropped it.

"Sykes?" she calls, but there's only static. We're either out of range or something blocked the signal.

*Or there's no one to answer*, Cherish suggests.

I suggest she shuts up.

"Was there another incident?" Col. Lutrell asks Tobin.

"Yes—Annie's overprotective reflex has officially reached insanity. I tried to stop her, but she wouldn't listen."

"Your mother's going to tear her hair out when she finds out you're gone." Mr. Pace is obviously relieved that nothing new has befallen the Arclight, but relief isn't what I hear in his voice. "She'd tear yours out if you had any left on your head."

Anne-Marie gives him a hateful look for the mention of her hair.

"I left a note," she says.

I can imagine:

> Sorry, Mom.
> Gone to see the Fade. I'll be back
> soon if we don't get caught. Then I'll

*be back later, but I'll probably try to kill you, so be sure to run as soon as you see me.*

*Love,*

*Anne-Marie*

Some note.

A dozen new fears take hold as the initial glow of seeing Tobin and Anne-Marie safe wears off. With them here, I'm one step closer to the scenario from my nightmare.

"How did you get here? There's no way you caught up with us on foot," Honoria says.

"Yes, we did," Anne-Marie says. "They just weren't our feet."

She giggles again. Honoria pinches the bridge of her nose.

"Whisper and Schuyler brought us," Tobin says. "They found us on their rounds and didn't want us wandering alone."

*Subterfuge*, Rue snarls, with a vague threat of pain for Honoria's brother. His marks swirl across his skin like swarming bees.

The Fade could have sealed the Dark up tight, so that neither Tobin nor Anne-Marie would have been able to see the way, much less follow it. Bolt came to protect his sister and used them for an excuse.

"Bolt wants you to drop the lights enough that they can come through," Anne-Marie says. "They need to talk to him." She points to Rue, and then sniffs the air in the direction of the fire, where Honoria's food has charred to ash. "Is something burning?"

"Your brain cells," Tobin says.

"It was not that bad, you big baby."

"Yes, it was—and it should have been worse for you! Since when does your claustrophobia come with an off switch?"

"I could see out," she says. "It was amazing."

"Not amazing. Never doing it again."

That's all he says, as though the memory's too terrible to recount. Anne-Marie chatters away at Trey and their father, speaking as much with her hands as her voice, in an attempt to describe what they've gone through.

*What happened to them?* I ask Rue.

He shows me Anne-Marie and Tobin's trip through the Dark in a blink, and it feels like they were moving that fast. Where born-Fade can break apart, slipping into the constant flow of nanite trails that thread through the Dark, the others move the way Rue and Dog did when they were sliding alongside the truck. For Anne-Marie and Tobin, they came up with an alternative method—enveloping them in a capsule of nanites and shuttling them along at high speed.

No wonder Tobin's still trembling. I'm surprised he hasn't blacked out.

"What do you think?" Col. Lutrell asks.

"That this is another bad idea in a long chain of them," Honoria says. "Make a path. If anything about this reads wrong, turn them back on." Then she addresses Rue. "Only bring faces we know."

She keeps to the middle, where she's got the best vantage point. Mr. Pace and Col. Lutrell make for the lamps nearest the spot where Tobin and Anne-Marie came through, and turn off two lights to create a walkway.

Bolt, Whisper, and Dog come out of the shadows, nearly incandescent where they pass close to the light.

"That's it?" Honoria asks. "Three?"

"Three you recognize," Rue says. The Fade follow him to a spot farthest from the lamps.

"How many are out there?" Honoria asks Tobin and Anne-Marie.

What does it matter? The Fade are infinite and are always adding more.

"Besides whoever came with you, a couple dozen followed us," Tobin says.

"Why so many?" his father asks.

*Reinforcements*, Cherish supplies; I repeat it out loud.

"They're a security detail. The hive senses danger and drafted more to keep us safe."

"You make them sound like an army," Honoria says.

They are—and they're ours.

"Anyone know what exactly is it that our soldiers are doing over there?" Mr. Pace asks.

Whisper and Dog stand facing each other, each clasping the

other's wrists. Bolt and Rue are doing the same. Their marks rush together and apart, mingling across their arms and hands.

"Status report," I tell him, but I'm not the only one. Tobin says it, too. So do Anne-Marie and Trey.

"We've got to get them out of here," Col. Lutrell says, glancing at each of us in turn.

"We can't send them back alone," Mr. Pace says.

"They didn't come alone," Rue says out loud. The Fade-caucus has broken apart, but their frustratingly blank faces show no clue of what's been said or decided. "They won't leave alone."

"Because we aren't leaving," Tobin says. His nerves tuck themselves neatly into their hiding place behind his temper, now that he has an opponent to spar with. "I'm not doing that again. Period."

"Go home, *Tibby*," Rue says.

"I will. In the truck, when this is done."

"You don't belong in this place."

"Yes, I do." Tobin pointedly takes my hand, threading our fingers together. "That's what's needling you."

"Enough!" Honoria shouts. "Get your hormones in check before I take after you all with a spray bottle. You are not starting a fistfight on the edge of hostile territory."

Very hostile. *Extremely* hostile.

"*You* keep watch on the perimeter," she tells Dog and Whisper. No one argues. "And you keep *him* away from *them*," she tells Bolt, pointing to Rue and then to me and Tobin. "This situation's volatile, but it's what we've got. We're going to make it work."

Rue actually growls.

"Save it for someone you're not trying to convince to like you," Honoria says before issuing orders to me and the others. "You four into the truck, and *stay* there."

The conversation's over before I realize she never demanded proof that Tobin and Anne-Marie hadn't been affected by their time with the Fade.

*She's different*, Cherish says, and I let myself mumble, "I know," back to her.

Rue doesn't speak as I head for the truck, but I can feel him watching me. I climb in through the back with Tobin, then turn to look through the flap. Rue's just standing there, separated from everyone. That's not what I wanted.

*Not your choice?* he asks.

*I didn't mean it to be*, I say, then close the flap, and snap it shut.

# CHAPTER TWENTY-NINE

## MARINA

I really do envy Anne-Marie's ability to turn anything she touches into a pillow. She's piled some canvas bags from under the seat into a heap against the door, and she doesn't even mind the smell—a musty combination of old socks and older mildew. There's no indication that her dreams are anything but happy

Trey's her exact opposite—awake and guarding his sister from the monsters in our shared nightmares. He's at attention in the front seat, with a rifle across his lap, exactly the way Mr. Pace would be.

"If I didn't know better, I'd think you were scared," Tobin says. He bumps my shoulder, trying to prompt a smile, but I don't feel like smiling. "Don't you think the payoff's worth the risk?"

"Being worth it doesn't mean you can't be afraid to take it."

We've taken refuge in the truck's cargo space. We have to shove a few things around to make room, but back here, I can pretend nothing's happening outside. We're simply sitting in the stillness of the Well, without the luxury of stretching out.

"Weren't you scared when the Fade came up with the capsule idea?" I ask him.

He nods, trembling.

"They were everywhere. I could see past them, but they were still there, making my nerves tingle where they touched my skin, and I'm pretty sure they touched all of it. I kept holding my breath because I was afraid I'd inhale some, but that made me light-headed, and I didn't want to pass out."

"You really hate them, don't you?"

"I don't trust them, not completely," he says. "With the ones like Honoria's brother, it's not so bad. You can see them coming."

"Most of the time," I mumble, wondering if who and what I am has ever fully sank in for him.

"It's the little ones I can't handle," he says, oblivious. "Not little like your sister, but tiny. Those other ... *things.*"

"Nanites."

"*Them,* I hate. That one word. It makes them sound simple. I still feel like shaking out my clothes and stomping my feet to make sure they're gone."

I remember that feeling. I had the same disgusted thoughts, and that makes me disgusted with myself.

"I don't think you have to worry." I ruffle my hands through his hair to show him nothing's going to flake off, but I understand his fear.

Rue told me once that his people weren't the ones who were faded, but the same isn't true of those pulled into the wild hive. They dissipate a piece at a time until there's nothing left but an echo trail. It's every bit as violent as the conversion that tore

272

me out of the hive. I can't stand the thought of it happening to anyone.

*I want to go home.*

Cherish and I think it at the same time, though we don't have the same destination in mind.

I want horrible, vitamin-infused cafeteria food and my pink-walled bedroom. I want to bury my hands in a bucket of dirt from the Arbor, where I can think of my sister and know she's safe with my parents. And I want *my* Well—the real one that's a sanctuary because we choose to make it one, not because we need a place to hide.

"Do you think . . ." I turn so I'm facing Tobin rather than beside him. He sits up straighter. "Do you think this is all because of the Fade?"

"Why else would we be out here?"

"No, you and me," I say. "You being friends with Anne-Marie. Her being friends with me. The only way Trey and I could share what we saw is if we're connected. Were we programmed to gravitate toward one another because we've all touched the Fade from birth?"

I expect anger for the suggestion that the Fade have any part in his life at all, but there's only contemplation of the possibility.

"I don't know," he says, leaning back so he's balanced on his palms against the floor. "I don't *think* so. If that was all it was, wouldn't we have clicked straight off? And you'd think Annie and I would have responded better to the nanobot."

"You can say his name, you know."

"Not until he stops calling me Tibby."

At least I don't have to worry about Tobin changing too much too fast.

"Besides I can't really say his name, can I? None of them have real names, except the ones like Dog who had them as humans."

"I don't think his name was Dog."

"They're not like us, Marina, and they have nothing to do with your choices or mine. You said it yourself—you took the path that was best for you, and it wasn't the one he *or they* wanted you to take."

I made the only choice I thought I had. Becoming Marina wasn't something I would have done as Cherish. Why can't he understand that?

"I wish we could see the stars," I say, glancing up the ceiling because it's too hard to look at him right now.

"What are you talking about?" he asks. "They're right there, over our heads. That bunch there looks like a fish."

He points to the truck's canvas covering, where snags in the weave and old stains have created patterns. One of them really does look like a fish.

"They're not very bright."

I get a grin for that.

"That's because they're a secret."

Tobin shifts, putting himself back beside me. I take the cue— our first trip to the Well—and rest against him.

"I see flowers," I say. "And trees."

Death Trees.

An old water stain near the center has the same branches as the mark on Silver's back, but I keep that to myself and let Tobin transform it into everything from Anne-Marie using an angry Arbor cat for a pillow, to one of his beloved snow globes.

Cloistered like this, with Tobin close enough that I can hear his heartbeat and feel his body heat, it's as cozy as under my lopsided quilt. I'm being lulled back to sleep.

"Sorry," I say through a yawn, forcing my eyes wide open. I snap myself with the band from my jacket again. "What was that last one?"

Hopefully, something exciting or funny enough to keep me awake.

"You can go to sleep if you want. I'll watch out for nightmares," Tobin says.

"Aren't you tired?"

"Too keyed up."

It takes some semi-painful maneuvering and a few kicks at the supplies to carve out a space long enough in which I can lie down and still hold Tobin's hand while he settles into a niche against a gas canister belted to the truck's wall.

"Tobin . . ."

"Hmm?"

"Do you think we'll make it home again?"

He picks up our joined hands, holding them in the space between us.

"My mom used to say that home was more people than place, so I guess we never really left."

Yeah, I don't think I'd have answered that one honestly, either.

# CHAPTER THIRTY

## TOBIN

Traveling by Fade left me drained. I don't know how long I lasted after Marina fell asleep, but it wasn't long. A second ago, Dad was working on the engine, but now the hood's down and we're idling. I guess he's testing the repairs.

At least Marina's not awake to know I broke my promise to watch over her. She's still out, like everyone else in the truck.

I just can't seem to get things in the right order. Girl sleeps over in my room—not Marina. Wake up with Marina—not in my room. We'd better survive this so I get the chance to get it right.

"We'll make it home," I whisper to her. "Whatever it takes, we're getting out of here."

It doesn't look like she's having a nightmare. When I slip my arm out from under her head so I can sit up, Marina doesn't move at all.

Is the other one sleeping, too? Or is she aware when Marina's not?

I reach for one of her hands and pull the edge of her glove away to check her skin. No lines, no dots, so where's it hiding?

I look out the backseat window, but there's no sign of Rueful and his bunch, either. They can't have left unless someone turned out the lights; maybe they're checking the buildings.

Dad's on the far side of our clearing with Honoria and Mr. Pace, shouting. Honoria shouts back, making wide gestures with her arm. Best guess: He wants to go home; she says no. Mr. Pace will have to break the tie, and they'll probably have to restrain whoever loses.

About-face and homeward bound works for me—not that they'd ask.

There's a flash of movement through the other side window, coming from a broken-down structure. At first I take it for a reflection of light on the glass left in the pane, or paint—like the numbers there, reading 24/7—but it shimmers.

There's no reason for Schuyler or Rueful to be incognito, so who—

*No . . .*

Did they trap one of those things in here with us?

*Wake up*, I tell myself, and check my hands, but there are none of the lines I see when I dream. I glance out the window again, and cock my head. Maybe at a different angle . . .

Another shimmer, and Trey screams bloody murder from the front seat, body seizing.

*We are so dead.*

"Marina, get up." I poke her shoulder. "We have to move."

Annie flies out of sleep and shakes Trey as hard as she can.

His screams settle into "They're here. They're here," repeated without stopping.

"Please tell me 'they' isn't who I think it is," Marina says, looking from side to side in the windowless cargo area. She scrambles for the back flap.

Trey's eyes pop open, but he keeps going. "They're here. They're here."

"Stop saying that!" Annie shouts. "Trey, wake up and stop saying that!" She tries to slap him awake. When that doesn't work, she puts her hands over his mouth.

"They're behind us," Marina says. "Check the side view."

I dive over the seat to get to the window.

"Do not tell me—" she starts.

"We're surrounded!" I shout back.

"I said don't tell me that!"

"In that case, we're fine. Go back to sleep."

"Shut up, Tobin."

What's beyond the glass warps the view like chemicals running down the pane. Shimmers appear in every tree past the lights, filling the branches and flowing down the trunks—mirages that have somehow clawed their way out of our nightmares. More fill the gaps between, tromping through the Dark where the trees give way to buildings.

*Shock troops.*

They're close to the lights, and pressing closer, despite howling in pain.

"Where'd Whisper go? Where's Dog?" Annie asks, leaning toward the window. "They're gone. Our Fade are gone."

She twists to look through the windshield, over the roof. She has to take her hands away from Trey's mouth, and he's still repeating those same two words.

"They can't be gone," Marina says, but I watch defeat take her face. I know the expression she gets when she's talking to one of them, and that's not it. She can't find Rueful, either. "But he promised," she whispers.

I knew we couldn't trust them.

"How did the wild ones get past our Fade?" Annie asks. "They were guarding the perimeter on the outside."

"What makes you think they're still there?"

She sinks into the seat as the truth finally gets through to her. They gave us up; we're on our own.

"Cherish says they have to stay quiet because of the wild ones, but they're there," Marina tells us stubbornly. "Rue and the others wouldn't have crossed the boundary without a plan."

"What plan?" I point to the trees above our lights, though she can't see them from the back. They're sprouting crystal leaves as wild nanites encase everything they touch, turning the terrain sharp and alien. "They have the high ground. We're in the kill-box."

Marina pulls the release for the tailgate under the truck's flap, but where can we go? We can't outrun them, especially with Trey in the shape he's in. We can't carry him, and no way is

Annie going to leave him after what it took to get here.

*Surrounded* isn't bad enough. We're buried.

My nightmares really were premonitions.

"The lamps are still holding," Annie says, but she's only thinking short term.

These Fade hit the lamplight and fall back, like the ones who attacked the Arclight and ran into our Red-Wall blinders, but it's not a full retreat. More come, pushing the front lines forward as the rest bank up behind them, using them for a shield. The ones above move down the trees, as close as they can get from overhead. Soon, one's going to risk dropping through the glare.

Marina can listen to whatever's left of that thing in her head and keep believing that the Fade care about everyone and everything, and maybe the ones she came from do, but not these. This is a suicide march.

The ones at the fore will burn, but eventually they'll overwhelm the lamps with the swarm. Those in the rear will pass the boundary without ever touching the light.

"We have to get out of here," Annie says.

"If your boyfriend's got any ideas, tell him I'm more than happy to follow his lead," I say to Marina.

"I'm trying," she says. "He won't answer."

"If they seal us in, it won't matter if the nanobot's out there or not," I say, stretching out the window. "Dad!"

He and the others are still in the open. Arguing—maybe

about the shadow crawlers bailing on us. I don't know; I can't hear them from here. Dad raises his head.

"Get inside!" I shout.

"Honoria!" Marina calls. She's leaned over the backseat. "They've found us!"

So many Fade have filed in that the Dark is nothing but shimmers running into one another. I can't make out specific shapes or individual bodies.

Dad and Mr. Pace race back toward the truck with the brightest lights they can carry, leaving the others where they stand and shrinking the safe zone as they flee. Honoria doesn't move yet, guarding their retreat.

Annie starts to clear the front seat, but that means uncovering Trey's mouth again. He still hasn't stopped babbling.

"They're here. They're here."

"Duck," I tell her finally, and hit him as hard as I can. His jaw pops, but it doesn't make a difference.

"What now?" Annie shrieks.

She keeps talking, but those are the last words I hear. There's a blast of noise so loud and jarring, it's unidentifiable. It shoots through my brain, shattering my thoughts and blurring my vision—I'm hearing this in my head, not my ears. Every nerve zings with the sensation of being turned to mush.

Shadow crawlers hate noise, why would they send—

"The horn!" Marina shouts. "Start the truck and hit the horn!"

Annie throws herself back behind the wheel and turns the key.

Rays of new, brighter light shoot into the Dark from the bulbs bolted to the truck's roof, and the gathering Fade reel backward, screeching. One continuous tone comes from the steering wheel under Annie's body, where she's pushed against it.

Trey stops screaming, his connection to the wild-Fade severed on the spot.

"Nice call," I tell Marina.

"Thank Cherish. It was her idea."

*Then how'd I hear her say it?*

Actually, I don't want to know.

The wild-Fade are rattled enough that they lose control of their camouflage, and we get our first real look at them beyond the perimeter.

"Sludge monsters," Trey mumbles.

These Fade look nothing like Schuyler or Rueful. They don't look human. They don't wear clothes. The hosts exist below an oil-slick coat of nanites. They rear up, flailing in the sound waves with clumps of black falling off their skin. Their joints are in odd places, bent at angles arms and legs can't match. Some of them aren't human.

A gunshot goes off behind us.

Dad and Mr. Pace both carry rifles, each requiring two hands to get off a shot, but Honoria's pistol only needs one. She sends a shot straight up, clearing the area above before she joins the rush for the truck. The next shot guards Dad's flank. She puts a bullet through one of the creatures, so the nanites burst off in all directions from the vibrations and hit the host animal below, leaving it dead on the ground. It brings one of the lamps down with it. The wild-Fade redirect their assault, turning as one massive entity to race for the gap.

"Get in the truck!" Annie yells, opening the driver's door. "They're still coming!"

I take Marina's hand to pull her over the seat and make room in the back for Mr. Pace and Dad as they haul themselves up through the tailgate and shut it behind them. Honoria heads for the driver's seat.

"Hang on to something," she orders, shoving Annie out of the way and gunning the engine.

Marina and I straighten ourselves in the backseat, where Annie landed. In the cargo area, Dad and Mr. Pace have their rifles through the flap, trying to knock the Fade off our tail.

"This isn't working," Dad says. "We'll run out of ammo before we make any headway. We need to take out their front line."

"Ever shoot skeet?" Mr. Pace grabs one of the reserve gas cans and slings it outside. One precision shot, and it explodes. The gas rains down as a hundred tiny fires, igniting every Fade it hits. The more nanites, the faster they burn. Behind us, the path is nothing but melting piles of fallen monsters.

We should have lit more fires.

# CHAPTER THIRTY-ONE

## MARINA

Our escape from the campsite makes the rest of our ride a peaceful overland tour by comparison. Without the open corridor created by Rue's hive, we have no path to follow.

"How long before they catch up again?" Anne-Marie asks.

"I'm hoping for never," I say. Between the fires and the noise, maybe we're not worth the trouble. Col. Lutrell and Mr. Pace keep firing at intervals, just to make sure.

Honoria hits a rock, pitching us up on one side. A ditch brings us low on the other as we drive through bushes and run over terrain that hasn't been touched by humans in decades. I hope Col. Lutrell knew what he was doing, or we'll stall out again.

"Annie, are you okay?" Trey asks. "And who hit me?"

He rubs his jaw.

"I'm fine," Anne-Marie says, doubled over with her head near her lap—until something lands on the roof, denting it in. "*Was* fine," she amends, head shooting up. "I *was* fine. What is that?"

"Please tell me that's Rueful changing his mind about coming with us," Tobin says.

"I don't think so." The indentions from this thing's feet are too broad and the wrong shape to be anything remotely humanoid. It's too big and too heavy. Two more land beside it.

"They're coming through the roof!" Anne-Marie cries.

Worse. They're taking the roof out of the equation.

Dark dots appear on the truck's covering, branching black along the grain. The cover disintegrates behind them, stripping our enclosure away. We'll be completely exposed.

Our elders shout orders from all directions.

"Get down" from Col. Lutrell.

"Annie, watch your head" from Mr. Pace, as a piece of the truck's canvas spirals down, covered in black. But the wind rips it out of reach, almost like nature is helping us fight the foe who bested her.

Honoria yells in bursts between the sounds of the road and our own startled yelps each time the truck hits a dip or bump.

"Silver case under your feet."

"What?" I ask.

"There's a silver case under the seat—open it."

I reach under the seat and find a bag with soft sides and a zipper. Inside is a refrigerated container filled with red-tipped darts.

"What are they?" Tobin asks, reaching for one. Five small dart guns are lashed to the side with elastic cords.

"It's the cure," I say. No one has to explain it to me; I can tell from the feel of its weight in my hands. These darts are filled with the serum that started me on my way from Cherish into Marina. And I don't know why I now choose to call it "cure" when I called it "poison" before. "It'll kill them."

"Point and shoot." Honoria points up before blasting the horn again.

The idea was simpler when we were still in the Arclight and all my potential targets were miles away in a place I thought I'd never see in person. The reality isn't so neat. Not when it's my hand on the trigger. Every human-turned-Fade ever treated has died from this stuff. If I fire, I'm ending a life.

A shot goes off beside me. Tobin's already taken a gun from the case and used it. One of the things above us roars, falling from the truck. I don't have the stomach to watch what happens next, knowing the creature will end up naked and abandoned like the Fade-animal Honoria killed.

Anne-Marie fires a dart with a squeak, and flinches at the slight recoil.

"Did I hit one?" she asks. The thud of a second body from the truck says yes, she did.

The last one's still there, its clawed feet clenching the cover's skeletal frame. It's not moving.

"Marina," Tobin prompts. "Shoot it."

I don't remember loading a dart into the gun in my hands. Or taking a gun. I don't . . .

"How do I know I'm not making it worse?" I ask.

One dose wasn't enough to bring *me* all the way across the

line. These things are huge. A single dart might leave the host in some kind of tortured limbo.

"Are you sure it's enough?" I ask Honoria.

"Yes."

"Real yes, or you-tell-me-what-I-want-to-hear-so-I'll-do-it yes?"

A clawed hand the size of a bear's paw swipes between us, caught in the canopy's skeleton. The creature snarls.

I raise both hands over my head, close my eyes, and fire. The creature drops off the roof.

Shaking, I let the gun fall back into the case with the others.

"Are you okay?" Tobin asks.

I don't know the answer to that question.

*Rue,* I call as loud and hard as a thought can be. *We need you, Rue. Cherish needs you . . . I need you.*

*Ours are coming,* Cherish says. *But theirs are listening.*

The wind blows through the truck, streaking my hair across my face. I brace for an attack from another creature, but instead comes the sound of cracking timber and the squeal of our tires straining as Honoria spins the truck to avoid a falling tree. Another comes down on its heels, then more, in a domino-fall all around us. The wild-Fade have changed tactics, using the terrain as a weapon rather than relying on the strength and speed of physical hosts that can be shot or outrun.

"We're dead," Tobin says. The engine's still running, but there's nowhere to go. They've put us in a cage.

Rue will come. He has to. He promised.

Right now, we've got our lights, but they won't last forever. The rifles are only good as long as the ammo holds out. Either we find another way, or I get to watch the closest thing to a human family I have be taken by the hive.

I don't think they can bring me in, not since the cure, but I don't know what they'll do when they figure that out. Maybe they'll kill me, maybe not. Maybe I'll be the last human left alive in the world.

Wouldn't that be something?

# CHAPTER THIRTY-TWO

## MARINA

It's no longer a matter of getting home, or even surviving. Our goal now is to take as many of the enemy down as possible before they take us.

Col. Lutrell and Mr. Pace are still in the rear compartment, each on one knee, with their rifles propped up and watching out the back flap. Nothing's moving yet, but it's only a matter of time.

The last time anyone spoke, Trey asked how much of the cure was left, and if there was a way to disperse it more widely than the dart guns, but there was no good answer.

Honoria's hands are clenched around the steering wheel and are no doubt bone white beneath her gloves and scars. I check the rearview mirror to see her face. She's defiant in the face of worse-than-death, but determination only goes so far.

Anne-Marie's on the floor, braced between the front and backseats. She's run out of fingernails to chew and moved on to reaching for phantom strands of hair. Her hand goes up, then clenches into a fist when she remembers she cut it. The fist drops back into her lap for a few seconds, and then repeats. Finally, she tugs on Trey's sleeve, wrapping her fingers around his hand when he lowers it.

Tobin and I share the backseat. Him next to the door, me in the center, with the space for Anne-Marie left empty in case she decides the floor's too confining. I wish we were in the cargo area, hidden among the boxes back there, but you need stars for a wish, and ours have all gone out.

We're out of options, out of ideas, and out of time. Out, period.

Will the end come quickly? Will it hurt? Will we all fall at once?

Waiting for death is worse than dying. Once you're dead, it's done. You can't be afraid anymore, but the wild ones torment us with time.

Col. Lutrell says this is normal. That they use military tactics gleaned from those they absorbed. In the first days, the Fade would attack and pull back to gauge an enemy's weakness. They want to make sure we're out of fire.

I think they enjoy taunting us.

When this started, I wondered if I'd be the last one standing in the wake of the wild-Fade, but now that my mind's had time to run rampant, I know I won't be. Honoria's used different variations of the serum on herself for decades. Diluted, sure, but it might be enough to make her immune to this hive, too. My friends will be lost, and in some twist of sadistic irony, she and I will be all that's left in a world gone dark.

I'm growing restless, my arms and legs buzzing with the

sensation of ants crawling along my nerves, but there's not a lot of room to move. I choose a selfish avenue and slip into Tobin's lap.

"I really thought we'd make it back," he says. I rest my head against him, so I can hear his heartbeat. If his aura, and the atmosphere of the immediate area hadn't already told me he was terrified, his drumming pulse would. "I would have locked Annie in a closet if I thought she'd never see her mom again. You and I could have hidden in the Well."

He squeezes me tightly as he tries to ward off his fears. I don't mind. It helps distract me from mine, too.

"Your dad knows where it is," I point out.

"He wouldn't have said anything. Marina, I'm sorry."

"You didn't do this."

"Maybe I did. I didn't really try to stop Annie—I could have. If we'd stayed home, the nanobot wouldn't have ditched you. You'd be safe. I really screwed up this time—I'm *so* sorry."

Ever since we woke up in the hospital after Tobin was shot, I've been searching for a way to end the awkwardness between us. I never thought it would take another near-death experience to get it done. It doesn't matter anymore that Tobin's father is within arm's reach, or that others can see us. There's no Cherish-born confusion to make me consider what Rue would think.

Rue's not here; Tobin is. And if this is where everything ends, then my last memory isn't going to be watching the shadows close in, as though we're cowering in our bunker inside the

Arclight. If I have only one choice left in life, then it's this: I lean over and kiss Tobin. If I have to die, then I'll do it with a taste of happiness.

No one says a word. Tobin and I exist in an infinite second, where the sky blazes with shooting stars so darkness no longer rules the night. We're inside that domed ball of water, sitting on my side table. If I close my eyes and hold on tight, then maybe—

"Hey, does anyone else see that?"

Anne-Marie pulls herself off the floor, tipping toward us in the seat and oblivious as she stretches over my head.

"The roof's gone, Anne-Marie. You don't have to use the window."

"I'm serious. Come up for air and take a look." She shakes my sleeve. "Is that light? I think it's light."

I look, but there's nothing.

"Where?"

"Right there." She jabs the glass with her finger. "There was a light. It blinked off."

"It was a reflection off the glass," Honoria says.

"No, it wasn't. It— There!" Anne-Marie stands up on the seat, putting her head through the open cage around us, where the canvas should be. She hoists herself onto the rails for a higher vantage point. "It's back!"

"Annie!" Trey shouts, scrambling to his feet in his own seat. "Get back inside."

Like that's any kind of protection.

"It's not a reflection," she insists, pulling on my shirt to get me to join her through the roof. I'd be furious except that she's right. Pale lights shine in the distance, not unlike the Grey, but they're not the sunlamps we use. These are ghostly, with rosy parts, and some are orange and yellow, like the bulbs on the Arc when they're about to fizzle. Pitch-black tree branches dip up and down in a distant wind, making them appear and disappear.

"What do you see?" Honoria calls up.

Tobin's standing now, and so is Mr. Pace.

"Security lights," Mr. Pace says. "Old school, no high beams."

"How far?"

"Mile, mile and a half, on your ten."

"You mean we made it?" Anne-Marie asks.

"Not yet, but we're going to," Honoria says. "Get on the floor and get your heads down."

She's moving before we have the chance.

Forward, back.

Forward, back.

Forward, back.

The truck tires tread the same line as Honoria tries to maneuver us to one side. Anne-Marie and I rattle against the canvas cover's skeleton, with our heads still poking through the ceiling, until there's a lull long enough to let go and drop.

Trey dives under the front dash, still hanging on to his rifle, while the men in the back tuck into balls with their hands over their heads. Anne-Marie slips back into her pocket between the seats, her face covered by her arms.

"What are you doing?" I yell at Honoria over the rumble of another pass.

She can't be doing what it looks like she's doing, because it looks like she's preparing to use a fallen tree for a ramp, to get us over the debris, and that's insane, even for a woman whose sanity I question on a daily basis.

Honoria grinds the truck into a different gear, changing the sound of the engine from its neutral hum to a roar. We're in the belly of some great, angry beast about to break free of its captors.

"You do realize there's no top on this thing?" Col. Lutrell asks.

"Hang on!" she shouts back.

Tobin and I slide onto the floorboard with Anne-Marie, squeezed so tight, I don't think we'll fall out, even if the truck flips.

I really hope the truck doesn't flip.

Every bit of jagged ground we cover slams against the bottom of the truck, making us hold on to each other tighter, and somehow, inside, Cherish coils herself around my consciousness so she can't shake loose.

"This is never going to work," Tobin whispers. "We're dead. She's going to flip this thing and kill us all."

"Shh," I hiss at him.

"We're riding on top of a tank of gasoline, Marina. Gas explodes!"

"Shut up, Toby!" Anne-Marie and I hit him at the same time.

We begin an incline, which means we're on top of one of the felled trees, and the shaking under the truck gets worse.

"This isn't going to work," Tobin says again. "It's not. It's—"

It's a moot point. We've left solid ground and tree, and I'm very happy I can't see it happen.

"We're dead," Tobin says. "Dead. Dead . . . dead . . . dead."

We hit the ground with a crash that makes us all scream together. The truck goes into a roll that has us hanging on to the seats, and one another, to keep from ricocheting off the doors, but when we come to a stop, my heart's still beating and the truck's right-side up. We're in a heap, with Tobin pinned against the door, me on top of him, and Anne-Marie on both of us. The girl may look like a twig, but she's heavier than cement blocks, and she's got bony elbows—one of which takes the air straight out of me.

"Are we dead?" Tobin asks.

If this is dead, I'm disappointed. We're still in the truck.

"Is everyone okay?" Col. Lutrell's voice calls from the back. "Tobin?"

"Still breathing."

"Annie? Trey?" Mr. Pace asks.

"I'm fine," Trey says from the front.

"Me, too," I say.

Anne-Marie starts screaming.

"Annie's fine," Trey says.

"No, I'm not!" She finally opens her eyes so she can glare at Honoria. "And you are a terrible driver!"

"I was fifteen the last time there were roads," Honoria says. "With all of one driver's ed lesson, I'd say I did pretty well."

From the back, Mr. Pace mumbles something about remembering why he blocked that class from his memory. He's got a cut on his cheek, and Col. Lutrell's rotating his wrist, like he's fallen on it. Honoria's got a red mark on her face from hitting the steering wheel, and my ribs are killing me, but other than that, it's scrapes and bruises.

*We heal*, Cherish intones.

I take that to mean that said healing is already in progress, so there's no reason to whine.

"Will the truck still drive?" I ask, hoping it fared as well as we did.

"This old girl hasn't lasted this long to give out on us now," Honoria says. "She'll get us where we need to—"

She's cut off by the sudden impact of a tree falling across the front of the truck. It hits so hard, the back end pops up, as though it might pitch fender over bumper, but it crashes back down, shaking us all into another shared scream.

We're dead in the water.

We're just plain dead.

# CHAPTER THIRTY-THREE

## MARINA

It's easy to think of the Wild-Fade as mindless. They have no will, no individuality, but as a hive, they're meticulous and methodical. Penning us in worked before, so they tried it again—modifying the attack so there was no chance of our duplicating our previous escape.

The tree's massive, more than enough to crush the front of the truck. Honoria tries the key again, but the engine won't turn over. How could it? She keeps trying until a hand reaches through the window to make her stop—Col. Lutrell. He and Mr. Pace had gotten out of the back and circled around.

"Enough," he says. She makes one more attempt, and he closes his hand on the key. "You've done enough, Honoria Jean. Let go."

It's another of those moments that remind me neither of them is who or what they appear to be. Honoria looks years older than Col. Lutrell and Mr. Pace, but they were already adults when they entered the Arclight; she was a kid. She takes a deep breath, and lets go of the key.

"Everyone out." Mr. Pace slaps his palm against the side

of the truck the way Col. Lutrell had earlier. "We've got to run for it."

"Run? Through here? On our feet with no truck?" Anne-Marie whimpers. "But those things are out there."

"This is why you should have stayed home," Honoria says bitterly. Mr. Pace is more patient. Maybe more patient than we have time for.

"We're sitting ducks, Annie. For now, we've got a few lights left, but once they're gone, that's it. And if the wild ones figure out they've crippled us, campfires and a few darts won't hold them back."

He opens the door for her, pulling her into the open. Tobin and I bail out on his dad's side.

Any safety afforded by the truck and its devoured canvas was an illusion, but I miss it. I feel more exposed. I'm breathing the same air, but it's fouler. Those ants crawling through my nerves are marching double-time, as though every cell in my body has started to vibrate, leaving me no choice but to shake.

"We're going to make it," Tobin assures me. He squeezes my hand, but it's little consolation, considering he was yelling about our certain demise a few moments ago.

The same doubt is in Trey's eyes. We've seen what's waiting in this deeper Dark. We know how massive and all-consuming it is. All the wild ones have to do is make one decision. They can drop from the trees or rise from the ground all at once. The only thing holding them back is habit and programming.

Or maybe they've developed a sadistic streak and want to play with their prey.

Getting out of here isn't going to be a simple matter of moving from point A to point B; we'll be running a gauntlet the whole way.

Occasionally, since I learned the truth of my origin, I've envied the Fade and some of their abilities—the strength, the speed, the connections. Right now, I'd trade all of them for the possibility of sinking into the ground in a billion separate pieces the way Rue can. It's Cherish's instinct, and knowing I can't do it leaves me feeling paralyzed.

"Why not light this place up?" Tobin asks.

"We're too far from the light, and Fade burn too fast," his father says. "We'd be running through an inferno. And you do not want to provoke a swarm. Trust me on that."

"Put these on." Mr. Pace hands Trey a wrinkled green field vest, and ones for me and Tobin. There's an ultra-bright lantern fixed to the top left shoulder of each. When the beams come on, the Fade pull back only as far as is necessary, churning in a mix of shimmering sludge, with no features or faces to tell us what they were before they were taken. Their bodies are too low to the ground for a human. They stand on all fours, with their back legs jointed backward to the front ones. Some have pointed snouts that drip with cycling nanites, like fresh-drawn blood in the maw of a predator. Some are smaller, with boxy heads and stubby legs.

They test the lights, stepping forward to see if they can push their advantage by another inch. Nanites sizzle and pop, like bugs against the Arc that fall sparking to the ground on collision. The smell's awful, but they keep trying.

*Inevitability*, that's the true nature of the Fade.

Anne-Marie's shutting down. She's so . . . I don't know.

She's moving slowly, as though there are weights or tethers on her arms and legs. Mr. Pace has to put her vest on for her, like the way she helps younger children in class when they get their buttons out of line.

"This is bad," I mumble.

"It was already bad," Tobin says. "I don't think Annie got that until now. She thought this was going to be like last time. Cute kids and happy reunions, you know?"

"Maybe she'll get better once we're moving," I say. Adrenaline will keep her focused.

Honoria and Col. Lutrell start pulling bags out of the back of the truck, tossing them to each of us in turn.

"I can't go out there . . . *I can't*," Anne-Marie says. The bag they toss her falls to the ground without her even trying to catch it. Trey picks it up and puts it on her shoulders. He buckles the strap around her waist, to make sure she doesn't drop it again. "We could barely stay ahead of them on wheels. They'll come as soon as we move."

"They'll come no matter what," Honoria says. From the look of things, she's about to snap. "Whatever fluke created the pocket of docile Fade around the Arclight hasn't spread. These are killers. Staying still only gives more of them time to arrive."

"Annie, listen to me." Mr. Pace stands directly in front of her, both of his hands holding tight to her shoulders. "We need to get to that light source before they attack again. You can do this. We've done it before, and we are not leaving you."

"The truck bought us a chance," the colonel says.

"Forget those things, and think about your friends and family," Tobin tells her. "You've gone into the Dark twice for us. You're fearless."

Anne-Marie nods along, trying to calm her breathing even as her eyes stay wide open and unblinking.

"Besides, the only one who really needs to worry is Tobin," I add. "We're both faster than he is."

That gets me a smile and a shallow laugh. I offer her my hand, and she holds tight enough that I can feel her pulse competing with my own through my palm.

Someone takes my other hand. I glance over, expecting to see Tobin, but he's still exactly where he was; my hand's gripped by empty air.

*Rue?* I ask silently, and my heart leaps with the possibility. *Are you here?* But he doesn't answer, and I can't see any shimmer-lines to suggest he's nearby.

I rotate my wrist to shake the drifting feeling of contact, and what I see when my jacket cuff moves chokes my breath off in my throat: Ornate lines circle my wrist like a bracelet. I feel the definite squeeze of another hand again.

*Cherish?*

*We will survive,* she says.

*How—*

I don't get to finish my question, or even decide if it's how we'll survive or how she's gotten strong enough to manifest like this. I'm afraid to ask her if I'm the only one who can see the lines.

Something hard and heavy drops into the pack on my back. I look back and find Honoria filling it with cans of water. A set of silver cases and that satchel full of the serum sit propped beside the truck as Col. Lutrell tears through the cargo space, tossing aside things that were essential when we left the Arclight but that are a burden on foot.

"Tell me you're okay, Annie," Mr. Pace says, shaking her shoulder.

"Can I carry a dart gun?" she asks, trembling.

He almost laughs with relief.

"Yeah. You can carry a dart gun."

He leans forward and kisses her on the forehead. I've never seen him do that before.

"Each of you take two of these," Honoria says. She's on her knees with one of the silver cases flipped open. "We've still got a couple of resources—and we are *not* losing our heads. Understood?"

She glances up to me and Tobin and then to Anne-Marie, waiting for us to nod.

"What are they?" I ask as she hands me a slim metal cylinder with a cap on the top. It's heavy and has an odd smell I can't place. Cherish doesn't like it.

"Flares," Tobin says, taking his.

"Anything gets close, and—" Honoria hits the base of the cylinder with her palm, igniting whatever's stuffed inside. Sparks and blue-hot flames burst through the capped end. "Do not drop it. The flare won't burn out before we're through, and if worse comes to worse—"

"What's worse?" Anne-Marie squeaks. "How is there a worse?"

Mr. Pace has retrieved the serum bag from the pile and handed it to her. She's got it hugged to her chest like a security blanket.

"They can't include anything that's burning into their hive," Honoria says.

"You want us to set ourselves on fire?" Tobin pales and rolls his shoulder automatically.

"No," his father answers, but it wouldn't surprise me if that's exactly what she means.

"If there's no alternative, you make the call you have to make," she says. "These flares burn hot and clean; it won't take more than a second. It'll hurt, but—"

"They're kids, Honoria," Mr. Pace breaks in.

"No, they're not! Not from the moment they chose to leave '

the safety of the Arclight and come after us." It's funny. The last time they argued over what we should and shouldn't be told, they were each on the opposite side, with Honoria arguing that there were things we didn't need to hear. "Stop trying to coddle them, and we might give them a chance to grow up." She looks to me, Tobin, Anne-Marie, and Trey, all standing in a clump. "You do what you have to in order to make it through this, and we'll deal with the aftershocks later."

She turns back to the ruined truck and throws the lit flare inside before striking another one.

"Move out. If we're lucky, the fire will hit the fuel tank before they figure out how to douse it. We don't want to be in range."

If we're lucky, it'll be the first time.

# CHAPTER THIRTY-FOUR

## MARINA

We aren't running. Not yet.

We're tiptoeing across a sheet of ice, while loose nanites crunch under our feet like the first cracks of an early thaw. My legs want to run so badly that it hurts, but pace is key. As long as we hold steady, and Honoria keeps that flare burning, we sidestep the coming melee.

Nanites roll under our feet, and we try not to flinch—even when they grab hold so that we have to kick them loose. A formation wraps itself around my boot, tugging back when I step forward. Tobin takes my hand and pulls, but the wild-Fade hold fast until Trey strikes the column with the end of his rifle as he passes, sending them back to the ground. Honoria waves her flare at them, and they scatter.

*Are they going to attack?* I ask Cherish. *Can you tell?*

*They do not speak to me.*

The truck should have blown by now, shouldn't it? How long does it take for a flare to burn through metal?

Long tendrils of moss and vine slip from the branches overhead, uncurling into our path at a lazy roll. It drifts back and forth, attempting to look accidental in the breeze that brings it close to our faces. Anne-Marie tries to move the one tracking her by blowing on it as she watches it from the corner of her eye.

"Easy," Mr. Pace whispers, wary of a possible panic attack.

He's watching his daughter the way she does the Fade. Beads of sweat have already gathered at her temple; soon they'll be spilling down her cheeks and nose, dropping to the forest floor.

The vine nearest Anne-Marie refuses to move, matching her progress inch for inch. She blows harder, cringing, and it still remains.

"Easy, baby girl."

"I can't breathe," she whispers back. "They're too close. I can't move when everything's this close."

"She's gonna lose it," Tobin warns, like I don't already know that.

Another flare hisses to life in Honoria's other hand. She holds it behind her and waits for Anne-Marie to take it. Anne-Marie lets go of my hand and holds it tight. Under her breath she hums the songs she uses to keep the babies in line in class.

"Everyone turn left," Honoria orders, keeping her eyes straight ahead as she motions for us to go right.

The Fade aren't fooled; they follow along.

Honoria's aura is dancing, cascading from bright to dim, wide to narrow, as far beyond her control as moths buzzing a lightbulb. Her injuries from the crash must be worse than we know. The nanites are replicating to fix them. Col. Lutrell and

Mr. Pace are stable, but Honoria's veins glow blue through her pale skin. I wonder if her eyes are shining, too.

The fall of crystalline moss that's shadowing Anne-Marie begins to flutter and trill. She raises her hand an inch, like she's going to bat it away, and I catch her hand. The ones who took Silver ate my gloves. Leather's nothing but dead animal matter.

"Don't touch them," I tell her.

"I don't want to touch them; I want to melt them." She swats at them with her flare. "Get them away from me," she bites out. Her free hand has a death grip on the dart case's strap. "Get them away. Get away!"

Trey and I move together. I hook one of her arms and he takes the other, so she's stuck between us and the Fade can't reach her. They fly into a fit, rustling and shaking with an awful racket that knocks nanite-encrusted leaves from their branches.

"Where's our explosion?" Tobin asks. "It should have gone off by now. This is weird."

"No weirder than that," Trey says. The path lightens in front of us.

It seems like an impossible mirage. Moss feelers recede into the trees, leaving our path free of obstructions. The coasting leaves fall back up.

"What's happening?" Anne-Marie squeaks.

"Something's drawing them off," Mr. Pace says.

The ground turns brown and rocky beneath our feet as the nanites there skitter away. They peel off trees and stones, leaving us with the eerie silence of a storybook wood in an enchanted sleep.

"Is it the other people?" Anne-Marie asks. "Did they find us?"

"We're in Fade territory," Honoria says as Mr. Pace and Col. Lutrell sweep the trees overhead with the red scopes from their rifles. "Whatever this is, it isn't human."

Cherish stirs to life inside my mind, opening shutters and raising the shades on our connection to the others.

"It's Rue," I say. The knowledge blooms up as a warm spring in my chest, confirmed by Cherish's agreement.

"He came back?" Tobin asks.

"He never left. None of them did." The block's gone. I can feel him, and Bolt and so many others. They've stayed out of range and out of my sight, but the wild-Fade could sense them, and so they've tread carefully. Now they've made their presence known in full, aggressive force to take the focus off of us. "They're giving us an opening."

"Then let's not waste it," Honoria says. "Go!"

We charge off, crashing through bushes and low-hanging branches. Overhead and underfoot, the flow's still in progress, but we proceed unhindered.

"They're going back the way we came," Tobin says, ducking to avoid the lower limbs. "Why would Nanobot be drawing them back to the truck?"

*The surest way to create silence is fire,* Cherish answers bitterly, adding the inferno she uses as Honoria's name to the end. *Ours will see their voices go silent. Ours may go silent with them.*

It's a horrifying version of Honoria's method for controlling the nanite population in her body.

Step one: create a disturbance to catch their attention.

Step two: draw them to a common point.

Step three: burn them out.

"The truck's about to go." The words fall out of my mouth in time with Cherish's breaking heart, and mine shatters, too.

Rue left to guard our retreat, waiting for the opportunity of greatest value. He knew I'd try to stop him—all of them. They're willing to die for us if helps right the balance thrown off in the early days.

*You should have told me*, I charge Cherish.

*Ours requested my silence.*

*Then you should have told them no!*

Free will works both ways. Humans have it, and so do Fade. Cherish shouldn't have to stand by and watch what she loves disappear any more than I should.

I grind to a dead halt, and the others don't leave me behind.

"Rue!" Out loud, or in my head, what does it matter at this point? "Answer me!"

He does, with one word: *Run!*

"Marina," Col. Lutrell asks. "Can you hear—"

His voice disappears beneath the rumble of an explosion.

A bleak and aching chill flows across the divide between me and Cherish, coming in the wake of a searing flash of heat. I cross my arms over my face to block the light, but it doesn't do much good. I feel the pain of agonizing death and hear the harmony of the hive stumble over gaps where there were once voices. Cherish forces it all into my head, as though she wants to imprint my soul with the cost.

"Rue!"

*Run,* he says again. *They are coming. We will follow.*

He urges me forward, willing me to find the speed I possessed as a Fade. The wild ones not consumed by the truck's sacrifice have realized the ruse.

"They're coming," I say as we scramble into motion again.

"Our Fade or the other ones?" Anne-Marie asks.

The answer comes as an enraged stampede. The wild ones stream into view, disoriented and tattered, swarming inelegantly without the cohesive motion of a hive. We're at the center of chaos, fighting our way out of whirlwind.

Cherish leaves the connection open. Weaker than it was when the hive welcomed me home, but enough to know Rue and the others aren't letting the wild ones go without a fight. Their well of shared strength flows into my arms and legs, turning my muscles to honed steel and reminding my feet how to race.

I am movement. I am speed. I am wind's current moving effortlessly from here to there. I'm definitely faster than a human girl should be. What I'm not is alone. Tobin and Anne-Marie have never left me behind; I won't abandon them.

*Stubborn,* Rue accuses.

*Just get here!*

The wild ones aren't touching us. Even without the truck or many weapons, they keep their distance. This hive could obliterate us, so why hide behind cheap intimidation tactics?

What's going on?

The ground begins to tremble, vibrations so strong they override the effects of adrenaline. More wild-Fade vault into what had been a clearing. A row of identical creatures forms; they look nearly human on the top, but the lower half is a huge four-legged something that has to weigh at least half a ton. Hot breath snorts out long snouts, tossing tiny plumes of nanites with the air. Their front feet paw the ground with the hollow whine of nanites grinding against nanites.

We're hemmed in.

"You've got to be kidding me," Mr. Pace says.

"Since when do they have cavalry?" Col. Lutrell asks, stunned.

*Cavalry.* Horse soldiers. These Fade are fused versions of horse and rider, twisted incarnations of the pictures in our history lessons.

A flare ignites to my right and another to my left. Mr. Pace and Col. Lutrell throw two of the slim canisters into the nanites pooling on the ground. They become a lake of fire, only going out when the hive withdraws, leaving the unfortunate to burn. Nearby, I hear a zipper opening one tooth at a time as Anne-Marie tries to reach for one of the serum guns without drawing attention to herself.

The creatures rear up, churning the air with hooves that drip nanites like blood from an open wound.

Honoria lights another flare and pitches it at the lead creature's chest.

It becomes a candle set alight, fire racing along its spine to catch its hair and tail. The nanites turn to molten bits and blow away, as though the creature underneath has shaken itself free. There's no scream and no twitch to its muscles as it falls—only a pair of ghostly white corpses whose skin hasn't touched the sun since the Fade rose.

"How can you be smiling?" Tobin asks me.

"Because they're here," I tell him.

The tide's turning.

Rue's Fade descend upon our enemy like angels of death. Eyes shining through the Darkness while their skin blazes with reflected firelight.

Rue, and those like him, born with nanites in their blood, are at a decided advantage. They go to pieces, crumbling away and reforming just long enough to inflict damage before dissolving again. They're faster than the wild ones, more agile. The wild ones try to strike, but hit air, the same way the Arclight's security forces could never seem to wound them.

Those like Bolt, who were human first, are slower but far from helpless. They're more evolved, and they have connections that go beyond the hive bond. They fight to keep those connections alive, and purpose is a mighty advantage.

Dog and Whisper move in perfect sync, with the grace of gifted dancers, each filling in the weaknesses of the other. And I see another familiar face—one I've only seen once before.

"Is that a general look of shock and awe, or did the nanobot tell you something I'm better off not asking about?" Tobin asks. He lights his flare and hands one to me.

"It's my father."

Cherish throws open every conduit, stretching toward the stoic Fade who guarded Blanca at their settlement. She reaches for his constant nature, striving to touch his voice so he can hear her, too. It must work, because he searches for me as he fights for us.

He nods at me, sending a sharp, curt: *Mine.*

My father came for me, and called me his, and that's enough for now.

I make my stand beside the rest of the humans, backing toward the lights we saw and whatever safety we'll find there.

Mr. Pace and Col. Lutrell fire their rifles, keeping the wild ones dazed with random bursts of sound.

"We're almost clear!" Honoria shouts. "Torch it!"

For Honoria, fire's familiar. It's been her guardian since she was a teenager, and she's not careful with it. She strikes another flare, flinging it into the trees so close to her brother that he has to dodge back. A fire blossoms where it lands, catching dry grass and wood and creating another obstacle the wild ones won't touch.

Anne-Marie lets the dart case hang around her neck and lights a second flare. She runs with the live ends pointed out, skimming the moss and weeds as she goes, blazing a trail in the most literal sense possible. And we run. Human and Fade together, flying away from the wild ones as the fire spreads.

It races up the trees and vines, toward the canopy that creates the upper limit of the Dark. An outer crust made of layers of nanites long dead from continual exposure to the light shields the lower levels. It's baked granite hard on the outside, but in here, it's tissue paper.

The canopy cracks in the heat, dropping bits of itself into the fire below.

"James! Elias!" Honoria shouts. She points up, her fingers in the shape of a gun, telling Col. Lutrell and Mr. Pace to aim for the canopy. Her pistol doesn't have the range to hit it, but their rifles do. They fire until they're out of ammunition.

The Dark crumbles around us, blowing away on the night air, so that in the end we don't escape—we're spit out. Unpleasant food the Dark no longer wants to taste. Fresh air, clean and cool, replaces the grit of ash, and I can breathe again.

# CHAPTER THIRTY-FIVE

## MARINA

"We survived," Tobin says, incredulous as he tries to catch his breath. Smoke from the blaze has created cover for Rue and his hive mates, but the wild ones don't risk following us out of their territory. They run in the other direction, widening the safe zone. Without them here, the fire won't burn long.

"How are we alive?"

He's on his hands and knees, beyond the burning Dark. I've got singe marks on my uniform, and a couple of holes where embers burned through. Trey's heaping dirt onto his pant leg, where a flare caught the cloth. Anne-Marie's lying on her back, staring at the sky. Everyone's smudged with ash.

"They're afraid of us," I say.

"Oh, yeah. Obvious terror," Tobin says. "I must have been thrown off by the fact that they kept chasing us!"

"They think we're contagious."

I struggle to interpret more of what I see through Cherish as she connects to her people. There are references to Honoria and how she burned herself. The wild ones know her. They know about Mr. Pace and Tobin's father and every human who ever injured himself to remain outside the hive. Rue's people broke away and closed themselves off.

Through Cherish's hive and Dante, the other Fade know about me and how I was taken out of the whole.

"They think dissent is a disease, and we're all carriers" I say. "They want to include us, but they're afraid it will spread like a plague and others will fall away." We'll bring chaos to their order. "They were only willing to risk herding us to keep us contained, or scare us off, but now—"

I stare into the smoldering Dark.

"Now we've drawn blood," Tobin says. "They'll retaliate."

When night falls and they're no longer confined to the Dark.

We may have survived the trip here, but they'll be waiting for us on the way home.

Mr. Pace is attempting triage. Whisper's on the ground beside him, shaking as she holds her arm up for inspection while Dog sits vigil, balanced on the balls of his feet.

Whisper's clothes have changed configuration. Camo-colored bits are stuck to her arm where the nanites forming her sleeve melted to her skin. The rest are gone.

*No pain*, Rue says.

Her nanites can trigger enough endorphins to keep her comfortable. She'll just have to wait for the skin to scar. She reaches up and touches the scar that crosses Dog's scalp, and he shakes his head, probably telling her hers won't look so bad, but theirs is a private conversation.

Bolt and my father stand to the side, hands clasped, also speaking amongs themselves. My father glances over at me and nods again. He hasn't even said my name—either of them.

"I need something for bandages and a sling," Mr. Pace says, and I shrug out of my jacket.

"You'll be good as new in no time," he tells Whisper.

"No, she won't. The nanites there are gone," I say quietly to Tobin as our teacher empties a tube of burn gel onto Whisper's arm. "She'll never get them back."

"It's better than dying," he says.

"Their voices have ceased," Rue says.

"Nanites replicate. She'll get new ones."

*But their voices have ceased*, Rue repeats, only to me.

*I know.*

*The ceased don't return. They are ceased.*

*I know.*

It's not better than dying. It *is* dying. Whisper will never be completely who she was before, and there's not a single human here who understands that. They should, our elders especially, but the nanites are still parasites to them, squatters in bodies to which they have no right.

Would Mr. Pace think things were "less" bad because one of his children died instead of both? Would he be thinking forward to a replacement for Trey or Anne-Marie? Would he forget they existed?

They have no idea what Whisper, or the hive, gave up to

help us. They are diminished and cannot reclaim their former number.

"Are you crying?" Tobin asks me.

I wipe my eyes and walk away. Rue follows me. The grief's too great to stay so close.

Before us is our prize. Looking at it, I can't believe it's worth the effort it took to get here.

"Is that it?" I ask Trey.

"I thought it would be bigger."

"Me, too."

The building's still standing, and it's outside the boundaries of the Dark, but I expected it to be like the Arclight. There's not even a real buffer; the lights aren't bright enough to make one.

There's nothing green here. No arbor or garden to provide food. The ground's covered in poured cement, but even that's marked with deep fissures where it's broken over the years. Scorch marks tell of likely battles in the past, where fire protected the people here like it did us.

"Let's move," Col. Lutrell says, slipping a pair of shades over his eyes to hide the silver color.

"Is she mobile?" Honoria asks, glaring at Whisper as Dog helps her to her feet.

"They move together," Rue says.

"But will they be able to keep up? We can't stay in the open."

Rue looks to Bolt and my father, now sharing their conversation with Dog and Whisper.

"Ours will watch from here. I will see inside," he says, looking up. He checks the sky, where the smoke's banking into drifts. "If danger ventures out, they alert me and I alert you."

"You're going with us?" I ask.

"I go with mine."

Honoria clenches her jaw, but by now, she knows she can't change his mind. Besides, it's hard to think of a convincing argument against the guy who just saved us from the Dark.

"Move out," she says.

Honoria stalks off toward the cement walkway in front of the Ice Cube, with Mr. Pace and Col. Lutrell behind her. Trey and Anne-Marie follow their father.

Whisper and Dog, my father and Bolt, and the others who survived break into teams of two and spread out so they can watch all sides of the perimeter at once. One by one, they blink out of sight, surrendering their true forms to the texture and color of their surroundings.

"Shouldn't that be your cue?" Tobin asks Rue.

"I go with mine."

"Maybe, but that doesn't mean we have to look at you."

Rue's marks stretch and flatten, taking a bit more of his features with each inch as they expand. Soon, all that's left is a shimmer-line where the edges of his body warp the light.

"Tobin! Marina! Keep up!"

The colonel's shouting at us. Our group's stopped a few meters off, waiting.

"We're coming!" Tobin shouts back.

We turn away from the Dark.

"You don't have to be so awful to him," I say.

"As long as he stays out of sight, I won't be."

I bite back my argument. The cement walkway is one of those places where speaking seems like a very bad idea. It's cold and dirty and gray. The closer we come to the fissures, the clearer it is that they're not cracks from age or use. Something broke through the ground, and inside the holes left behind, it still wriggles just enough to make itself known. The Dark is here, a great sleeping beast below our feet.

Our group packs in tight, moving fast. It doesn't take long to cross the walkway, but every step comes with the certainty that something's watching.

"Is anyone else creeped out by this place, or is it just me?" Trey asks as we climb the front steps.

His words are met by the whine of sharp wind swirling between us, and the crash of a piece of debris falling from the roof.

"Definitely not you," Tobin says.

Definitely.

# CHAPTER THIRTY-SIX

## MARINA

The door opens easily. I expected a barricade or guards, but it's not even locked. I wish I could convince myself that's a good thing.

I shift my pack as we cross the threshold.

"Tighten the straps," Tobin whispers.

He grasps my pack at one shoulder and pulls the slide so the strap shrinks down.

"Thanks."

I hadn't needed to adjust the straps. Moving the pack was just something I could control.

Suddenly the other strap shrinks to match the first, making Tobin scowl.

"That isn't invisible," he snaps, then goes ahead to inspect one of the piles of debris scattered around the room.

"You can't do that, Rue," I say.

"Talking to him isn't invisible, either," Honoria says without looking down. She turns sideways, cutting between Rue and me.

*Repentant*, Rue says. *Tibby's solution was incomplete.*

*Be more careful. Maybe they'll forget you're here.*

*Maybe you'll forget, too.*

*Never happen.*

*It already did.*

He stops talking, and at first I mistake his silence for a reminder that there was a time when I *did* forget him. But he's only doing what I asked—he's being invisible.

*I never forgot,* Cherish insists.

"Marina," Anne-Marie calls. "Get over here."

She's keeping to the space between her brother and father, still bunched up and shaking like she's got a sour stomach.

*Compromise?* I ask Rue before I move, sending him the image of a hand grasping my pack strap the way students hold on to one another's uniforms during class drills.

*For now.* He tugs on the strap, and we join the others.

The Ice Cube's entry is a central junction where all of the building's passages meet. The off-shoot halls are straight, turning around corners in the distance. A cement wall brackets off a set of stairs leading to the upper levels. Each side of the entry is flanked by a glass wall that's caked with grime and age. There are rooms on the other side, visible through the broken frames.

There's light here, but not bright. Col. Lutrell and the others ignite the point lamps on their rifles to add a few feet to what we can see. Everything's the color of dust.

The Arclight's a palace compared to this. I can't imagine feeling safe here.

Trey's light lands on something reflective in a swept-aside

pile of debris. I lean closer, until I can make out the shape of a dented cup. Tobin bends down, poking at a child's shoe. It's as dirty as everything else, but the same pink as my walls and Blanca's flowers, so I put it in my pocket. I need all the good thoughts I can find.

"There's nothing here," he says.

"Don't be so sure." While the rest of us are focused on the ground and the walls of this level, Honoria's looking up, scanning the ledges of the rusted safety rails above. Something's caught her attention.

Thankfully, she's refrained from shooting at it.

I nudge Cherish, hoping she'll oblige in the use of her senses, but all she says is: *The sound is not ours.*

Does that mean we're alone, or is she telling me there's something lurking in the shadows? If there's anything worse than the wild ones out there, I don't want to know.

"You kids stay put and stay together," Col. Lutrell says, following Honoria's line of sight. "We're—"

"You're leaving us?" Anne-Marie cuts him off.

"We need to check the rooms," Mr. Pace says. "But we don't know how stable this place is."

"And we don't know how stable *Annie* is," Tobin whispers low enough that only I can hear him.

"The fewer bodies in motion, the better. Stay with your brother. We need to see where we stand."

Mr. Pace starts down one of the hallways while Col. Lutrell

eases his way around the broken glass to enter one of the rooms here in the entry. Honoria takes the stairs, treading gingerly until she's over our heads, boots clicking across what I hope is a sound floor. Her weight could bring the whole thing down on top of us.

"I don't like this," Trey says, once they're gone.

"Me, either," Anne-Marie echoes. "I feel like we're being watched."

"We are," Tobin says. "By the transparent tagalong." He grimaces at an empty spot in the room, reconsiders, and aims his disdain somewhere closer to me, trying to hone in on Rue. "This place is dead, Annie. Not even cockroaches."

And yet, at the first unexpected noise, we move closer to one another, backs to the center, so someone's looking in every direction. Tobin takes my hand on one side, and while I'm not going to hold on to someone who can't be seen, and risk exposing him, I don't object when Rue tugs my pack again.

I also don't object when I feel his hand on my back. I tell myself it's a concession to keep Cherish quiet, but that's a lie I'm finding harder to believe. *I* want Rue with us—I didn't realize how much until I thought he'd gone. It's not just Cherish he makes feel safe, and knowing Rue's got my back can only help in the long run.

"I can't breathe in here," Anne-Marie says. "It's too hot. The air smells weird."

Vile would be more accurate. It's definitely not the

ultrapurified air from the Arclight, where the only thing that smells are the animal pens, and we both avoid those.

But the air quality isn't half as disorienting as the lack of running commentary. Normally, Anne-Marie would be chattering nonstop to use her own voice as a distraction. It's too quiet here.

"Hot's a good thing, right?" I prompt her, so some of the weirdness will evaporate. "It means they're keeping the heat on."

"It's hot because we're not in the Dark, anymore," Tobin says. "That's all."

*The light is weaker here*, Rue tells me, disagreeing with Tobin's assessment. *It doesn't burn.*

For the strangest moment, Rue is both visible and invisible to me, as if each of my eyes is seeing things slightly different. I can't see him, but Cherish can. She's trying to show me something, and she's trying to make me understand his point.

"What'd he say?" Tobin asks, tugging on my hand to get my attention.

"Huh?"

"You're doing the blank stare into nothing, which means Nanobot has something to say. And you can tell him that I know exactly where he's standing."

Tobin scowls in Rue's general direction—so general, it's probably a guess.

*This light won't repel the Darkness*, Cherish says, to make sure I understand. *But the Darkness hasn't followed.*

"The lights are too dim to hurt Rue," I say. They aren't sunlamps like the Arclight's perimeter or Red-Wall blinders. "The wild-Fade haven't come inside, but it's not the light keeping them back. This place isn't abandoned, and they know it. I can feel it."

"Me, too," Anne-Marie says. She's biting her nails, clicking at her teeth with her thumb.

"You feel your nerves, Annie," Tobin insists. "And you're making the rest of us jumpy."

"It's a safe bet that if this section's sound, some of the other overhead lamps should work," Trey says. More of Mr. Pace comes through in his voice and mannerisms. He's been methodically inspecting our corner of the entry, shining his light up into the ceiling and tracing cracks along the walls. "Spread out, but keep in sight. Test whatever switches you find. Maybe we'll get lucky."

He reaches for one mounted on the stairwell, only to have his hand seized by black-gloved fingers before he can flip it. Honoria's leaned over the side to grab him.

"Careful," she says, releasing his hand. "I wouldn't trust the wiring around here."

She comes the rest of the way down the stairs, then stops to inspect the switch panel. It's nothing but a dummy that comes away easily when she slides her finger under the wires hanging out beneath it. She tugs gently and the wires pull loose, exposing a painted-over knot of more wires, with leads that run up and around the door frame to continue on down the hall.

"Someone set a trap?" Trey asks.

"Or rigged an alarm." She nods. "There's no way to tell without following the lead lines. For now, we'll stick with the 'don't touch' approach."

"Still think the place is empty?" Anne-Marie asks Tobin.

"We don't know how long that's been here," he says. "It could be ancient—from the first days."

"That's not ancient," Honoria growls.

Something I've learned from the way Cherish, and even Rue, consider the world is that the longer someone lives, the less time means to them. Perceptions of a day in relation to a week or a year warp until the words lose meaning. It's easy to pretend they don't exist at all, but here, the clock never stopped. No one's kept it clean enough to foster the illusion.

A piece of glass snaps on the wall opposite us as Col. Lutrell climbs back through the broken window. Mr. Pace returns light on steps so he's practically tiptoeing.

"The office is nothing but old furniture and trash, but there are disturbances in the dust that look like shoe prints, so not likely Fade," Col. Lutrell says.

Rue agrees; Fade hate the restrictive nature of shoes.

"They've got the door wired." He looks around. "I'd say the place is staged—a few things left in plain sight, meant to draw people through where they can be contained. But the display hasn't been kept up for a while."

"Nonexplosive, then?" Honoria asks.

"Contact magnets set against the door frame, possibly a hot wire to stun whoever activates it—fairly rudimentary. It's similar to the setup we had on the supplies for the first few years back home. When you're not sure who's friendly or how long your goods will hold out, it's best to take new faces and grabby hands out of the equation."

Honoria nods. For this conversation, no one exists other than our elders. We're just the dumb kids in the background who nearly tripped the alarm.

*We don't use alarms,* Rue muses. *Everyone is welcome to home.*

There are no locked doors to his Fade. They live a shared existence where there's always enough to go around. All it takes is teaching one a fact or a skill for all of them to learn it.

*You watch for the Darkness,* I tell him. *You don't let the wild ones pass unannounced. Alarms announce for us.*

"We've got what used to be the science labs down that hall." Mr. Pace twitches his head back the way he came. "The gas lines are hot. There's no way the municipal systems are still active, not with downtown and most of the outskirts under the canopy. Someone's got their own sources, and they're keeping them online."

"So someone's here," Col. Lutrell says.

"Someone's here."

"Then where are they?" Tobin asks.

"Hiding," I say. "It's what we'd do. If a group of people walked into the Arclight, we'd be in the bunkers."

"A group this large would never make it into the Arclight," Honoria insists.

I don't bother to pass along Rue's rebuttal. He shows me Fade who've been inside the Arclight's boundaries more than once since the lights went down. It was the only way they could be sure the wild ones hadn't breached the perimeter.

Now I know why the cats down there were so fond of me and mistrustful of Tobin—they were carrying nanites.

I also know that Rue came with them. He was there almost every night while I was on duty in the Arbor. How could he come that close and not tell me? Cherish mourned for weeks, thinking he'd left her behind. How could he not tell *her*?

"As long as they think we're a threat, we won't see anyone," Trey says.

Anne-Marie breaks from the group and plants herself in the middle of the entry, where she can look up to the other floors.

"Hey! Is anyone up there? We're friends! We—"

Trey dashes over and covers her mouth. She shoves him off.

"What?" she demands. "No one else had any ideas."

"Shut it, Annie."

"Make me."

Honoria's already sour mood gets worse. She glares at Trey and Anne-Marie, then Mr. Pace.

"Fix that before we can't," she says.

Mr. Pace nods, somewhere between exasperation and embarrassment. I've seen their mother shut down a full-scale temper tantrum with one look and zero words from across a room, but they don't even register his presence. Maybe this is the first time he's ever had to referee them.

"You're a blink older than me," Anne-Marie snaps at Trey. "You can't tell me to shut up just because the color of your sleeve patch changes."

"*I* can, and *I* am," Mr. Pace says. "Quiet—both of you—or the next time either of you sets foot in a nursery class, you'll be there as a student, naptime, diaper and all."

Sibling discord turns into a block of solidarity. Anne-Marie and Trey stop shouting at each other and direct their mutual scorn at their father. It's another of those weird displays where they look so different and so much alike at the same time— feet planted and eyes narrowed, as if to dare Mr. Pace to act on his threat.

"Nice try," he says. "But I've been dealing with teenagers longer than both your ages combined, not to mention dealing with your mother. I'm immune to the hate face. Get back to the group before I decide to tell her about this when we get home."

Both of them snap to attention, and Anne-Marie's back with me and Tobin without any further argument.

"You didn't really think that would work?" I ask her.

"It could have." I can hear the desperation in her voice, and fear. "If they're worried that we're some kind of invasion force, shouldn't we at least try to tell them differently?"

"They won't believe you. Not when the Fade can take any face they want."

Assuming the hosts' faces have survived all these years beneath the nanite shell.

"Oh. I didn't think of that."

"We need to move," Honoria says. "We can set up in the lunchroom, if it's still here."

With Col. Lutrell and Mr. Pace in agreement, we wander off as a group down one of the halls at the far side of the building. Unlike the others, this one doesn't have doors along the wall. There's only one room, at the end.

This lunchroom looks like the Common Hall, with one large area full of tables and chairs, only less clean and more chaotic. Nothing matches. Everything here's been salvaged and tossed together. Honoria unstraps her bag and drops it on the nearest table; the rest of us do the same.

"Check the kitchens," Col. Lutrell says. "With power and gas, they might have provisions. We might as well use the time until dawn for something productive."

"We can't just steal it," I say. "If there are people here, they need it."

"Unless someone wants to come forward and make themselves knows, everything's fair game," Honoria says. "Settle in."

Trey sits at the table with our bags near the wall.

"I'll do an inventory. See what made it and what we need to replace," he says.

"Good," Col. Lutrell says. "We'll start searches in teams of two—one of us and one of you."

"That won't work," Tobin argues. "There's four of us, three of you, and one of him."

He jerks his thumb to a random spot in the room where he thinks Rue is standing, but Rue's not there.

I don't need Cherish to tell me that; he answers out loud from the space between me and Tobin: "I stay with mine."

"You're not supposed to talk." Tobin tries for intimidating, but he's unnerved from hearing Rue's voice so close—something Rue doesn't miss.

*Tibby is scared again.*

Fade aren't much on facial expressions, but if I could see his face, I'd bet there's a smug grin to go along with that statement.

"We can stay with the bags," I say. "It's safer if Rue doesn't go exploring."

I can imagine finding someone and having to explain a floating dust blob following us. Rue may be invisible, but the stuff that settles on him isn't.

Tobin's got a comeback ready, but as he starts to speak, new lights switch on overhead—white hot and bright enough to startle us all as they blare on and off rapidly.

"Strobes!" Col. Lutrell yells.

Rue and Cherish scream louder.

# CHAPTER THIRTY-SEVEN

## TOBIN

Rueful hisses from the sudden flash. The rest of us hit the floor. This isn't the Common Room, but it's close enough to trigger our usual response to danger—hide under the tables. I pull Marina down beside me.

"Where's Rue?" she asks.

"I don't know," Annie says. I shrug.

I couldn't see Rueful before the lights came on; I can't see him now.

The lights are disorienting. They're faster than ours and starker, giving every movement a choppy, half-frozen appearance.

Reflective panels—no, people wearing reflective clothes—fill the doorway. Honoria doesn't miss a beat; her pistol's out of her waistband and in her hand, pointed at the closest target. If this happened at home, she would have dropped three of them by now.

Marina looks like she's in pain.

"Close your eyes." I squeeze her hand. With my other, I reach for Annie, who's hanging onto Trey's trouser leg to keep him close.

I hear Trey's gun slide lock into place.

"Nobody shoot," Annie shouts. "We're friends."

"There aren't any friendlies left," a man's voice shouts back.

"We've got kids, here," Mr. Pace says, quickly. Dad hurries to back him up.

"We came here looking for help."

I hope he still has his shades on. Of the seven of us here, three have the light blue eyes that peg them as Fade-touched; his are silver. This is already going bad enough without having to explain that.

"Our weapons are for self-defense."

Dad slips the rifle strap off his shoulder, using his thumbs to lift it without touching the gun. He drops it onto the nearest seat. Mr. Pace lowers his weapon to his side, then makes a motion behind his back like he's patting something down. Trey places his on the floor.

Honoria doesn't budge.

"Who are you?" the man's voice demands. "Where'd you come from?'

"We're happy to talk, but we'd rather do it face to face," Dad says.

"I can see your faces just fine."

"We're human." Mr. Pace steps to Dad's shoulder. "We received information that there was a group hiding here."

"What information?" The man separates from the group, entering the room. He's small for an adult; Dad could take him easy. His clothes are ratty and dirty; his shoes don't even match.

"Long story, but we're willing to tell it."

"Blood first, then words," the man says.

Mr. Pace cuts a slash across his palm. The man examines the blood, then looks to Dad.

"What about you?"

Dad holds his hand out, and the man nicks his finger, watching the blood as it gathers.

"And those two?" The man points the knife at Trey, then down at Marina. "Where'd they come from?"

"He's my son," Mr. Pace says.

"And she's with me," I say, shifting my weight so Marina's crouched behind my shoulder.

"What about before she was with you?"

"Another long and complicated story," Honoria says. To my complete surprise, she replaces the hammer on her pistol and puts the gun away at her back before holding a hand out to the stranger. "Shall we tell it?"

He's hesitant. Shaking her hand means taking one off his rifle, but he's wavering. We're human, and he's probably never seen strangers.

"Cut the lights!" He swipes his fingers in front of his throat, and the flashing stops.

One by one, the people in the doorway creep inside, only to clump together in the lunchroom's main space.

"They're kids," Trey whispers.

Aside from the speaking man and three others, most of them

are our age, and behind them, there's a group whose ages have to still be in single digits. They look awful.

This can't be everyone. How would they have the wild ones nervous?

"Annie," Mr. Pace calls. "Show yourself. Tobin, Marina—you, too. Show them we're not an invasion force."

Annie crawls out the end of the table. Marina and I come over the seats.

"He's here," she whispers, and I know she means Rueful. "He's okay."

She squeezes my hand and I squeeze hers back. Let her think I'm happy for her—at least if he's guarding her back, he's got mine by default.

"See?" Mr. Pace continues. Honoria finally puts her hand down without shaking the man's. "They're kids. *Our kids.* We're trying to keep our kids safe."

"Where'd you get your supplies?" the man asks.

"We brought them from home."

"No one comes through Death. It's impossible."

"Not easy," Honoria corrects. "Not advisable, but possible. Unfortunately, we lost our transport on the way in. I don't suppose you have any working vehicles here?"

I don't think they have much of anything.

"Hey!"

Everyone's attention turns to Trey when he shouts, then to the girl who skirts his grasp to slip under the table and out of reach.

"Get back here, you little thief."

But she scrunches up, guarding something.

Annie snaps back to herself and slaps Trey in the head. "That's not going to work, idiot."

She kneels down on one side of the table, waving Marina to the other in case the kid tries to make a break for it.

"Hi there," she says.

The girl's tiny and mostly hair. It falls long and wild, hiding her face and body except for the hands holding whatever she took, and her feet.

"Can I see what you've got?" Annie asks. "There's some sharp stuff in my brother's bag. I don't want you to cut yourself."

The girl sweeps her hair behind her ear on one side, peeking out with deep-set, dark eyes. She's shy, moving so timidly that I'm afraid one of her people might intervene if we don't hurry up and coax her out.

"Come on, baby, let me see what you took."

The girl looks down in her lap before hoisting her treasure into view. Annie grins, crawling backward until she's clear of the table's edge. She gives the room a thumbs-up,

"No worries," she says. "She snagged a jar of peanut butter."

"*My* peanut butter," Trey complains.

"Your stomach will get over it," Mr. Pace says.

The man says something I don't understand, repeating himself louder when he gets no response. The girl scrambles out, bringing the jar with her. Reluctantly, she hands it to him and slouches back to the others.

Annie acts like the guy's a student and she's in class. She walks right up to him and twists the top off.

"It's peanut butter," she says. She holds the lid close to his nose, then sticks her finger inside the jar and scoops up a taste for herself. "It's good."

"It's food?"

"It's high protein, easy to carry, and doesn't need cold. Good for survival rations," Honoria offers.

"They brought food?" a boy's voice asks from the crowd.

"It's yours if you want it," Honoria says.

The man sets his rifle aside, so he can pull the hood off his face. Like the girl, his hair is dark, long and tangled. His eyes are hard and brown, and he's not smiling. But he lifts the jar to his nose and takes another sniff. He dips his finger in for a taste.

It's like someone flips a switch inside him.

"You have more of this?" he asks hopefully.

"We can make more. We grow the nuts and crush them."

"You have crops?"

"We've had to get creative with the space we have, but we've done all right," Dad says. He signals for Trey to hand him his bag, which he passes to the man. "Everything in here's edible. Take it."

The kids from the doorway are closer now, some stepping up on tables for a look over the others. They make a pitiful security force.

The man takes Dad's bag as he hands off the jar for them to pass around and taste.

"Can we talk?" Honoria asks.

"I think we'd better," he says, sinking into the nearest seat.

She holds her hand out again. "Honoria Whit."

"Hector Ramirez," the man says, taking her hand. "Call me Rami."

# CHAPTER THIRTY-EIGHT

## MARINA

"We don't live here, not normally," Rami says. "This is an emergency fallback position. We can't hold it much longer."

He's spread the things from Col. Lutrell's pack out on the table in front of him, picking at a cracker packet while he talks. Another adult, a woman, touches the end of her finger into a can of protein powder, then brings it to her tongue. The others sniff at containers of dried fruit and shake vitamin bottles.

"It's never been easy, but we were doing okay. Then a little over a month ago, there was a surge. No reason. No warning. Those things came boiling out of Death like someone poured hot water on an anthill."

The Arc went down less than two months ago. Did we cause the surge?

"Where are the rest of your people?" Col. Lutrell asks.

"Scattered. It was my job to get the kids out. I got them here safely and went back. I've picked up a few stragglers, but the Homestead's obliterated. We were preparing to relocate to our secondary site when our lookouts reported the fire. I hoped you were some of ours, but—" He stops and shakes his head;

exhaustion whittles his face into something drawn and haggard. "We don't set fires much anymore. They always make things worse in the end."

That doesn't bode well, considering the blaze we set.

"Where will you go?" Col. Lutrell asks.

"Why?" another of the adults asks suspiciously.

"You've got nothing we want," Honoria says. "Relax."

Rami scoffs.

"A group of armed strangers walks through Death with supplies I thought were myths my grandfather made up, food, clothes that look new—" He bites back something he refuses to say. "We're a step above stone soup. You came here looking for something, lady, and if there are more where you came from, you could destroy us as easy as the Killers to get at it. This is as close to relaxed as we can afford."

"This isn't going well," Trey mutters.

He, Anne-Marie, Tobin, and I have been banished to the kiddie corner, sitting at the end of one long table. Rue's beside me, his hand on my shoulder. Rami's kids are at another table, staring at us and talking among themselves.

I'm the only blonde here. No one besides our group have blue eyes—even the ones with light and reddish hair have brown or dark green. Trey and I are getting a lot of curious glances. I don't know what they'll do if the colonel loses his glasses.

I wish I could mimic my surroundings to change my hair and eyes the way the Fade change their clothes.

"They can't keep us here," Tobin says.

"We'd be suspicious, too," I tell him.

"No, I mean they aren't capable."

"He's right," Trey says, leaning in. "I'm surprised they've survived at all if this is the extent of their facility."

I don't know. Those strobes seemed pretty effective to me.

"Maybe they've got their own secret base underground like we do."

"A secret base without food or working showers?" Tobin asks, tossing a disdainful look at the others as they try to scrape more peanut butter from the empty jar.

He doesn't like being treated like an outsider. He's not used to it, and for Tobin, the unknown is met with derision. I should know—it's how he treated me in my first days inside the Arclight.

When I was isolated and untouchable, Anne-Marie risked sharing a meal with me. It could have cost her friends, even her safety for all she knew, but she did it. Maybe the same tactic will work here.

"What are you doing?" Tobin asks when I stand. He clamps down on my hand.

"Trying to convince them we know how to smile."

He gives me a mock-laugh, but doesn't let go of my hand until I make him.

"You're not going over there alone," he says.

"No, I'm not."

Rue's with me, and Cherish.

"Stay here, Tobin," I tell him. "They can't see Rue. You've been glaring daggers at them since they appeared. Which one do you think makes for a better impression?"

"Fine, but be careful," he says

Rami's kids tense up as I approach. The bigger ones stand up, flanking the smaller without saying a word, but I don't bother with them. The one I'm interested in is the little girl with the long, dark hair, who's made a fist inside the peanut butter jar. She's banging it on the table because the way it rattles on her hand makes her laugh.

She's kicking her feet off the edge of her seat, missing one shoe identical to the one I found in the entry. I take its mate from my pocket and hold it out. She stops kicking, but one of the older boys shakes his head, and she slumps. I set the shoe on a seat, turn, and walk back to my own table, watching over my shoulder. Once the girl decides I've gone far enough, she snatches her shoe and runs.

"Was there a point to that?" Tobin asks.

"I gave her back what was hers. Besides, she reminds me of Blanca."

"Only because she's short."

"This is why you should stay home when we go to meet people. Right, Anne-Marie?"

Normally, she's the first to call him out for being a creep, but she's sitting by the wall, with her back against it and her knees pulled up to her chin. She gives no indication that she can hear me at all.

In Cherish's eyes, she starts to dim as a stifling depression sets in. The bright colors the Fade originally attached to her dull.

"Annie?" Trey asks. A sickly sweet amalgam of concern hovers around him, more intense the longer she stays quiet.

"I want out of here," she says finally. "I can't stand it. I just want them to stop talking and let us go home, but I don't know how we'll get there. What if we have to live here forever?"

"We won't. It won't be much longer."

He doesn't get it. Anne-Marie's being crushed by reality closing in on all sides. There's nowhere we can go that she won't always know the wild-Fade are out here.

I'm so focused on the meltdown I expect at any second that it's a surprise when Rue nudges me.

*You have visitors.*

It's a curious way to put it, as we're actually the strangers here, but the little girl from the other table is standing two seats away, holding the hand of the boy who wouldn't let her approach me before, Both of her shoes are back where they belong.

"Look, Annie, a kid," Tobin says a little too enthusiastically.

"Seriously—stop talking," I say.

Getting Anne-Marie out of her fog is going to take more than a curious little girl.

"Hi," I say to the girl. "I'm Marina. What do they call you?"

*Peanut,* Rue suggests.

*You stop talking, too*, I tell him.

The girl reaches for my braid and pulls it, so I'll bend down and let her whisper in my ear.

"Your name's Noor?" I ask.

She nods happily.

"She wants to know if you have any more of that," the boy with her says. He points to the jar, which is still on the girl's other hand, and she shakes it at me. "The rest of us want to know why your hair is white."

"It grows that way." I shrug. "My body doesn't make the stuff that gives hair its color."

Slowly, two others from their side of the room straggle in, trying to find ways to peek around him without being fully in the open themselves. A girl my age with a serious face glares at me, like maybe she knows it's our fault the wild ones attacked. The other one, another boy, just looks hungry. His face and his eyes carry an emptiness that goes deeper than his stomach needing food.

These kids aren't surviving; they're pictures taken at the point of death.

"You were born like this?" the first boy asks.

"What's it to you?" Tobin asks, crowding closer.

"You ever see what happens when a Killer burns?" the boy challenges. "All the black stuff melts off. What's left behind looks like her."

*We are not a killer.* Cherish fumes, boiling through my blood like a fever. This would be the absolute worst time for me to find out if I'm the only one who can see the random patterns that appear on my skin when she's upset.

"If she was one of those things from in the Dark, you'd already know," Tobin says.

"I still want to hear her say it."

"I'm not a Fade," I say.

Any longer.

"Is she okay?" I nod to the girl whose serious face has changed. She's staring off at the corners of the room, grinning as though she's seen the most beautiful thing in the world.

"She's as good as she gets since the surge."

Noor pulls my hair again, shaking the jar at me, in case I've forgotten what's really important to her.

"I think Trey's the only one who packed peanut butter, but how about these?" I tell her, fishing through my bag for the container of dried berries I brought along. "They're my favorite."

I pick one out of the container and offer it to the boy, figuring he won't let Noor eat something on my say-so alone. He pops it into his mouth and starts chewing—then his eyes light up. He reaches out for the container automatically, but draws his hand back just as quick.

"You can take them," I tell him.

He grabs a handful as he passes the container to Noor. Like the boy, she's hesitant to taste the first berry, but after she has, dashes back under her table.

"I think she likes them," Trey says.

"I guess she does."

Trey resumes his position as our leader by default and stands up to introduce himself.

"I'm Trey," he says. "The grumpy one's Tobin. Marina's the blonde. This is my sister, Annie. She'll never be this quiet again, so enjoy it."

His attempt to rile her fails.

"Michael," the boy says.

He introduces the other boy as Javier and calls the girl Gina. She's drifted off into her own world, walking two steps one direction and turning to go three in another, swaying to music no one else can hear and laughing at things that aren't there.

"She'll do that all day. You get used to it."

No, I don't think I will.

"Where'd you really come from?" Michael asks.

"We call it the Arclight."

"Is that New Mexico? My folks said there used to be people in a place called New Mexico, at a university."

"That's out west," Tobin says. "We're east."

Gina's watching us again, cocking her head like she's tuning an antenna between our conversation and our elders'.

*She's listening,* Cherish says.

"Is it a prison? We heard there were some prisons in the northeast that survived. All cinderblock and cement."

"It's a military base."

Michael keeps firing questions, and Trey and Tobin keep answering.

Something here isn't right.

Our elders are still negotiating with Rami. Most of Rami's kids are still at their table. Noor's given up the berry container, and they're passing it around.

Javier has taken the seat across the table from Anne-Marie. He drags one of our bags closer to inspect what's inside. He takes out a knife, flicks it open and shut before stashing it in his pocket.

Rue's exactly where he's supposed to be, holding his tongue while keeping an invisible hand on my shoulder.

Things *seem* fine, but they're not.

Tobin leans in close and whispers, "Where's the ink blot? I think that girl's tracking him." He cuts his eyes at Gina, who's gone creepy-still beside Javier. She's fixated on the spot over my shoulder where Rue's head would appear, if he was visible. "Tell him to move; I think she can see him."

"She's lost her mind, Tobin. Don't stare."

If Rue moves, he could create a shimmer-line, and *that* everyone could see. It's too much to risk because one girl's gone spacey.

*Affirmed,* Cherish says. *Gina has gone Spacey Tracey. Hide. Flee. Conceal.*

Spacey Trac—

*The girl from Honoria's book?*

*Affirmed. She's listening.*

"Gina?" I call her name out loud; she turns the fraction of an inch it requires to look me in the eye, and but it's enough. The irises of her eyes are running with vertical lines of metallic gold.

She's turning.

# CHAPTER THIRTY-NINE

## MARINA

"Gina, listen to me," I say cautiously. My hands are up, noncombative. "I know you're confused, but you don't want to hurt anybody."

*Flee.* Cherish cries. *Run.*

My legs tingle as I stand, nearly giving in to her commands, but I make myself walk closer. If I can reach the real Gina, maybe she'll fight for herself before she's consumed completely.

"I know you can hear me. Fight *them*."

"Marina?"

Tobin steps forward; I wave him off.

"Get help," I tell him. "If she snaps, she could end up feral, like Dante."

If she was looking anywhere else, I'd say open the door and let her run, but she can see Rue. She'll run straight at him or straight at me.

"Gina, we'll help you. Back up and sit at the table."

Her chest rumbles with an all too familiar growl.

"Okay, no talking . . ."

Crap. Now what?

*Flee*, Cherish says.

*She'd be on top of us in two steps.*

"What's wrong?" Michael's stopped grilling Trey for information. The remainder of the Ice Cube's children have joined him, closing ranks to protect one of their own.

"Don't touch her," I warn Javier when he tries to coax Gina back among them. "She's turning."

"That's ridiculous," Rami says. I hear him approach from the adults' table. Hopefully, our people are with him. "We would have noticed. She's been with us for days."

"Has she been distant?" I ask him. "Talking to herself, wandering around like she's stepped outside reality?"

"It's called shock."

"It's called *inclusion*," I snap. "You *did* notice. You ignored it."

Like we did with Dante, until it was too late.

Our alliance ends before it has a chance to gel. The Arclight's people form a line on one side and the Ice Cube's on the other. Gina and I are stranded in between. At least Rue's still with me.

"How can you be sure?" Rami asks.

"She can't," Honoria answers for me, as though she's afraid I'm going to cite Rue as my source. I'm not that stupid.

"Her eyes are turning gold," I say. "Listen to her. She's growling." Every person from the Ice Cube—except Rami— backs up a step.

Rami doesn't know what to do. He's probably known Gina since she was born. Sentiment can be as lethal as a bullet.

"When you found her, was she wounded?" Honoria asks.

She turns her head, gauging how far she is from the weapons we surrendered. All of them are out of reach except the rifle Rami never put down and the silver pistol she refused to give up.

"She came in on her own, but the only blood on her was from someone else."

"Didn't you screen the survivors? Check for branching? Anything?"

"I know a human when I see one," he says. "Gina! Get over here where you belong."

But she *doesn't* belong there anymore.

Cherish shows me the grid of blue lines growing inside Gina, strongest at her pulse points. If I could see her back, I know there'd be a Death Tree in full bloom.

"Gina!"

"You've got to get her isolated," Honoria says. "We can give her a shot to beat this, but—"

*"Beat it?"*

Rami pulls up short. He looks from Honoria to Trey to me. Back to Trey. Back to me.

"What did you do?" he asks.

"We have a serum," Honoria says. "It's not perfect, but we've tested it, and—"

Gina shrieks, high-pitched and horrible; her expression turns hateful. She launches into the air as nanites flood her skin, appearing and receding like kinetic bruises.

"Rue, don't!" I shout out loud because it's not going to matter if the others hear me or not. He's let go.

Gina's becoming a Fade, but Rue was born one, and he's a lot better at using Fade abilities to his advantage.

By all appearances, she hits a pane of glass and crashes back with the wind knocked out of her, but once he's got her on the ground, Rue's focus splits. He can't restrain her and keep up his camouflage at the same time. One has to go—and there's no way he'll give her another shot at me.

"Oh, this is so not good," Tobin says.

Rue's camouflage blinks like a faulty connection in a wire, revealing his presence to the rest of the room. He's sitting on Gina's legs, pinning her hands down by the wrists, over her sleeves and through his robe, so she can't scratch him, but his presence triggers the wild-Fade's self-defense mechanism. The same black protrusions that came out of Silver shoot through her skin and clothes to ward him off, knocking her unconscious. He lets go before they can touch him.

"She needs to be contained," Honoria tries, but it's futile. You can't just pretend there's not a Fade in the room.

I understand now why "getting stunned" is called that. A pulse goes off through the room, with Rue and Gina at its center point. It passes through everything—concentric rings of electric current that freeze everyone where they stand. The air's buzzing with it, creating confusion in those who aren't prepared for what they see. All they can do is gape and scream.

"I'm sorry," Rue says nervously. "I cannot aid her."

*Repentant. Apologetic. I cannot change the outcome. I desire to change the outcome.*

He tries to convey how sick he feels, but even if I pass his anguish along word for word, they'll only see a monster hovering over someone they love.

"We can deal with this, but you have to act," Honoria says, trying to keep Rami's attention on her. "The nanites are going to replicate double time to deal with the damage to her body."

Below the surface of Gina's skin, thick glowing lines of nanites wind through her veins, flowing into her tissues.

"Gina?" Rami calls. I think he knows she can't answer.

I pull out of Tobin's grasp despite his tightening grip, and reach for Rue, to draw him to his feet.

*Run,* I tell him.

*I'm sorry. Attempting aid won't be successful.*

*Get yourself out of—*

"Get away from that thing!"

Rami swings his rifle up, locking tight against his shoulder. People are always trying to shoot me.

"He's not dangerous." I say.

"You brought that thing?" Rami asks. His hands are sweating so much that they slip on the rifle. "You knew it was here?"

"Calm down." Mr. Pace's voice is softer, less threatening and more rational.

"He won't hurt you," I say. "He was protecting me from Gina, that's all."

"Get away from it." The rifle shakes in Rami's hands.

"No."

*Rue, get out of here. Disappear and run.*

*You run; I run.*

*I can't leave.*

"I will not abandon mine," Rue says out loud.

His marks are in motion. Responding to his agitation and temper, the nanites tighten across his skin and clothes. There's definitely no way to miss the change in his face, where the lines become finer and sharper. The silver bands in his iris widen out, a signal to beware.

"What was that you said about branching, lady?" Rami asks.

Cherish chants *guard* and *protect*, calling out to her hive mates, but they're too far away. She and I stand in their place. Together, we are unmovable.

A rock unmoved by water.

Rue's arm closes around me.

Honoria's hand goes to her back, and for once I'm glad she's got that stupid pistol on her.

"Do something," Anne-Marie calls out to Mr. Pace.

Rami's focus snaps to where she's standing with her brother.

"There are an awful lot of blue eyes in this room," he says, staring at Trey before turning back to me and Rue. "Nothing much on its own, but I've never seen anything like you, girl.

Nothing but what crawls out of a Killer's skin when it's dead. I've never seen anything like him."

He fires.

I actually see the shot emerge from the flash off the end of the rifle. Nanites explode from Rue's skin at the same time to create a veil around us both.

He pushes me down until my knees and hands hit the tile below us. The bullet strikes the veil and deflects, but the resonance of impact shimmies across the weave, passing along thin wires that disappear into—*my* skin?

"Not possible," I say, staring at my hands. They're covered in whirling Fade-marks, connected to the veil. Where Rue's hands are wrapped over mine, the lines mingle into braided cords, stronger than one created by a single Fade.

I lay my hand against the veil on the inside and feel it pulse with the heartbeat Rue's played for me a dozen times or more. On the other side, Tobin lays his hand palm-to-palm against mine.

"Marina?" He's looking at my face.

Are there marks on my face, too? Can he see the ones on my hands?

My *Fade* hands.

I was human two days ago.

Cherish is singing. A wordless song of unbound joy and relief fills my head, drowning out screams of horror as Rami fires another shot. The impact resonates along the veil, but Cherish is still singing. She has what she wants.

Rami's at a loss. The third shot has no more impact than the first two. Col. Lutrell pounces on his hesitation.

One quick strike to his side, and Rami crumples enough that Col. Lutrell can get his hands on the rifle at the stock and barrel. They grapple for it, but the colonel has better leverage, and gloves that protect his hands from the heat off the barrel. He wrenches the rifle from Rami's hands, sending the smaller man sprawling.

He also loses his shades.

Honoria stands over Rami, her arm outstretched with the pistol in her hand, pointed at his head. I still hate that thing, but I'm starting to appreciate its advantage.

"We are *not* your enemy," she says. The creases in her face are shallower than they used to be; her complexion's brighter. That can't be right, a person can't age backward . . . but she is. "So long as everyone keeps their heads, we will remain *not* your enemy."

Rue takes that as his cue to stand. The veil shrinks in. My stomach sinks when half the nanites slide into my hands, and I can't help but hide them behind my back.

Cherish will *not* win. I will *not* wither inside my own body. I search for Tobin's hand and hang on tight.

*My choice*, I tell her stubbornly.

All she does is remind me that I haven't stepped away from Rue. I made that choice, too.

Rami, still on the floor, doesn't blink.

He and Honoria are mirror opposites, matter and antimatter on the verge of detonation.

"We're going to do what we can to contain that child," she says. "And you are going to stop pointing weapons at the people trying to help you. Understood?"

Rami stands, pushing up from the ground with his palms, staring at Col. Lutrell's face. He was wary of blue eyes; silver are worse.

"I suggest you say something," Honoria says.

Honoria gets her answer, but it's not what she's hoping for. Rami pulls his lip in under his teeth to create a long, variable toned whistle. His people spring into action, and we're not ready for it.

The Arclight concentrates on defense, making sure nothing can break through, but these people expect a breach. They're prepared to face a swarm. They don't hold their ground; they attack.

Groups of them encircle each of us, pushing, pulling, shoving, keeping us stumbling as they jostle us. The complete randomness of the assault works in their favor. It's not a fight in the traditional sense, but we're losing.

"Stop!" Anne-Marie cries somewhere to the left.

"Annie!" Her father and brother call out.

"Tobin!"

"Marina!"

"Trey!"

"Dad!"

They separate us, nudging us in different directions. I try to grab for Tobin or Rue as they're taken away, but I can't get my arms up. If we were outside, Rue could return to the ground, but in here, they'd trample him.

The only one not participating is Rami. He crosses the room and covers Gina with his coat, so he can carry her out. I barely get a glimpse before a jab in my side sends me spinning.

Trey's still with me, not close enough to touch, but we're being herded the same way. He tries to get his arms around one of his captors, for leverage or a shield, but another hits him in the face, knocking him backward and most likely unconscious.

Anne-Marie disappears from view, dropping to the floor; I follow suit, thinking I can crawl out between their legs, or topple someone, but I only fall halfway before I'm caught and propped back up.

My head's pounding, the room spinning from the constant motion. Everything I see flickers with spots of light and dark. It all ends with a sharp crack against the side of my head.

This time when I fall, no one stops me.

# CHAPTER FORTY

## MARINA

I dream of the desert. Or maybe I'm dead, and heaven is sitting on the sand under a night sky. The stars swirl and fall to the ground as pieces of silver I can pick up in my hands. They're so bright, I know that they'll protect me from the monsters, but there are no monsters here. The desert's safe. The desert's secret. It's protected by stars and sun and moon.

It burns.

Heat comes first, and then the light as I open my eyes. My whole body aches with the dull throb of an old wound brought to life.

This feels familiar. Hospital lights glare like this. Maybe we've made it home.

"Doctor Wolff?" I call.

Out of habit, I reach for my long-gone inhaler to quell the rhythmic ache inside my skull. It's beating harder than my heart.

"Doctor Wolff?"

But no. The beating pain is shaking things loose, including my last moments before I was in the desert. Now, I'm slumped against the wall, with a crick in my shoulder, not lying in a bed.

There's no IV stand or pinging machines, and the pounding isn't my pulse. It's broadcast through the air and floor. Here, wherever here is, the light's solid, hard and unyielding. It crushes me into the wall and grinds the air from my lungs.

*Cherish?* I try, but every thump and vibration destabilizes her.

The room's a near perfect rectangle with built-in shelves and stacked chairs. One wall's nothing but windows. Beyond it, smoke from the Dark still hangs thick and black over most of the sky, but it's definitely daylight.

I must have been out for hours.

Sunlight filters through every pane; they've done something to the glass to amplify it. Bits of highly shined metal have been fixed to every wall, reflecting everything back to the middle. Speaker boxes near the door keep the low-level hum going to make any possible communication between Fade and hive difficult. It's a low-tech White Room.

A whimper comes from the far side of the room. Someone hiccoughing after a crying jag.

"Anne-Marie?"

"Marina? I thought you weren't ever going to wake up!"

"You okay?" Trey's sitting with his sister.

"Yeah. You?"

"Peachy."

Anne-Marie moves closer, on her hands and knees, but doesn't get to the center of the wall before something stalls her progress. She tugs on a chain that's cuffed to her arm before shoving Trey in my direction with an order to "go hug her."

When I try to move, I find a metal cuff encircling my own wrist and burning like a lit torch; it's attached to a line bolted through the glass of the window wall. It's not long enough to really go anywhere, but I can inch closer to Trey. He seems to be the best off of the three of us. His lead's in the middle, so he can go from side to side.

"Where are we?" I ask.

"Upstairs guest room, courtesy of Rami's bunch," Trey says. "They think putting us in here until sunset will tell them if we're dangerous or not."

"Where's everyone else?"

"Other rooms, I guess. This one only held three."

"How long—"

A triangular shadow appears on the floor, enticing as the hallucination of water in the desert heat. It grows long across the room as someone opens the door. Cooler air breezes through, and the vague shape of a person forms.

"Who's there?"

"It's me, Michael."

He steps forward, and the jittering thump from the speakers cuts off. In my head, Cherish slumps, as exhausted and dizzy from it as I was from being prodded by the people who knocked me out and locked me up.

"Tell me it's true," he says.

"You have to let us out of here," I say instead.

"I just need to know if what the woman said is true," Michael says.

"You mean Honoria?" Trey asks.

This could be bad. Honoria and truth aren't categories given to much overlap. Who knows what she's told Rami's people since they split us up.

"Were you really a Killer?" Michael asks me.

"Marina's never hurt anyone," Anne-Marie answers.

"Is she lying about the cure? If that woman gives Gina the medicine, will she be like you and the other one?"

"You mean Rue?"

Cherish flies into a panic, firing questions at me, but I have my own. Did Honoria tell them Rue was a transitioning Fade? Did she dose him to demonstrate the serum? Does Michael know anything at all?

"Rami doesn't trust her, but that other thing doesn't look much like a Killer anymore. It doesn't act like one, either. Something happened to it. If it was really a cure, then tell me. Rami will let that woman fix Gina."

"Yes, I was born a Fade," I tell him, standing up to move closer. "Yes, Honoria used that serum to make me human, but—Ahh!"

I pull too far, and a sharp pain cuts through my wrist.

"Sorry," Michael says. "I didn't think the sunburns would come so fast."

When I first opened my eyes and looked at my hands, all I could see was the stark white of reflected light. I dismissed the sting as an effect of the handcuff. I can't believe I missed the glowing pink and red splotches.

"You didn't put that girl in a room like this, did you?" Trey asks.

"It's the only safe place."

"She's too far into the change. If you've exposed her to extreme light and heat, the nanites will die. They'll poison her."

"The woman said you use light as a deterrent in your hospital."

"In a controlled environment! With a doctor and medication!" I pull forward, but the handcuff won't let me get closer. Michael still steps back. "You know what sunlight does to a Fade—you're killing her!"

"Gina can last until sundown. Then she'll be cured and your friends will be released."

"Friends?" Anne-Marie asks.

"Michael, where's Rue?"

I got sunburns; Rue will get worse. The veil won't hold. His nanites will die in the light. If he loses enough, he'll die, too.

"I'm sorry," Michael says, backing toward the door, nervously. "Rami will keep his promise—I swear. It's only a few hours."

"Rue won't last hours!"

He's gone. The shade from the door disappears, resealing our cell into an endless cubicle of light. He was in such a hurry to get out of here, he didn't even turn the speakers back on.

"Michael, get back here! Michael!"

The cuff's cut into my wrist. I can feel the blood as it slides. It drips on the floor, but knowing it's red is small comfort.

"Hey!" Anne-Marie shouts. "Do I need to have Trey smack you, or will you snap out of this on your own? You're shredding your hand."

"I don't care."

I truly don't, not when Cherish is screaming for Rue so loud, she's making my throat hurt. Snatches of her time in the White Room spill across the barrier between us. I can smell the charred skin and singed hair; the unmistakable odor of Fade-rot stuffs itself into my windpipe with every breath. If Rue's in a room like this, he's burning. And if Tobin's in the same room, that means he's locked in and chained beside a Fade who won't be in his right mind.

A Fade who already can't stand him.

I brace my feet against the glass and pull with everything I've got, but it's useless. Rue's going to die down the hall and a locked door away from me.

"We don't even know if one day's enough to kill him. Toby said the archives on you ran for almost a week before they took you out of the cage."

"That was because of the serum."

I switch tactics, slamming my feet against the window glass to kick it out, but it's too thick, or whatever they've treated it with makes it unbreakable.

"Hurting yourself isn't going to make things any better."

*Escape. Flee. Find.* Cherish says, showing me Rue's face.

She's settled under my skin, like insulation. Another layer of consciousness that wasn't there before.

*I'm trying!*

*Attempt without success is unacceptable.*

*I'm open to suggestions.*

*Seek them beyond us.*

She expands, spreading her plea for help beyond the barriers of my mind. Cool water drifts into the room, ankle deep, and only experienced by me. There's a stone in middle, forcing the water to flow around it.

"What is it?"

Anne-Marie and Trey and I are as close as we can get in the middle of the room. They're watching me as I listen to things they can't hear.

"It's my dad."

*Remove the obstacle,* he says, and my bloodied hand begins to heal. I wipe the blood away on the side of my pants to be sure, and I witness the last of the cuts knitting shut.

"Whoa," Trey says.

"Good start. Now what?" Anne-Marie asks as though this is completely normal.

*Remove the obstacle,* my father repeats.

I've seen born-Fade change shape. Maybe he wants me to try that. I stare at my hand, willing it to shrink.

"Is something supposed to be happening?" Anne-Marie asks.

"It's not working," I say, shaking my arm.

*Your focus is misguided.*

*The cuff won't go over my hand.*

"I can't remove it," I add out loud.

*The water goes around what it can't move,* Cherish chimes in. *It doesn't fight what it can't best.*

I stare at my hand again, watching the nanites form lines at the cuff to cover my sunburnt skin. I cup my other hand over them to shade them from the light.

*Stop fighting,* Cherish says. *Don't pull back. Release. Don't shrink. Expand. Don't doubt. Trust. Trust me. Trust yourself.*

*Remove the obstacle.* My father says one last time. He calls my name—all of it, from the joyous wind that marks me as an adventurous soul, to the rebellious crash of waves against rock, for the times we've disagreed. And he calls me Cherish— Beloved, Adored, Embraced . . . *Missed.*

He calls me Marina.

*I'm* the obstacle. *I'm* what's standing in the way.

I stop reining Cherish in, and let go. And it's not the unconditional surrender I feared. I'm still me.

*We are Marina,* Cherish amends. *We are Cherish. We are free.*

Nanites flood the cuff, picking at the locking mechanism and hinge; it falls to pieces—useless.

"You have got to show me how you did that," Trey says as I rub my wrist and head for the door.

"Maybe later," I say, laying my hand against the door to let the nanites—*my nanites*—deal with that lock, too. Having them run off the ends of my fingers doesn't feel like anything at all. It's a nerve pulse I wouldn't even notice if I wasn't looking for it.

"Marina! Let us out!" Anne-Marie tries to whisper and shout at the same time.

"Not yet."

The lock clicks. I nudge the door open, slowly with my foot. Michael's still here, across the hall, jiggling doorknobs to make sure they're secure. Thankfully, he's got his back to me.

A pair of women who had been in the lunchroom walk down the hall with Col. Lutrell between them. Neither of them glances at my door, but Col. Lutrell does. He locks eyes with me. A momentary startle gives way to a pointed look at a door down the hall before one of the women notices.

"Your kid'll be fine come sunset," she says.

They march out of sight, leaving Michael by himself.

"Tobin and Rue are two rooms down on the other side," I say as I ease the door shut. "Michael's alone out there."

Anyone who would enter a locked cell without permission or backup has no business being left on watch, but inexperience and carelessness works for me.

I knock lightly on the door, then harder when there's no response.

"You don't really think he'll—" Trey says, but then the knob turns. "Oh. I guess he will."

Michael's head pokes through, looking in cautiously.

"Hello?"

He's not worried yet. Trey and Anne-Marie are still tethered. He can see them, and so he assumes all is well, but when he tries to shut the door, I pull back and hold it open.

"What—"

He comes farther into the room to see what's in the way. His eyes are wide open when I swing the door and smash him in the face with it so that he stumbles back, holding his nose.

I set my feet and curl my right hand into a fist, in an imitation of Tobin's fighting posture. When I throw my weight into the punch, Cherish throws hers, too.

Michael goes down, stunned enough that all he can do is roll side to side on the floor. I snag the keys out of his hand and toss them to Trey so he can release himself and Anne-Marie.

"I don't like being locked up," I tell Michael, and kick him in the side.

"Me, either," says Anne-Marie. She gives him one to match.

We shut the door behind us, and run.

# CHAPTER FORTY-ONE

I crack the door Col. Lutrell showed me, and stagger back. Fade have died in this room.

When an included voice falls silent, there's a signature left behind. Feedback. An echo. That remnant's here. More than the few voices Whisper lost' this is a colony of nanites. A whole person's worth.

Maybe it's old, but it feels as fresh as a ripped-away bandage, and only one Fade was locked in here recently.

Cherish is already calling out to Rue, fretting over the lack of an answer, but the speakers have her spinning again. They're making me nauseous.

And why hasn't Tobin said anything?

"Shouldn't it be brighter in here?" Anne-Marie asks.

She's right. Heat roars out of the opening, on par with what we felt in our own cell, but toward the left corner, farthest from us, someone's built a blockade in front of the window.

The crude lean-to is made of broken shelves and chairs, with other bits of unused material laying scattered on the floor. Sections of hammered metal have been pried loose from the reflective walls, but they've been abandoned in favor of one long strip that came completely off.

"Marina." Trey nudges my arm and points.

"Tobin!"

He's kneeling, half falling from the top of the lean-to.

"Tobin!"

He still doesn't answer.

"Cut the speakers," I tell Anne-Marie, and start for the pile. "If Rue's hurt, he won't be able to heal with that racket."

"How long do you think he's been like that?" Trey asks.

"All day." I'd bet my life on it—and Rue's.

Tobin's cuffed arm drags sharply down on one side, cutting into his skin so deep that there are trails of dried blood where the wound has closed and broken open throughout the day. His other arm steadies the piece of sheet metal braced against his back and shoulders, and tilted toward the window to prevent sunlight from filtering through to where Rue's hiding inside. He's turned himself into a human sun shield, balanced on the top of the stack and blocking the light from above.

*It's enough*, I tell myself. Tobin's determination and Rue's resilience have kept Rue safe. It has to be enough.

"Tobin," I call as Anne-Marie guts the speakers behind us and the room falls silent. He's about a foot over my head. "You can come down now."

"M-Marina?" He blinks. "Am I hallucinating? How—"

"Escape now, questions later." I jingle the keys at him. "Let's go."

"But—" He glances from the window to the pile of chairs under his feet.

"Rue can handle the light long enough to get to the door."

He moves stiffly, after hours of keeping his muscles tensed in a single position. Trey reaches up to take the piece of sheet metal, and the entire structure groans.

*Tear it apart*, Cherish says.

*It could hurt Tobin.*

*Reassemble him later.*

She's joking—*I think.*

Tobin lets the sheet metal slide off his back so that it hits the floor. He moves his weight to one foot and jumps, dislodging two chairs as he goes. When he lands, he holds his chained wrist up so I can unlock the cuff.

"Tell Rueful we're even," he says, wincing when it comes loose. His wrist is mangled below the cuff.

"You're insane for even thinking about standing up there like that," I tell him.

"Nanobot would have fried without a shield. He never made a sound, but it was like I could feel him baking in there. I had to cover the gaps, but the metal wouldn't stay in place unless I held it. Pretty stupid, huh?"

"Not stupid." I shake my head, lean over and kiss him. "Brilliant, and amazing."

"Less kissing, more rescue." Trey claps his hands the way Mr.

Pace does to call for attention in class. "Thank him when we get home."

Tobin laughs, but I feel myself turning red. He reaches his hand up for help getting off the ground but groans as soon as someone touches his hand.

"I don't have anything to put on it," I tell him. I'd suggest letting Rue help, but that's probably not an option.

"I'm still better off than her." He turns his head to the other side of the room, and so do I.

Gina's dead.

She could be sleeping, the way she's lying on her side, knees tucked in with one hand stretched over her head, bolted to the wall. But her eyes are open and murky. Ashen Fade residue surrounds her body. When the nanites died, and the protrusions that ripped her skin crumbled, she bled out.

"Is she—" Anne-Marie falters when she catches sight of Gina's body.

"She's lucky," Tobin says, accepting Trey's offer of a hand up, now that he's caught his breath. "Those things started jumping left and right looking for a new buffet table. Made me glad I was out of range."

We've come into a world where death is a sign of good fortune. If this is what's out here, I'd rather live inside the Arc.

"Sorry, that sounded cold," Tobin says. "But—"

"No, you're right." I say. "They're Killers, like Rami's people call them."

And that's why we still have an edge. They have reasons to kill; we have reasons to live.

"Has Rue said anything?" I ask.

"Not since we got the tower built." Tobin's testing his arms and legs, shaking the kinks out. "It took a lot out of him, but the stack blocked most of the light and some of the sound. I think he's hibernating."

"Someone should wake him up, or this is going to be the shortest rescue mission in history," Trey says. "Curing Gina was Honoria's only leverage."

"Right." Tobin reaches for a chair and wriggles it out of the stack. "Start high, otherwise you'll bring the whole thing down on his head. I'm not sure what shape he's in."

The four of us become an assembly line, picking the lean-to apart a chair at a time until there's an opening big enough to see that Rue managed to erect a veil around himself.

*Emerge!* Cherish shouts, but he doesn't drop the veil.

"Something's wrong," I say.

"Maybe it was the speakers," Anne-Marie says. "Give him a minute."

"We don't have any to spare," Trey says.

"It's not from the speakers." I move closer, almost touching the veil. Through the side, Rue looks like he's trying to hold himself together, arms clenched around his middle. A tremor cycles through his arms and legs, and even though his head is bowed, I can tell his mouth's moving. If any words are coming out, they fall unheard on the other side of the nanite wall.

Rue hates talking like a human.

*Speak*, Cherish prompts me.

"Rue?"

It's not enough. Cherish's urgent cries for speech become more forceful and more clear. My right hand begins to tingle. I shake it like I would if it fell asleep, but the sensation gets worse, turning warm.

"Hey! Sleeping Beauty—rise and shine!" Tobin bangs his fist against the veil, then pulls it back, hissing. "Is that thing supposed to be hot?"

"Hot?"

"Yeah, like burning." He holds up his hand, and the whole side is blistered.

No, the veil shouldn't be hot. It also shouldn't have been solid enough to hit. The nanites' strength is in their flexibility. They absorb force and distribute it. Tobin's fist should have bounced off, like Rami's bullets being deflected in the lunchroom

I lay my hand against the cocoon and it scalds me, too.

*What is this?* I ask Cherish.

The tingling feeling spreads from my fingers and into my wrist and on up my arm, mimicking Rue's contact with Silver.

My throat closes off, stuffed from diaphragm to mouth with something coarse and sandy.

I can't breathe!

*Strangled*, says Cherish. *Choked*. Cherish's words are joined to the squawking cry of a bird as it soars from my memory.

*Rue.*

"He's under attack," I say with a gasp. The wild ones are attacking Rue. "When he went into hibernation, they latched on to him like they did to us when we fell asleep in the truck." He can't take the veil down; they're using it to restrain him."

I reach for one of the chairs, hoist it over my head, and bring it down as hard as the combined strength of a worried human and an angry Fade can manage. It's like hitting solid steel; more of the impact reverberates through my hands and arms than the veil itself, until I feel it from teeth-to-toes. Each strike's the solemn ring of a death knell.

My hands are numb. My body aches, but I keep going, pushing aside my concerns over whether or not Rue can tolerate the clanging.

Tobin's beside me, using the legs of a chair as a battering ram. Trey's dismantling the tower from the back, in an attempt to expose it to the window and direct sunlight. *Something has to work*, I tell myself. There's always a way through.

Suddenly, someone grabs my arm, stopping my next swing.

"Marina!" Anne-Marie shouts in my ear, as though she's been trying to get my attention for a while. "I said, try this."

Pinched between the thumb and forefinger of the hand not gripping my arm is a tiny silver dart with red feathers on its end. *Fade suppressant.*

"Where—"

"I put some in my pocket in case I lost the satchel." Anne-Marie slides her hand into her pocket and brings it out with a half-dozen more. "It's not like they'd hurt me, even if I stick myself. Will it work?"

*Death!* Cherish screams. *Poison!*

She hurls the "poison" so fast and hard, I'm surprised it doesn't appear on my forehead. The serum will definitely break the veil's bonds, but the veil's attached to Rue.

I could kill him.

"You risked me turning Fade to save my life," Tobin says. "Don't tell me you think him maybe turning human is worse."

"You saw what happened to those things on the road," I say. "If the serum reaches his body—"

"Chance of death or certain continued torture—which would you pick?"

"Fine." I take the dart from Anne-Marie. "But we can't just stab him."

Minimal damage—that's the key.

I press my thumb against the needle end, to snap the tip off the dart, but I stop. What will the serum do to me now if gets into my bloodstream?

"I need something to crush it," I say, laying the dart at the edge of the veil.

"Stand back," Trey says.

He straightens and then slams his foot down, crushing the glass chamber at the center of the dart and releasing the serum.

It wicks along the seam between veil and floor, deceptively small in quantity for the effect it has. The veil dissolves on contact. Woven threads of nanites erode, exposing Rue's body to the open air.

As soon as the space is wide enough, I scoot inside and take his face in my hands. His skin's ice cold.

"Rue?" I call.

His eyes pop open, unfocused; full of pain, but also confusion and loss. Accusation.

My stomach churns yet the first answer comes in Cherish's voice: *Necessity*.

I'm surprised it's not a condemnation.

"There was no other way," I tell him.

The distant haze leaves his eyes, so they're shining with that familiar silver-cast blue. Quickly, he pulls the remainder of the veil back into himself, and I feel his heart break when he draws the line on those he has to sacrifice. The ones left behind cry out, knowing they're lost. I don't think nanites experience physical pain in their individual state, but there's no question that they're capable of anguish. They know fear, and that's how they die.

A body seems a solitary thing until each cell inside it gains its own voice, and when thousands of those voices all shriek in terror at the same time—when they all dim to nothing after that last brilliant flare of emotion—perception of the whole can never be the same again.

The hive outside takes up the lament, bringing tears to my

eyes I have to fight. Cherish can sob on the inside; Marina has to compartmentalize.

"Rue, say something."

He's on his feet, stepping clear of the residue on the floor, careful to let the dead lie in peace.

*Rueful*, he answers, and he doesn't mean his name. A well of pain springs to life inside my chest, weeping like a wound too great to stop the bleeding. *Sorrow*.

"Finite words are insufficient for infinite anguish."

His marks are different. They bear gaps no bigger than freckles where the lines are irreparably broken.

"I'm sorry," I say.

"The anguish remains infinite. We should leave this place."

"Hey!" Anne-Marie grabs his arm as he passes. "You don't get to pretend Marina did something wrong and sulk away."

I expect a response. Vitriol, rage, insults involving the name "Tibby," but Rue's . . . *diluted* is the only word I can think of.

"We should leave before more is taken," he says, glancing at Gina's body.

"That's low, even for you," Tobin says, blocking his path. "We saved your life."

*Affirmed*, Rue says, confused.

"You saved many," he says. "You lost many. Many more will be lost if we remain." His eyes cut up, searching. A gentle nudge in my mind, and the word *leave* turns more dire. *Evacuate. Remove all life.*

He's not being cruel. He's warning us.

"What did you see?" I ask him.

*Darkness. Silence. Void.*

An infinity loop snaps in half. The pieces become shackles, tying Rue's hands and feet, so he's powerless.

*Failure,* he says. "My ending. My Cherish's ending. Marina's Tibby. Our others."

"And I thought human nightmares were bad," Trey says.

"They're just dreams," Tobin insists. "Intimidation tactics. Psychological warfare—nothing that can hurt you, unless you let it get to you."

It's more than that.

"Show me." I grab Rue's hand.

Cherish pounces on the connection, asking a thousand questions and getting the answers at the speed of thought. Anne-Marie's voice, and the others', fall to the back as Rue's nightmare gains definition and focus.

It's not what I saw, nor is it some idle threat. There's no looming beast to represent the nature of the wild hive; it's no testing of Rue's limits. It's far more immediate.

It can't be . . .

I'm shocked straight out of our connection.

"Well?" Tobin asks. Anne-Marie and Trey crowd closer.

"Is it real?" I ask. "As in actually happening and not an image you're using to get your point across?"

"We should evacuate," he answers solemnly.

I run to the window wall, hoping he's wrong, but a swarm of nanites is growing in the distance. This is the wave rising up to drown us, a monster shadow blocking the sun.

"What is that?" Tobin squints toward the horizon.

"We need to get out of here," I say. "The Dark is coming."

# CHAPTER FORTY-TWO

## TOBIN

"The Dark is coming."

This is the swarm Dad said we didn't want to provoke. He was right.

"But it's still daylight," Annie says.

"I don't think they care," Trey says. "Not if they're like the ones we saw before. They'll sacrifice the first wave to cover the ones behind."

Dr. Wolff's theory that the nanites are part virus makes more sense after seeing the wild hive in action. There's no room for reason or mercy. They compute, but they don't think.

I take another look out the window.

Loose nanites, which usually cover the ground and trees, are creating a mobile canopy to cover the ones with hosts.

"I don't know how long it will take for them push forward, but I'd bet on sooner rather than later," I say; I do not want to be here when they arrive.

"But we don't have the truck anymore," Trey says.

"Ours have come," Rueful says. "Ours are faster than the truck. Ours are faster than theirs. You accompany us."

He looks at me.

There's only one way Rueful's bunch can outpace the wild ones with us along for the ride—Fade capsules.

"I can't. I—I just can't."

"It'll be okay," Marina tells me, but she wasn't inside one. Those things basically swallow us whole.

"You are even with me," Rueful says. He holds out his hand, like he wants to shake on it, but instead, he grabs my wrist and won't let go.

"Get off!" I shout. Marina tries to pull him away, but he hangs on tight. "What are you—"

The sting from the handcuff stops; my wrist doesn't hurt anymore.

"What did you do?" I ask him.

Rueful removes his hand, and I pull mine away.

"You healed him," Marina says.

"Even," he says again. "Trust us."

How he makes those two words sound like "You saved my ass, we'll save yours," in my head, I've got no idea.

"Anything involving the word *home* is okay with me." Annie bumps past us, for the door. But when she opens it, she stops and closes it again. "Slight problem. All those people who weren't out there when we left our cell are back. They brought friends."

How could I have forgotten we're still in the middle of an escape attempt? The wild-Fade aren't the only ones we have to get past.

I take a peek through the door.

Michael sits on the floor, leaned against the wall and holding his head, while Mr. Pace checks him over.

"My fault," Marina says, biting her lip.

He's got at least a broken nose and a busted lip. He's holding his ribs. "If we live through this, I want details."

Honoria's backing away from the room Michael's outside of. She walks deliberately slow, despite the person trying to move her out of the way.

"Steel doesn't fall apart for no reason," Rami snaps, waving his rifle and oblivious to the way Honoria's actually controlling his movements rather than the other way around. "I locked her in myself."

"Then you should have guarded them, too," Honoria says. "She was in that room for hours. Were she what you believe, she wouldn't have walked out of it under her own power." What happened? She sounds different, and she looks nearly fifteen years younger than she did when we were captured.

"Then why not wait until sunset for us to let her out?" Rami demands.

"Ask her yourself."

"You think she's still here?"

"Putting that girl in one room and the two troublemakers in another guarantees that there's only one place she went once she was free." She glances our way. "And, oh look, she left the door open."

The nonchalant way she alerts Rami and his people to our room startles them. He swings around full-body, so we're face-to-face.

Honoria steps forward and into his turn, using her height and momentum to throw him off center. He tries to compensate, locking his grip on the rifle, but she clips him in the jaw with her elbow, knocking him down. The rest of his people, few as they are, are easily overwhelmed by Dad and Mr. Pace before the shock wears off.

Honoria tosses Dad the rifle, preferring to keep her pistol once she takes it back from the woman who had it.

It's still hard not to flinch when I see it in her hands.

"You have a lot to learn," Honoria growls, advancing on us. "Even the troublemaker knew to knock out the guards and lock the door behind him when breaking out."

She nods to Rueful.

"I knocked him down!" Marina protests. "I just forgot the lock. If I'd waited until sundown, Rue could have been killed."

"He looks fine to me."

"We must leave here. Hastily. Immediately." Rueful takes her mention of him as his cue to speak. "Here is danger."

"As much as I hate to agree with the nanobot," I say, "he's right. We need to bug out before the bugs get here."

"Bugs?" Dad asks.

"The wild ones are swarming," Marina says. "Look for yourself."

Honoria reaches for Mr. Pace's sleeve and pulls him closer, whispering about a roof-access door.

"Get a visual," she tells him. "Every approach line to the building."

"Trey—with me," he says, and they tromp off down the hall together, though Trey gives Annie an uncertain look at the idea of leaving her behind.

"I know what I saw," Marina says.

"Me, too," I agree.

"I saw clouds," Rueful says. He thinks he's helping.

"Clouds?" Rami stands slowly, edging around Dad and Mr. Pace. "That's it?"

Marina shoves her way out from behind Rueful and me. "Rue sees it as thunderclouds breaking overhead, but it's not rain and lightning that's headed this way—it's them."

"Killers don't move like that."

"They tried to take us out using their host bodies, but we used the serum," Marina argues. "They tried using the terrain, and we burned it. They tried a direct assault—Rue's hive proved to them that they're inferior, hand to hand. They think we're a threat. This time, they'll bury us."

"How long?" Dad asks.

"I don't know, but with the sun going down; they'll only go faster."

"Then we're safer inside," Rami insists. "With the lights on, the doors locked, and *them* out there." He throws Rueful a disgusted look. "I'm just supposed to believe that you're not luring us into an ambush?"

"Yours may choose to remain. Mine return to home." Rueful takes Marina's hand and starts for the stairs. She tightens her grip on me, so I'm pulled along.

"Yeah, I vote we leave, too," Annie says, hurrying after. She whispers, "This is a bluff, right?"

But Dad and Honoria come with us.

"I've got people to protect," Rami argues, following us. "I can't ignore that because you—"

"Gina's dead," Marina blurts. He stops talking, and we stop walking. "We offered you a way to save her, but you wouldn't listen, and so she's dead. You killed her as soon as you locked her in that room. Now you're still not listening, and that's going to kill the rest of them."

Rami races into the room where Rueful and I were chained up. I don't need any weird Fade sixth sense to know what he's feeling. I wonder if Gina was his kid.

"She's silent," Rueful says, approaching Rami cautiously. "Untormented. Other voices can be preserved, if you flee." He's trying to show compassion and get the man moving at the same time. "Ours will assist yours."

"You honestly want us to go with *you*?"

Rami's kneeling beside Gina, one hand hovering above hers but afraid to touch. With his other hand, he wipes his eyes. I feel sorry for her, but she's dead. The rest of us still have a chance.

"Yours are welcome. Ours will inflict no damage," Rueful finishes as Mr. Pace runs back in.

"We've got incoming."

# CHAPTER FORTY-THREE

## MARINA

"Incoming?" Trey scoffs. "The Dark's on a march straight for us. They've all but ripped the sun down out there."

It's a good thing Anne-Marie didn't go to the roof, too. Being boxed into a safe room causes her enough trouble; witnessing the wild ones close in would probably send her over the edge.

"Is there an escape route?" Honoria asks.

"None that I could see," Mr. Pace says. "But your brother and his buddies are headed this way. Maybe they know something we don't."

"You've got more people out there?" Rami asks as he drapes a dusty cloth over Gina's face. "How?"

"They aren't *our* people," Honoria says, just as a woman's voice screams for Rami outside our door.

"Maya?" Rami yells back, shooting to his feet as the woman appears at the door, frantic and still screaming.

"Killers." She leans on her knees, breathing hard. "Four of them, at the front door. More beyond, closing fast."

"Like the ones who razed your Homestead?" Col. Lutrell asks.

"No—like him," Maya spits at Rue. "They look like him."

"Our way to home," Rue argues.

They ignore him.

"The ones behind," Honoria says. "Do they look like him, too?"

"They're dragging Death with them," Maya says. "You can't see anything but darkness."

Rami must not be used to making decisions in the moment. His last twenty hours have been a condensed version of our last months. He doesn't know what to do, so he hesitates, but Honoria's in her element.

"Elias, Trey, go down the halls and open the gas lines in the science rooms. I'll head for the basement and see if there's anything useful there. James, rig me a switch."

"Localized or remote?" Col. Lutrell asks.

"I'll take whatever you can give me."

"We've got these." He pats his pockets, locating the ones where he's stashed flares. "I can use my alert bracelet for a timer, if nothing else."

He tosses one flare to Tobin, one to me, and one to Anne-Marie.

"Just in case," he says, and I drop mine into the long pocket on my pants.

"Did we salvage any phosphorus rounds?" Honoria asks.

"With our gear."

"Good. Now, the rest of you—"

She turns on me and Tobin, Anne-Marie and Rue, glaring down with the icy stare she's had so long to perfect. Anne-Marie and Tobin automatically snap to attention.

"I need you to—"

Rami steps between us and her.

"This is *our* facility, not yours."

Honoria levels that horrible stare at Rami. I've got to give him credit, he doesn't back down, but battles of will against Honoria rarely end in the challenger's favor.

"Unless you've got a viable means of defending this location, it's about to be *their* facility," she says. "If we blow the gas lines, we can take enough of them down to cripple their advance. It should buy us a window to get out of here."

We balance a half second on his pause, waiting to see which way things will fall.

"Do it," he says.

Honoria nods to Mr. Pace again, adding, "Go. Radios on channel six. Meet up in the lunchroom."

Mr. Pace, Trey, and Col. Lutrell leave. Rue pulls away, toward the door.

"Rue?" I ask along with Cherish's: *Leaving?*

"I must speak to ours," he says. "We must prepare our retreat."

"You go, she stays." Honoria clamps a hand on to my shoulder.

She really is a gifted strategist. If I stay with her, and the rest of the humans, Rue will wait no matter what happens.

"Mine will hold the Darkness back as long as we are able. Make certain yours are ready when we return," Rue says, and then he leaves. Maya flinches when passes her.

"Our facility isn't overlarge," Honoria says to Rami. "But it's sufficient to incorporate those of you here."

"Our secondary Homestead is out there," Rami says resolutely. "Maya, get the kids," he says.

"You're not seriously considering this?" Her eyes flick to Gina's covered corpse on the floor.

"We couldn't hold the Homestead with everyone fighting. What chance do we have with one building, one rifle, no ammo, and a bunch of kids barely old enough to understand that their parents are gone for good? Get them to the stairs and tell them we're going home."

There's a pause after Maya leaves. Rami remains standing beside Gina's body, refusing to look at it. He still doesn't want to leave her.

"Can your kids handle this?" Honoria asks. "They're going to have to get close to the creatures like the boy who was here with us."

This is the first time she's referred to Rue as an actual boy, the creature part notwithstanding.

"They can do what they have to," he says.

She nods, but it's not so much acceptance of his answer as an indication that she's moving on. I can almost see her thoughts as they spin in different directions behind her eyes. Each possibility shines like a silver thread. She weaves them together until they form a cohesive reality. The Fade in her body have become a tool she can access, like I do with Cherish.

They're helping her, and she's letting them.

Dark auburn lines thread through the orange-tinted strands of her hair. Her posture straightens like someone suddenly relieved of a heavy burden. Her voice becomes stronger. I swear five more years just fell off her face.

"You three stay with their children," she tells us. "You're the closest thing to a liaison with the Fade that we have, and I have a feeling we may need you to get through this."

"High ground is safe ground for us," Rami says. "My kids will be calmer if—"

He's interrupted by a distant rumble that turns into something much closer. The room shakes, throwing us all to the floor and toppling the remnants of Rue's chair cocoon so that the window's no longer obscured. I pull up as far as my knees.

Honoria, Rami, Tobin, and Anne-Marie are all in almost identical positions, staring at the now unmistakable cumulous mass of Death headed in our direction. It rolls forward, shunting more nanites to the top to bolster the outer layer destroyed by the sun. And beneath it all, hosted Fade approach at a slow march in time with the covering protecting them.

The building shudders again; a jet-black geyser bursts through the ground beyond the parking area outside the building. It streaks upward to join the cloud. The wild ones are calling on the dormant nanites we saw through cracks in the ground; they're waking up.

"We really need to get out of here," Tobin says.

"I agree," Honoria says.

Her words start a scramble for the door. It feels wrong to leave Gina's body behind in an empty room, but at the same time, it's inevitable.

Such is the nature of Death.


The Ice Cube's children are already at the stairs, waiting with Maya and another woman. They hold themselves together better than I expect—until they see Rami. Half of them come running to meet him.

"Rami!"

"Why is the building shaking? Is it Killers?"

"Are we going to die?"

The ones who rush him are panicked, with wide-open eyes that never blink; the rest, like Javier, share the stoic calm of those who've accepted their fate. They have no questions, because they know the answers.

"The Killers aren't here yet, but they're coming," Rami tells them.

Michael separates himself from the silent ones, with Noor following along, her hand gripping the back of his shirt.

"What do we do?" he asks.

"Keep everyone together," Rami says.

He dispatches the two women, but he's cautious. The words he uses aren't only softly spoken, but make no sense. Like their whistled cues, these are secret things he doesn't trust us to hear.

"What shook the building?" Michael asks again.

"When you hear the signal, get them moving," Rami says, leaving the question unanswered.

"You three stay with them," Honoria says. She drops her voice, knowing I can hear it, but Rami likely can't. "Our priority is our own people. Keep yourselves safe, even if it means keeping *only* yourselves safe." She cocks her head, acting like she never said that last bit. "Understood?"

"I understand," I say.

But that doesn't mean I'll do it.

She heads down with Rami, leaving the rest of us with nothing to do but wait and worry. Tobin, Anne-Marie, and I stand closer together while the others shy away from us. I close my eyes to see if I can hear what's happening outside.

When I did this in our bunkers, it was easier. My other perceptions were mostly human then, and didn't interfere with my concentration, but now, a toxic swirl of danger and emotion has created a vapor that's spread to every corner. It makes it hard to concentrate.

"I wish they'd let us wait downstairs," Anne-Marie says.

"So do I," I say. Cherish echoes me. Downstairs, we'd be closer to Rue and the rest of the hive. We'd be closer to home and freedom.

"Why do they keep staring at us like that?" Tobin asks, but he shouldn't have to. The Ice Cube's children use the same expressions he used to give me. "It's like they're waiting for us to attack them."

And why wouldn't they? The last they saw of us, Rami was having them lock us up.

"Do something, Michael," a girl in the crowd whispers. "She'll bring the others, and it'll be just like the Homestead."

*We are not destroyers,* Cherish says, stung. *We restore.*

I thought I was done with feeling regret for others' actions, but the guilt comes back exactly as strong as in my early days inside the Arclight. The whispers come next. I heard the same from Jove and Dante and other members of our year at school. They think if they sacrifice me, then somehow everything will become better for them.

I can't take the blame for anything else; it's too heavy.

"Are you really that stupid?" I storm across the short distance left between us and the Ice Cube's children and jerk the mouthy girl's arm so hard, she falls to the floor. That was an accident, but I'm not helping her up, and neither is anyone else. They leave her to her fate as easily as they'd toss me out the front door. "Do you really think a wild-Fade could be in here with you, and you still be human?"

"Javier said—"

"Javier doesn't know me, and neither do you," I tell her, letting my frustration boil over. "I'm trying to *help* you, and you're making me not want to do that anymore. Stop it!"

I'm shaking.

"Help how?" Javier steps forward into the space between our group and his. Tobin and Anne-Marie join me, so one of them's on each side. Three against thirty. "How are you going to get us out of here if the Killers are coming?"

"The same way we came in."

"Through Death?" he asks, and another wave of that noxious fog rolls through me as the others whimper.

"It's not Death," Anne-Marie says.

"Prove it," Javier challenges. "I bleed red, how about you?"

Tobin shifts his weight forward, onto his toes, curling his fingers into fists. "Even think about trying to draw blood on my friends, and the first drop that falls is going to be yours."

Michael steps between them, facing Javier.

"You're making things worse," he said. "People are going to panic."

"What do we know about these people? They show up out of nowhere. They *say* they're human. They *say* they survived. They *say* we can trust them. And we're just supposed to *believe* them?"

"Rami does."

"Maya told us what she did to Gina."

"I wasn't even in the room when Gina died," I snap.

"He was." Javier jerks his head at Tobin. "And so was your freak friend. Where is he?"

"What do you care how we get out of here, so long as no one's left behind?" Anne-Marie asks. Her arms are crossed, and she's got the same tilt to her mouth that her mother uses when someone's in serious trouble. "The sooner we leave, the sooner we all get back to where we belong."

"Shorter trip for you, isn't it? All you and your Killer-brother have to do is step outside and you're there."

Javier has just accomplished the impossible: He's put a taste for blood in Anne-Marie's mouth. Her aura turns to blue flames that burn darkest around her body. Even the hive reaches out to ask me what's wrong. They can feel it, too.

"Anne-Marie, don't." I snatch the back of her jacket, pulling her back a step as she advances.

*Vengeance.* The word weaves into the other pieces of a name the Fade have attached to Anne-Marie. Now when they speak of her, they call her *Fury.*

"Why not?" she asks.

"Yeah," Tobin says. "Why not?"

One, we're outnumbered. Two, knocking someone's teeth down their throat is counterproductive. Three—

"Rue's back," I say.

Cherish trills, but Tobin's breathing faster in anticipation of going back into one of those capsules to escape. He makes another fist, driving his fingernails into his palm.

"We'll go together," I tell him. "They'll have to carry pairs to get everyone out, anyway."

"I'm fine," he whispers. "Can't expect them to go if I won't."

The pulse is jumping in his neck.

"It's no different than the Well or the spot we made in the back of the truck," I tell him, forcing him to look me in the eye. His pupils are dilated.

"I hope it's a *little* different than the truck." His forced laugh is too harsh.

"Close your eyes and it's you and me in the Well on a night without stars."

"What are you talking about?" Michael asks.

"Our ride."

I nod to the stairs. The youngest scream at the sight of Rue and Bolt coming up, and I knew they would—Rue and Bolt knew they would; it doesn't faze them in the least. It's nothing but common, even understandable, panic. It should burn itself out when the people involved realize there's nowhere to go.

The problem is *Javier.* He's moving against the flow, *toward* the stairs. Selfishly, even morbidly, I hope he gives them an excuse to defend themselves, and so I let him go—all the way to the wall, where he reaches for another of those hidden switch plates like the one downstairs. The one Honoria warned us not to touch.

"Stop!" I shout, but no one hears me. I can't get to him with everyone else running wild.

Javier slams his fist sideways into the plate, hard enough to crack it.

Honoria was wrong. It wasn't an alarm.

The stairs and the Fade on them disappear into a deafening boom, and a cloud of dust.

He blew them up.

# CHAPTER FORTY-FOUR

## TOBIN

Marina lunges for Rueful and Schuyler, crying "No!" as they fall. I have to catch her before she goes over the side after them.

"Rue!" She screams. She elbows me in the stomach, and I drop her so she can skid to the edge. The stairs are gone. There's nothing below but open space and the promise of a hard landing.

"What did you do?" I shove Javier backward into the wall; he's smug, like he did something worth applauding. "You could have killed them."

"That was the idea." He shoves me back.

"They're our ride, you idiot!"

"Did you get them?" One of the younger children darts forward to look down.

Marina's on her knees, watching the dust settle, scanning the wreckage below. Fade may be resilient, but that's got to be half a ton of rock and cement.

"They're all right." She nearly laughs, and the child beside her gasps.

"Do it, again, Javier," he says.

"Cherish says they're fine. They're annoyed, but not hurt." Marina's beaming.

Rueful and Schuyler shake themselves to get rid of the debris. Dog and Whisper help them out of the heap.

"What was that?" Annie asks.

"A fail-safe," Michael says. "If things went bad, we could make a stand on higher ground without giving them a way up, but it was supposed to be a last resort."

"More like our last way out," I say.

"He thought he was helping," Michael insists.

"Don't put apologies in my mouth," Javier snaps. "I did exactly what I meant to do."

"Our exit's on the ground floor, moron," I tell him.

"All of you shut up," Annie says. "We need another way down. There're stairs to the roof, so there have to be more to the ground floor, right?"

"The auxiliary stairs were sealed off in the first days," Michael says. "They took the escape ways off the sides of the building at the same time. Roof access is all we have."

"That's no good," I say. That canopy will be right over our heads.

"Maybe we can lower the little ones down. It's not that far, if someone catches them," Annie suggests.

"And then what?" Michael asks. "The rest of us jump?"

"Yes!" Marina says. She's got that look on her face that means she's talking to the hive; it's nearly electric. "We can jump, and they can catch us. Rue!"

"Wait—I wasn't serious."

"I am. It's not a wide jump from here to the wall. Rue can catch each of us easily. Bolt can take the center point on the wall, so we're almost to the floor before we have to drop—it'll work. Rue! Bolt! We need you up here," she calls down.

Claws appear at the end of Rueful's fingers, and Schuyler's, and they begin scaling the wall.

"High ground." I give Javier a thumbs-up. "Great idea. The Fade can't reach you at all if you're on the second floor."

*Idiot.*

I swear I hear Rueful say: *Affirmed*, just before Marina giggles.

Behind us, the Ice Cube's children are in a huddle, with only Michael and Noor standing apart from the rest. They're shaking, faces stricken with an unhealthy tint to them as they stare at Rueful, like he's death itself come to collect their souls.

"Evacuation would be simpler with the stairs intact." Rueful stops at the high point, nearly parallel with our position on the top step.

"We're improvising," Marina tells him. "Go with it."

"He's a Killer," Javier says.

"No, he's not," Marina says. "Rue's a Fade, but he is nothing like the creatures you know. He saved Tobin's life, and now he's trying to save you."

"I'd rather die human."

"You do that," I say. "The rest of us opt to not die at all. Who's up first?"

They all cringe back.

"Six months ago, you would have cut off your hand before touching a Fade too," Marina says. "If you want to get them moving, go first and show them it's safe."

Another tremor hits hard enough that I have to grab the wall to keep from toppling headfirst into the gap. I catch Marina by the elbow as she steadies herself, and the youngest children scream again. Noor grabs on to Michael's leg.

"I'll go, you bunch of babies." Annie slips between me and Marina. She eases out onto the remaining steps, hanging on to us, with her attention on Rueful rather than the empty space at her feet.

The marks on his face and arms draw tighter. Annie lets go of Marina first, using that hand to brace herself on the wall.

"Easy as breathing," Marina says.

Annie squeezes my hand, lets it drop and leaps.

"Nice catch," she says, and I realize I've closed my eyes. When I open them, she's hanging off Rueful's arm, clinging to his neck, but the continuing rumble from outside the building leaves no time for celebration. She drops from Rueful's hands to Schuyler's, and then sets her feet on the ground.

"One at a time's too slow!" she shouts at us.

"Right," Michael says, as though he's convincing himself of

his own resolve as he speaks. "Noor, get on my back and hang on tight. Don't look until I say."

I lift her so she can get her arms around Michael's neck.

He turns to the others, doing a quick survey. "Those four are too small to go on their own," he says of the younger children. "They'll have to go tandem, and they need to go next."

One of the teens grabs a little boy and puts him on her back, but most of the little ones kick and scream, even being held.

"Running after them like lemmings isn't going to help anyone." Javier steps forward.

"If you want to stay here, then do it." Michael steps into the place Annie's vacated, steadied by me and Marina.

Rueful reaches out.

"Hang on," Michael tells Noor.

She smashes her face against his back. He leaps, leaving the ground as another rumble rolls the floor.

"Keep moving," Michael yells back. He hands Noor off to Schuyler and then follows her down, still shouting orders. "Youngest to oldest. Now!"

The rest become well-orchestrated line, jumping in time, and turn so that as one is released to the floor, Schuyler's passing down the one behind him and Rueful's catching another while the next readies for the jump. Javier is the last of them to go, and I swear he only makes the choice because with both me and Marina up here, we outnumber him.

"Now you," I say, bracing my hand against the top step to help Marina into position.

"Not a chance—you first."

"Don't argue with me, Marina. Jump."

"Listen to Tibby. Marina should be less stubborn," Rueful says.

"Oh good. Call her stubborn. That'll help." I let the "Tibby" slide this time.

"You could have both been on the ground by now!" Annie shouts. Most of the Ice Cube's children have fled. "Just sayin'."

"Go," Marina says as the next rumble comes. "I'll be in the air before you're on the tile."

"You're making me agree with Rueful. That's got to be a bad sign." I kiss her quickly, shifting to her ear to whisper: "If he misses, I'll catch you myself."

I lean forward to jump, but the roll of the floor spreads up the walls, throwing the whole structure into a seizure. The stair crumbles, and I fall spinning, arms windmilling. I close my eyes and make a mad, stretching grab for what's left of the ledge.

Someone catches me; the hand's too small to be Rueful's.

"Marina?"

My weight should have pulled her over the edge.

I open my eyes.

"Impossible . . ."

I'm hanging suspended beyond what had been the stairs, my hand clamped tightly by another, but it doesn't belong to Marina or Rue or even Schuyler. Marina's stretched out, lying on her stomach. Between us is . . . *impossible*. She's just impossible.

"Is that . . . are you . . . *Marina*?"

A hand's tucked inside mine, the fingers so real, I can feel the nails, but they're nothing but nanites. Just like the arm attached to them, and the body that could be a shadow, if it wasn't solid.

Cherish caught me; she looks exactly like Marina.

"How—"

"I don't know," Marina says.

"Drop," Annie orders. "Toby, get out of the way!"

Cherish disintegrates as fast as she appeared, tucking herself back into Marina's body through their linked hands, and as she crumbles, I drop. The fall's not enough to hurt me from here.

"Marina!" Annie and I are both screaming. "Jump!"

She does, bypassing the Fade to land on her feet. Rueful and Schuyler land on either side.

"Are you okay?" I ask. "Are you . . . *you*?"

"It's me."

Cherish was supposed to be gone—an echo that Marina could still hear—but she's still in there. *Literally*. But where? If Cherish is back, then what happens to Marina?

"Get everyone back to the entrance," she tells Michael.

"What are you?" he asks, holding Noor away from us.

"She's hard to explain," Annie offers.

She's more than that.

"I'm a friend. And I want to go home. Rue's people are ready to take us out of here. Once we're gone, Honoria's going to blow this place to ash. We can't—"

The sudden muted pop of gunfire rolls over the end of her warning.

"They're here." The words, obvious as they are, fall out of Marina's mouth.

The first sounds are like rain, but then come solid thumps. Things with feet impact against the roof and hit it running.

"Okay, that's bad." Annie's turning in place, tracking the sounds as they multiply. "We need to hide."

Somewhere in the rooms above, glass shatters, and one of the few kids who stayed with Michael screams, but cuts herself off by holding her hands over her mouth. She backs away, gaping at the precipice of the second floor; three creatures now prowl the ledge we leaped from.

One balances on the top rail. The one nearest the edge flattens its body, growling in a graceful stretch at odds with its bulk. It springs off its front feet, launching itself high.

The creature falls unnaturally slow, and we scatter. Marina, Annie, and I take shelter behind the ruined steps with a handful of children. Rueful and his Fade blink out of existence. And the wolf-thing finally hits the ground on all fours, snarling as its nanite coat expands to make it even larger.

No one moves. The creatures on the second floor remain

in position. They act like scouts rather than invaders, likely funneling information back to the rest so they can map out their assault in earnest.

The first creature takes a step, tilting its head.

The screaming girl's still holding her mouth. She, and those with her, cringe because it's so close to them, but it keeps going, uninterested.

Another step. Metal strikes the hard surface of the floor in the silence, a grating whine as its heavy body scrapes the tile. It swivels its head the other way, and stops again.

"What's it doing?" Annie asks. Her attention darts between the wolf on the ground and those above.

"It's looking for our Fade," Marina says.

The wild ones are smart enough to know that Rueful's people are our greatest advantage, and their strongest physical adversary. They want to take out the biggest threat first.

"It can't see them."

"Can you?" I ask.

The wolf sniffs the air, snout turned up. Marina eases Dad's flare from her pocket.

"What are you doing?" I press her hand down between us.

"It smells Whisper's wound. It's almost on top of her."

The wolf moves forward.

Behind its shoulder, Rueful starts bleeding into view.

"Give me the flare. I'll do it," I say, but she's already moving.

"Hey!" she shouts, stepping away from our shelter. She

blows out a shrill whistle that makes the creature turn. "Looking for me?"

The instant it begins to charge, she flicks the cap off the flare with her thumb. It's burning bright by the time the wolf's in the air, and Marina gets a clear shot at its underbelly. The wolf's dead before it crashes onto its side; its nanites perish in clumps of charred glop.

"Nice," Annie says. "Now do it again." She points up.

With the first wolf down, the next leaps down to take its place.

It lands facing us, now treating Marina as the threat of greatest importance, the obstacle to be removed before all others.

It never sees the Fade coming.

Dog appears out of nowhere, hurling a piece of debris from the stairs at the creature. It turns on him, and Whisper strikes from the other side. The wolf roars, and Schuyler responds with a blow to its head.

"Where's the nanobot?" I ask.

My answer is a whistle mimicking Marina's. Rueful appears standing in the creature's path. The wolf puts all of its effort into a lunge, and Rueful goes to pieces, dropping to the floor as though he'd been made of sand, and a wind came up to blow him away. Once he's gone, there's nothing between the second wolf and the flaming carcass of the first.

It lands on top of the one Marina torched and goes up, too.

"Two down," she says as the third wolf howls above our heads, and springs.

# CHAPTER FORTY-FIVE

## MARINA

The third wolf crashes down, away from Rue and the others, and onto a pile of rubble Michael had been using for cover. The impact flushes him out, along with the children he'd rounded up. He's now directly across from us, and frantic, searching for something.

*Peanut,* Cherish says, filling my nose with the scent.

"Noor," I say with a gasp. That was Rue's nickname for her. "She's not with them. Where—"

"Michael!" Noor cries.

She's taken refuge in a shallow stairwell across the entry. The steps lead into the glass-walled room full of shelves we saw when we first entered the Ice Cube, and have a short, railed wall on either side. She's boxed herself in.

"Michael!"

He whips toward her voice, but so does the wolf.

Dog throws a chunk of broken stone at the creature; Tobin a piece of metal. Michael runs into the middle of the room, waving his arms and making noise, but the wolf's learned from its predecessor. It ignores him.

*Make it cease.* Rue broadcasts the command with a *Shh!*, to direct it at Whisper. *Make it still.*

She's scaling the wall with one arm, barely visible, and dragging a long piece of shorn metal from the stairs along with her. Her wounded arm can't grasp, but the nanites there hang on to it for her. Once she's high enough, the nanites let it drop. Between the weight, gravity, and the sharpness of the metal, it cuts straight through the wolf, into the floor, holding it fast.

It howls, bucking against the beam, but it can't dislodge itself.

"Michael!" Noor screams, desperately tucking into a ball to escape its snapping jaws. She takes off the tiny pink shoe I returned to her and flings it with all the strength she can muster, but it bounces off the wolf's snout.

The wolf can't get closer, but she's still trapped.

"One dart's enough, right?" Anne-Marie asks, dropping her hand into her pocket for her stash. "That thing's smaller than the ones we hit on the road."

"Do you realize how close you'll have to get to use that?" Tobin asks. "The Fade could jump to you as soon as you touch it."

Anne-Marie stabs herself in the palm with the dart and then pulls another out of her pocket.

"Now they won't," she says, and launches herself toward Noor's hiding spot. She clenches the dart in both hands and hits the wolf full force in the back flank. The creature roars one last time. Fault lines form in the nanite shell along its legs and back. Nanites blow off in all directions, and Anne-Marie dives for Noor to protect her.

"I cannot believe that actually worked," Tobin says.

I feel as stunned as he sounds. The wolf's dead.

Anne-Marie hands Noor up out of the stairwell, shaking black powder from her clothes.

"Gross," she says, spitting onto the floor.

I grab her for a hug; Tobin grabs us both.

"Never do anything like that again," he says, but our moment is broken by renewed gunfire.

An eclipse overtakes the windows one by one. Shadows pour over the floor as the sun's blocked, dragging an impossible chill along behind them.

"They're covering the building," I say.

"Where is everyone?" Anne-Marie asks. "They should have met us by now."

"I don't think they're coming," Tobin says, casting a long look down toward the hall leading to the lunchroom. "There's got to be another breach point where my dad and the others are."

"What do we do?"

"If they can't get to us, we go to them," Tobin says.

*Affirmed.* Rue echoes.

*Negative.* "Evacuation is our priority," Bolt says, sounding nearly like his sister.

"We have no weapons." Javier speaks up for the first time since the incident at the stairs. "What good are we in a conflict?"

Michael uses Noor as an excuse to stall, bending down so she can climb onto his back, but Javier isn't standing for it this time.

"You know the rules," he says. "And we know where to go. They haven't sealed the door yet. We can run for it."

The wild-Fade have stopped short of covering the main doors. A single strip of sunlight filters through, creating a pathway that looks clear.

"That's bait," I say. And this time, I'm not biting. "They're not stupid. Do you really think they've staked out the rest of the building and left the door unguarded?"

"We go to home," Rue says resolutely. "Home is safer."

"*Anywhere* is safer." Javier turns to Michael again. "You know I'm right."

And I know we've lost them. They've been through too much too fast; I can't blame them for taking a long shot as their only shot.

"My dad's down there," Tobin says. "I'm not leaving."

"So's mine," adds Anne-Marie. "And my brother."

"Rami will know where we've gone. He'll bring your families to us."

"Your brother, but my sister," Michael says apologetically, clinging tight to Noor. "Come with us."

"No," I say, but he persists.

"There's communications equipment. It hasn't been used for anything other than broadcasting noise into Death for decades, but we might be able to reach your home base."

"And they *might* take one look at us and lock us up."

"We came together; we leave together," Anne-Marie says.

"Suit yourselves." Javier heads for the door, and most of the Ice Cube's children go with him. The rest wait for Michael, who finally gathers the nerve to speak to Rue face-to-face.

"Can you keep those things off our tail?" he asks.

"Mine can distract, but they won't engage. To engage endangers mine."

I can tell it's hard for Michael to even ask for help, much less extend the hand he reaches out toward Rue, waiting for Rue to take it.

"He doesn't want to talk, Rue," I warn him.

Rue nods, then tugs sharply on Michael's hand.

"I *am* sorry," Michael says.

"So are we," I say.

He turns to join the rest of his people, but Anne-Marie pulls him back by the sleeve.

"Take these." She drops three darts into his palm.

"Thank you," Michael runs out with the others, and I can only hope the shadows on the ground all belong to them.

# CHAPTER FORTY-SIX

## MARINA

I'm starting to take comfort in the sound of gunfire. At least it's a human sound.

"Can you tell how many there are?" Tobin asks as we pick our way over the rubble.

The Fade are in front, claws out for traction. They pull Tobin and Anne-Marie and I to the top of the pile.

"Their voices are chaos," Rue says. *Discord. Confusion.*

"Is that a no?"

Rue glares. The lines across his stoic face tilt in toward the center point, the way a human's eyebrows would draw together.

"What'd I say?" Tobin asks.

Rue hops down on the other side of the pile and reaches back to catch me as I drop behind him. Dog and Whisper come next, bringing Anne-Marie along with them, and then Bolt and Tobin.

"Seriously, what'd I say?" he asks me again when we're clear on the other side. "Half the things he says make no sense to anyone sane."

Inwardly, I bristle at the implication that I'm crazy, but I know that's not what he means. He's struggled with understanding Rue from the beginning.

"It was a no, Tobin," I say. "Their number is in flux; you can't count them."

"How hard is it to say that?"

"Their voices are chaos," Rue repeats, with a derisive puff of air through his nose.

We're close enough now that the sound of gunfire bounces wall-to-wall along the hall leading into the lunchroom. Despite the volume we lower our voices. There's nowhere to hide here, so we move in a collective crouch.

I don't smell gas.

Black Fade-lines branch along the greenish surface overhead and on the walls. A whispering rush signals the arrival of more nanites, filling in the gaps and forming dimensional ridges, but that's as far as they go. They're watching us.

Anne-Marie absentmindedly twirls one of the serum darts between her fingers; everywhere she steps, the marks recede, only to fill back in when she's passed.

"They fear the void as we do," Rue says. "You carry the void."

"Cool." She swipes her hand through the air, causing a mass retreat.

Our order shifts, with Tobin pulling to the front of the line. He and Rue both stop at the entrance so that we bank up behind them.

"Annie, how many of those things do you have left?"

"Five, I think."

"Then we have a problem."

The room looks like a diorama of the Dark. Nanites coat every surface, from ceiling to floor, except the one our people have managed to hold, which is nothing but a table and the area around it. They've kept the Killers back by burning them. Hosted ones mill the edges of the room, growling and snapping

"It's going out!" Mr. Pace shouts. He's standing back-to-back with Honoria, Trey, and Rami.

Rami reaches for one of three small jars on the table and throws it straight down into the waning flames. Some kind of oily substance rushes out from the shattered jar, and the fire flares up, spreading wider.

Definitely no gas.

"Not to rush you, James, but we're down to two cocktails," Honoria says.

"I'm doing the best I can," Col. Lutrell answers back. He sits on the table in the center, with the two women from the Ice Cube, tinkering with some kind of small device. I guess that simple switch he was going to come up with turned out to be a bit more difficult. "Most of the wire we salvaged is completely corroded. It won't hold long enough for a charge to pass through. Just give me—"

"I know, I know—five more minutes."

As the fire flares, the nanites closest to it catch and burn. In response, the hosted Fade against the wall lunge forward, only to run directly into the rifle shots, which drive them back again. It's a standoff, but it shouldn't be; the humans should be dead.

"I don't want to sound like I'm complaining, but shouldn't there be more?" Anne-Marie asks. "That swarm was miles wide and more than a thousand feet high."

"Their voices are chaos," Rue says again, straining the words for emphasis, as though we're being intentionally dense. "Is there a better word?" he asks me.

*Discordant*, he says. *Disagreement.*

*The cohesion has eroded,* Cherish says. *Fear causes chaos.*

She tries to show me in terms I can process. A signal drew the wild ones here. They all heard it, and all responded, but once they arrived, some tried to leave. Even now, scores of them want to flee, but they can't because the hive bond won't allow it.

"They're still afraid of us," I say. "Too afraid to attack and risk the void. The hive mind won't give them the freedom to run."

"Anne-Marie, hand me a dart," I say.

We're at the very edge of the room, along the border the wild ones have set in place. A step forward will put my foot right in the middle of them. I take the dart from Anne-Marie and hold it by the feathered end, like a bomb I could drop at any second.

"You know what this is, don't you?" I ask every nanite close enough to hear.

Before my foot strikes the ground, they flee.

"And you know who I am. You know my voice was removed from the hive."

I take another step, and the same thing happens.

Anne-Marie fishes another out of her pocket and steps sideways; the Fade retreat, extending our safe zone by half a foot. She produces another dart for Tobin, and we arrange ourselves so that Rue, Bolt, and the others are inside a loose triangle. The wild ones won't come near us.

"Annie?" Trey calls from the table. He's nearest, and so he's the first to notice us.

"Annie!" Mr. Pace echoes. "Get out of here."

It must be a dad response—desired outcome before logical thought. Where does he think she's going to go?

"Do you have any darts left?" Anne-Marie shouts to him, louder than she needs to, then wiggles her foot like she's going to take another step to show him how the wild-Fade respond.

"They were with the rest of the gear we never recovered," Honoria answers for him, directing her anger at Rami. Spread out. See how far you can stretch the clearing."

Anne-Marie and Dog stay near the door, with Rue and Whisper stopping five feet off. Rue holds his dart carefully, but his marks leave his hands all the same. Bolt and I take the next leg, leaving Tobin to go all the way. The wild-Fade along the walls step in closer, but those who come too close get shot, leaving sickly pale corpses along the edges of the room.

"How—" I start to ask.

"Phosphorus rounds," Tobin answers. "They burn like flares."

Mr. Pace nudges Trey to step off the table, onto the bench

seat, and into the safe zone, where he can jog to his sister. The rest of the adults come behind him, with Col. Lutrell putting the final flourish on the device he's rigging.

"Got it," he says, and centers it on the table. "Tobin toss me yours."

Col. Lutrell smashes the final jar of oil on the floor to start a new fire near where Tobin's standing. Tobin pitches his dad the dart he's been holding, which the colonel places on top of the device, hopefully guaranteeing the wild-Fade will leave it alone until it goes off.

"Let's go," he says. "The gas from the boiler won't take much longer to reach this far."

"Where are our kids?" Maya demands once everyone's within the clearing.

"They left," I say. "They said you'd know where to find them."

"How long?" Rami asks.

"Right before we came looking for you."

"Move faster," Honoria says as we make our way to the doors.

This isn't some tornado's eye where we can pause for a breath; it's not even the safety of being hidden within a Fade's camouflage, where the enemy can't see us. The wild ones are following.

"What happens if enough of them change their minds about chasing us out of here?" Anne-Marie asks.

Behind us, and on the sides, the walls close in, making sure we can't get out through the lunchroom. By the time we're halfway up the hall leading to the main area of the Ice Cube, I hear locking pins and pieces of a machine coming together.

"You had to ask, didn't you?" Tobin says.

I glance back, already knowing what I'll see, but it's impossible to look away. The beast from my nightmare forms behind us. It grows paws and claws, and a set of sharp teeth. It grows legs, and that means it can—

"RUN!" I scream. Anne-Marie and Trey are farthest ahead. She turns to see what's wrong, and suddenly, her eyes are twice as big as usual.

Cherish cries out for our father, who's waiting with the others beyond the Ice Cube.

*We're coming,* she says.

*Be there. Please be there.* That's me.

Rue and the rest of our Fade drop back, trying to take the rear guard position, but Honoria refuses to relinquish it, and she and her brother end up running side by side. The bear-beast lowers its front shoulder to ram her, but Bolt jerks her out of the way, so he's between her and the creature. She's furious at first, but better sense and survival prevail. She raises her pistol and fires past Bolt's ear, straight at the creature's head, but it has no underlying body to kill.

A few scorched nanites fall dead, and the creature's edges blur, but the bullet goes straight through into the facing wall.

We could really use one of those jars of burning oil about now.

"Look out!" Tobin shouts, and I turn forward again, where

I'm about to plow into the rubble pile left behind by the stairs.

Rue yanks me sideways as the creature smashes down with its paws. The beast can't get through the debris, so it goes for Maya and the other woman.

"Over." Rue points to the pile of rubble.

"We'll be too easy to pick off."

"And here, we're trapped," Tobin says.

"Over," Rue says again.

He means to be reassuring when he shows me his plan to help us escape. One long, veiled shield, created by all four Fade, slowing the creature down enough that we can get out of here.

*But you'll be in direct contact with the Killers*, I say. *You could lose your voice.*

"They fear us also," Rue argues.

"That monster doesn't fear anything. It has no mind, Rue."

He shows me a retreat plan. Once we're over the rubble, the Fade will follow, trusting speed and agility to give them the advantage they need. But it's only an advantage against the wild ones with hosts, the ones hindered by physical bodies beneath the shell. We don't know what will happen against something like this bear-beast.

"Marina!" Tobin shouts, and I realize he's moved. "You're up."

"Rue!" I shout with every voice I have. He distracted me while the others went to work.

Bolt, Dog, and Whisper have formed a line—one Rue joins. Anne-Marie and her brother are already climbing over the top of the pile, with Rami and his people behind. Midway up, Mr. Pace and Col. Lutrell are reaching back for Tobin and me.

"Up you go," Honoria says, dragging me up the pile so Tobin can get a grip on my hand and pull me with him.

I should be down there, standing beside Rue and the others. I'm the least likely to be absorbed, but if I go back, Rue won't retreat. I fit my hands solidly to the rubble and start to climb.

It was hard to tell the size of the bear-beast on the ground, but up here, it's worse. There's no back half. It stretches on forever, down the hall and into the lunchroom, filling every space.

On the other side of the pile, the wolves we killed are smoldering, their carcasses filling the entry with the stink of burnt flesh and nanites.

"Our kids lived through this?" Rami asks, astonished. He fixates on something near the wolf that Dog and Whisper speared to the ground—Noor's pink shoe—and bends to pick it up.

"No one fell," Anne-Marie tells him as Tobin and I scramble down the steeper chucks of rock. "Our Fade distracted the wild ones. They had a fighting chance."

"Go get your kids," Col. Lutrell tells him. "We can handle ourselves."

He and the woman whose name I've never heard nod and run out after a quick thank-you. Maya stops.

"We have com equipment," she says. "If you feel like listening—"

Before she can finish, Mr. Pace is unclipping his radio and tossing it to her.

"We use channels two through six, on a rotation. Keep shouting."

She stares at the little black box in her hand like it's a magical thing, then hugs it to her chest and sprints off after Rami.

*Where's Rue?*

Cherish blasts the question through my brain, trying to shame me for letting my ears hear anything besides his voice, and my eyes watch anything but the pile of rubble Honoria's now descending. He has to be right behind her; she wouldn't have left until everyone was on the move.

But there's panic on her face.

"Go—go—go!" she shouts, waving her hands toward the door, her eyes wide and more silver than I've ever seen them.

I still don't see Rue.

Honoria wobbles. She pitches forward as the pile beneath her feet begins to shift and then blasts apart from behind. A glistening black paw swipes a section of rubble out of the way, trying to dig a big enough hole in it to allow the bear-beast through.

Honoria claws her way to her feet, but I don't see any of our Fade. The creature couldn't have reached the blockade without going through them first.

"Rue!"

Any possible answer is drowned in a trumpeting shriek from the other side of the heap.

"Let's go, Marina," Tobin says, trying to pull me toward the door by the hand.

"But Rue—"

*You run, I run.* Hearing Rue's voice so suddenly and so clearly actually makes me yelp in surprise. *You lead, we follow.*

Very pale hands appear in the gap created by the bear thing, grasping at rubble for leverage, and I see something I never thought possible. Honoria leans in, crawling across the pile, and pulls the Fade through—Rue, Bolt, and Whisper.

"Where's Dog?" I ask, but the only answer I get is a nudge to keep running.

Honoria runs toward us, hooking my arm; she nearly knocks me off my feet. I have to turn midstride to keep from stumbling backward. She doesn't let go until we're outside and jogging down the front steps.

The Ice Cube looks nothing like it did when we approached. The Dark stretches over it, leaving the building inside giant cobwebs of nanite strands. The only evidence of Michael and the others are the discarded dart casings left from the serum Anne-Marie gave him. They're empty.

"Where are your people?" Honoria asks her brother, scanning what we can see of the horizon.

"There," he says, pointing to the emerging shimmer-lines of two dozen of his hive mates.

She locks down as they approach, knowing there's no way home that doesn't involve contact with them, but she at least tries to hide it.

"And this works, how, exactly?"

"They are my voice. You are my other. Mine doesn't hurt mine." Bolt puts a hand on her shoulder.

"Where's Dog?" I ask again.

"He remained," Whisper says out loud. She stands apart, her aura in turmoil, turning its usual blue-toned sour green. Rage explodes red and burns into a wash of despondent yellow. My bones feel brittle, about to shatter from the echoes of her pain. This is how a Fade cries. "He promised to follow, but he remained to hold the darkness back."

"Dog's holding that monster back?"

"I hear him, but he doesn't answer my voice. I would have remained also."

The marks on her face morph into a replica of his scars, and a smaller version of his dog tattoo appears on her arm, in nanites.

I knew that one determined Fade could be a relentless adversary, but Dog's standing on his own against that thing.

*Not alone,* my father's voice breaks in. *Until he falls silent, never alone.*

"It's still only Dog's hands, feet, and butt on the line!" And if *hold* means physically holding, then it's a matter of death or absorption into the wild hive. "How much longer can he last?"

Another screech answers the question for me. The bear-beast

charges through the rubble pile like it's no more than a stack of pebbles. The creature's separated from the rest of the wild-Dark so that it now has hindquarters. Dog broke it in half; this was the only piece that could get around him.

"Let me guess," Tobin says. "That's a group that all agrees we should die, isn't it?"

"You had to ask," I say.

Rather than pursue us down the steps, the beast throws itself into the air from the top one, landing on the other side of Anne-Marie and me. Between us and our way home.

The bear-beast roars, a blast of hot foul air so intense, it leaves my ears ringing. It hoists itself up on its back legs and splits in two again. One creature adjusts its height so that it's exactly as tall as Anne-Marie. The other's mine.

Rue disappears from my peripheral vision, *Don't*, I warn. He can't fool these things by being invisible.

"Annie—" Trey starts, but she throws a hand up to tell him to stop.

"Nobody move," she says, but our elders don't listen.

The creatures grow taller, towering up and up. Honoria, Mr. Pace, and the colonel blast straight through them, and their shapes warp further, starting to bow over. Those of us who've already had this nightmare know what's coming next.

Anne-Marie shakes, jamming her eyes shut. I take a breath to hold, and raise my hands in an *X* over my head as the bear-beast falls forward and flattens me to the ground.

Darkness. Everywhere

*Help me!* I scream. Cherish screams: *Help us!*

I can't open my mouth to say it out loud.

I hear the Killers, but they're all saying different things, interrupting, talking over, having a dozen arguments at once. Where the nanites touch my skin, they burn, biting my flesh with electric shocks.

I kick my legs and pound against the ground with my hands, but I'm drowning in the sludge that destroys everything.

I wish I had another flare.

I call out for Rue, but can't hear through the wild ones' insanity.

*Cherish*, I call, and she calls for Marina.

I twine my consciousness to hers. In every dream I had, this was what saved us—both of us, working together. *Not* human. *Not* Fade. Together, we will *not* be destroyed.

Cherish rises to the surface. I feel her emerging as she did to save Tobin and becoming armor the wild ones can't break. I can't be included. We refuse.

*No!* We shout.

Our choice.

The nanite cocoon's surface ripples; I feel it like a flag popping in high wind, but soon it slows down and turns rigid. The sound is that of freezing water, but I'm not cold. The wild ones voices soften until they're less than a whisper. Once more, I kick out and claw at the sludge around me, but this time it crumbles to dust.

I'm free.

Someone drags me away by my vest. I can feel my father, and Rue, and all the others again. They're here, ready to take us home.

"Marina?" Tobin's walking beside me.

"Don't touch," Honoria says—she's the one dragging me. "Not yet."

He's on his knees beside me. "Marina? Are you still you?" he asks.

"Shut up, Tobin," I say, trying to sit up, but I can't. "Where's Anne-Marie?" I turn my head sideways and see she's out of her cocoon, too. Mr. Pace is next to her, on the ground, with Trey on the other side.

"How—"

Anne-Marie blinks. She tries to raise her hand, but it falls limp beside her. A crushed serum dart lies in her palm, mixed with the blood she spilled smashing it open on the ground.

"Look at me, Annie. Open your eyes," Mr. Pace says.

"Dad?" Definite shock, but I'm not sure about pain yet.

He tears at her blood-soaked vest. The more he moves the material, it's clear that there are rips in it. The kind that come from the claws of a large animal ripping through. I glance at my stomach—I've got them, too. Blood's pooled red across my stomach and chest, where the bear-beast's claws cut me; the slashes are already healing. I can't tell if the black specks are from me or the broken cocoon.

Right now, I don't care.

*Heal*, I hear. My father kneels on my other side and takes my hand. *You heal.*

Tobin bends down, putting his mouth next to my ear. "Can you and . . . *the other you* . . . can you do anything for her? Like Rueful did for me?"

*Negative*, Cherish says. *Interference. Obstacle.*

"No," I say.

"Can he?" Tobin looks at my father.

"Not while the serum's in her system," I say. "She's had two doses."

"Get them on their feet," Honoria says. "We'll patch Annie up at home."

She knows I'm healing.

Anne-Marie tries to sit, but barely makes it halfway before she gives another sharp cry. She tries to raise her hand again, pointing this time. The nightmare hasn't ended yet. We've faced the beast, but not the flood.

The rumble starts up high, with the cobwebs that tether the Ice Cube to the Dark. They rain down from the building into drifts that reach the second floor. They're amassing, taking on oddly geometric configuration. Hosted Killers appear in the doorway of the school and on the roof. One of the animals moves apart from the others, growling low in its throat and ready to pounce, but the others turn on it, hissing and driving it back.

"What are they doing?" Tobin asks as Mr. Pace lifts Anne-Marie from the ground.

"It doesn't matter," his father says.

Col. Lutrell raises the trigger he's kept in his hand since the lunchroom and presses the button. Another tremor shakes the school, but this one's a lot bigger than the others. Glass shatters as the first explosion goes off, then it's a chain reaction from room to room as each gas pocket ignites, racing along the lines through the school and back to its source. The Killers try to flee, but the fire's faster. Those in and on the building burn.

Our Fade are in motion, surrounding us, creating capsules that grab each member of our group. Tobin takes my hand so we're together, and the last thing I see as the nanites fill in the space before my eyes is the flash from center of the school that brings it down.

# CHAPTER FORTY-SEVEN

## MARINA

The trip from the Ice Cube to the Arclight's nothing but a blur, no matter how I try to slow it down. All I see is the flash of trees through the nanite capsule that keeps me safe. Their voices try to lull me to sleep—my father pretty much insists on it—but I refuse. I force myself to stay alert so I can keep asking about Anne-Marie.

When we reach the relative safety of the Grey, she's still unconscious in her father's arms.

I've never been so happy to see someone I care about soaked red with their own blood. She's lost a lot, but still—it's red. I can almost convince myself the wounds haven't shrunk to a quarter of the size they were a few hours ago. I can almost believe her eyes will be brown the next time they open. I just can't help but know that a cure isn't the same as a vaccine.

I wonder if it did Michael or Noor any good.

Honoria's on her radio as soon as the Fade let us out, telling Sykes to get the lamps back online and not to leave any gaps.

"Don't wait for nightfall," she says. "If night falls, so do we."

Sykes wants details, but she won't give him any. She tells him

433

to "get it done," and turns her radio completely off.

Time warps, this time speeding up, and after what feels like mere steps, we're home. Mr. Pace has Anne-Marie in his arms. Lt. Sykes and Dr. Wolff are waiting for us, along with a scattering of others, including Jove, but it's Anne-Marie's mother I notice first and keep going back to. She's bouncing, the way Anne-Marie does when she's nervous, and chewing her fingernails, standing as close to the boundary as possible without crossing it.

I will never get the sound of her wailing out of my head.

"Annie!" Her mother rushes forward, trying to check for injuries.

"Don't touch her, Nique," Mr. Pace says, and dodges her.

"Elias? What happened?"

She already knows what happened—there's only one reason you don't touch the wounded. He heads toward Dr. Wolff, whose shoulders are slumped.

"No . . ." Her eyes, already red and wide seem to take over her face, but I can't look away as she turns to Trey.

"Mom—"

"No." She starts shaking her head.

"Mom, please—"

"She can't be, not with you and Elias there," she says, trying to force a smile. Her head shakes harder. "She can't. She's not. She's just—"

"Mom!" Trey catches her as she tries to touch Anne-Marie again. He shakes her, and she crumbles.

The sounds she makes can't be called words or even a scream. They're a dirge, already anticipating the end of a life that was just beginning. Her arms and legs go limp so that the only thing holding her up is her son, and as he drags his mother toward the main building, he looks back at me.

It's more horrifying to see guilt in his eyes than it would have been to find the accusation I expected. He blames himself for this.

The others who've gathered, realizing that this isn't a false alarm or a drill, return to the buildings, too. Honoria heads straight for Lt. Sykes.

"Where do we stand?" she asks him. He doesn't even mention how young she looks. Maybe it's happened before. "Has it spread?"

"No. It was just the two kids. Tess's boy ran. We tried to keep him sedated, but—"

"And the other one?" she cuts him off. Excuses don't do any good, and she already knows what's coming after the "but." Dante's a Fade. No, that would imply Dante still exists. The Fade took his body, the way they're trying to take Anne-Marie.

"Silver's still fighting. She hadn't gone critical when Doc got her on the meds, so if Annie's a recent case—"

"Good."

"We'll have the White Room viable in forty-eight hours. We can put them both there. He's going to try the dialysis again."

"Better."

"Honor"—Sykes chokes on her name, glances at me, and

turns sideways so they're closer together—where he can whisper and I can pretend I don't hear "Jeannie, are you okay?"

"Get it done," Honoria says. "Please."

He nods, jogging off toward the main building, and she watches him until he's out of sight.

"James, I would appreciate a thorough check of all the power systems, starting with the main generator," she says.

"You got it."

Tobin looks like he might say something to me, but pulls back at the last second, following his father.

I can't make myself move.

I stand with my toes at the line between light and dark, watching the sun lose power in the Grey, and it's like I'm looking through a window I've never used before. Familiar and different.

There are people out there. Are any of them standing at their boundary, trying to figure out where we are? Maybe Michael and Noor are safe. Maybe we're looking at one another, but we can't see because the Dark's between us.

Honoria steps up beside me, sharing my view of the Dark, now that the Grey has lost its natural light. Is she blaming me or herself at the moment?

"We'll be lighting another row of watch fires until we're sure the high beams will hold," she says. "Would you like to be assigned to a shift?"

I turn to face her.

"If that's a joke, it's not funny."

"Of the thousands currently residing within this facility, you are one of ten people with the experience and motivation required not to consider the fires a secondary defense. You know their value, and you know the potential cost if they go out." She looks down at my shredded vest and shirt. "Would you like me to assign you a shift?"

"Yeah. I think I would."

"Good," she says. "We're at true night; you should get inside before the doors lock."

Is it that easy? I'm an asset because I've seen how bad things are out there?

Honoria presses a pair of buttons on either side of her wristband. The face of mine, and every mounted emergency beacon, starts blinking Red-Wall scarlet as the sirens blare.

"This is going to be bad, isn't it?" I ask her.

"You read my journal?"

"Yes."

"You're about to live it."

She walks off, arms crossed, with the light glinting off the silver pistol at her back, and leaves me standing at the divide.

Alone.

*Never alone.*

"Rue?" I can't see him, but I can hear him. "Are you there?"

*I remain. You are healed?*

"Pretty much."

*Pain?*

"Not the kind you could fix."

He reminds me of the state Whisper was in after we lost Dog.

"Something like that," I say. "Is he really gone?"

*He no longer speaks to us.*

"I wish I could see you," I say, and strain my eyes as far as they'll go, on the chance that he's hidden out there where I can find him. "They have to seal the tunnels. How will I see you again?"

*There are always ways,* he says.

"Always?"

*Affirmed. Always. Infinite.*

Forever.

"Marina!" Honoria shouts from the doorway. "Inside, now!"

I nod, but take one more look at the Grey before starting her way.

It doesn't look like there's a war coming, but there is. We hurt the Killers, and once enough of them decide to mobilize, they'll come after us with worse than bear-beasts and nightmares.

*Can you tell what's happening back there?* I ask Rue at the door to the Arclight. *Is it still burning?*

*Burning,* he says. The door closes behind me. *Destruction. Fire.*

Fire always makes things worse in the end.

## EGMONT PRESS: ETHICAL PUBLISHING

Egmont Press is about turning writers into successful authors and children into passionate readers – producing books that enrich and entertain. As a responsible children's publisher, we go even further, considering the world in which our consumers are growing up.

### Safety First
Naturally, all of our books meet legal safety requirements. But we go further than this; every book with play value is tested to the highest standards – if it fails, it's back to the drawing-board.

### Made Fairly
We are working to ensure that the workers involved in our supply chain – the people that make our books – are treated with fairness and respect.

### Responsible Forestry
We are committed to ensuring all our papers come from environmentally and socially responsible forest sources.

**For more information, please visit our website at**
**www.egmont.co.uk/ethical**